MW00775393

THE PERFECT CANDIDATE

A *LANCE PRIEST* NOVEL

CHRISTOPHER METCALF

TT Tree Tunnel Publishing

Published by
Tree Tunnel Publishing, LLC
Tulsa, Oklahoma

ISBN: 978-0-9837447-0-2

www.treetunnelpublishing.com

For Diana

It's not a lie, if you believe it.
— G. Costanza

ACKNOWLEDGMENTS

Too many to thank. Diana is supportive, always. I'm blessed to call her mine. To me, she is love. Kids who let their father put on headphones and disappear into a computer screen and keyboard are more than treasured. Ann is reliable and an example for all. She's also Mom. Mike is generous for allowing me to steal. Phil blazed an inspirational trail. The Internet, Wikipedia® and Google Maps® are constant companions. But long before the World Wide Web, there was the *CIA World Factbook*. It is online now. Do yourself a favor and see what interesting things it has to say about your favorite countries.

Prologue

Patient was the killer.

He was stealth and strategy and confidence. Most of all, he was composed. No question or hesitation in his resolve.

His target was deserving of death. Deserving of much worse than the brief moment of pain he was soon to endure. But there simply wasn't ample time to perform a procedure proportionate to his many offenses. This kill needed to be carried out in an expert fashion that left no trace of evidence. This job demanded nothing less than flawless execution -- a bad pun, but still.

Planning was over. It was time. Peering around the corner, the killer reviewed the scene. No change in' the last half-minute. Nothing much had changed in the four minutes since he silently entered the structure.

He evaluated his target one final time. The man was comfortable, seated with legs propped, at ease in his blissful ignorance. His attention forward, seemingly absolute. The guy was oblivious to his surroundings, hypnotized by the television his eyes were glued to. Two empty bottles on a side table provided evidence of his chemical-induced stupor. He had left himself unprotected. Vulnerable.

The killer reached up and turned the dial on the thermostat to 72°. Significantly cooler than the sweltering 90-degree-plus evening temperature outside. His extensive surveillance and reconnaissance of the location revealed useful details such as the obnoxious noise produced by the aged air conditioning condenser unit when it kicked on. Right on cue, the rattle and hum outside was immediate. That noise would conceal the sounds of execution.

Consummate preparation brought the killer here this evening at this time. His patient, exhaustive observation of the target and location identified this precise window of opportunity when the man would be alone, defenseless.

The killer was silent in his approach. He had removed his shoes outside to further dampen the fall of his feet on the floor. He held the target's own gun gripped in a gloved hand as he stepped closer. His advance recon of the building had uncovered the gun in the bedside dresser. It was perfect.

Peripheral vision confirmed what he knew already. No one else was here. No witnesses.

The killer was in position, just behind the oblivious target. His approach undetected. He had practiced this kill, trained for this moment. Silently, he stepped to the right to gain the proper angle. No hesitation now. In one fluid motion, the killer leaned to the right and forward to allow his outstretched right arm to move around the target and bring the barrel of the gun up until it made contact with the unsuspecting man's chin. Not the chin per se; the area between the chin and Adam's apple. The submaxillary triangle, for those familiar with human anatomy, like the killer.

The target tensed as the cold barrel jammed into his skin. But there was no time. No time to move or scream or plead. The trigger was levered and the bullet exploded up through and out the top of the man's head. The killer simultaneously stepped forward and to the right to avoid the matter that followed the bullet up to the wall.

A fine mist of blood droplets was still settling as the killer moved the gun from under the corpse's head down to a lifeless hand. He placed the gun into the dead man's right hand with the pointer finger inserted into the trigger space. He aimed the weapon at the television a dozen feet in front of the chair and applied the pressure necessary to pull the trigger.

The television tube suffered a quick death just as a running back avoided tacklers and stepped out of bounds on the sideline. To anyone examining the scene, this second bullet would be interpreted as the first shot fired. The gunshot also left microscopic amounts of gunpowder residue on the man's hand. Proof the deceased had indeed fired the weapon.

The killer then brought the gun and sagging hand back up under the deceased's chin and released them. The appendage and gun slid naturally with gravity's help down to the dead man's protruding belly where it now rested.

The count in his head was up to 11 seconds since the first shot. Right on schedule. The killer quickly exited the room the way he had entered 21 seconds earlier. The accomplished killer stepped out the sliding glass door next to the kitchen table onto the patio and closed the door behind him. He slid his shoes back on and listened to the sounds of the night before moving. Nothing.

Once on the backyard lawn, his movements were precise. He jogged diagonally across the yard and climbed the fence at the corner. His motions sure and fluid, as if he'd done it hundreds of times.

Once over the fence, he continued his trek into the blackness of a clearing and then onto a quiet street. He removed the leather gloves and put them in his back pocket for the moment. They would be disposed of properly in a dumpster a quarter of a mile away. The dumpster sat in an alley behind a small shopping center. Situated in the middle of the center was his destination, his alibi.

The killer didn't dwell on the job just completed. It was simply a function necessitated by the target's irresponsible, dangerous actions. The reckless man had placed too many in danger with his selfish desire for dominance. His predilection for violence and abuse of power had signed his death warrant. Threats against innocent bystanders and those beyond reproach required decisive action. His recent escalation of terrorizing behavior to include death threats toward those who dared oppose him was simply the last straw. He had crossed a line.

There would be repercussions. There always were. There would be tears and pain and glowing sermons even though this target had alienated or offended most everyone in his sphere of influence. Even those who were now free from his oppression and constant torment would be in pain for a period. But it would pass. This was, at its core, a righteous kill. But the killer knew that was for someone else to decide. He had merely done a job, a service.

He reached the shopping center in a comfortable minute and 49 seconds. The gloves were placed in the dumpster under several broken down cardboard boxes and full plastic garbage bags. Twenty three seconds later, the killer entered his destination through a back door propped open with a pencil 12 minutes earlier. A good many pubescent and adolescent boys, heads down playing games, populated the video arcade. A smattering of young girls waited for the boys' attention. A few adults could be seen, mostly playing pinball and electronic darts. The chubby shopping center security guard sat on a stool talking with the arcade's manager as the killer walked past. No new faces in the room since he slipped out the back door.

The killer took in the room in a flash, cataloging hundreds of details as he stepped over to the Galaga machine. Before dropping his quarter into the coin slot, he surveyed the room again. One of the young girls looked his way and smiled.

Didn't need that. Last thing he wanted right now was a pre-teen girl crushing on him. He smiled back though. If nothing else, her look of longing reinforced his alibi. The killer turned back to the game and proceeded to kill hundreds of alien ships. They all deserved their demise.

Chapter 1

Tuesday, November 10, 1987 – Dallas, Texas

"Damn. This is really happening."

Lance said it as much to himself as he did to Geoffrey Seibel. The older man was seated across the small conference table Lance stood leaning over. He took a quick survey of the facts, the new reality enveloping him. Two men alone in the room, a table between them. A threat with a definitive and immediate timeline had been issued. Elton John singing a classic in his head. Oh, and Lance held a gun to Seibel's head.

Lance Priest was undeniably the worst shot in his family. Worse than his little brother, his mother and even his aunts. But even Lance wouldn't miss from this distance with the gun's barrel making a little circle-shaped indention in Seibel's left temple.

He just wished Elton would wrap up the song. He needed to think, to plan. Sometimes songs just start playing in his brain at the most inopportune times. Like this one.

He would be running soon. In a matter of minutes, he'd run for his life, burst from the room, from the building and break into a full sprint once outside. His lungs would ache; his legs would scream at the pace he pushed them down streets and alleys in downtown Dallas. But right now Lance needed more information. He'd missed too many details already today.

In the seconds preceding the current situation, Lance had gone out of body to look down on the scene from above, formulated a plan and executed it to perfection. It surprised the heck out of him how well it worked. Lance was simply faster with his gun and turned the tables on Seibel, if that was even the dude's real name. He didn't linger on the fact he held the gun to the guy's head. It had just worked out that way. He pushed the barrel deeper into Seibel's temple. The song was into its final chorus. What now? He needed to think. The seconds hesitated, time slowed.

He'd basically lied his way here today. Hell, truth be told, and it wasn't often told by Lance Priest, he'd fibbed and lied and B.S.'d his way through most of his 21 years. A half-day of whoppers and white lies told to others during the Foreign Service Officer oral assessments was nothing. It was fun.

That is, up until about two minutes go when Seibel pulled out a gun and put in on the table. He followed this surprising action with the equally surprising words, "You will be of no use to your country or anyone for that matter unless you can survive the next 72 hours." Damn. Didn't look like Lance could lie his way out of this one.

No time to think about where this all started. Lance could cram a lot of thinking into a second or two, but this was going to take time to figure out. Time he didn't have if what Seibel had said moments earlier was true. Lance had apparently walked into a shit storm and now had just over four and a half minutes until two brutal killers somewhere else in the building started chasing him, hunting him, like an animal. It would be a whole lot easier to think, to devise a plan, if the guy sitting in front of him with a gun to his head wasn't smiling like he knew a secret. It was slightly unnerving.

Seibel turned his left wrist that Lance held pinned to the table to look at his watch. "Four minutes and 29 seconds. You need to move Mr. Priest." He smiled as he said the words. He almost giggled really. The guy did know a secret.

Lance snuck a glance at the clock on the wall over Seibel's head. Something about the clock wasn't right. He'd noticed it when he came in ten minutes earlier. It didn't belong there.

But no time for those thoughts now. He didn't have the time to process every detail. Ten minutes. Man, his life had changed in those few rotations of the hands on a clock.

Rewind. He went out of body and back to 11 minutes earlier. Lance walked out of a large conference room on the fifth floor of a nondescript federal office building on Commerce Street in downtown Dallas. Gathered in the room behind him were U.S. Foreign Service Officer candidates who had passed the written exam portion of the process and traveled to Dallas from around the region for group and individual oral assessments.

They had been placed in pretend situations during the morning and asked to come up with responses. They had all participated in a full-group exercise followed by smaller group sessions. Lance's small group had been tasked with handling the repercussions of a deadly tourist bus crash as members of the U.S. embassy staff in Zimbabwe. Lance had dominated the session by literally making stuff up on the spot, like usual.

After lunch, the next phase of the day was individual interviews. Lance was ready. He lived for moments when he was challenged to create characters and build backstories, traits, wants, needs and desires. Lance was a born liar. Leopards have spots. Fish swim. Lance Priest lies.

He walked down the hall to a room marked "3" with a piece of paper taped to the door, took a breath, opened the door and entered. He was only mildly surprised to see Seibel and the liar who called himself Marsco sitting behind the lone conference table. Drew Marsco wasn't his real name. Lance was sure of that. The man, who had sat in on Lance's small group session earlier this morning, had been in Tulsa on a rainy Saturday at the University of Tulsa eight weeks earlier when Lance and 40 others took the Foreign Service Officer Written Examination. Marsco, not his real name obviously, was across the room watching Lance most of the time instead of filling out answers on his exam. And in Tulsa, the guy wasn't wearing a wig, fake mustache and glasses like he was now. Bad disguise.

The two men didn't get up and didn't speak as Lance entered. He closed the door behind him, stepped forward and sat in a chair facing them. Seibel's eyes drilled into him. Seibel was a different person than the jovial and dapper gent who greeted all the candidates this morning. In fact, as far as Lance could tell, this was the fourth different persona Seibel had played today. Lance was impressed. The changes Seibel manifested at different times during the day were subtle – hunched back, drooping mouth, bright shining smile, a locked, furrowed brow. Lance seldom encountered people who could "chameleon" like he could. Seibel was good.

"What color is the wall on your left?" Seibel asked pointedly.

Lance responded immediately. "Green, like the one on my right and behind you. The wall behind me is yellow for some reason."

"Are my shoes loafers or wing-tip?"

"You're all wing-tip, all the time."

"Where is Grisham from?" Seibel asked. Grisham, or whatever his name was, had led the small group exercise Lance had participated in this morning.

"He said Billings, Montana." Lance returned Seibel's glare.

"But you don't believe him." Seibel's left eyebrow rose.

"He is from somewhere east and north. Not Montana. No doubt." Lance replied.

"Why would he lie to you?" Seibel's right eyebrow rose to join the left one.

Lance let the question hang in the air and smiled. "I think the question is why did Grisham, Sarah, Mackenzie, Waters, you and Mr. Marsco here lie to me."

"What do you mean?" Seibel's eyebrows furrowed.

"What do you think I mean?" Lance asked.

"How did everyone lie to you?" Seibel's eyes now squinted.

"First things first, none of those are their real names."

"How so?"

Lance's smile widened. "People aren't born with names. They are given them. They become them. A Jim is named James at birth but ends up a Jim. Michael stays Michael instead of becoming Mike. Elizabeth becomes Lisa or Liz. Either way, you become that name. It's who you are. You carry it with you, wear it. When people lie about their name it is easy to tell. It doesn't fit. I see it all the time on the car lot." Lance sold used cars part-time at a dealership when he wasn't in class or studying or running. Yes, a used car salesman.

"So just the six of us lied to you, not the rest?" Seibel just smiled.

"Just five lied about their names. You have lied every time you've opened your mouth, but not about your name." Lance smiled.

"How could you tell they lied about their names? Exactly please?" Seibel inquired.

Lance shrugged his shoulders. "Sarah gave it away with her eyes first thing this morning. She simply had no investment in the name. It wasn't hers. Grisham worked too hard to be Grisham. Said it too many times. Mackenzie doesn't wear glasses and didn't need them. They were just glass, no magnification. You could see it from the side. Just like you could see the lie in his name. Waters simply didn't dress the part. And the gentleman playing the role of Drew Marsco here decided to put on a wig and mustache today to disguise himself."

Seibel turned to Marsco whose real name is Braden, Stuart Braden, psychologist and talent evaluator. Braden is a human lie detector, or better, spy detector. And he was stunned, flabbergasted yet again by Lance's performance. Just like he'd been eight weeks earlier in Tulsa. The glance between Seibel and Braden was its own language. The psychologist shook his head, closed his notebook and placed it in his briefcase. He got up and walked out of the room without a word. Seibel followed.

Outside in the hall with the door closed, the two stood only inches apart. They had obviously been in tight spaces together. Seibel pulled a tiny recorder from his jacket pocket and whispered.

"Seibel, Geoffrey, NCS-SAD number 347 dash 9. Braden, Stuart NCS-SAD psych ops, number 4561 dash 7. November 10, 1987. Do I have approval to proceed with candidate number 1 dash 713, Priest, Lance P. age 21, Tulsa, Oklahoma?" The question was steeped in formality as if it were spoken for documentation purposes. And obviously it was.

Braden's reply was just as dry and formal; it too wrapped in government bureaucratic legalese. "Braden, Stuart 4561 dash 7. Candidate Priest meets or exceeds all position and agency NDC requirements under Directive 718H. You are approved to proceed."

Seibel snapped off the recorder, shoved it into his pocket and turned to re-enter the room. The door closed behind him louder than it should have, but the effect was nice. He moved back to his seat and after sitting, reached down beside him to pull something out of a small leather bag on the floor. It was a gun and Seibel put it on the table right in front of Lance.

"What is that for?" Lance kept his eyes locked on Seibel's pale blue eyes. He also managed to keep his cool. He was annoyed at the moment. Not by Seibel or the gun. A classic Elton John song had started playing in his head while Seibel was out of the room. His personal mental soundtrack picked a lousy time to kick in. But there was no stopping a song once it started. It had always been like this.

"For shooting." Seibel replied.

"Why is it on the table?" Lance nodded. His foot tapped to the beat of the song playing in his head.

"Do you recognize this weapon?"

Lance leaned down to get a closer look. "It looks like mine."

"It is yours. Beretta 9 mm model 92 chambered for the classic Parabellum bullet with a 13-round magazine. A little light, but still a nice gun. Given to you by your stepfather three years ago and given to him by his uncle who lives in Fort Smith, Arkansas."

"How did you get it?" Lance's face showed nothing, but he had been knocked slightly off kilter by the gun appearing first of all. Seibel's accurate telling of the gun's life story was a gut blow. *What the hell?*

"Does seeing this gun now really surprise you?" Seibel was the ultimate in cool.

"Yes. How the hell did you get it?" Lance squinted and played the role of an angry young man. His foot tapped away. He fought the urge to go out of body.

"How do you think?" Seibel raised his hands slightly with the question.

"Obviously from of my bedroom closet."

"Precisely. Off the shelf above your hanging suits, which were grey, blue, blue and seersucker. Your navy blue sports coat is missing a gold button from the left sleeve." Seibel said this last line with concern, like he really cared about that missing button.

Lance tilted his head and squinted his eyes. "What the hell is going on? Who are you?"

"Are you sure you didn't know we had been in your apartment?" Seibel's look was telling.

"I knew someone had. You knocked the red koozee off the armrest of my plastic deck chair."

Seibel furrowed his brow. "That sounds like some kind of code. But regardless, your instincts were right as I expected." Seibel paused to gather himself, and for effect. He was something of a showman.

"Mr. Priest, you have been under surveillance for nearly two months. Your every action has been captured or documented in some manner. Quite an investment has been made in you already. But of course we expect a great return on our investment.

"We have followed you to school, to work, out on the town with your very few friends and back home again. We followed your early morning or late night runs, which never, and I mean never, follow the same path. A team followed your drive from Tulsa to Dallas yesterday and was quite impressed with your recon of the area surrounding this building last evening. We were in the room next to your motel room last night and beside your vehicle on the drive in this morning."

"For what? Why?" The smile was gone from Lance's face.

"Please let me finish," Seibel raised a hand. "We have indeed looked into a great many aspects of your life, from your childhood in Florida and then Texas, right through high school and now college in Tulsa. We have interviewed people in your distant past you have forgotten. We have collected sufficient data to tell your life story. I have mounds of paperwork detailing the family history, education, health and finances of Lance Porter Priest." During this last part, Seibel leaned forward for further effect. His face was within 18 inches of Lance's blank stare.

But Lance's mind wasn't blank. It was working, collecting, cataloging. Processing.

Lance sees people the same way he views, or better, devours maps. People are maps of their life. The decisions made, hardships endured, lies told and hidden are like roads and topography and landmarks all there on and below the skin. And like maps, Lance can memorize every detail.

His knowledge of human anatomy had been memorized from a number of reference books on the subject. Looking at Seibel, he watched his favorite of the 20 facial muscles -- the procerus -- do its thing. Located right there on the bridge of each human's nose between the eyes, this small muscle helps people flare their nostrils or furrow their eyebrows to look angry. A great little muscle.

He took in every feature, every facet of Seibel's visage in a flash of a moment. He was 56, maybe 58. Six-feet tall and solid 195 pounds. Blue-grey eyes, broken but distinctive nose, light scars on left cheek, below left ear and left side of his neck. Good-lookin' guy, but hard, tough, smart. Kind of guy you'd see on cigarette billboards. *A drill sergeant with a Harvard MBA.*

Seibel broke a slight grin and placed his hands flat on the table, again for effect. "But, here's the thing. I don't think we've uncovered even a quarter of who you really are Mr. Priest. Your ability to both create and maintain stories, identities and advantageous relationships is…" he searched for the correct word, "extraordinary. I think that best captures it. Your capacity to lie, to create intricate fabrications, is nothing short of remarkable. You are very, and I mean very, talented. So, after all this time and investment in man hours and surveillance technology and psychoanalysis we have come to the conclusion that you make an excellent candidate."

"For what?" Lance was damn sure it wasn't Foreign Service Officer.

"Please let me finish," Seibel lifted a finger this time. "You are an excellent candidate to help us do great things in the service of your country and the cause of freedom around the world."

Lance just looked at him and waited for more. "Are you done? Can I interrupt now?"

"Excellent. You really are extremely adept. You picked up my cadence. You read my body language and decided it best to play stupid or dumb, of which you are neither."

"You lost me."

"I highly doubt that. Mr. Priest, you are indeed very impressive, especially for a 21-year old who should be more interested in sports and girls and partying than getting yourself into this situation. But for some reason, you have chosen in your life to play a series of roles and characters that require you to live a number of well-constructed and intricate lies. You are a student, a salesman, but most of all a chameleon. You are adept at change and flexibility and creativity. And that makes you something and someone we can use."

"We?"

"Not just yet Preacher." Seibel let the word, his in-depth knowledge of Lance's life, including his ironic nickname, hang in the air. He leaned back a few inches and gestured toward the gun. "I am guessing you know how to use that weapon."

"I have shot it a few times." Lance told the truth. He didn't tell Seibel that he was a lousy shot, really bad. Broad side of the barn bad.

"Good. You will want to take it with you."

"Where?"

"That is entirely up to you. Where you go and what you do can keep you alive."

"Alive?" Lance whispered. His procerus muscle pulled his eyebrows together.

Seibel reached back down into the leather bag and pulled out a manila file folder. He moved the gun to the side and laid the folder on the table. He spun it with a flourish and opened it. On each side of the folder was a sheet of paper and a photo of a man paper-clipped to the side. They both looked tough, weathered and mean. They weren't Americans.

"These two men are veterans of many challenging incidents, primarily in eastern Europe, although they know the United States well from several assignments. They are possibly the best hunters of men to come out of Europe in the last two decades. They have been extremely useful for both sides. Hired guns if you will, mercenaries. They are an excellent team."

"And?" Lance waited for more. This thing had moved from interesting to a little scary.

"And, can you disappear Mr. Priest?"

"Disappear? From where, here?" Lance tilted his head.

"Where is not the question. The real question is when, and when for you is right now." Seibel replied.

"What do you mean?"

Seibel paused for a moment, a dramatic pause. The smile faded from his chiseled face. "I will tell you this, all of this, only once. Listen carefully. These men are here, in this building in fact on another floor." He stopped and looked at his watch. "In six minutes and 24 seconds they are to be handed a file like this one that contains your photo, name, address, driver's license number, social security number and last known whereabouts. Which of course, is right here in this room."

"And?" Lance was spinning, but didn't miss a beat. His foot still tapping in rhythm.

Seibel couldn't help but smile at this kid, this consummate liar. "They will be given the assignment to find and apprehend a wanted package -- you. They are very good, very capable. Our preferred method of capture is alive and unharmed, but they will be given sufficient leeway to complete their assignment since they are apprehending an armed individual." The words hung in the air like a flashing neon sign.

"Leeway?" Lance, still cool, smiled back at Seibel. This was now definitely scary.

"They will be authorized to use any and all means, including deadly force."

"Jesus." Lance sat back in the chair and ran his hands through his hair.

"He won't be able to help you, unless he knows a good hiding place or is armed to the teeth. And after reading through your life story, I don't think you'd call upon him anyway."

"Why? Why me?"

Seibel continued in his formal manner. "Mr. Priest, you are apparently a gift sent to us by someone or something that wants you to contribute to the betterment of mankind, at least American mankind. I can tell from my short time with you and my hours and hours of examination of video, audio and dead trees that Lance Priest is a patriot. You have a deep respect for your country. You came close to joining the military out of high school but couldn't handle the structure. You are truly a very promising candidate. Maybe one of a kind. But you will be of no use to your country or anyone for that matter unless you can survive the next 72 hours."

Maybe he should already be running for his life. Elton's song was only halfway through. It was making it a bit hard to concentrate on what Seibel was saying.

Chapter 2

He should be scared. Scared to death. Maybe convulsing, bending over to hurl his lunch. He should be sweating bullets -- another bad pun, but still.

But he wasn't. He wasn't scared or nauseous or sweating. If anything, Lance was excited, like those eager moments before the starting gun fired prior to the 400-meter race at the Oklahoma high school state track meet. Right now, in this moment, Lance was more alert than he'd been in years, maybe ever.

Lance could feel every joint in his body, every surface or fabric touching his skin. Even with the song playing in his head, he was able to concentrate on his senses. He was about to go out of body, could feel it coming on.

He couldn't see them, but Lance could sense the layers of reality comprising the situation he now found himself in. Like sitting across the desk from the school principal in 9th grade telling a lie-filled epic tale with dozens of moving parts, he knew there were multiple agendas in play here. Seibel was much more than a well-dressed bureaucrat. Each word spoken by the man carried numerous meanings.

"Seventy-two hours. Three days?" Lance shook his head as he said this. He also pushed his chair back a few inches, readying himself.

"Three days," Seibel pulled a business card from his suit jacket and set it on the table next to Lance's gun and looked at his watch again. "Here is a number that you are to call at precisely 2:17 p.m. three days from now. The number will be active for only 10 minutes and only I can answer it." With that, Seibel sat back in his chair. "I hope to hear from you then."

"That's it? I just leave now?"

"You have 5 minutes and 20 seconds head start. I would use it." Seibel was relaxed.

Lance corrected him without looking at his own watch or the clock on the wall. His internal clock was keeping time like it does when he runs. "It's 5 minutes 11 seconds. Again, why are you doing this?"

"Now is not the time to ask why. Now is the time to fly. Good luck Preacher." Seibel was done with his performance. He had just told a 21-year old kid that two killers were about to hunt him down, but at least he did it with a smile.

Lance's next few moves were sudden and surprisingly confident despite the desperate situation. Seibel watched every infinitesimal detail of Lance's actions. Assessing everything.

First, Lance stood, scooting the chair back as he did so. He grabbed the gun with his right hand. Even though he hadn't held it in a year or fired it in two years, he pressed the clip release and popped the magazine out the bottom of the handle. It was fully loaded and had been oiled. He shoved the clip back in and swiped the card from the table with his left hand, shoving it into his right breast jacket pocket. Seibel remained completely passive.

And then Lance reached for the file folder. This changed things.

Seibel smacked his left hand flat on the manila folder. It was a loud slap. Definitive in its intent and effect.

"I'm afraid I'll need to keep this." Seibel smiled up at him.

Simultaneous to stretching out to the folder with his left hand, Seibel did a deceptively fast thing with his right. The motion was swift and smooth and utterly natural as he reached his right hand to lift his suit jacket and grab the handle of a gun resting in a holster midway between his armpit and waist. He didn't pull the gun, but was ready to. His eyes never left Lance's.

Preacher watched Seibel's right hand movement with his peripheral vision but kept his eyes locked on Seibel's. The gun in his own right hand was currently down at his side. This was suddenly an old west showdown. No doubts now, this was really happening. Lance was closer to death than he'd ever been, but felt more alive than ever. *Damn.*

With his eyes locked on Seibel, Preacher's mind slowed the world around him to stop-motion. He went out of body, above the fray for a clearer picture. In his mind's eye, he looked down on the scene from a vantage point near the ceiling. His ability to see the world below like examining a map had simply always been a part of him. Preacher couldn't actually see anything more than he could from behind his hazel eyes, but the visual acuity process taking place in his unique mind gave him another, more detailed view of the world around him. Preacher sees things others don't.

From above, he saw himself leaning over the table with a hand on the file folder. He saw Seibel sitting with his left hand on the same folder, his right hand hidden under his jacket gripping the handle of a gun.

Preacher looked for details, for the clue he needed. He saw it. The folder. A flash bulb went off and lit up the room with a burst that showed Lance his next move, his next series of moves. His plan was formulated and ready for execution. Two whole seconds had passed.

Back inside his head, Preacher executed the next three motions naturally with lightning speed and no forethought. He lifted his left hand from the folder while slightly lowering his shoulders -- a microsecond of resignation. Seibel's reaction was to relax his own left shoulder just a fraction.

Still locked on Seibel's eyes, Preacher saw the shoulder ease in his peripherals. This was his cue. He suddenly grabbed Seibel's forearm and violently slid it to his left, to Seibel's right. The secret to this move was the folder. Seibel was strong and tried to resist the movement, but the manila folder's paper cardstock made it slick as all hell sitting there on the printed vinyl wood grain of the tabletop.

The effect of Seibel's left arm being jammed to the right was a twisting, a wrenching of his body, made even more so because he was seated. It pinned Seibel down for the tiniest moment. A moment was all Preacher needed.

Now, if Preacher had only grabbed the arm and shoved it sideways, he might have just pissed Seibel off. But simultaneous to the arm slide, he swung the gun from beside his right hip up to where the Beretta's barrel met Seibel's graying temple. The entire sequence of motions, from the slight fade upon releasing the file to gun barrel pressing against flesh, took less than a second and a half. Funny how life can change in a second or two. It makes 10 minutes seem a lifetime.

Seibel kept his eyes locked on Preacher. When his arm had been suddenly gripped and shoved across his body, he squeezed the handle of his Glock 17 but didn't get it out of the holster before the younger, faster and stronger man had a cold barrel pressed against his temple. *Damn.*

The older man's reaction was another surprise. He smiled. He friggin smiled.

The smile broadened and became quiet laughter. "Excellent," he whispered, giggled really.

Lance wasn't sure of his next move. He had no idea his manila folder forearm-slide plan would work so well. Standing with a gun pointed at a man's head, he needed to think. Elton was thankfully into the song's final chorus and musical crescendo. His foot still tapped the beat.

Lance couldn't help his next action. He leaned in close to Seibel's ear. But before he spoke, he did a strange thing. He winked at the clock on the wall, particularly the small round hole where the 12 should be. From the angle, Seibel couldn't see the wink.

"I should pull the trigger," Lance lied. He had no intention of making a mess like that. "I don't know who you are, but you are one messed up dude for doing this. Let me get this straight, you watch me for two months, invest hundreds of man hours, record my movements, follow me down here to Dallas and then decide to sick two killers on me to bring me back in a body bag. Seems like a waste." He smiled at the clock, "I think I might be doing folks a favor by putting one in your brain."

Seibel was not shaking, not nervous. "You need to be challenged right? Well this little test will challenge you. Especially your survival skills."

Lance leaned back to look Seibel in the eye. "You can stop this. Pick up a phone and make a call. Stop it." Lance raised his voice well beyond a whisper.

"No stopping. Operation is live," Seibel removed the smile from his face for this last part. "You need to think through your next actions. You need to be gone, now. These men are not known for their mercy."

Lance's next action was decided for him by something and someplace deep inside. He didn't know its source. But this unpredictability, this embrace of chaos, this need for instability, was a vital and driving force in his life. Always had been. Lance thrived in unsettled situations.

He moved the gun five inches from Seibel's temple and squeezed the trigger. The clock took a direct hit. A pretty good shot for him. The explosion in the small room was deafening. Seibel's eardrum took the brunt of it. He cringed but took no aggressive action.

Preacher also got the proof he needed. The gun was indeed loaded with real bullets.

Lance stood up while keeping the gun leveled at Seibel's head. He gestured to the clock with a nod. "No witnesses now. I should do it."

"Go ahead. No one's stopping you." Seibel was serious. "You can surely make up a beautiful lie about shooting in self-defense. I have no doubt."

Lance smiled down at Geoffrey Seibel, super spy. Top secret and classified CIA legend in his own time. Master of his own universe. "Bang. You're dead Geoffrey. Enjoy your time in hell. I'm sure I'll be joining you soon." Lance smiled for another reason as well. The song was finally over.

Seibel could only shake his head. He was the sole witness to the birth of something special, something truly unique. Something he would have to harness and train and release into the world. But something he knew he could never control, never break.

Lance grabbed the folder from under Seibel's hand and stepped back from the table. He shook his head and jammed the gun into his pocket. The expected footsteps ran down the hall. Who ever it was, took a position just outside the conference room. Lance stepped sideways and raised his hands. The door smashed open and the man playing the role of Grisham expertly entered the room by rolling to his right. He rose with both hands holding a gun pointed directly between Lance's eyes. He didn't look much like a State Department trainer.

"Stand down," Seibel held out the palm of his left hand. Grisham looked from Lance to Seibel and back.

"Where is the gun?" he demanded. A strange accent accompanied the question. Sounded a little like German.

Seibel spoke in a voice irrationally calm for the situation. "There's no time for that now. He needs to be out of here in four minutes. His clock has started. He is active as of now." Grisham lowered his gun a few inches. Lance somewhat brazenly walked directly at him, stopping just an inch from the gun.

"What the hell did I get myself into?" He asked. Grisham only looked over Lance's shoulder at Seibel. Lance leaned his head to the left to block Grisham's view and continued, "I came down here for the Foreign Service Officer oral assessment and now I've got four minutes head start on a couple of European killers."

Recognition flashed in Grisham's eyes and he lowered his gun. "Krachovs?" he asked Seibel.

"Yes." Seibel nodded. "No time for chit chat."

Grisham stepped out of the way and holstered his gun. Lance noted that he had missed the bulge of the gun during the day. How did he fail to spot that on both of these guys? What else had he missed? No time now to be ticked off by this oversight; but he told himself it wouldn't happen again.

Grisham motioned to the door. "Then you'd better run kid and don't stop. Get out of this building and out of town. Stay low, keep running. They never stop tracking once they have a scent and they don't have the word quit in their vocabulary."

"Great, friggin great. Thanks a bunch, assholes," he pushed Grisham aside with enough force to nearly knock him to the floor. He turned back to Seibel from the doorway to give him a middle-finger salute. He was a 21-year-old kid after all. "Just be by the phone Geoffrey."

"Three minutes 20 seconds," Seibel tapped his watch.

Lance took off like a bat out of hell down the hall. People stood in doorways and at the front reception desk. Everyone on the floor had undoubtedly heard the gunshot. He saw someone else with a gun and was even more pissed at himself for missing all the hardware. He hated missing details.

When he burst out the door into the waiting area, Sarah, or whatever her real name happened to be, was seated in the same chair she sat in this morning as they chatted. Except now she was white-knuckle gripping both arms of the chair. This was out of her league and pay grade. *"Oral assessments!"* he huffed as he ran out the door and down the hall to the elevator. The surprised and shaken look on her face told it all. She only thought she was in the know on this exercise. It looked like the rules for the day's session had changed. Still, she bit her lip.

Lance kept the count going in his head as he reached the elevator lobby. Seven years of running track and cross-country in middle and high school had given him a fairly static cranial timepiece that counted off the seconds quite accurately. He could do it in the background while his mind wrapped around other issues, like how to stay alive. He counted 22 seconds since running out of the conference room. That meant just under three minutes until Boris and Boris get their assignment. He turned from the elevator and threw open the door to the stairs. Five flights should take about 30 seconds. They actually took 28. Two and a half minutes to go as he burst into the mostly empty ground floor lobby.

He didn't have time to pause and think and examine all the angles. If this was a normal situation, he would stop someone, maybe the security guard, ask for the time and comment on his watch or shoes. He'd start a conversation that led to a stranger telling Lance everything he needed to know about him. He would catalog the story, the details, and use them somewhere with someone else, as someone else. It wasn't stealing. It was borrowing. Telling lies was all about the details.'

But he needed to move. No time for spinning a web of lies. He'd gotten himself into something that he couldn't bullshit his way out of. Words wouldn't do it this time.

He should have been scared, petrified even. He felt anything but. Instead, from the moment he'd grabbed Seibel's arm and put the gun to his head, he'd never felt more excited, more alive. This was indeed real. This was a challenge, something he'd been waiting 21 years for. No time for grand statements and eloquent thoughts. *Damn. This was fun.*

Chapter 3

Out the front doors and onto Commerce Street, no time to get to his car out of the lot across the street. Too risky.

He recalled his reconnaissance of the area the night before and maybe more so, the OU-Texas weekend two years prior. If only that crazy thing were going on now, he'd have no problem melting into the crowd of thousands on Commerce Street the night before the big game.

He knew that diagonally to the left he could make his way to Dealey Plaza where a certain president met his untimely demise. Not good karma right now. Further to his left were the spires at the top of the Old Dallas Court House, but that area was too wide open. He needed crowds and walls and windows to look through. Two blocks west, the Greyhound bus station offered a crowd, but was way too obvious.

Three blocks to the right was the incredibly over-priced Adolphus Hotel where he had party-crashed that night before the big game two years ago.

He went right. Figured to stay on Commerce for a block and then cross and go north over to Main where he could get behind a wall or a car or tree and still see the entrance of the federal building. The slow jog and jaywalk across Commerce took 26 seconds. If Seibel was correct. The two hunters would be given their mission within a minute. They would likely come storming out of the building two or three minutes later.

He took Griffin over to Main Street and positioned himself beside a short wall just east of the intersection. Two female office workers sat 20 feet away solving the problems of the world and complaining about their bosses.

From his vantage point, he could duck down and still see the front doors of the building. He opened the file folder and re-examined the faces of the two gents who were supposedly out to capture or kill him. He closed the folder and folded it into his pocket. He rolled his neck and exhaled all the nerves out. Well, most of them at least.

He couldn't stop his mind from going out of body to look down on his position from a couple thousand feet. The aerial view put a little mental red "you are here" circle at the northeast corner of Main and Griffin. He could see the streets going in all directions like asymmetric arteries. He had originally memorized downtown "Bid D" several years earlier when he and a small group of teenagers drove down for a ZZ Top concert at Reunion Arena just a few blocks over from his current location. He knew his immediate surface road options and maybe a few secrets hidden in the urban terrain. He returned to his head at street level.

Another minute passed and he allowed himself to think maybe this was just a hoax or some screwy test or possibly even one of those dinner theater murder mysteries where everyone in the audience plays a part. But this little respite from reality was quickly shattered by the emergence from the glass double doors of a man he had just seen in a photo folded in his pocket.

What happened next was definitely not cool. The guy, instead of scanning the horizon and looking up and down the street, put a walkie-talkie to his mouth and did the most amazing thing. He looked directly at Lance from over 250 yards away. No mistake; he picked him up immediately. Impossible, but true.

Boris Number 1 spoke into the walkie-talkie and glanced up at the building before jogging toward Lance. Preacher glanced up and couldn't be sure from this distance, but he thought he could make out someone standing in a window on the seventh floor with a pair of binoculars. His best guess was it was the Boris Number 2. He looked back at the hunter heading directly his way and stuck his hand into his pocket to grab the handle of the gun. Boris would reach him in about 30 seconds. Lance thought of the odds. Here's one guy coming at him. Likely armed and more than likely skilled in weapon use. Boris probably wouldn't let Lance walk up to him and put a gun to his head. Better to move.

He turned from his perch and walked briskly to the north. His brisk walk rapidly evolved into the jog of a young businessman late for a meeting. His sightline of the building on Commerce was lost when he rounded a corner of another building, which meant the watcher in the window could not see him either. Behind him, Boris crossed Main a block and a half back. He could follow Lance, but he didn't know the secret Lance knew. And he hadn't run at least five miles virtually every day of his life since he was 13.

Preacher broke into an all-out sprint, which immediately put distance between him and the hunter. No contest. After turning another corner, Preacher came to the intersection of Main and Field. For the briefest moment, he thought of stopping right there and plastering himself against the building with the gun aimed at the corner, at the height of a man's head.

He could put a bullet in the guy's brain and turn and run. But the problem was witnesses. There were no less than 50 people within view. Shooting a guy right there on a downtown Dallas street corner would likely raise attention. He'd have a hell of a time getting out of the area without dozens of witnesses identifying him.

He stuck with his plan formed the minute prior. He crossed Field diagonally and ran into a parking garage entrance. His visit to Big D for OU-Texas weekend had left him with more than a few bits of precious information. One of these little jewels happened to be a secret back entrance into the aforementioned Adolphus Hotel.

He had been introduced to the virtually unknown and totally discrete entrance by a bellman who appreciated a $50 bill and no hassles. Lance had made a little wager with the fellas he had come down with that he could not only get into the heavily-secured grand dame of Dallas hotels; he would stay the night with one or more of the guests and meet back up with the guys at the game the next day. As usual, Lance came through and had another great story to share with the gang. Always leaving out the intimate details. He was a gentleman, of course.

All of that fleeted through Preacher's mind as he ran through the parking garage and out a back door into a tiny alley between tall buildings. He stepped into a doorway out of view if Boris happened to see him enter the parking garage. Not likely though, he had turned on the burners pretty good and left the hunter in his dust back on Main Street. But still, he listened for footsteps and the crackly voice on a walkie-talkie. Maybe, just maybe there were more of them out there hunting him.

He thought about walkie-talkies and how he and his little brother had played with them as kids. They usually didn't work very well, but damn they looked cool tucked in your belt while you pointed your toy machine gun at the bathroom mirror. *"Roger that, over and out."* He whispered.

He leaned against the wall beside the door and jabbed his hand back into his pocket. The gun calmed his nerves. He stayed out of site and listened for any sounds in the alley. None came. Approximately four minutes later, a door with no outside handle opened and an employee stepped out for a smoke. Lady luck shone on Preacher yet again. He didn't believe in luck. It was being in the right place at the right time. And lying helped, a lot.

The employee's name was Philip, the hotel's French-Canadian concierge. Lance put a hand on the man's bicep gently forcing him back into the building. The cigarette would have to wait.

Lance was quite convincing as an anxious assistant to a Texas businessman who needed to arrange special accommodations that required absolutely secrecy. He implied he had been watching the facility for a couple of days and knew Philip would be stepping outside for a smoke at this location and time. Lance was very persuasive, as always.

He lent a great deal of credibility to his story through his in-depth knowledge of the facility. Lance led the way walking the concierge down the hall, up a flight of stairs he shouldn't have known about and onto an elevator restricted to VIP use. He kept eye contact and often put a hand on the Philip's arm or shoulder. He so completely took the concierge into his confidence that he was able to tell him a couple of highly personal and completely fabricated facts about Lance's fictitious employer. Lance convinced Philip that room 614 would be ideal for his employer's needs and would greatly appreciate it if the concierge could use a house phone to confirm the availability of that particular room.

Lance described the suite's layout, traditional American furniture and priceless chandelier over the conference table as the perfect setting for his superior's needs. Philip was quite taken with Lance's details of both the room and his employer's delicate situation. Philip was fairly certain the room was unoccupied and used a house phone on a table near the elevator to confirm the fact. He asked the registration staff member to send up a key immediately. Lance interjected to ask for three keys. Details. It's always in the details.

Lance pulled out an American Express card belonging to Jimmy Lee, the car dealership's owner. He had been given the card under the table because of his exceptional sales performance the previous quarter. Jimmy was particularly impressed with Lance's handling of a long-time family friend going through a delicate personal situation.

Lance had made a point of using the card several times so as not to appear rude. He wasn't concerned that the card had someone else's name on it. If anyone was alarmed enough to call American Express, who would in-turn call Jimmy, the dealer would simply tell them Lance was using the card with his permission. Lance didn't know the card's credit limit, but assumed a few thousand dollars over the next few days wouldn't break the bank.

But a credit card may be called in for verification and a computer record generated. Anyone who knew much about Lance Priest, and it appeared Seibel knew just about everything, could possibly see a charge for Jimmy Lee at the Adolphus. He needed to delay card verification for a little while.

He inched closer to the concierge, took the man's hand, affected a conspiratorial tone in his voice and a look of utter and complete trust in his eyes. Lance asked Philip to handle all pertinent details but not run the card because that might trigger an action that could bring unwanted attention for his superior. He told Philip a cash payment that would cover all expenses as well as a generous gratuity would arrive in two days.

Lance added, if anyone, anyone at all, asked about room 614 or its occupants, Philip was to report this to Lance immediately. There could be no leaks, no loose ends. The concierge assured him these situations happened all the time at the Adolphus. Confidentiality was the hallmark of the institution.

As they stood outside room 614, Lance piled detail upon detail and added elements of intrigue that captured Philip's imagination. The hairs on the back of the concierge's neck stood at attention. He was sold.

Lance informed his new confidant that if anyone came looking for someone resembling himself, it would be rival interests who had only cracked the code up to Lance's level. "Do not divulge anything about me to anyone." He grasped Philip's upper arm to emphasize the point as they shook hands.

He let Philip know he would only deal with him. Aside from room service, no other employees were to come to 614. No maid service would be required. Secrecy was demanded at all times. Lance asked Philip for his home number so he could reach him after hours. Lance had the hooks in.

The concierge committed himself and the resources of his closest and most trusted associates to secrecy. For their confidentiality, Lance told him, they would be rewarded handsomely. And if they earned his trust, they could expect repeat business and even greater rewards in the future.

A bellman stepped out of the elevator with three room keys. Philip immediately intercepted the Hispanic man while Lance turned away to conceal his face. Philip quickly dismissed the bellman and turned to unlock the door. During the walk-around, Lance pulled out his wallet and fished out the secret $100 bill he always kept folded in with photos. He had about $300 in $50s and $20s but wanted to award the larger bill for full effect.

Back at the door, he placed the bill and the American Express card in the concierge's hand to seal their deal. Philip left the room with the credit card, the $100 bill and a sense of pride. Before he closed the door, Lance called out to his new friend, "And Philip, we would love to have a good U.S. road map. A road atlas would be even better."

As the door closed, Lance walked over to the windows at the corner of the room to look down on the street. He didn't expect to see anything suspicious and he didn't. No sign of either Boris. He could see Commerce Street in both directions. Nothing. He pulled the drapes closed and sat in a chair beside the bed to do some calculations. The room was going to cost at least $300 per night and room service would need to be ordered for three or four people each day to keep up appearances. He estimated that the next 72 hours would cost him about $3000. There went the commissions on the 280Z and Fiero he had sold the weekend before. Oh well.

He fell. And kept falling, rolling, tumbling, crashing and didn't stop until he struck the bottom of the hill. Hell, it was a mountain really. The ravine at the foot of the hill would be his grave as he lay bleeding, broken.

He had outrun them, escaped. Breathlessly, he'd run through day and night, never stopping. Their bullets had whizzed by overhead and smashed into walls and rocks. He'd made it out into the open, into an arid desert climate with clear skies and billions of stars shining. But he'd chosen the wrong route somewhere along the way and had to make a deadly choice minutes earlier.

Turn and fight, face an onslaught of bullets. Or step off the edge and see where gravity took him. He chose to fight gravity.

He lost. Every bone felt broken, shattered. The pain well beyond excruciating. Those stars in the night sky above would be the only witnesses to his lonely death.

His eyes opened. He was alone in the dark, but not the desert. He was in the hotel room. Alive, for now.

Chapter 4

5,496 miles east and north.

She pushed it a little further than planned. But not too far. She had him.

It took 11 weeks to get to this point, to his multi-million dollar apartment in Vienna. They were alone, which was a tragic mistake on his part. His two bodyguards were outside in the hall instead of in another room where they would usually be. The couple sat across from each other at a table on his balcony overlooking Stadtpark and its exquisite statues below. It was a beautiful chilly November evening and should have been a very romantic pre-seduction moment between an attractive young blond woman and an older man, a business tycoon.

But instead of a confident look of impending conquest, Herman Briouk looked scared to death, or worse, scared he was about to lose it all. And he was.

The young woman across from him with a pleasant demeanor about her and a glass of chardonnay in her hand smiled and continued. Her eyes though, were anything but pleasant. They were cold, icy, deadly. "So the choice is yours Herman. Do you want a bullet between your eyes or a blade across your throat? Either way, you are already dead. You were, the moment you welcomed me into your beautiful home."

In the preceding minutes, the young woman had told Briouk, not his Russian birth name of course, a short tale of oil and gas and pipelines and Soviet government contracts. Her knowledge of Briouk's vast energy empire was deeper than his own. She commended him on winning a recent government contract for oil fields along the Caspian Sea. She was especially impressed with his ability to bribe local officials while blackmailing others. "Impressive work by your people," she had said.

She finished her tale by telling the billionaire about a new corporation established under his umbrella holding company. The new firm had been commissioned by Briouk's chief financial officer and his vice president of Asian operations and was ready to take ownership of several Briouk corporations. Only his signature was required to complete the transaction. She had the papers with her now, in her purse.

Audacity of this nature was nothing new for Briouk. He built an empire by doing the same. The tycoon wanted to laugh this amateur stuff off. But the young woman's eyes, along with the photos she had just laid on the table, altered his bearing. Pictured in each photo were the aforementioned CFO and vice president. The thing was though, in these photos taken just hours earlier, each of the men had an extra hole in his head. Actually two holes; one where the bullet entered and a larger one where it exited the skull.

"You are a murdering wench," Briouk said in German as he disgustedly threw the photos back on the table and reached for his wine glass.

"We are both business people Herman. I have merely had the benefit of following men like you. Your examples, your practices have been enlightening. I thought you would consider this scenario a compliment."

"A compliment? You killed two men. They have families, children."

"And of course you thought of families and children every time you ordered the murder of government officials because they stood in the way of one of your acquisitions. I could list at least 14 deaths in which you and your people were involved. Please don't insult me." She shook her head.

"You have no proof." He fumed.

"I'm not here to put you on trial Herman. I am simply here for your signature or your life." She stopped and leaned toward him, "And before you think of screaming out for your guards, I would caution you that mine is not the only gun on you at present." She pulled her left hand from under the table and showed her small firearm. "Others have your forehead in their sites. And the moment your guards open the door they will be annihilated. Nothing personal. They appear to be good men, but good men die all the time."

"So you think I'm just going to sign over my companies to you without a fight. You think I will simply give you all that I have fought and bled for?" Briouk began to rage.

"Of course not Herman. We are not taking all your companies. In fact, we are only taking four. You keep the rest and go on about your business as usual. You will continue to receive significant compensation from their value, but we are acquiring ownership." She was professional, very mature.

"This is ridiculous, insulting. Why did they send a girl to do their job? What are you 25, 26? You are just a child, barely out of school. Why don't they show me their faces so I can tell them to go screw themselves in person." Briouk's anger caused him to switch to his native Russian for this last part.

He wasn't far off. She was 24, a mere child in most circles. But in a world of abandonment, life or death, of cruelty and deception and winning at all and every cost, she was anything but a child. Marta Illena Sidorova was ruthless and calculating. She was in control. And she was deadly to anyone standing, or even sitting, in her way.

He had it wrong. There was no one above her, especially since she went rogue from the KGB three months prior. And in this moment, she was actually being generous. She didn't really need Briouk's signature. His now deceased underlings prepared the transaction in such a manner that it was essentially completed. She merely wanted Briouk to know he was beaten. Marta thought again how quickly this operation had progressed. Eleven weeks from planning to implementation and now consummation. She was too professional to gloat or even smile.

She reached into her pocketbook and pulled out a stack of legal papers and a pen. "Herman, I need to leave now. Another appointment. Would you like to sign these papers or should I splatter your blood on them to seal the deal?"

She pushed the papers toward him with the barrel of her gun. "Now. Please."

He shook his head but still picked up the pen. Her gun helped convince him. After he signed away several corporations valued at hundreds of millions of dollars, Briouk spat on the documents. "You are nothing, you have nothing." He spoke in Russian.

Marta answered him in her native Russian, "We are all nothing; just dust and smoke my friend. We live then die." She leaned in close to whisper in his ear. Her voice was silk. "You were dead the moment you met me Herman, actually the moment I set my sites on you. Consider the rest of your days a blessing and live them to the fullest. Kiss your wife. Hug your children and grandchildren. Make love to your mistress. If we ever meet again, if you ever see my face, it will be your last vision until you open your eyes in hell."

As she stood up, a metal clang behind her allowed Marta to continue the showmanship of this little performance. She put the papers in her purse, the purse on her shoulder and pivoted to leap over the balcony railing. The clang was a hook attached to a rope anchored by a man dressed in black on the sidewalk three stories below. Because Marta wore leather gloves, she easily grasped the roped and descended to the street. As her high heels hit the pavement, she looked back up and smiled, smirked really, at Briouk leaning over his balcony.

And in the next moment she and the other individual were gone. Like dust and smoke.

Three hundred yards to the east, a man watched through binoculars. From the fifth floor of a building with a nice view of Stadtpark and Briouk's apartment, he had watched Marta and the tycoon on the balcony. He witnessed the older man begin to twitch, to shudder. She had done it.

Gregor Smelinski smiled to himself as Marta descended the rope to the street below Briouk's apartment and then disappeared into the dark of night. He looked back up at the Russian mogul reduced to a quivering idiot.

Smelinski witnessed his plan, his most secret mission take wings and now take flight. He had overseen Marta's training, her development and now her departure from his beloved KGB. She was now a weapon for him to wield. Marta would be his finest weapon, his greatest secret. He could change the playing field with her working outside the system. It was brilliant.

Marta's ascent into infamy was nothing short of spectacular. She had joined the agency only five years earlier, fresh out of university. In the ensuing half decade, Marta Illena Sidorova had proven to be extra capable, extra proficient at her duties. From a safe, yet voyeuristic, distance, Smelinski had kept tabs on her development from the very beginning. He'd recognized her potential within moments of meeting her during her initial language training in Moscow.

He had spoken to a new class of recruits and been drawn to her in the crowd. She wasn't particularly beautiful, but her intellect and ability to attract and incite others was obvious. It was in her eyes; that something, whatever it is.

She'd quickly moved from an assistant to an under secretary in Minsk to a perfect cover as a translator in Vienna and then right to the big leagues in Paris, where her position in the Soviet embassy put her in touch with agents and operatives and enemies at every level. That she'd done all this in a matter of five years was an amazing achievement for anyone, let along a young woman. But alas, her aspirations far exceeded even those of Smelinski and others supposedly guiding her career. She had been building a network along the way that allowed her to virtually disappear this past April. After going off the radar for a couple of months, she emerged in September in Vienna and worked Briouk in less than three months. Spectacular.

He said a silent prayer thanking whoever brought Marta to him. She had followed her orders to the letter and built a façade as a rogue agent, a wild card, a lethal loose cannon. She was his secret alone. Or so he thought.

Her success was amazing. Even more so when one considered her upbringing. Smelinski knew some of the sordid details. At least the pieces he could dig up. Her backstory out of abject poverty, abuse and basic torture at the hands of her father and family in Novosibirsk was the stuff of which survivors of Nazi concentration camps would empathize and maybe even shudder. She was strong in a way a tree that had been chopped but refuses to die only knows. Those tiny, scraggly branches grow out of the torn stump in multiple directions and then become strong trunks supporting other branches. She found a way to survive hell in childhood and then state foster homes.

Her strength was adaptability. She was a chameleon on par with the greatest actors of any generation. She was a method actor who took abuse and turned it into laughter, somehow turned heartbreak into joy. She was never the same person any of the times Smelinski had encountered her.

A childhood on the outskirts of Novosibirsk under the iron thumb of a frustrated and fiendish factory worker father with absolutely no morals and a mother willing to turn her back on any semblance of reality, forced a young Marta to fend off all males in her life. And fend for herself.

She knew in the moments after killing her 13-year-old brother after he tried for a second time to take her virginity before her 12th birthday, she had what it takes to provide for her meager needs. She rid the world of her parents' stain and left the next day to make her way as an orphan. Tough times from an 11-year old.

Marta still sees her parents' faces when she closes her eyes. It was horror, but it was also something else. They had just lost a son and their only daughter was now dead to them, but the look in their eyes was not sadness. It was acceptance. They knew they deserved to suffer for what they had done and what they had allowed themselves to become.

Marta could see her parents' eyes so clearly because she had seen them time and again on the faces of others she'd faced down or those she was about to dispatch unto the great beyond. People were really all the same. Most lived unrealized, unhappy and unrelentingly wasted lives. When faced with their demise, they all realized this. The look was always the same.

Chapter 5

The secret to playing and winning hide and seek is knowledge of the terrain. Young Lance Priest became the neighborhood expert, the aficionado in the intricacies of "hide n seek" by the age of seven in Winter Park, Florida.

He and the other children living on and around Monmouth Way participated in some of history's epic hide n seek battles. Lance was almost always the final hidden participant. The rules of competition were even changed because of his skill in locating and occupying the most secret of places. The traditional rules of the game, as most will recall, involve one seeker setting out to find the hiders after closing his or her eyes and counting slowly to the pre-determined number, usually 25. The counting was followed by, "Ready or not, here I come."

The seeker would leave home base and work methodically to locate others. Hiders could either stay hidden or come out and make a break for home base. When they reached it, they were deemed "free" or safe.

This is where young Lance changed the rules of the time-honored game for those on Monmouth Way. His prowess at hiding became so absolute that the seeker was allowed to enlist the help of the others he or she discovered along the way to search for Lance. The rules clearly stated that kids could hide anywhere on the block, but not inside any of the houses or garages. Lance followed these rules like everyone else. But his advantage was knowledge of the environment, terrain, landscapes and any new developments.

His dedication to the sport demanded his total commitment. He would awaken at 4:30 a.m. some mornings and sneak out of the house to search for the next great hiding spot while others slept. He had several unique locations that had befuddled the other kids, but he was always seeking that one perfect location that could simply never be discovered. On many occasions, the other kids were heard saying that Lance just plain made the game no fun at all.

Eventually the seeker and his enlisted searchers would return to home base and call out the inevitable, "Olli olli in come free!" The dreaded surrender. Lance would take as much care in emerging from his hiding spot as he did finding it. He would climb a fence, cut through a back yard and appear three houses down from where he had been concealed.

And another rule Lance changed about the sport, at least in Winter Park, Florida, he was never allowed to be the seeker. The other kids had learned by the time little Lance was six that you simply could not hide from him. He would find kids up a tree, down a hole and easily behind a row of bushes in front of the Munroe home. It was useless to even try.

Lance thought about those legendary hide n seek games during that first night's stay in the Adolphus Hotel. He had done the legwork on this particular location a couple of years earlier during OU-Texas weekend when he was 18.

After sneaking into the hotel through the hush-hush door around back, he wandered the halls for half an hour or so mingling with a few groups, chatting with employees and ducking out of view of hotel security. All the while, a classic song by The Who was on repeat in his head. He hummed along as he crept about like a burglar in training. Lance found the VIP-only staircase and the permission-only elevator and stepped on to ride to the top floor with an elderly and obviously well to do Texas Longhorn patron.

Stepping off the elevator, young Lance ran into a group of ultra-affluent college age offspring of Lone Star State aristocracy. The group of boys and girls reeked of wealth and privilege and a good bit of arrogance. They were gathered in the hallway outside their rooms as late evening turned to early morning and the partying was still in high gear. Security kept their distance and turned their heads when these young adults, many definitely under the age of 21, consumed alcohol, a lot of alcohol. As Lance stepped up to the group and grabbed a beer from a cooler, several of them noticed his crimson colored shirt.

"Hold on, hold on, what the hell are you doing here?" A stoutly built boy of approximately 20 turned and bowed up his chest to Lance.

"Got bored with the party downstairs and heard they were still kickin it up here," Lance replied with a warm and trusting smile as he twisted the cap off the bottle.

"No way, no friggin way we let a goddamn Sooner up here." Another young man stepped over beside the stout gent. The girls in the group giggled. They had been bored a few moments earlier and now this looked like it might be interesting.

Lance looked down at his shirt and then back at the two fellas standing in front of him and did a completely unexpected thing. He handed the beer to a boy and pulled the shirt off to reveal a burnt orange shirt with a large UT and longhorn pictured on front.

"Sorry about that. It was an OU crowd downstairs and I didn't want anyone to be uncomfortable." He kept the smile on as he took the bottle back from the boy.

"Wait a minute. You don't just change colors and say everything's okay. Either you're all for Texas or your against." The guy slurred the word "against" so it sounded like "ahginn." The beers and tequila and whatever else his daddy's money had paid for showed up in his speech and wild eyes.

"You see, that's the beauty of it. I am truly not for either one," Lance looked from the big boy to the other and the three more standing behind. His survey of the group told him they all came from big money and had known nothing but privilege in their soft, short lives.

They knew nothing about living in apartments with their single divorced mother and annoying younger brother. They had never eaten a bowl of cereal sitting on the floor using a cardboard box as a table. They couldn't know that one bowl was the single favorite meal that one would ever eat because it was born of freedom. The constant fighting and violence of the relationship between mom and dad had taken so much away from him that a mere bowl of Cheerios eaten while kneeling on the floor amid moving boxes had left an impression that would never be replaced by filet mignon or poached salmon.

Yet none of that flashed across Lance's face as he looked over the group in front of him and smiled. "I'm just here for the party mates."

"Where do you go to school?" A particularly cute young lady standing to the left and behind the puffed up boys asked and bit her lower lip.

"Notre Dame." Lance perused a mental database in the flash of a moment to select a school about which he knew several key facts learned from movies and a books.

"What the hell are you doing here then?" The boys demanded.

"To party with some of my friends."

"Just to party? You came all the way to Dallas to party?"

"Where the hell else would a professional partier be? This is it man. I've been coming down here since I was a kid."

"Where are you from?" The girl asked and inched closer.

"Wichita." He smiled back at her.

"Wichita sucks." Stouty blurted out.

"Damn right there. That's why I got the hell out and went to Notre Dame." Lance's smile was brilliant. He'd already won this one.

This particular conversation lasted another few minutes but Lance had altered the mood of the crowd and turned it into a monologue he delivered in perfect pitch. Lance was required to tell them a few more particulars about Notre Dame, Wichita, his major and other "shit." He passed the test and moved into the middle of the crowd to share their beer, shoot their tequila and sneak off with the cute girl who had to give Stouty the slip.

At about 4:15 a.m., Lance pried himself apart from the sleeping young lady and left the room. He grabbed some rich kid's navy blue sports coat flung over a chair to be sure he looked the part. For the next hour, he wandered the Adolphus picking the best hiding spots, just as if it were the old block on Monmouth Way. On the 6th floor, he found the door to 614 standing wide open and not a soul inside. There were suitcases and clothes on the still made bed, but no one home. He stepped in and inspected the room. It looked like a couple had started the evening together and then either left or split up during the night and found other quarters to shack up. He spent just over a minute in the room to catalog details and then stepped back into the hall.

As Lance stepped into the same hall three years later, he surveyed both ends of the corridor for any activity. Nothing. It was about 4 a.m. again and he wanted to investigate the premises for anything that should make him worry. This time, however, he had a gun in his pocket. "Come on trouble," he snickered to himself.

In the lobby, he smiled at the female attendant behind the opulent front desk. A fast scan of the space showed it to be empty as it should be at this early hour. He kept his hand in his front suit jacket pocket gripping the handle of his gun as he crossed the room to look out a front window at Commerce Street. Nothing.

Lance smiled at the front desk gal and again fought off the urge to go tell her a series of intricate lies all aimed at learning any and everything she knew. He wound his way back to the private staircase and privileged elevator and back up to room 614. He passed out quickly after laying his clothes out on the chair.

He awoke the next morning and stepped out the door to welcome room service for three ordered the night before. Over the next several hours he wrote down everything that had happened the previous day. Every detail he could recall.

Two things stood out. First, he had been handed a loaded gun and just minutes later he held the gun to Seibel's head. But Seibel's response was approval, not fear or anger or panic. Strange.

Second, everything he had been through yesterday was more than likely an act, a play, a charade put on for his benefit. Not all the players were in on it. Seibel was the director giving the other actors directions. Lance wanted to walk down the block and back into the building to see if there would even be anyone there. Had it all been fake? Who were these people? CIA? FBI?

KGB? Some big scam? Certainly not State Department or Foreign Service.

Right about now is when most people would call or at least think of calling the police. Not Lance. It never crossed his mind. He was going to figure this one out on his own.

In reviewing his notes, another prominent question came into focus. Where did this start? How did they learn about him? Seibel said several months of surveillance. *When did it start?* He wrote the question and circled it.

It had to be either during the written exam or just before. Marsco, or whatever his name was, had given himself away there. Was he in Tulsa during the exam only to watch Lance or was he picking others as well? What did they really want from him? He didn't have much money and most of what he did have he owed to the University of Tulsa.

He took a break and stood up to stretch his back, then took a shower and put his clothes back on. He considered walking over to his car parked just a few blocks away to retrieve his stuff, but thought it unwise. He'd already missed his morning class back in Tulsa and luckily wasn't scheduled to work at the dealership until Thursday afternoon. He picked up the phone and asked the operator to connect him with the concierge.

Six minutes later there was a knock at the door. Lance grabbed the file folder from the desk and opened the door only inches to step out. Philip greeted him with a new North America road atlas. Lance thanked him with a high five.

Lance learned Philip hailed from Montreal and chose to relocate to Dallas for the climate and the women. Lance agreed with him about the women, but Texas was even hotter than Oklahoma and there were plenty of days over 100 in Tulsa. That was hot enough.

"How are your meetings progressing? I hope your party is finding our accommodations acceptable. I hope the private entrance is working for those not staying with us." Philip said.

Lance liked that. Philip obviously knew that four people, especially executives, were not staying in the room together. "Everything is moving at a good pace. No real breakthroughs, but lots of positive dialogue that required face-to-face conversations. The accommodations are perfect and the private entrance is indeed working well." Lance replied in a tone that reflected complete confidence in Philip. "I trust our presence here has gone undetected by anyone other than yourself?"

"Room 614 is registered to Mr. Buckner as you requested. No one has inquired about the room or its guests to my knowledge."

"Excellent. I am going to have to ask you for an additional favor." He looked directly into Philip's left eye. He'd learned from his time at the dealership to look into only one eye so his own eyes did not shift from side to side. No one likes, let alone trusts, someone who is shifty-eyed. And automobile sales requires a modicum of trust as its foundation.

"Anything," Philip replied without hesitation.

"I would ask that you please take a look at these two photos." He held up the file folder and opened it to show Philip the two mug shots of the men hunting him. "These two individuals have presented a significant challenge for my employer in recent months. They have disrupted several transactions and made it difficult to complete our business. If you should happen to see either of these men, I would ask that you first call the police and then call me."

"The police? Are these two dangerous?"

"They have committed crimes in several countries, including some very violent acts. In fact, one of their more spectacular incidents took place in Montreal several years ago." Lance added another layer of detail to cement the story. The Canada connection was sure to hit home with Philip.

"I see." The concierge reacted differently hearing his hometown mentioned.

"I don't want you to be afraid. I just want you to be aware of the situation. I am sure you and your security staff have dealt with similar circumstances. We would have brought additional security ourselves, but didn't want to upset the delicate balance of the negotiations. Both parties agreed to this stipulation."

"I understand," Philip took another look at the photos to memorize each face. "Do you have reason to believe that these two are in the area?"

"They were spotted at DFW three days ago and just a few blocks from here yesterday."

"Thank you for bringing this to my attention. I feel with this information, I will be required to extend my shift each day for the duration of your visit." Philip nodded to assure Lance. And with that, Preacher succeeded in bringing a resource into his sphere of influence. He had just employed one of the oldest tricks of the trade by placing confidence in another; thereby gaining trust and loyalty.

Before Philip shook Lance's hand and turned for the elevator, they discussed the current occupancy level, expected activities over the next couple of days and of course, the weather. Lance got the concierge to talk about his car, a BMW 3i that cornered like an animal. Car talk is always good for male bonding.

Lance didn't leave the room the rest of the day. He enjoyed sampling four different lunch items. Because he was holed up in the room, he jogged barefoot in place for 30 minutes and did his usual 200 push-ups and sit-ups. He also devoured the road atlas Philip brought. In honor of his new Canadian friend, he memorized the arterial streets in Montreal.

He paused a few moments at 2:17 pm to mark 24 hours completed in his 72-hour survival assignment. No reason to celebrate. When evening arrived, he enjoyed most of a porterhouse steak, a medium rare filet mignon, chicken picatta and only one bite of the veal.

At 4 a.m. the next morning, he followed the same routine from the previous day. The same attendant was at the front desk. No one else stirred in the stately hotel. On this excursion he stopped and read several pages of a coffee table book about the hotel. He learned of its rich history spanning 70 years and was surprised he hadn't put two and two together about the hotel's name. Lance was a big fan and had been for a number of years a regular drinker of Anheuser Busch beer. The hotel was built by Adolphus Busch, founder of the beer conglomerate. There weren't many people named Adolphus around. He'd raise a cold one in honor of the old fella if he made it through this. Lance returned to room 614 and began the third day of his exile.

The man with one eye darker blue than the other fell to his knees in slow motion. His left hand kept him from falling all the way to the ground. His right hand clutched at his chest. The cut, a deep, slicing gash gushed blood. He had only minutes.

The chase had lasted nearly an hour and the man never caught his breath. He never would. His chaser was too fast, too relentless. The chaser bent down on one knee to get closer now, to look into a dying man's eyes and share the last moments.

Lance had never looked into a man's eyes as he took his last breaths. He'd chased this stranger through the deep dark of endless night and caught him. Without a moment's hesitation, he'd thrust his cold blade into the man's chest. His eyes opened and looked about. The world was dark. The hotel room unchanged. He waited for the remorse. None came.

Chapter 6

5,859 miles to the east and north.

It wasn't quite the firefights they'd been in during their time in that hell on earth known as Afghanistan, but this was good. These were real bullets flying around them, creating little explosions in the walls and leaving craters behind. They nearly had them cornered now.

Soon to be former KGB agents Evgany Korovin and Nikolai Kusnetsov were in their element tonight. They hadn't forced this violence, but were ready to end it. Instead of the streets of Kabul or frozen high mountain passes, this little battle was taking place on their home turf in dark alleys and abandoned apartment buildings in Kiev.

The 2 a.m. meeting was scheduled to facilitate a transfer of Israeli-made weapons in exchange for a significant amount of opium. Korovin and Kusnetsov, often referred to by the catchy acronym K&K, brought the opium to the party. Their access to large quantities of the narcotic was a remnant of their time in the heart of opium country.

Their objective in this particular transaction was twofold. They wanted to obtain the weapons, of course. But they also wanted to exploit a black market source. They'd been hunting this channel for six months and had maneuvered their way into a number of nefarious dealings to reach this point.

Rewind seven minutes. Korovin drove the car to the designated location. It was a secluded street in an empty, dilapidated district. They knew it well from their childhood. Although they both grew up in Kiev, they didn't meet until they were each recruited into the KGB from the Red Army in the early 70s. They had both been to this very location as children three decades ago. One with his father to visit a black market source for salmon. The other with a gang of street toughs pursuing another gang.

Tonight, the neighborhood was silent. There were no gangs, no fathers, no sons. The other vehicle waited as Korovin approached with headlights extinguished. Kusnetsov was 70 yards to the west in a darkened doorway; a radio held close to his mouth. Korovin held another radio just like it. At three other locations surrounding the site, men held similar radios. They also all held guns. Their sightlines triangulated to create a nexus of death at the center should they begin firing.

As expected, just over 45 seconds after the transaction commenced, one of the longhaired gentlemen who had emerged from the other vehicle pulled a weapon. The KGB veteran had his radio in his right coat pocket. He simply said the words "Okay then," in Ukrainian. The weapons dealer lost a good bit of brain matter when three bullets entered his forehead and exited out the back. As shots were fired from four separate locations, Korovin took this opportunity to dive and roll to the rear of his vehicle. The guy standing next to the first to die then took four bullets to his head, neck and chest. Neither Korovin nor Kusnetsov were thrilled with this development. It meant they would likely be killing people instead of gathering information on their network and connections. But maybe if they were lucky, they'd capture one of these guys and keep him alive long enough to mine him for usable data.

The rolling gun battle moved to the next block and then the next. At the beginning, there were six of them against the five K&K brought. Moving from doorway to doorway to alley, the other side's numbers dwindled to two. K&K had with them veterans of the Afghan war who had fought and killed hundreds. The other side fired randomly with little effect. None of their bullets reached their intended targets. The only thing keeping the remaining two alive was the pitch-black night as they hid, huddled really, in whatever alcove they could find. It was only a matter of time.

One of the two took off to the east in an all out sprint. K&K radioed to the others to stay with the runner. Korovin called to Kusnetsov over the radio with his next move. He really didn't need to though. They knew each other's tendencies like they knew their own. K&K were elite among the league of killers populating the ranks of the KGB. Their skills and reputations were unsurpassed. The black market weapons dealer they were chasing along a deserted street this early morning had no idea who he and his team were dealing with.

The weapons dealers did not know they were dead the moment they were contacted by men acting as conduits for K&K. This job and maybe one more would be the last K&K would complete as salaried employees of the KGB. They had built up their network, established multiple spheres of influence and stashed millions in accounts throughout Eastern Europe, the Middle East and Southeast Asia. Running now like they were was exhilarating, refreshing. They hadn't been in a firefight since Afghanistan. They had participated in shootings. Mostly the two of them killing others quickly with no shots fired back.

This was actually kind of fun. K&K came together against a wall. The man being chased had stopped up ahead and lay flat on the downward slope of a loading dock. He fired 25 or 30 rounds in seconds. The bullets exploded on the wall above Korovin and Kusnetsov. They looked at each other and couldn't help but smile. They could hear the man get to his feet and take off running again. K&K silently signaled each other their plans. One went directly after the man, the other peeled off to approach from the north.

Four minutes later, they had him cornered. Korovin leapt to his feet and angled across the street. He drew fire and Kusnetsov zeroed in on the muzzle flashes. His good ol' AK-47 put a hail of bullets square in the weapons dealer's chest. Hopefully they hadn't killed him. K&K rushed him from their separate locations, staying low to the ground in case he recovered. Once they arrived, it was obvious Kusnetsov's aim had been lethal. They wouldn't get to interrogate this one.

Korovin bent and picked up the man's gun to remove evidence from the scene. Without the high-end rifle, the dead man would look like any other dead drug runner. As they turned from the body, Kusnetsov brushed his hand against Korovin's. The gesture was quick and could not be seen by anyone else as the two walked beside each other in the dark alley. But the gesture carried with it the commitment of two people devoted to their shared mission and to one another.

Chapter 7

Preacher was lost in thought.

He'd been thinking for hours. Just lying there in room 614 of the Adolphus Hotel. But his mind was elsewhere. He'd gone out of body big time, reliving the last eight weeks. He knew he'd get it. He'd figure it out if he could just get a hold of a few of the details missed along the way. He started at TU.

It was a simple one-page flyer pinned to the bulletin board outside the Career Counseling Office at the University of Tulsa. Lance stopped to look at the notice. He didn't know why. Something about it caught his eye. It announced the upcoming Foreign Service Written Examination or FSWE in government acronym talk.

The test would be held in two weeks on Saturday, September 26, 1987. He thought about it for a few seconds. Foreign Service. Could be interesting, exciting even. He had just turned 21, was a junior with unremarkable grades, a part-time car salesman. He was in need of a new challenge. Maybe even a career.

The female work-study student at the counseling office reception desk was named Lori. He could see it on a graded exam atop one of her stacks. She was 19 or 20. Her clothes were casually unfashionable. And as she raised her head to greet him, Lance saw contacts, acne scarring and a smile improved by orthodontics. Details.

She blushed red with embarrassment at the mess she'd made all over the desk with her studying. After a brief exchange with Lori, featuring a delightfully assortment of white lies, Lance assuaged her embarrassment and turned around to wait for a counselor. Her smile was replaced with an ever so slight bite of the lower lip. Lance didn't have to see it. He knew the look. He'd seen it on countless faces.

The counselor's name was Janine. He heard a co-worker call to her from across the room. Lance hated to ask people their name and instead preferred to learn it through other means. It was a silly little game he played with himself.

Her greeting was perfunctory as she walked him back to her office to get him information about the exam. Lance took in the postage stamp of an office in a flash. Kandinsky prints, husband with a paunch, two grown daughters, no grandkids yet, undergrad at the University of Missouri, masters' at Creighton. Left-handed, flower doodles on the desk pad. *If Music be the Food of Love, Play On* streamed across the screensaver on her computer monitor. Lance recognized it as the opening line of Shakespeare's *Twelfth Night*. More details.

Janine handed Lance a one-page questionnaire with 11 questions.

"Here is a little form they ask that you fill out when you register for the exam. Can I ask why you are interested in the Foreign Service?" she asked.

"Foreign policy has always interested me." He lied. Lance had never considered a career with the US Foreign Service prior to six minutes ago. He had read a number of foreign relations reference books in the library. He blurted out details of US-

China affairs and Thomas Jefferson's exploits in Europe during a time of revolution. But he was making it up on the spot as usual.

"Interesting," she replied. "I've always wondered what it would be like to immerse myself in another culture. Like the Middle East or Indonesia."

"Absolutely," Lance kept the beat. "Have you ever visited those places?"

"No. Just Mexico and Canada," she sagged her shoulders a little. For a moment her eyes misted over and she was off someplace.

Lance went with her for the ride. In fleeting moments when people speaking with him lose focus and drift to someplace visited or only dreamed about, his innate ability to disengage, to go out of body, wander the world and return in a split second allowed him to bond with strangers as if they were lifelong friends.

The secret, learned as an infant looking up at the faces of those around him, was a brief smile and a moment of unfocused gazing into the distance. A subtle sigh or exhale adds to the effect. Complete strangers often share their dreams, their fantasies with him. Happens all the time.

Lance filled out the questionnaire in a few minutes. His short answers were a mixture of interesting facts and complete fabrications, like most of his life. He walked the form back to Janine's office and she handed him the Foreign Service Written Exam prep envelope. Her parting smile and bite of her lip were not unlike Lori's a few minutes earlier.

Lance opened his eyes. He could feel it. He'd missed something there. Something to do with Janine. He shook his head and closed his eyes to try to go back into a trance.

What he couldn't see were the moments after he left the counseling office. Janine got up from her desk and walked across the office to the fax and copier room. She inserted Lance's Foreign Service questionnaire – Form No. T12A - into the fax machine and dialed the number on the fax cover. A number, by the way, that does not appear in any listings with the university, the U.S. Foreign Service or any official government agency. The number existed for this one purpose.

A fax machine at the other end of the line fired up. The ensuing hiss and whine of internal modems resulted in two sheets of paper printing out in a nondescript office in an otherwise nondescript building on a very nondescript street on the northwest side of Arlington, Virginia. Just across the Potomac from Washington, D.C. and about five miles southeast of Langley, the headquarters of a little government entity known affectionately worldwide as the CIA.

Chapter 8

Lance was out of body again. He was watching himself take the Foreign Service Written Exam eight weeks earlier in Tulsa.

He put a few details into the vault. The guy in the back row across the room was a pencil chewer. He'd made a mess of his No. 2. The gal two rows over could not stop blinking, absolutely could not stop. She was going 200 to 250 blinks per minute as if a blink was required after each letter of each word she wrote. And the gentlemen in the flannel shirt on the second row across the way had looked at Lance at least 80 times since the start of the exam. Lance knew now that gentleman sometimes went by the name Drew Marsco.

He watched from above as Marsco eyed him. It didn't bother Lance much, he was quite used to garnering the attention of others, including those of the same sex. It had just always been like this. But the way Marsco was watching him was different. The guy was trying to keep it undercover, but he was constantly watching. At the time, Lance had struggled to come up with a word to describe what Marsco's watching felt like. He knew now. It was surveillance.

What Lance couldn't see were the thoughts going through the psychologist's head. Indeed, surveillance is half art and half science. Stuart Braden had mastered neither. As a psychologist and a subject evaluation specialist, he is an expert in the intricacies of the human condition, with an emphasis, or specialty, as he likes to call it, in body language.

For Braden, the human body is a book with a cover that does tell a story – often the whole story. He trained alongside the elite psychologists in the country in evaluating a person's feelings, state of mind, desires, hidden secrets and greatest fears – all visible in the furrow of a brow, flutter of an eye, rise and fall of the chest and bounce tap-rate of a foot. Braden is a walking, talking lie detector.

Instead of going into practice for himself, he practiced his craft on behalf of the intelligence-gathering arm of the U.S. government.

Braden found himself in Tulsa on a rainy Saturday in mid-September to do what he does best – evaluate people. In this case, one person. The subject in this instance being a candidate. But this particular setting in a university classroom was not ideal, not even close. Instead of evaluating a subject in a controlled and secure interview or interrogation room or even a somewhat secure courtroom, he was asked by Seibel to examine this candidate in a pressure setting.

His mark was Lance Priest, male, 21, student, part-time car salesman. The young man set off a few alarm bells with his T12A questionnaire response. It was the first time Braden could recall this particular trigger.

Looking across the room now at young Mr. Priest, Braden tried to be as discrete as possible, but field surveillance was simply not his bag. His notes, written on a single piece of notebook paper so as not to stick out among the other exam takers, detailed a mixture of observations recorded over the past two hours. Looking over his notes again, one word kept showing up. *Comfortable.* Braden had written comfortable multiple times across the page. *"Comfortable, is that the best word to describe candidate Priest?"* he furrowed his brow.

At ease, casual, stress-free; all applied, but comfortable best captured the kid's essence. Glancing around the room, Braden could play his one-word association game with everyone taking the exam. *"Bored"* fit the heavyset woman two desks over. *"Flummoxed"* best detailed the young man dressed in denim. *"Perched"* most accurately described a female student with a long nose and glasses. *"Lonely"* applied to the boy trying very hard to be a man directly across from him.

But *comfortable* just fit Priest. A detailed observation h2t, or head-to-toe for non-government intelligence professionals, revealed a healthy, attractive young man completely at ease in a potentially stressful situation. Braden's notes had captured the following details -- breathing normal, no fidgeting, eye movement steady, facial expression relaxed. Yet, there was something that Braden couldn't quite nail down that lay just below the comfortable quilt of sorts this kid had wrapped around him. If he had to say, he would call it *awareness*. This kid was comfortably aware of everything going on around him. It was not overt, but it was there in his eyes. Braden wrote *comfortably aware.*

And the psychologist had no doubt Candidate Priest had caught him several times. In field surveillance instances such as this where he is detected, protocol calls for playing gay. He had become quite good at it. One time in a delightful seaside cafe in Majorca surveilling a team of Serbian arms dealers to determine which one was a KGB agent, Braden was nailed cold by one of the men. The man rose rather abruptly and approached him in a menacing manner. Braden escaped harm by affecting a lilting French accent and commenting on the guy's excellent choice in slacks. Interestingly, the chap turned out to be both KGB and homosexual.

His current evaluation subject didn't present any obvious danger. If anything, Mr. Priest looked the nonviolent type. Braden wrote *possibly unable to act with violence* on his sheet. He returned to the word comfortable.

He had sat in on interviews with cold-blooded murderers who were also incredibly comfortable. They sat by calmly as insults and threats were hurled at them by interrogators. But below the surface and only flashed in the briefest of moments with a squint or a fleeting eye roll, was a torrent of evil. These moments gave bad guys away. In these situations, Braden was able to step out of the interview room and give the investigating officer or interrogating agent a sliver of insight to use as a wedge to begin unraveling the subject. He'd done it dozens of times over the years.

His now bulky file on Subject Priest held a number of details indicating levels of narcissism and detachment, but nothing in stone. Priest was just a naturally calm and at-ease individual. *And then there was the lying.*

But just like that, Braden knew he was made. No doubt about it. Candidate Priest met his glance and smiled. The exchange lasted a fraction of a second, but in that moment, Braden knew his attention and focus had given him away. He followed protocol and averted his eyes for 30 seconds and then brought his attention back to Lance. The kid's second smile at him made it clear he was aware. Not good. Impressive on the kid's part, but not good. Not a real big deal because of the logistics of the classroom and the absence of firearms, but the next phase would need to be timeline advanced. Further observation would be completed by video surveillance. Braden didn't like videotape. Didn't trust it. Preferred to see his subjects in person to be able to catch the details that two-dimensional video and its accompanying bad audio often missed.

As planned, Braden dropped his pencil and bent to pick it up. When he returned to sitting position he' and the exam monitor exchanged a glance. The exam monitor, a man of 50 or so with unruly hair, dirty glasses and jacket with elbow patches, stood. "Your attention please, you have two minutes to complete this portion of the exam." He announced to the room. Most had finished, but a few still working on their answers released sighs of exasperation and ran fingers through their hair or rubbed their brows.

The exam monitor moved closer to Lance and took a position directly between him and Braden, creating a momentary visual barrier. He then cleared his throat to get Lance's attention. Lance glanced up and Braden got up and walked out the door. The professorial gentlemen smiled down at Lance and turned to finish his rounds of the room.

All of this went as planned. All of it except the part where Lance saw the entire thing unfold. He watched the replay again from above. At the time, he couldn't be 100 percent certain the guy he knew as Marsco was only watching him. Now he was sure.

He was used to it of course – the watching. Even though he worshipped anonymity, Lance had always garnered the attention of others. Girls in elementary school stalked him in games of kissing tag on the playground. Older girls whispered to their friends as he walked by in high school hallways. And dudes who liked to kiss other dudes could never be sure if he was one of them or not. Marsco appeared on the surface to be this type. But something tugged at Lance and told him there was another element at work here.

The next few actions were subtle. Marsco dropped his pencil – a signal to the test monitor. He left when his friend Mr. Exam Monitor made a little human wall. Why would someone just get up and leave when the rules given at the beginning of the exam stated clearly that leaving the room forfeited the test. He knew the reason now. Lance noticed Marsco's test still lying there on his desk, but his scratch paper was gone.

Just what the hell was all this about? He knew that now also.

"And that is time ladies and gentlemen," Mr. Elbow Patches made his way back over to the podium. "Please close your exams if you haven't already done so. I invite you to stand up for a few moments. Take a few deep breaths and maybe stretch your legs. Please do not talk to each other though. The third and final portion of the test will begin in five minutes and will last one hour and ten minutes."

His fellow exam takers did various forms of stretching, exhaling, yawning. Lance did the same. He stood up and raised his arms over his head to release a little pressure in his back. He waited for another student to approach the exam monitor and then casually made his way over near Marsco's desk. He quickly reached out and opened Marsco's test to see the first few pages and what he found surprised him indeed. The faker had not answered any of the questions in the test.

Lance turned ever so slowly and walked back to his desk. It was all one fluid motion. From above, Lance thought it was pretty slick work.

Lance's replay of the scene didn't include Braden being impressed with the move. The psychologist was also watching from above. Two floors up, he stood next to contract electronic surveillance expert Frank Wyrick who sat in a chair in front of a video monitor. They both smiled at what they had just seen.

"Pretty good." Wyrick whispered.

"Pretty good is right," Braden replied.

The video cameras for this particular surveillance opportunity just happened to be inside the two 21-inch televisions hanging from the ceiling in the corner of the classroom. Whichever side candidate Priest had chosen to sit, the cameras concealed behind see-through opaque glass, could zoom in on him.

"Did you get enough?" Wyrick asked while still watching the screen.

"More than."

"You sure he made you?"

"Positive." Braden confirmed

"How long?"

"Tell you the truth," Braden rubbed his forehead. "I think the little shit made me within minutes. I think he knew I was there from the git-go and was trying to figure me out."

"Think he took you for a friendly kind of guy?" Wyrick smiled and winked.

"That's the vibe I was giving, but I'll tell you what, I think that I was the one being evaluated here. I don't know if I recall anyone this aware with his surroundings."

"What, you mean ever? In all your years digging through people's minds?" Wyrick asked.

"Ever." Braden replied.

They both watched the monitor as Wyrick zoomed the camera in on Lance. His eyes gave nothing away, just like a professional. "The word I kept coming back to is comfortable. He is like a throw blanket on a couch or maybe a robe." Braden added.

"Or like a friend you can open up to. Almost like a shrink you can trust."

"That really hurts man." The psychologist shook his head. The two of them had worked together dozens of times.

Wyrick laughed. "I'm just wondering if you are going to write the word 'blanket' or 'robe' in your TER?"

"I might." They laughed a moment. "It fits though doesn't it?"

"Yep. This one is a natural," Wyrick added. "You can see it inside of a minute. Like we did the first time. The moves, the recognition, the assessing going on; it is like a computer program running in his head. And then there's the lying. Man that's artwork."

"From everything I read in the file. He's a liar on par with the greatest." Braden added.

"You got it," Wyrick leaned back in his chair for a moment and put his hands behind his head. He had spent a good part of the last two weeks reacquainting himself with Lance Priest and had become an expert of sorts. "This kid's entire life is a lie. You interview five different people and you get five different stories. Very subtle differences. Totally believable, totally detailed; amazing. I've been with more than a dozen so far and I can tell you this kid, Preacher, is the real thing."

"Preacher. Can you believe that nickname? That's irony for you." Braden sat down in a desk and stretched out his legs. "I felt like I was reading in layers in his file. One set of lies, built upon another level of falsehoods which was in-turn built on a foundation of 100 percent prevarication."

"And that's doctor talk for good lies, right?" Wyrick giggled and leaned back into the monitor to work the video joystick.

"Yep." Braden replied and rubbed his eyes. The camera zoomed in even tighter on Lance's face. His eyes took up the entire monitor screen. Braden leaned in to look over Wyrick's shoulder at the screen. "The best ones are able to work in the most intricate details. Just like an artist works in oil or water or clay. This one builds a house of lies on a frame of details that is mind-boggling. I don't think I've come across anyone at his age that is half as skilled at it. Such nuance, so much dedication to it. It's not pathological though. Its something else driving him. Either way his methods are very impressive."

"Most get caught when we're young and don't stay committed to it like him. Or if they do build a life of lies, they have to move around, skip town. He is completely comfortable staying put and building the web around him." Wyrick kept the camera tight on Lance's eyes. "Man, I'm looking forward to seeing what he puts down in this test. Did you read his essay on Marcus Aurelius from his freshman year? I believed everything he wrote… Had to pull out an encyclopedia to see if it was true. And when I found out it was horse shit, I remember thinking Priest's version was better. I wanted to believe it instead of the facts. Now that's good."

"I didn't read that yet. But his letters of recommendation to TU were phenomenal." Braden giggled. "They gave excellent recommendations and spoke of him as a young man with much potential to be fulfilled. They were each different, felt like truly different people wrote each one. Very good, especially since none, not one of those people exists."

Braden sat back. "You know what is really beautiful though is when Preacher does get caught. Doesn't happen much, but when it does he just rolls with it."

"Yah. No squirm." Wyrick added.

"None. He is able to convince others that their facts are wrong or at least suspect. Brilliant I tell ya. I like him." Braden smiled again. "And that nickname."

"Preacher. Man that's perfect." Wyrick smiled and added, "Too bad his government has to kill him."

"All the good ones." Braden added. "He might do some good before he's gone though."

The psychologist unfolded his scratch paper and wrote a few more notes while they were fresh in his mind. He'd transpose them into his TER back in Virginia.

T.E.R. stands for Talent Evaluation Report. And Lance Priest's life would truly never be the same when Braden submitted it to a few key people in charge of clandestine operations for a small government agency tasked with gathering intelligence for the nation.

Lance Priest might think about declining an offer, but he wouldn't. How did Braden know? He circled three words he had written earlier in the upper right corner of the page – *born for this*.

He then wrote three last words – *the ideal candidate*. But then he furrowed his brow. Wyrick had said the more appropriate word a few moments earlier. Braden scratched out the word *ideal* and wrote *perfect*. That fit better. *The perfect candidate*.

Chapter 9

"Right there. Just like I told you. The kid friggin smiled at the camera."

Three men were gathered in a small room, a video-editing suite. Wyrick and Braden sat. Standing behind the two of them was Seibel. They were watching video captured in Dallas three days earlier.

Wyrick paused the video right at the moment Lance leaned in to whisper in Seibel's ear. Lance's hunch about the clock on the wall having a video camera was right. In fact, each room Lance had been in during the fake Foreign Service Officer candidate oral assessment had been rigged with video and audio equipment. All to capture Lance Porter Priest for further evaluation.

"Can you believe his cajones? Kid never ceases to amaze." Wyrick added.

"I'll say it again, like I did in Dallas, his performance was pitch perfect," Braden said.

"True, that's what he said. And I have to say that is an excellent description for Preacher. His performance is always spot on. I'm still looking for his weak spot." Wyrick smiled at the frozen image of a winking Lance Priest on the screen. He'd captured hours of video and days of audio on Candidate Priest. The veteran surveillance professional probably knew more about the subject than anyone else in the world. He'd spent more time with Lance than many of his family members and most of his friends. He, like Seibel, also knew a secret or two about young Mr. Priest.

"Take it back to just before he makes his move and play it again," Seibel ordered. He had replayed the scene in his head dozens of times. Looking up at Lance's completely passive face as he feigned resignation lifting his hand from the folder. And in the next moment, the kid was a blur, pinning Seibel's arm to the table, shoving it across his body and jamming the gun into his head. It was poetry in motion. Embarrassing as all hell for the CIA veteran of three decades, but poetry nonetheless.

Seibel thought he was ready for anything in the moment before Lance took control. Yes, the kid had the high ground because he was standing. But Seibel had a number of options. He could explode upward and throw the table. He could reach up and grab the kid's tie and yank it down until his nose smashed into the tabletop. Or he could simply pull his gun and put it to the kid's head.

But Seibel had been wrong. Grabbing an arm and shoving it sideways while keeping hundreds of pounds of pressure on it was something Seibel had not foreseen. In his replays of the scene over the last 69 hours, he still could not see this move as an option. *It was unnatural.*

The other things he kept seeing were Lance's eyes. What he saw in the moment before Lance acted was emptiness. Lance literally went away, disappeared for a moment. His eyes unfocused. Seibel wasn't sure about it, but the video he had just seen confirmed it. He didn't mention it to Wyrick or Braden. He'd look deeper into this aspect in the future.

Seeing the whole thing again on sanitized video gave Seibel a new perspective. This kid did the unexpected at virtually every turn. He was unpredictable. After all the parameters had been plugged into the complicated formula, the computer algorithms had been wrong about him. They predicted he didn't have it in him, didn't have what it takes. The computers said his correct responses on the questionnaire were just an outlier, a fluke. His IQ, school records, demographic background and genetics all said he was not a candidate. But the computers at Langley couldn't hear, couldn't see the lies. Couldn't understand the layers of detail this kid worked into his vivid storytelling. A computer couldn't feel just how strong Preacher was as he held Seibel's arm in a vice against the table. And most of all, the computer didn't look into his eyes when he put a gun to your head.

Seibel leaned in between the other two to watch as Lance, with a completely passive look on his face, took total control of the room. "Damn." It was all Seibel could say.

The video continued to play. Lance leaned in close to Seibel and winked at the tiny video camera in the clock on the wall. Lance's menacing words that followed the wink took on new meaning seeing it from this vantage point. Seibel could see the performance, the artist at work. All he could do was smile.

In the next video frames, Lance moved the gun and pulled the trigger. Seibel instinctively cringed like he had days before when the gun exploded beside his ear. It was still ringing. The screen went blank. The video camera didn't make it.

"And this is all we have from Dallas. Our resources are still gathering security camera footage from buildings near the federal building." Wyrick paused the static onscreen and looked up at Seibel. "Do you want to go back and watch the small group session again? I love that part where he stands up and starts directing the room. Awesome stuff."

"No, I'm okay." Seibel looked at his watch. It was 11:45 am. Three and a half hours until Lance was to call the designated number. "I think I'll get going. Need to visit with Marvin before this afternoon."

"You still think he'll call?" Wyrick asked.

"He'll call," Seibel and Braden answered in unison.

"I'll be ready," Wyrick turned back to his equipment and ejected the tape.

Walking out of the room, Seibel thought of his dream the night before. Soon after reaching R.E.M. sleep, he had been inundated with visions of Lance Priest. The kid was running at breakneck speed for hours on end. He could see the horror in Preacher's face as he looked back over his shoulder. He saw Lance round a corner, trip and fall. He rose back to his feet with a bloodied face and hands. Up ahead, as he rounded another corner, he stopped and plastered himself to a red brick wall. He held a gun in his hand, but he was no killer. He would be no match for the experienced murderers tracking him.

Seibel wanted to shout at him, tell him to keep running, don't stop. But he couldn't. The kid was on his own. But in the next moment, he was off running again. He turned corners, hurdled boxes and emerged from an alley onto a dimly lit city street. He could feel the kid's heart pounding, his lungs aching from the effort. The kid was pretty much spent but he kept moving.

The dream ended there. Seibel wasn't able to get back to sleep and see what happened or if Lance made it. Reports from the field were sketchy, but the two killers he'd put on the case were not very credible or ethical gents. He'd have to wait until 3:17 p.m., 2:17 p.m. Central, to see if Lance was still among the living. This was a brutal trial by fire, but a necessary one if Seibel's chosen candidate was truly worth the effort.

His eyes were closed, but he was moving, racing. Constant motion with wind whipping through his ears and lungs spent. How much more did he have left? The bullet struck him from behind. It hit his left shoulder. The pain was immediate and radiated outward as he continued at an impossible pace.

He had to keep running or he'd be dead. Wait. Maybe he already was. His eyes opened. It was dark in the hotel room. Another dream. Another death.

Chapter 10

Candidates who achieve a passing score on the Foreign Service Officer Written Examination may, if they choose, progress to a second round of evaluation by the United States Information Agency. Candidates invited to participate in an oral assessment may travel at their own expense to Washington D. C. or a number of regional locations where the oral assessments are conducted.

From over his own shoulder, Lance watched himself read the letter that arrived in the Thursday mail. He froze the scene and looked around the tiny room; positive he'd missed something.

He watched as Lance below him immediately flipped to the next page in the packet to see the host cities for oral exams. Dallas was right there third from the top.

"Cool, Big D," he said to no one. The date for the oral assessments in Dallas was next month on a Tuesday. He'd have to take off from school and the dealership. But that should be no problem, he expected to be well over his sales quota and missing a class or two was no big deal. He left the other pieces of mail unopened on the kitchen counter of his small and

Spartan apartment and plopped down on the couch to read the letter again.

He'd half forgotten about the Foreign Service and taking the test six weeks earlier. But the idea of getting in front of others and pitting his creative talents against a bunch of educated folks intrigued him. He'd put his B.S. skills up against the best, anytime, anywhere. Reading through some of the frequently asked questions on the third sheet, he learned about the format of the oral assessment, the panel makeup and key areas he should study beforehand.

He put the letter on the coffee table and turned on the TV. He'd been at it since 7:30 that morning and he'd be able to catch the last half of the 10 p.m. news. His days were usually a combination of school each morning, an hour or two of studying, or at least wandering the library, and then a shift at the dealership. He was number two this year in used car sales, which really pissed off the full-time guys. It had been extra cold this afternoon and he was as surprised as the other guys to close two deals, an 86 Corolla and an 85 Mazda RX7. And best of all, both the buyers drove onto the lot asking for him by name. Referrals are gold in this business.

The female news anchor read from her teleprompter that new details were just reported on the downing of Pan Am 103 over Lockerbie, Scotland. A link between luggage and Libyan terrorists had those in Washington calling for immediate action against Gadhafi.

"Muammar, Muammar," Lance muttered. "Survive a missile attack from Ronnie and now you let these pricks blow up an airplane. Not smart."

Lance turned the volume down and leaned forward to pick up one of three road atlases sitting on the coffee table. The particular one he chose was a detailed compilation of roadways in the U.S. He thumbed through the states to T for Texas and traced his finger from the Oklahoma border southwest along Highway 75 right into downtown Dallas. He flipped the page for the close up view of the Dallas/Fort Worth. Another close-up map showed downtown Dallas, just what he was looking for. The letter listed the address of 900 East Commerce Street, looked like it was just a few hundred yards off I-35 and just west of Highway 75. Lance already knew the area, but just loved to look at maps.

"Three and a half, maybe four hours door to door, just need to pick a motel." He started backing up Hwy 75 to areas north of town. He considered the idea of staying with his aunt in far northwest Fort Worth, but that was an hour from downtown Dallas, with little or no traffic, which wouldn't be the case at 8 a.m. on a Tuesday.

He chose Richardson just north of the 635 Loop for his first motel location. He got up and grabbed the yellow pages from a kitchen drawer and plopped back onto the couch. Under "motels" he found the familiar Motel 6 and Best Western logos and chose Motel 6 for this one. Lance was about to pick up the phone when something caught his eye.

On the floor, under the deck chair against the wall, was a foam beer koozee. Now, the fact that a beer koozee was in the apartment was no surprise. He and his occasional guest would use the foam rubber sleeves to keep their beer cans cool out around the pool. But this particular koozee had been sitting on the armrest of a cheap white deck chair for five months without being moved. Lance hadn't had anyone over in a long while and more to the point, he had said to himself the night before that he needed to put that thing away. As usual, he didn't and it was sitting there on the armrest 14 hours ago when he left for school.

Two explanations he could see. Building maintenance, in the form of the nosy apartment manager, had come in for some reason, like changing out the air filter in his HVAC unit. Or someone else had been in the apartment. He knew now, it was the second explanation.

A quick scan of the room saw nothing else out of place but he stood and paced the junior apartment just to be sure. Walking into his bedroom, he saw nothing out of place. He opened the small door in the hall to take a look at the heating and air unit. The sticker on the metal panel holding the air filter was dated six months earlier. Lance stepped into the kitchen and could not detect anything amiss. The female anchor said sports and weather would be next and to stay tuned for more news.

"Stay tuned," Lance said to no one. The disembodied Lance floating above watching a replay of the scene mouthed the words.

Lance couldn't see him, but someone else was listening to the news anchor. Approximately 150 yards from where he stood in his apartment, a plain white van sat parked. The van looked like any other electrician van with a panel behind the front seats. But behind this particular screen sat special agent Wyrick hunched over a small radio unit listening intently to the activity taking place in apartment 7C. Wyrick had been in the unit hours earlier. He had confirmed Lance's presence at the dealership by calling and asking to speak with Mr. Priest. The receptionist put him on hold and when Lance picked up, Wyrick hung up the pay phone and drove across the street to Lance's apartment.

While in the junior size apartment with a small kitchen, sleeper sofa, bedroom with no door and surprisingly clean bathroom for a single male tenant, he placed several small radio transmitting devices. One was inside the lid of the smoke alarm, which was conveniently located high on the wall across from the couch. Another was in the bedroom adhered to the underside of the base of a bedside lamp. The third was in the phone handset hanging on the wall. Wyrick had been successful in planting the devices, but upon leaving the unit, had bumped the thin plastic deck chair that rightly should have been out on the small balcony. In doing so, he knocked a red koozee with a radio station logo off the chair. Because it was made of foam, it made little or no sound when it landed. It was the only visible evidence of his invasion.

Wyrick wrote 'stay tuned' on the legal pad sitting on a small counter next the radio unit and smiled to himself. "I am." He said to no one.

Bugging, wiretapping or otherwise delivering clandestine obtained information via audio from a subject or group of subjects inside the borders of the United States is not normal procedure for the CIA. In fact, it is illegal. Any information gathered through such means would be spotty at best if presented in a court of law. But Wyrick wasn't collecting evidence for use in a court case. And he was not actually an employee of the Central Intelligence Agency. His contract status prevented others from tracking his activities and therefore made him and his impressive skills in undetected surveillance quite valuable.

His sought after skills had brought employment in unique, isolated and exotic locales around the world. His job had also gotten in the way of two marriages and raising two kids who were mostly grown now. Wyrick spent more time on the road sleeping in motel rooms or the backs of vans or on hillsides or in building basements than his own bed back home in Maryland.

His current contract assignment was filling in the missing pieces in the growing subject profile for one Lance Porter Priest, aka "Preacher." Wyrick had a feeling he would be spending more time than usual on this candidate during the FSWE in September. His hunch had proven correct and he arrived back in Tulsa a few days earlier to begin planning and now executing a week of intense surveillance procedures. The secret Wyrick shared with Seibel about their young subject meant that this, all of this surveillance and investment, was not really a surprise.

Experience had shown him that one week, two at the most, was more than sufficient for candidate evals. Really, a day suffices in most cases. In 24 hours, he can usually uncover enough information to build a case for rejection. People give away their weaknesses and potential problems for the agency during private moments alone at home, at work or with their partners or families.

The candidates he is assigned to invasively inspect are not traditional personnel contestants. Wyrick hadn't kept track of those he has seen pass this particular portion of their unbeknownst evaluation, but he knows of a few who are now in the coveted DCCO – Deep Cover Clandestine Operations. One thing he had learned during these assignments was that these are not candidates being considered for CIA office assignments or communications intel. They needed to possess certain skills and mindsets that permeated their conscious. They needed a rough edge to them.

In two days of tracking Lance, Wyrick had witnessed nothing unusual about this particular candidate. Yes, this guy is quite a bit younger than most of the others, but there were a few even younger, none under 18 of course. But 21 is still a boy in most circumstances. He had come to like this one though. Something about Priest's character was chameleon-like which made Wyrick want to learn more. This candidate had a number of layers to him. It was evident on the surface there is more to be discovered beneath.

But getting close to college students is not an easy assignment. Many live on campus or right next door to campus and a man in his 40s hanging around college campuses can lead to police calls. Securing a maintenance or security uniform can work for short-term stakeouts. Wyrick had seen these scenarios blow up in his face on several occasions, especially since he happened to be a black man. Call it profiling or prejudice or fear; people are just naturally more suspicious of a black dude hanging around.

He had turned to surveillance technology back in the 70s and became something of an expert in long-distance audio monitoring. Listening devices utilizing small battery-powered transmitters which could be placed just about anywhere had become his favorite surveillance tools. Video has improved throughout the 80s, with the size of cameras finally coming down to a manageable risk in certain situations. But still not to a level Wyrick was comfortable placing them in dicey remote locations.

No video for this one though. Wyrick was certain he'd get what he needed by tailing Lance for a few days, planting the transmitters in his apartment and using the long-range microphone to capture the candidate's conversations at school, and more importantly, at that used car lot.

"Used car salesman," Wyrick muttered to no one and smiled. "Too much." The fact that this kid basically bullshitted his way through junior high and high school and right into college and now sold used cars really cracked Wyrick up. He and the small group he worked under contract with back in Virginia all had a good laugh around a table in a roadside diner about Priest selling used cars. "Perfect!" more than one of them had said and then joined the others in a laugh.

Funny thing though, in listening to Lance via a directional microphone for three days on the lot, one thing became obvious. The damn dealership appeared to be the one place the kid didn't lie. Just yesterday he steered a young couple away from a particular Mazda because it was making a disconcerting sound. He sold them a Nissan Sentra at a lower price, therefore a lower commission. And then there was the guy Lance had to talk out of buying a Ford pickup because it was just plain too much vehicle for him. Wyrick chalked Lance's behavior at the dealership up to eccentricity. The kid had definitely turned out weird.

Wyrick listened to the sounds emanating from the apartment 150 yards away. He had tuned up his ears 20 years earlier sitting in an undisclosed location in Europe listening to transmissions bouncing around the Soviet Union and Eastern Bloc. Through his experience, he was able to pick up on and discern between the slightest noises. Like Braden, who preferred to see his subjects in person instead of on video or film, Wyrick liked to hear it first-hand. He recorded everything for further analysis by others, but more than a little quality is lost when sounds are captured on tape. So he usually sits hunched over his little counter as he did now with his 1960s headphones mounted on his slightly balding head. He listened to the paper shuffling, the occasional belch and television programs viewed by this latest candidate. His listening skills allowed him to build a mental image of his subjects. He could basically "see" Lance sitting there on his couch reading and watching TV.

Wyrick's legal pad on the small shelf in his van contained the usual bulleted outline format he had used for two decades. During moments of silence or inane dialogue of the sitcom now on Lance's television, Wyrick reviewed his notes from his surveillance. In doing so, he came to a conclusion that he had missed something. His in-depth knowledge of candidate Priest included reams of school records, occupational history, credit reports and analysis prepared by Braden and his psych eval team. He knew he would not likely get what he needed in 24 hours of observation, but a scan of his notes concluded that this kid didn't have the car in drive. He was stuck in neutral. Wyrick recalled his discussion with Braden and follow-up conversations with his contacts back at the ranch that it all, and by all, everything, seemed to come a little too easy for Priest.

Wyrick drifted for a moment as the two characters on Lance's TV discussed some ridiculous situation they now found themselves in. He thought about Pete Marivich, the Pistol. "Pistol Pete" would take and make shots both in college and the pros that no one should have. Time after time, he set scoring records, often breaking his own. Wyrick, like so many others sitting in stands or glued to television sets, had marveled at Marivich's scoring prowess. He truly made it look easy. The Pistol obviously worked at his craft, but the way he floated from top of the key to the wing and back and then turned in a flash to catch a pass and shoot another swishing basket was sheer poetry. Wyrick remembered watching an after-game interview with the young Pistol where he was asked how he does it. "Practice" was the one-word reply, but between the letters was a subtle code that simply stated some things just come natural to certain people. For Pistol Pete, squaring up and sinking a shot was as natural as putting one foot in front of the other.

Priest had this same naturalness about him; the same confidence the Pistol exuded every time he eyed a shot. A confidence that said he'd make this shot and the next and the next. Priest excelled in pressure situations as well. And probably most important, when he missed or was knocked off kilter in some way, his recovery was quick and confident, almost without skipping a bit. Yet, it wasn't overtly obvious to those who had not been through 611 pages of candidate Priest's life. This young man's success in building a cover was so complete, that he gave little or no hint of his prowess. He stayed humble and modest while putting others to shame or getting by with a whopper of a story. This undoubtedly required practice.

Yet practice is different for each of us. For some it is repetition to build muscle memory. For others it is experiential to prepare for the actual event and the physical and psychological elements. For others, practice can involve deep visioning to essentially rehearse the event, whether a speech before a board or a 100-meter hurdle race. Coaches will encourage athletes to envision success so that it can come easier. From what Wyrick had seen, Lance Priest practices in a manner that borrows aspects of each of these methods and more into a process that psychologist Braden had labeled "personality borrowing" and sometimes "stealing." He basically became another person by copying them, by copying their actions, movements, facial expressions, speech, laugh.

From what Wyrick could discern, Lance's practice methods revolve primarily around reading. Books, maps, catalogs but most of all, people. The kid seems to possess a photographic memory and is able to grab certain aspects of everything he sees, hears, smells and touches. His practice involves borrowing these aspects and putting them into action. He plays different characters from minute to minute. It showed up mainly in the interview transcripts Braden and other compartmentalized agency members had gathered in just over six weeks. Interviewees would depict different people when describing candidate Priest. Utterly and totally different with detail piled upon detail. That took practice.

Wyrick thumbed through Braden's report for a 10th time and stopped on the passage he liked most. It read, "Candidate is perhaps most comfortable when faced with a challenge or set of challenges. He appears to excel, even live, for these moments when his current paradigm is challenged and a creative, improvised response is required. He has purposefully placed himself in these situations time and time again. It is as though he views these challenging situations as opportunities to practice, or better, perfect his performance skills." Wyrick smiled to himself and put his finger to the headphone on his ear to get a better "view" of the room.

One hundred and fifty yards away, sitting in front of his television with made-for-TV characters regurgitating lame lines followed by laugh tracks, a road atlas of the United States beside him, a phone book open to the yellow pages on his lap and an architectural reference guide in his hands, Lance put in motion plans for his next practice and envisioned success. The winning moment he saw in his mind was not being offered a Foreign Service job at the end of a serpentine bureaucratic governmental process. No, his goal was fooling them all into thinking he had a clue where he was going and what he was doing with his life. He practices for this particular result each and every day. The thrill for him is in the chase, not the end.

A disembodied Lance floating above could only look at himself on the couch below and try like hell to see what he'd missed. He searched for clues he'd missed. Was there a bug listening to him? Was there a video camera somewhere in the apartment? He knew something was there. He just couldn't see it. *Frustrating*.

Chapter 11

Nondescript. That was the word the floating, hovering Lance used to describe the federal government building in Downtown Dallas. He was back where the fun had started three days before; watching from above as the earthbound Lance entered the building to begin his new life.

Lance rode the elevator to the fifth floor at 7:45 a.m. The gal in her mid-20s riding up with him was headed to the same session. He now knew her as Sarah Ridenour, not her real name. They smiled at each other upon entering the lift and casually looked away during the ride.

He couldn't help but read her. Twenty-five. No ring left hand third finger, but there was an indent from a band. Blue contacts. Designer knock-off suit and size 7 ½ two-inch heels. Soccer player back in high school – medial collateral scar below her left kneecap. But the smell didn't fit. She wore Diorissimo perfume, the fragrance Annette, Jimmy Lee's wizened secretary at the dealership wore. It didn't fit a 25-year old.

Lance did a little recall assessment during the slow upward drift of the ancient elevator. He had scouted out the building, available parking and multiple traffic options the previous evening. His drive in from Richardson before 7 a.m. was pleasantly uneventful as he beat much of the morning's rush-hour traffic aiming towards the glass and steel skyscrapers of downtown Big D. The parking lot he chose offered all day for $12. He tipped the lot attendant an extra $5 to make sure no one parked behind him, potentially blocking him in until 5 p.m. The interior of the building was as vanilla as its exterior. Grey walls, greyer linoleum floors, no surprises.

He politely held his hand in front of the opened doors allowing his fairly attractive but fake co-passenger to exit first. He then followed her down the hall to room 510 where they checked-in with a cordial, but cold receptionist who obviously found this day's assignment of welcoming nobodies below her low pay grade.

"Please have a seat and someone will be with you shortly," the receptionist gestured to the chairs lining the wall and immediately returned to her newspaper.

Lance and his elevator partner sat in two of the 10 chairs lining the walls of the small waiting room, an open seat between them. She proceeded to pull out a folded copy of the New York Times from her purse and continued a story she had started reading earlier. Lance craned his neck to scan the headlines on the front page. She caught his eye and smiled.

"I only get to read the New York Times in the library," he apologized.

"No problem. That's what I did back at school. Are you still in college?"

"Yes," he smiled back, "University of Tulsa." He told the truth.

"Really, I had a friend graduate from there." Sarah lied to add detail to her story.

"Really, who was that?"

"Tina Stempler was her name in college, now she's Tina Mayes. Mrs. Brad Mayes as she likes to joke."

"Don't think I recognize the name. What degree did she graduate with?"

"Marketing," she replied and turned back to her paper.

"Great."

"I'm Sarah Ridenhour by the way." She turned back.

"Oh, I'm sorry, I'm Vance Porter." They shook hands. From above, Lance giggled at the little twist on his name. Stupid really.

"Nice to meet you. I guess we'll get to know each other a bit today." Her smile was very nice.

"That's what I hear. Supposed to be six or eight of us, right?"

"Yep." And she turned back to her paper while turning the page.

The door opened and two more candidates who made it to the oral assessment stage of the Foreign Service Officer applicant process entered. The gentleman was in his late thirties with tiny gold-rimmed glasses. The woman was probably 32 but had a premature grey streak in her black hair.

Ann Bancroft. Lance thought to himself. The grey streak in her hair made him think of the movie *The Graduate*. Lance thought for maybe the 20th time in his life that it was amazing that Bancroft was only six or seven years older than Dustin Hoffman but was masterful at playing a seductive older woman. The opening chords and "doo-dooing" of the movie's theme song started playing in his head and he had to listen to Simon and Garfunkel sing for a few minutes. Lance recalled reading somewhere that Joe DiMaggio had been really pissed when the song and movie came out. Joe didn't think he had gone anywhere. Lance laughed at yet another bit of useless trivia rambling around his head. He would *kill* on Jeopardy!

A moment later, another chap walked in. This guy was dressed for business with a navy suit, striking white shirt and deep red power tie. He was followed a few seconds later by two women in their late 20s who had struck up a conversation riding up in the elevator together. The heavier one finished their conversation with an exclamation, "Now, wouldn't that be perfect."

The dour receptionist welcomed them and directed them to join everyone else by being seated.

Lance scanned the group again from above, taking in details that hardly mattered to most but amounted to something more than nothing. Clothing, accessories, shoes, haircuts, eyewear and other minutia came together to create a whole, a complete and comprehensive visual portrait. Little things like being right or left-handed, cologne and leg position told him most of what he needed to know about his fellow oral assessees. Or so he thought at the time. Dumb.

Sarah finished the front section of the Times and decided to put her paper away since the clock on the wall now read 8 a.m. sharp. Her timing was impeccable because less than five seconds later a door to the right of the receptionist opened and out walked Geoffrey Seibel. Lance didn't know that was his name at the time, but would in a minute.

Lance paused the image in his brain to examine the details. Seibel exuded travel, experience, sun-baked desert and steamy tropical intrigue. Lance could hear an ocean breeze blow in behind as Seibel walked out through the door to greet the group. He wore a very expensive suit. Lance guessed it cost significantly more than the $1,200 custom-tailored suits that Jimmy Lee loved to wear. And like the car dealer, Seibel wore gold on a couple of fingers and his wrist. Those props disappeared for his performances later during the day.

"Well, good morning everyone." Seibel's smile was electric, a flashing neon light.

A chorus of reciprocal "good mornings" went up and everyone adjusted in their chairs. The nerves kept so well in check suddenly came to the fore.

"I am Geoffrey Seibel and I am one of your prompters today for the oral assessments portion of the Foreign Service Officer evaluation process. Seibel took another pace to the exact center of the small room just as an actor doing Shakespeare in the round might do. He made sure he smiled at each and every one of the candidates before going on.

Lance paused the replay in his head and did a quick 360 around Seibel frozen in the middle of the room. No bulge in his jacket. No gun. Must have come later. He restarted the playback.

"Congratulations on passing your written exams. You all have likely read how today will unfold. You will participate in a group session to start. Then we will break up into three smaller case management groups and then your individual assessments will round out the day."

His smile broadened and he continued. "You should expect to be here until approximately 3 p.m. today. But don't worry, we have drinks, snacks and Uncle Sam is picking up your boxed lunch today. Please be sure to let us know if you have special dietary needs."

Smiles and gentle laughs ensued. "Before we bring you back, are there any questions?" No reply. "Okay, then I'll rephrase it, who wants to break the ice and ask the first question?"

The group exchanged glances, but no one was willing to step up. Lance broke the awkward silence, "Bathrooms?"

"Very good, thank you Mr. Priest for asking a very important, albeit short one-word question. Restrooms, lavatories, the lue or el bano in most of the countries south of where we now stand are located just down this hall we are about to walk through."

"Thanks." Lance let it go that Seibel knew his name already though they had never met. He knew better now.

"No, thank you for asking sir. You receive no prize, but you have earned my gratitude and that of your mates here for breaking the proverbial ice that is silence." Seibel moved back to the open door. "Now then, please gather up your bags, briefs and paraphernalia and follow me through this first doorway to the rest of your lives. If you dare that is." His smile even broader.

They all traipsed down a hallway, indeed passing bathrooms approximately halfway, and walked to the end of the hall where they entered a large conference room with a number of tables pushed together forming a large "U." An open space on one side allowed someone to walk into the middle of the space. Lance expected Seibel to be in there shortly.

A group of three individuals stood to one side of the room where a pot of coffee and a tray of breakfast goodies waited. The three of them split up to welcome the members of the arriving group. By the looks of them, they had done this gig dozens, maybe hundreds of times. In turn, the three made their way around to introduce themselves to the group.

The first to approach Lance was a small woman who appeared to have a good bit of Native American Indian in her. Lance, living in Oklahoma for several years now, had spent a lot of time with people of Native American descent. The trail of tears brought their ancestors to Indian Territory, now the Sooner State. She extended a hand to him and smiled. "Good morning, I'm Isabel Russell with the Department of State."

"Good morning, I'm Lance Priest, department of state of denial."

She smiled and laughed at that, "Oh really. And how long have you been with them."

"Permanent assignment."

"I like that. Might have to see about a transfer there myself." She squeezed his hand and released.

"We accept all types. No real requirements that I know of, at least none based in reality." Lance added.

"Very interesting Mr. Priest. I look forward to getting to know you today." She smiled wider.

"You too, thanks for letting me come." He returned the smile.

"You're very welcome."

And she moved on with a wink. She liked him. One down.

Lance turned to face number two approaching. He was a black man in his mid-fifties. Lance glanced up and down and immediately knew the gentleman drove an older model foreign make; probably a BMW 528i. Maybe 1976 or 77; just old enough to be considered a classic.

"Hi there. I'm Brad Renfro."

"Morning. Lance Priest." He replied.

"From Oklahoma, right?" Renfro asked.

"Tulsa." Lance nodded.

"I was there maybe 15 years ago for a couple of days. Very pretty as I recall. Green Country."

"Right. I like it. Place has changed with the oil bust and all. But where are you from?"

"All around I guess. Grew up on a bunch of military bases around the world. Dad was in the Navy." Renfro added.

"So now you still get to travel round the world in the Foreign Service."

"Used to. I'm stuck in D.C. most of the time. I'd love to get back out there in the field doing embassy work, but they say I'm more valuable as a trainer."

"Very good. Can't beat a good teacher."

"Don't know if I'm any good or not."

"I'm sure you are. If they have you training others, that means they trust you with the future right?" Lance nodded.

"I like that. Trust me with the future. Think I might find a way to use that." Renfro patted Lance's arm above the elbow and moved on to meet and greet the others. Number three approached him and did an even worse job lying than Renfro had.

"Good morning Lance. I'm Pete Grisham."

Lance paused the playback in his head. From above he looked down at Grisham. In particular, he looked at the man's right side. He was sure there was no gun. Thank goodness, he hadn't missed that detail. Grisham, or whatever his name is, had added the gun to his wardrobe sometime after this point. Looking at him from this vantage point, Lance could see there was a lot more going on with Grisham than meets the eye. He was serious.

"Hi Pete," he put emphasis on the name during the handshake. "I'm Lance Priest but I guess you know that already."

"Indeed I do. Been looking forward to meeting you. Excellent work on the written exam."

"Thanks. They didn't send me a score just told me I passed and to show up here. Don't know if I did good or not."

Grisham nodded. "You did very well. High marks; excellent writing skills. We don't discuss particulars with candidates at this stage, but I think I'm safe in saying you nailed it."

"What do you do for the State Department?" Lance asked.

"Personnel mainly. I recruit and train."

"Like Brad?" And that was all it took to confirm the lie. In the next 10th of a second, Grisham had to process the question and fabricate a response. Lance had seen it more often than not in his conversations on the car lot. It was in the eyes.

"Yes, like Brad." But there was no conviction. The response was a cover-up; a delay tactic before a more refined reply. "He and I cross paths quite a bit."

"I'll bet." Lance meant it. He didn't know why, but he was sure of the truth behind Grisham's lie.

"Very nice to meet you. I'm looking forward to today."

"Me too. Thanks."

Grisham moved aside to allow Lance and the others to find their seats at the conjoined conference tables. Lance sat beside Sarah. She welcomed his presence with a nervous smile. He smiled back.

Seibel, as if on command, walked into the center of the conference tables, but if it was possible, he was not the same man from minutes earlier. His shoulders, so broad moments ago, were slouched. His smile had given way to a furrowed brow and his suit even looked different. It looked oversized, like he had lost 40 pounds in five minutes. And the multiple gold rings and bracelet were gone. Only a wedding ring remained.

Lance paused the playback and looked around the table to see if anyone else noticed. On the seven faces, he saw no signs of worry but did catch one smile that was anything but natural. It was Sarah and it was forced. He had missed this on Tuesday. She gave herself away with the look. She was in on this thing. He restarted Seibel's performance.

"Okay then," Seibel started in. But instead of jovial, he was serene, weary. He looked beaten down. Lance had been stunned by the transformation at the time. Replaying it now in his head, he was simply impressed. "Again, thank you all for coming. We have a very full day ahead of us." *Peter Falk*. That was it. Seibel was doing the tired investigator, Peter Falk style. He even had a different accent than he did in the lobby. The only thing missing was the trench coat. Damn. He was good, really good.

"We will begin in a moment with the group exercise. I hope you all met your prompters for today's session. I will have them each introduce themselves to you officially in a moment. I will be stepping in and out throughout the day and participating in various capacities during your sessions so don't be surprised if I jump in and ask you a question on the fly."

With that, Seibel asked each of the prompters to reintroduce themselves. Isabel was first followed by Pete and Brad. When they were done, Isabel asked everyone to introduce themselves to the group. As each individual gave a short introduction, Lance took his usual mental notes. He also had the hair on the back of his neck prick up several times as people lied. He kept his face in check with a stone smile that didn't change for the five minutes it took to work around the table.

When it was his turn, he looked everyone in the eye and gave the standard name, rank and serial number. He purposefully turned up the Oklahoma accent. Couldn't be positive if he caught a smile flash across Seibel's face, but he was pretty sure.

After the introductions, they jumped into the group exercise involving several scenarios presented for discussion and group member interaction. The scenarios dealt with situations embassy and state department personnel may be faced with during their time overseas. They included plane crashes, crimes, missing persons, government coups and more. The prompters sat quietly watching after setting up the scenarios and only spoke when things got really off track.

Lance kept score in his head throughout and contributed a fair share of insight and humor. The session lasted an hour and a half.

Chapter 12

After a short bathroom break, the eight individuals were broken into two groups of three and one group of two. Lance was paired with Sarah and Carl, the 32-year-old gold-rimmed glasses guy from Albuquerque. Grisham escorted the group down the hall to a small conference room.

Waiting in the room was the liar Marsco. Lance wasn't supposed to recognize him. His hair was lighter, almost blond and he had a mustache and tortoise shell glasses. Lance paused the playback and looked at Marsco again from above. It was a lousy disguise. Too easy.

"Hello, I'm Drew Marsco," Stuart Braden lied.

Without skipping a beat and with nothing but a boyish smile, Lance shook his hand and shot right back. "Hi, I'm Lance Priest."

"Nice to meet you Lance." Braden then turned to Sarah and Carl to introduce himself. Lance gave Braden a complete look over. The suit was expensive and looked radically different than the jeans and flannel shirt he wore during the exam in Tulsa. Lance turned away to take in the room. Grisham was right behind him with a smile.

"Okay guys. We've been joined for this portion by Drew. He is with the Department of State and is a veteran of many of these sessions.

"Too many." Marsco/Braden joked. "I should probably get a real job."

"And miss all this?" Grisham replied.

The group took a seat around the table. Grisham stayed on his feet and walked around the room as he read a scenario he pulled from an envelope. After reading the document, he smiled at the three candidates. "You've got a good one guys. I'm to read you this scenario and then let you three work out an initial response. Then Drew and I will prompt you with a series of questions to evaluate your reasoning, understanding, response and strategy."

He stepped back over to the door and closed it. "For this session, you are all U.S. embassy staff in Harare, Zimbabwe. You have just received word via telephone that a tour bus loaded with international passengers, including 14 U.S. citizens, has been involved in an accident on the outskirts of town. The area is particularly impoverished with no infrastructure or government resources. The bus collided with a vehicle carrying a family with three small children. All passengers in the car were killed. Several of the tourists have been injured but more importantly, and certainly more dangerous, a crowd, or better yet a mob, has surrounded the bus and is attempting to remove passengers to gain a certain amount of monetary retribution for the loss of the local family."

Grisham moved to the other side of the room. "Local authorities are slow to arrive on scene. By the time they show up, several of the passengers, including US citizens, have been dragged from the bus and taken away into the surrounding village. This information has just been phoned into the embassy by a local resident whose wife works in the embassy as a housekeeper."

"There you have it. You now have your scenario and you are to discuss the situation and develop a response plan for 30 minutes. At that time Mr. Marsco and I will begin asking you questions."

Lance, Sarah and Carl looked at each other for a few moments and then each turned to their notes just jotted down. Sarah had the best notes; Carl's covered three quarters of a page and Lance had a few bullet points.

"Can we have that sheet?" Sarah asked Grisham.

"Afraid not. You are to respond to this situation as if the brief phone call is your sole source at this point," Grisham answered and pulled back a chair across from Braden to watch the action around the table.

Preacher jumped right in with what he knew and what he saw as the best course of action. "First of all, we know that we don't know much."

"Right," Carl added.

"And we probably won't have any more information for awhile so we need to confirm what we do know." He added.

Sarah recited the facts as she had recorded them. It took about two minutes. Lance became acutely aware of the time crunch. Only 27 minutes left.

"Okay, first things first, who do we need to call and bring into this?" He asked.

Carl and Sarah looked at one another and back to Preacher. In a matter of minutes, he had become the leader of the small group as the other two's brief exchange transferred leadership to the youngest candidate at the table. "I imagine there is a shitload of protocol we have been trained to put in place in this type of event." Lance looked to Grisham and Braden. No reply. They were playing their roles of unobtrusive observers. "But since we don't have all that background, let's write a list of who we should call real-quick."

"The embassy director first." Sarah followed.

"And then we would call back to Washington right?" Carl tacked on.

"Don't know if that would be our job or not," Preacher surmised. "Who would we call outside the embassy? Where would we start?" The question was to no one in particular and with it Lance's wheels started turning. He stood up. The stratified layers of the situation started coming into focus. In the next two minutes, he dictated calls to local government officials, law enforcement, the tour bus company and most importantly, to the embassy security detail to arrange for protection for one of them to be taken to the scene. His research of embassy operations came into play.

He continued, "It would probably be best for the Marines in the embassy to be accompanied by local police or army in a little convoy out to the accident site. We should get eyeballs at the scene as quickly as possible."

In the next seven minutes, the three of them decided on roles, responsibilities, a communication plan and timeline to follow. Preacher peppered the other two with questions throughout, but half of them were really rhetorical in nature as he processed information out loud.

Grisham stood up at 29 minutes and announced one minute remaining to get notes and assignments in order. Sarah feverishly wrapped up a ninth page of notes. Carl nailed down his roles and Lance returned to his initial bullet points to add three more on his single page.

"Okay, time." Grisham stepped back from the table and looked to Braden. "Drew, please go right ahead."

For the next hour, Grisham and Marsco/Braden asked the group dozens of questions. The quick-hit nature was purposeful in that its aim was to shoot holes and enlighten dark spots. On several occasions, the two prompters exchanged looks that confirmed what Braden knew already and Grisham had read in a file. This Priest kid had it. The rapid-fire approach he had employed with the others had sewn up loose ends that usually dangled for others in this drill. The plan he had led the others in developing covered nearly every angle.

"What about search and rescue once onsite at the accident?" Grisham asked no one in particular.

"We would be limited to relying on local police and military," Lance responded. "Our marines could show up and use some force, but five or six of them against a crowd in the hundreds and then hundreds of houses the tourists could have been taken to. No good. We would have to rely on local cops who knew the area."

Sarah and Carl smiled at his response. He made them look good.

"Very good," Grisham concluded the session by standing. "Very good work by all of you. We are now finished with the small group portion of your day. You are going to head back down the hall and join the others for lunch and then it will be individual exams to wrap up the day. We will join you down there shortly."

The three candidates stood up from the table and were surprised to see Seibel leaning against the wall by the door. He had silently entered the room at some point and neither Grisham nor Marsco/Braden had given any indication he had joined them. Lance watched from above as Seibel moved, performed.

"Very impressive, very solid analysis," Seibel said to everyone and no one in particular. "I especially enjoyed the decision making on several levels in a time crunch. I could see this scenario unfolding pretty much as discussed here." He stepped from the wall and moved to the other side of the room.

The way Grisham and Marsco remained motionless told the other three that their session was actually not quite over. Seibel turned back to the group and his smile was replaced with something of a sneer; not menacing, but certainly a changed point of view from a few seconds earlier.

"I wonder though," he let it trail off as he looked from each of the three and settled on Lance. "What if you didn't have time to wait for local authorities? What if you had arrived on the scene and it was obvious which home a hostage had been taken to because of the crowd gathered around it? And that property was just across the street from the accident, only seconds to get there for the Marines. What would you do if you were giving the orders?"

Lance was probably expected to think about this for a few seconds, to contemplate options and reply with something less than an assured outcome. But he didn't take a second to reply.

"We make sure the other people on the bus are secure and we hold that position or even fall back from the scene of the crowd." He looked from Sarah to Carl. They both nodded in support of his response.

"You leave a hostage in danger when he or she is right there in front of you in a structure you could easily enter and take control?" Seibel looked only at Lance.

"Easily?" Lance furrowed his brows. "What's easy about hundreds of people going crazy? Six Marines against that would mean lots and lots of people hurt or killed for a hostage that we don't know is in there. That's easy. Stick with what you know and stay in control."

Seibel let the sneer fade into something of a frown and then moved his gaze from Lance to Sarah and Carl. "Do you two agree?"

Carl and Sarah nodded again.

Seibel continued, "A bird in the hand, huh?"

"Better than two in the bush with a bloodthirsty crowd between you and the bush," Lance added. He was confident, maybe too confident. Maybe.

"Potete credere questo capretto?" Seibel turned and posed the question to Braden.

"Nada surpreende-me," Braden replied. Grisham nodded.

He turned back to Lance, "I think I would have to agree with you. Keeping those we have safe is first priority before launching any kind of rescue mission, regardless of the numbers or support. Tactical gamesmanship aside, going into that crowd is an absolute no-win. Casualties would be expected and repercussions would extend well beyond a local flare-up. Probably turn into an international incident." Seibel moved back to the door.

"Congratulations again, you have averted an international pain in the ass for our government and probably saved lives. Now wouldn't it be fun to get to do this in real life?" The smile came back and Seibel turned and exited the room.

Grisham laughed a personal little laugh and moved to the door. "Congratulations for passing a little test within a test. Sometimes they are more important than the results that show up on paper." He gave Lance a fake punch to the gut walking past him. Lance smiled like he was supposed to.

The lunch around the pushed-together conference tables in the large conference room involved lots and lots of small talk between oral exam candidates and prompters. The civilians in the room shared their stories from the morning session and the small group exercises. Lance made small talk with those around him. Sarah sat next to him again. She kept her eyes on him. He could see her glances and outright staring from his peripheral vision.

From above, he paused the scene and looked around. He had not noticed at the time that neither Seibel nor the guy he knew as Marsco joined them for lunch. Grisham was there along with the other prompters.

Video cameras were also watching from above. This lunch gathering, like the morning session and Lance's small group exercise, was being captured for analysis. Two video cameras, one in the fake clock on the wall, the other protruding ever so slightly out of a smoke alarm on a pillar a few yards from the table, watched the room. Both cameras were trained on one individual as they had been during the written exams, while he spoke with customers on the car lot, while he ate dinner on his one date over the last three months and during several of his classes. At the other end of the video cable sat Wyrick peering into his monitor. Braden had just joined him and sat eating his boxed lunch sandwich. The psychologist found it difficult to eat with the fake mustache, but didn't dare take them off and have to fight to put them back on again. That tried his patience more than anything.

"Anything new here?" Braden whispered to Wyrick.

"Nope. More of the same perfect pitch performance. He's talking football with Number 7; accepting adoration from Number 2 and doing a flawless job of ignoring Number 3's stare."

"Anything at all I need to take to Papa, last minute wise?" Braden asked.

"You see what I see, right?"

"Yep. I like perfect pitch as a metaphor. It fits." Braden scratched his head. The wig made him itch.

Wyrick continued, "I struggled over what it was I've been witnessing with this kid. And perfect pitch with its ability to replicate a note seemed most appropriate."

"Like I said, I like it," Braden finished his sandwich and stood. He smoothed his mustache and wig and left the room.

As lunch wrapped in the conference room, Grisham stood to give the candidates their orders for the afternoon's final sessions. "I hope you all enjoyed your government-issue lunch. Better than bologna but no filet mignon right?"

Everyone laughed. "As you know, your last session will be an individual oral assessment. Some of you will go immediately to this session, while others wait. The order of these sessions has already been determined prior to today, so please don't read anything into the fact that you have to sit around for an hour or so before your turn."

Grisham finished by giving each of them their destinations. Lance was assigned room three right now, no sitting around. He liked that.

"You should all say your goodbyes to each other now. Once your session is complete, you will be free to leave. These sessions will all last differing times so you won't come out together."

Lance turned to Sarah. She was already facing him.

"It was very nice to meet you," she stuck out a hand first.

He accepted it. "You too. I enjoyed going to Africa with you."

"It was a blast and you were great." Her smile wider.

"Thanks, you too. Very impressive," he did a spot-on imitation of Seibel. Sarah smiled and held his hand a little longer than customary.

"Maybe we'll see each other some time," she added.

"If you're ever in Tulsa, please look me up." He pulled a business card from his breast pocket. "I work at a car dealership to pay the tuition bills."

"New or used?" She looked at the card.

"Mostly used. I get to deal with real people that way."

"A used car salesman. Now that is something I would have never guessed. Then again, maybe it makes sense. You were awesome on your feet. I'll bet you do great selling cars."

"The secret is to never lie," he winked.

"Okay, Lance Priest, car salesman," she read off the card. "Good luck on the individuals."

"Thanks Sarah Ridenhour, graduate student," he held up a pretend card. "Good luck on your individual session. You'll do great."

"How did you know I am a graduate student?" Her procerus muscle tugged her eyebrows together.

"Easy. The clothes, the hair, no business card; you're all grad student."

She let a look of surprise flash across her face as if she wasn't supposed to. "You nailed it."

"See ya," he smiled and stepped away. He walked out of the room after saying so long to a couple of others, including Grisham.

Lance paused the playback. Instead of looking around the room at others, he looked at himself. He moved in close to look at his face. He didn't like what he saw. This Lance was good looking and all, couldn't help it, he joked. But this Lance from a couple of days ago was oblivious, inept. He was so intent on impressing others, on stealing the show and playing his little mind games, that he missed detail after detail. It was hubris. Good old-fashioned arrogance.

Lance opened his eyes to release the image of himself about to walk down the hall and be introduced to a new life at the end of a gun. He sat up in bed drained from his review of the last two months of his life. And he still didn't know the trigger, the thing that started it all. He'd missed it.

It was just after noon. His room service lunch would be delivered in a few minutes. Two hours later, he would make a call. He had survived the 72-hour test. Now he needed to find out what this was all about. Who were these people? What government agency did they work for?

Most importantly, he wanted, needed really, to know more about Seibel. He wasn't close to being done with him.

Chapter 13

"Congratulations Mr. Priest."

The call was routed through four switches in three area codes. Not just difficult to trace, it was designed to be untraceable. On the third ring, Geoffrey Seibel, walking across the floor of his library study, had picked up. The call came in three minutes late.

He got no reply from the other end of the line.

"I imagine you have been moving constantly the past three days Lance. I pictured you in bus terminals, train stations, hitching rides beside the highway. Always on the move, constantly looking over your shoulder. I'll bet that was exciting for you." Seibel remained silent for a few moments and continued. "The reports received from the field have been most impressive. Only two potential sightings; in Mobile, Alabama and Lakeland, Florida. But neither were confirmed."

Still nothing from the other end. "I didn't think you'd head for Orlando, but I am never really surprised by how people under pressure react. Fort Worth was too easy and too close, but you certainly recall the lay of the land from your three-plus years there as a pre-teen. You're much too smart to go to Tulsa."

Seibel's one-sided conversation served two purposes. He kept Lance on the line allowing the computer acting as a caller ID verifier to process the location of the call. Seibel had another telephone handset to his other ear and from it he heard a voice detailing location confirmation details. That voice said a surprising word, "Texas." Seibel's eyebrow arched. *He's still in Texas?*

"But as I said three days ago, you are indeed something of an enigma Lance. We can usually pin someone down to a certain set of character traits and value structure, but you have remained a mystery."

"Dallas County," the voice in the other handset updated caller location. Seibel let out an audible chuckle at the mention of Dallas. *Holy shit, he's still in Dallas. Unbelievable.* The conversation with himself in his head carried on.

"I think we may need to develop a new set of analysis parameters to come up with an adequate label for you."

"Downtown, 645 prefix." Seibel rolled his eyes and broadened his smile at the mention of the location. He bit his lip to hold back a chuckle. "Phone number range 645-5200 to 5500. Locale is southeast quadrant of downtown Dallas. Address range involves Commerce to Main in the 600 to 900 blocks."

And with that, Seibel burst out laughing, belly laughs. He couldn't control himself. "You've got to be absolutely friggin kidding me," he said out loud this time. "Don't tell me you're in that same building Lance."

"I assumed you had some way of tracking this call," Preacher finally spoke.

Able to get control of himself and stifle his laughter, Seibel answered. "Yes, technology is coming along nicely. And the little green men in the telephone lines tell me you are calling from Commerce Street in downtown Dallas. I can't tell you how surprised I am."

"This is where you yell 'olli olli in come free.'"

"Ah yes. I remember well. Hide and seek; and you obviously did one hell of a job hiding. Did you travel all across the country and then circle back? Or maybe just tool around the Lone Star state on those endless Texas roads?"

Lance remained silent.

"I am looking forward to hearing about your adventures but I don't fault you for not sharing the details at this point." Seibel added.

Lance continued, "I've been on this line for one minute and 15 seconds now Seibel. I'm guessing I need to get moving quick-like before you have someone here."

"Oh, not to worry, not to worry. You have completed your mission. The assignment has expired for those involved. I can assure you that no one is coming for you. Those tracking you are hundreds, in fact thousands of miles from where you are. You had them chasing ghosts. Very impressive for a newbie, not yet even a rookie. Our deal was 72 hours and you have exceeded that requirement. Congratulations."

"Three hours." Lance was curt.

"Yes, go on." Seibel replied.

"I'll call you back at this number in three hours."

"No need for that." Seibel's voice was soothing and soft.

"Three hours."

Lance's line went dead in Seibel's ear but the line stayed active for the others on the call. "Assessment?" Seibel said into the handset as he leaned back in his leather chair.

"Surprising, but not," Wyrick chimed in.

"Two sightings, none confirmed…" another voice said with a chuckle. "We all know we had absolutely nothing. Zero. Zip. He was gone the moment Krachov lost site of him on Main Street in Dallas. This kid disappeared and did not surface on any databases. Nada, zip."

"Yes, yes I know Marvin. He is living up to full potential on all aspects of the evaluation matrix." An edge in Seibel's tone.

Wyrick cut in, "I was reading over third-party abstract analysis this afternoon on candidate Priest. The latest assessment by this particular team of analysts is that of an individual with multiple personality disorder. I laughed when I initially read it, but after a couple of more read-throughs I see where they were heading with their assessment. They were 100% unable to get a fix on Preacher's underlying psychological make-up. It says 'unable to categorize him in one or two or even three personality segments.' They stated, and I'm reading from their written evaluation here – 'candidate possesses multiple or dissociative characteristics or personalities evidenced in varying levels of perception and interaction based on particular environments. Subject exhibits potential sub-clinical narcissism, Machiavellianism and psychopathy.'"

"Horseshit," Seibel replied.

"I know," Wyrick added. "I've watched hours of video, listened to weeks of audio and read every detail of this kid's life. He is remarkably consistent in his inconsistency. It is calculated, not based on the environment. He is a-"

"Chameleon." The voice Seibel identified as Marvin cut in.

"Perfect." Seibel added for both confirmation and effect. "We have history here gentlemen, you know what I mean. You both know we have been looking for someone like this for a great many years. Hell, I'll bet if we would have given the hunters the order to engage, one or both of them would have ended up like the mother's boyfriend back in Fort Worth."

"You know Braden and I disagree with you on that point," Wyrick cut him off.

"Disagree all you want."

"He was 13." Wyrick was insistent.

"Twelve," Seibel corrected. "The guy picked the wrong single mom with two young boys to rough up. Bastard never knew what hit him."

"All circumstantial," Wyrick replied. "Braden agrees with me on this one."

"Braden's not here and you know perfectly well that everything we do is circumstantial. I saw it in his eyes when he put a gun to my head. He evaluated the circumstances, calculated the related risks and wanted to punish me for putting him in a difficult situation. He was cold and calculating and I'm pretty damn sure he enjoyed it."

"So what happens when he is placed in a situation significantly more difficult?" The disembodied Marvin asked.

Seibel replied, "He put the gun to my head to achieve a goal, but he was also intrigued. He wanted that file folder but he didn't want a murder on his hands that he couldn't immediately work or talk his way out of."

"So you think he was intrigued by all this, but in some way not surprised?" Wyrick asked.

"Gentlemen," Seibel deliberately spoke slowly now to emphasize his point. "I think that for just as long as we have been looking for young Mr. Priest he has been looking for us. Funny, he was under our noses all along. He may not have known exactly what he was looking for, but the desire for a challenge, a real opportunity to push himself, is what has been lurking below his many surfaces. Frank, you've read everything I've read and then some. I appreciate you playing Devil's advocate." Seibel paused for effect.

"You know this subject better than any of us. You've been with him longer than anyone else by a long shot. You don't believe for a moment he was going to shoot me. His reaction was quick, efficient and effective." Seibel added. "We can discuss his reaction and my aching eardrum all we want. I have made my decision and Account One has given me operational authority on this matter. Isn't that correct Marvin?"

"Correct." Marvin replied without emotion.

Seibel continued. "We will proceed with full acquisition, training, development and deployment of this asset under the directive."

"You know I agree with moving to acquisition and training, but I think maybe you should give him more time to mature before comprehensive development and field deployment. We just don't know what we're buying here. He's unquestionably talented, but this kid's a loose cannon if there ever was one. I've got weeks of video and audio to prove it." Wyrick gave his final view on the subject. He didn't really have a vote, but Seibel trusted him and his senses.

"We already have Braden's opinion on this matter. Marvin, anything more from your end?" Seibel asked.

Marvin's voice was matter-of-fact, "You've already made your decision. Just remember that your plans for this role within the agency have been developed and implemented before with less than stellar results. Your 'Fox in the henhouse' project has done well, but not as well as you'd hoped. Patience is a virtue and the proof of your record cannot be denied, but we will need to see a return on this investment."

"Understood, as I have always understood the directive," Seibel chaffed a little at Marvin's comments that made it clear he was Seibel's superior. He brought his hand up to rub his still numb ear. "One can never guarantee ROI, but mark my words on this chilly fall day gentlemen. You and every member of Account One will one day consider this acquisition the finest in the history of the intelligence community."

"Damn, you're sold on this one." Marvin's tone was now surprise.

"Bought and sold and will not have an iota of buyer's remorse. Neither will you." Seibel was matter-of-fact.

"You've said that before. That Belgian situation."

"Don't bring that up Marvin," Seibel giggled a little. "For confirmation purposes, I have approval and am proceeding with plan ALEX."

"You have approval and undoubtedly have an interesting candidate here," Marvin answered with both authority and sarcasm. "Good luck."

The phone lines went dead and Seibel placed the receiver in its cradle and eyed the clock on his large oak desk. He had two hours and 50 minutes to kill. He reached for the bulging file on the corner of the desk and pulled it to him. It sure had fattened up since he was first handed the folder a little over two months prior with only one sheet inside. He'd been through it dozens of times. Like his confidant Wyrick, he too could not pinpoint the source of his sense of awe with this one. It was between all the written lines.

He'd seen outstanding and overqualified candidates before. In fact, he'd recruited and personally trained several of the very finest deep cover agents ever placed in the field. Seibel was renowned for his ability to recognize and develop talent. But he had never seen a package like this.

The gypsy background, the ability to move from conversation to action and back to over-lapping layers of lies was just astounding. Seibel had always been a little more in the nurture over nature camp, but when faced with something or someone so amorphous, almost enigmatic, it makes one wonder. After nearly 30 years is this particular form of clandestine priesthood, he had supposedly seen it all. Seibel also thought he had a good idea of what God intended for perfection.

And that is the word that just kept seeping up through the pages in the file laid out before him. Just as Wyrick kept going back to that concept of ease when he poured over the life of this particular young man and Braden focused on the word comfortable in his evaluations, Seibel was stuck on the word perfect.

Never one for absolutes, he didn't want to get ahead of himself. But the old pro was excited for the first time in a long time. Maybe even more than he was nearly a decade ago when he discovered and launched his greatest espionage achievement. Certainly more excited than his identification and development of his most trusted pupil two decades ago.

He knew from the first moment he read about Lance Priest that he was something. The short answers on the questionnaire confirmed that gut feeling. He had finally found what he had been searching decades for. He'd found that perfect candidate. And if he had to be completely honest, it scared him a little. Kind of like holding a 50-karat diamond or a tiny premature infant in his hands. One wrong move and it could be dropped, shattered, destroyed. Perfection is always amazingly delicate.

Chapter 14

Twenty-seven hours later, when the phone on his antique cherry desk rang, Seibel was waiting. He had been sitting there staring intermittently at the phone and the clock beside it.

The desk phone he had brought from one of his many offices rang precisely 24 hours after the second call the day before; exactly when Lance told him to be here. This time Seibel played coy. He picked it up on the third ring and put the receiver to his ear without saying a word.

At the other end he heard an assortment of noises that immediately led him to assume Lance was calling from a public area, most likely a pay phone. Seibel didn't have anyone tracking this call. A few moments of silence passed at each end before Seibel spoke.

"Are you there my boy?"

"I'll assume this is being recorded like yesterday so I'll keep it short. McLean, Virginia."

"Yes I've heard of it." Seibel's eyebrows rose. The old pro didn't skip a beat.

Lance continued, "Of course you have. You're there right now."

"If you say so my boy." *Damn.*

"If you'd like, I can call you back in about twenty minutes with your address."

"And how would you do that Lance."

"Just like I did to get as far as McLean, I'd ask nicely." Lance was sparse with his words.

Seibel remained silent this time. He was processing the information and working through protocol to see how Lance could have possibly tracked him down through a line that was sterile, switched so many times it was beyond traceable.

Lance broke the silence, "You probably want to know how, but you know I won't tell you. And you also know I won't be at this phone for more than another 30 seconds so tracing this one probably won't work."

Seibel finished with a few calculations that had taken him away for a moment. "Lance I'll ask you to please not hang up. I need to speak with you for just a few minutes. We have some items to discuss."

"Don't feel much like talking right now." Lance was short.

"I'd rather talk right now. Shouldn't take long." Seibel implored.

"No let's talk later. How about 8 o'clock?"

"Actually I have a dinner appointment this evening." Seibel lied.

"In McLean or maybe over in D.C?"

"I'm not in McLean or anywhere near Washington," Another lie.

Lance replied, "How about 7 then, before your dinner meeting? That's only 45 minutes from now."

"Lance, why don't we speak now? What's the point in delaying?"

"Because I prefer to speak with you in person." The words were a thunderbolt. He had been under the assumption that Lance had likely made his way back to Tulsa or somewhere near; or was still hidden in Dallas. Seibel did a completely natural thing for a veteran of three decades of espionage. He stepped to the window and looked out. The street was clear.

"In person?" Seibel played it cool.

"Yep. And I have just the place." Lance's turn to be coy.

"You're in McLean?"

"No. I figured you just lived over there but worked either in D.C. or close by. Maybe up in Langley. Am I right?"

No reply at the other end of the line, just silent processing.

Lance continued, "I'm sure you want to hear all about how I tracked you down to McLean and the 837 prefix for your home phone. But not right now. I need to hang up in nine seconds."

"Where do you want to meet?" Seibel blurted out.

"Ah-hah. Got you?"

"Got me, yes." Seibel shook his head.

"I'm thinking a very public place with lots of people."

"There are lots of them in Washington, but you really don't need to worry about your safety Lance. You passed the test with flying colors. We don't want to harm you, we want to get to know you better and see about possibly working together."

"So that's why you had those guys trying to kill me?" Lance's voice cold.

"That was a test. Merely a trial of your innate survival skills. And as I said, you succeeded on all parameters. We have placed a great amount of value and invested significant time and resources into learning as much as we can about you. The exercise in Dallas was a stress test to see how you'd react under pressure, that's all. We wouldn't want anything to happen to you." Seibel was indeed a skilled and experienced liar.

"Great. So you won't mind meeting me at the Washington D.C. police station on 4th Street."

"Very good, excellent choice. You assumed that you would be safe there with all those uniforms and guns right?"

"Something like that. Do you know the place?" Lance asked.

"Yes. Just a few blocks off the mall." Seibel knew the place.

"That's right. Between School and E." Lance replied.

"You must have been there before, huh?"

"No, just standing right outside now. I'm going to step inside the station in 30 seconds. See you here at 7 or any time you'd like before then."

The words hung there. Seibel was flabbergasted, knocked out. *How the hell did he do it?* He asked himself as he turned to hundreds of books on the shelves beside his desk. He would have known by now if he had asked communication ops to monitor and track this call. He still would have been amazed. But nonetheless, this kid had somehow tracked a virtually untraceable call. He'd left Dallas yesterday afternoon and traveled to Washington D.C. What a find.

"Very good. I'll start heading that way shortly." Seibel covered up any emotion in his voice with years, decades really, of experience and countless times like this in which he was presented with a situation bordering on the impossible.

"And you'll come alone right?" Lance suggested.

"Yes, just me. You'll recognize me from the smile on my face."

Lance remained deadpan in his response. "I'll be looking for you, Smiley. Come alone."

Seibel added, "In the meantime Preacher, I want you to think about something."

"What's that?"

"Joining the Army."

Chapter 15

Lance hung up the phone and looked both directions up and down 4th street just off the National Mall in Washington, DC. He could see the top of one of the buildings on the mall, the Smithsonian, he guessed.

It was his first time to the nation's capitol. He'd devoured the road atlas folded in his jacket pocket and memorized the streets surrounding the mall. No time to go up to 5,000 or 10,000 feet and take in all in. He closed his eyes and caught his breath.

Lance had been riding a whirlwind for just over 27 hours and more than 1,300 miles. A half hour earlier, he was dropped off by a nice trucker from Anderson, Indiana. The police station seemed like a naturally safe place, but he'd just come up with that about three minutes ago. On the fly. Seat of his pants.

It had worked for about 21 years. He didn't see an immediate reason to change. He looked briefly at the phone booth he'd just used. It was hanging up a phone yesterday that started him on his cross-country journey.

Twenty-seven hours earlier and 1,371 miles to the west and south.

He didn't know where he was going with it, but right after hanging up from the first call to Seibel, he picked up the phone again and pressed "0." Talking to operators had always been something of a treat for him because he could be anyone in the world and take the conversation in any million directions with the nameless, faceless Ma Bell operator at the other end of the line. They were almost always female.

"Operator, how may I help you?" A friendly female voice came on. Lance guessed her age at 39 or 40. He put her accent south from where he now stood which meant Louisiana, maybe Mississippi.

"Yes ma'am," Lance affected an accent equal to or even more southern than the operator. "I just hung up from a call on this line with my brother and I'm afraid he's going to hurt himself."

"What's that?" The operator asked.

Lance's voice dripped with emotion and quivered. "I think he might kill himself. He just flunked out of boot camp and his girlfriend back home broke up with him. He just hung up on me a few seconds ago and I need to call him back or find out where he was calling from so I can get him some help." His voice cracked.

"Oh my, oh my, okay just a moment sir. Let me do a quick check on that line." The operator clicked away on her CRT keyboard.

"Thank you so much ma'am. I really appreciate it."

She came back on the line. "Can you please confirm the number you are calling from sir?"

"Yes ma'am," he picked up the phone off the reception desk in the office he had come to take the oral assessments. The lights were out in the offices. He hadn't turned any on after breaking in. He'd actually been a little surprised to find a working phone. It seemed not every prop had been cleared off the stage. "It is 214…"

"Okay. Thank you honey. Please remain on the line and I will get with my supervisor and a technician to research that call. Just a moment, you hold on now."

"Thank you ma'am. I will." He sniffed to stifle a cry.

When the operator returned to the line four minutes later, she had a supervisor and a network technician on as well. They were stumped at first by the number and relay process of the call that the phone had just made. The 800 number Lance had dialed had evidently gone into a transfer station that then moved it to an alternate network before returning to another terminal and in the process switched to another protocol before terminating in Virginia.

All of this went way over Lance's head. He heard the operator and her supervisor hem and haw as the technician traced the call across the country. It was obvious from the technician's voice that he found this one challenging. His approach was methodical, but his tone spoke of the urgency he was employing.

"Mclean, Virginia." The technician stated with confidence. "Prefix 837, but I am having real difficulty getting to the actual post. Do we know if this is a home or a pay phone?"

"No sir. I called the number he gave me. I thought it might be on his Army base." Lance took a wild swing at that one.

"I don't see any military codes attached to this one, but I am sure of the terminal point." The technician typed on his keyboard and read the information off his green screen.

"Mclean, Virginia?" Lance asked.

"Yes sir. Mclean."

"Where is that?" He knew, of course. He'd seen it many times when memorizing roads in and around the nation's capitol.

"Right across from Washington D.C." the technician replied.

"Thank ya'll so much." Lance replaced the handset on the phone base and made his way out of the empty office and down the stairs he had raced three days earlier.

On the way down, he thought about Mclean, Virginia and its proximity to Washington, D.C. It could only mean government. Had to be. And government meant something like CIA or FBI. He cracked a smile as he rounded the stairwell onto the first floor and opened the door leading into the lobby. "This is just like the movies," he whispered to himself giddily. Spooks, spies, espionage, assassinations. "Damn. This might get interesting yet."

Walking across the lobby, he thought of his next steps. He could grab a taxi be at Love Field in 15 minutes, but the airlines had computers and tracked names. He needed to travel at a much lower profile and pay cash if possible. He still had $300 or so, not forgetting the $2,700 he owed the Aldolphus. The bus station was just a block away, but he still thought that too public a means of transportation.

No, he knew what he needed and he knew where to find it. He hit the street on Commerce, after saying so long to Alfred, the federal building security guard from Beaumont, Texas who enjoyed fishing for bass up on Lake Texoma. Alfred was Lance's newest friend and let him enter the building with no problem after learning that Lance was a bass man. Lance wasn't, of course. But he could tell a good fish story.

He jogged over to the Hilton and caught a cab. The driver was a little surprised to hear that Lance wanted to go to nearest truck stop. Once there, it took Lance exactly seven minutes to convince a trucker, George P., enjoying a cup of coffee that he desperately needed a ride east. George P., the guy insisted on including the "P," listened with compassion as Lance spun his yarn about an uncle and prison and regrets for things left unsaid.

George P. and Lance were on the road nine minutes later bound for South Carolina along Interstate 20. From there, the George P would hook Lance, who was calling himself Billy for this performance, with a fellow trucker heading north on 95. With good traffic, the route would take 23 hours.

Lance did more uninterrupted listening on that drive than he had in years. He devoured George P.'s road atlas along the way, paid for dinner, coffee and breakfast 13 hours later on the east side of Atlanta.

He did a bit of thinking as well, but only when George P. stopped talking. Did he really need to go to Washington? Was he doing it for spite or fun? He thought of Seibel and his knowing smile and firing the gun beside his head to try to wipe the smile off.

He didn't hate the guy, but wouldn't mind the opportunity to point a gun at him again. Lance reached into his pocket and grasped the handle of the gun for maybe the hundredth time. If George P. saw him do it, he hadn't mentioned it.

One thing just kept rolling through Lance's mind, turning over and over. *Why did they pick him?*

Chapter 16

Seibel was early. He parked his car, a silver Mercedes, at a meter on School Street just around the corner from the front entrance to the First District Headquarters of the DC Metropolitan Police. Lance took a guess it was Seibel approaching from the west on School Street in the German make a few minutes earlier. When the car pulled to the curb, Lance was sure. And he was positive when he saw Seibel reach down and pull a phone up to his ear.

"He's got a car phone. Now I know he's a big shot." Lance snickered to himself and then took a look around to see if Seibel brought anyone else to the party. He didn't know exactly what he was looking for.

There were a good number of people around. Many on foot; many more in cars. Washington D.C. was a busy place at rush hour with thousands of workers leaving their government jobs and heading to homes outside of the Beltway. Lance couldn't keep track of everyone and everything he was seeing but he didn't pick up any patterns. He thought his position, standing in a doorway kitty-corner from the police station, was as good as any to survey the landscape.

He didn't really have a plan, just wanted to see what would happen over the next few minutes. The fact that Seibel had a phone in his car changed his thinking a little. As he watched the government man walk up the sidewalk and stairs into the police station, Lance decided to take action. He pulled out a receipt from a 7-11 down the street and took the pen out of his jacket pocket. In the 40 minutes it had taken Seibel to arrive at the police station, Lance had walked the surrounding perimeter and stopped at two other pay phones and written down the numbers. The number he now wrote down was for a phone at the corner of 6th and E. Street. He also wrote "Call me from your car phone."

He walked directly across 4th Street and then j-walked across School to Seibel's parked Mercedes. Lance placed the receipt with the phone number under a windshield wiper and walked away casually. He stopped at the end of the street and positioned himself just at the edge of a building so that he could see down School all the way to 4th.

Seibel came around the corner less than five minutes later. From this distance, about 300 yards, Lance couldn't really make out the look on his face, but he was sure he saw a little frustration. It took Seibel about 20 seconds to make it to his car. He spotted the piece of paper on his windshield and stopped to look in all directions before grabbing it. He pulled the receipt off the glass and looked around.

Seibel opened his door and got in his car. Lance took his cue and turned toward the phone booth about 75 yards away across 6th Street. He was pleased to see that no one was on the phone, but wouldn't have minded keeping Seibel waiting with a busy signal for a few minutes until someone got off the line.

Lance arrived at the phone and expected it to be ringing already. It wasn't and didn't ring for another four minutes. Strange. He stepped away from the phone toward a crowded bus stop 60 feet away. The phone rang and Lance took the few steps back over to it. A few people gathered round the bus stop looked up in curiosity at the ringing. But he noticed some of the people nearby didn't look up because they were already looking at him. Uh-oh.

Preacher picked it up after the second ring.

"Look to your South and East across E Street." The voice was not Seibel's. "See the gentlemen with the black cap?" Preacher stepped back from the phone booth and looked at the man in jeans, blue denim jacket and black ball cap with a big yellow Pittsburg Pirates "P." The guy was looking right at him. Preacher still had the phone to his ear as the voice spoke again.

"Now turn around and look at the two men sitting on the building steps."

Preacher turned to see two men in business suits with ties loosened. From this close, he could see the matching earpieces each had in their right ears. Both just looked at him with expressions unchanged.

Preacher kept his eyes on them as he spoke into the phone. "Any more?"

"About six. All within 200 yards of your location." The faceless voice at the other end of the line waited for his next question. A city bus pulled up to the curb on E Street. The assembled mass cued up to get aboard. Lance looked at the bus then back to the two gents on the steps. They both stood up as if prompted by sounds in their ears. His mind raced.

The voice spoke again, "You could get on that bus, but our people would just get on with you."

"But at least I'd be moving. A moving target is tougher to hit." Preacher replied.

"It's very likely that a D.C. Metro police patrol car with another patrol in support would stop that bus very soon to detain and if necessary arrest a suspect in a recent robbery or maybe it's a homicide."

"Don't they need a warrant for that?" The line to get on the bus was moving quickly now. He would have to move within 10 seconds to get on.

"Not really. Not when national security is a concern."

"National security? What did I do to threaten national security?"

"There are lots of things one can do to place the security of our great nation in danger." Sarcasm tinged the voice on the phone.

The line at the bus was down to two people. The two suits on the steps took several steps toward the bus just in case Preacher bolted for it. The last bus rider was about to step on the bus but then turned back to look at Preacher. It was a black woman and surprise, surprise -- she had an earpiece in her right ear. Preacher looked from her to the two suits now only steps from him. He then glanced to his right and to no one's surprise, saw another nice looking guy in slacks, sports coat and black earpiece.

The bus pulled away from the curb.

"What now?" Preacher asked.

But just as quickly as the bus pulled away, up pulled a silver Mercedes with Seibel behind the wheel.

"Looks like your ride is here." The disembodied voice was probably attached to a man with a smile on his face. *They had him.* "No scenes, no funny stuff Lance."

The passenger side window rolled down and Seibel's smiling face greeted him.

"What if I don't get in?" Preacher spoke quietly into the phone.

"Just get in." The voice was a little gruff.

With that, Preacher hung up the phone and whistled as loud as he could. In seconds, six men approached from different directions. Unlike the well-dressed men in suits and earpieces, each of these gentlemen sported black jeans and flattop black heads. Each had various amounts of gold around their necks and each obviously carried weapons under baggy clothes.

"Whadup G?" One of the men shouted from the middle of 6th Street. "We ain't got no problem do we now?" He raised his arms in the air and beckoned each of his friends to take a position at the perimeter of the corner. One stood just off the bumper of Seibel's Mercedes. Another stood just behind the guy in the blue sports coat. Another stood on the sidewalk behind the black woman. Each of the young men kept one hand tucked in clothing, gripping firearms.

"Don't really know G." Preacher affected an accent that sounded part Long Island, part Boston. "Like I said, I knew some folks was after me, but I didn't know they was fake fuzz."

"Fake fuzz. You got that down. These ain't cops. You can tell by the threads. No cops got suits that nice. These here look like feds, but like you said, you ain't done nothin wrong so the feds can't just grab you."

Lance moved from the phone toward the two suits. His walk had a definite saunter to it. Just a step away from them, he could tell by the blinking of their eyes they were getting messages in their earpieces. "I think these boys don't want any kind of a scene out here G. I think they probably want to turn and walk away real quick like, don't you think?"

"Yeah, that's right. If they ain't got no warrant and no cops backing them up then they ain't got cause and need to step off." The gang leader made his way into the center of the scene a few steps behind Preacher and only a few paces from the Mercedes.

Preacher turned to see Seibel talking on his phone. He spoke a few terse words into the receiver and hung up.

Preacher yelled at Seibel, "Hey man, that's a no parking zone. You know you gonna get yourself a ticket hombre."

As Seibel got out of his car, his jacket flapped open to reveal the gun holstered under his right armpit. His demeanor was now totally different from the multiple personas Preacher had encountered in Dallas or on the phone. Seibel walked past the young black gangster standing at his rear bumper and past the ringleader to Preacher. His smile now gone.

"Another excellent job Lance." He was within two feet of Preacher and spoke in a low voice just above a whisper.

"How's that?" Preacher tilted his head.

"This little circus; I assume you found your friends on some street corner and paid them a little tip to join in on some fun with folks in authority?"

Preacher smiled and looked over Seibel's shoulder to TJ, the gang's leader. "These fools think they got everything figured out man. They think you all are a street corner gang."

TJ replied, "Oh I been on a few corners and this one right here just happens to be one of ours, especially after 6 p.m. You know we charge a permit fee to assemble here."

Preacher laughed and turned back to Seibel. "What do you think about that? You all are going to have to pay a little tax for your show here Seibel."

"How much?"

"TJ, what's the goin rate for a… circus? I think that is the word for this?"

"This here looks like at least a $200 circus. That sound right boys?" TJ turned to his gang and received general agreement if not a plea for a higher fee.

Seibel just smiled and laughed. He then looked to each of his team members and nodded at each. "Lance you do not fail to surprise at every turn."

"Thanks, I try."

Seibel leaned in close and TJ took a step closer. The gang leader was now invested in this deal. Seibel whispered in Preacher's ear. "You have some very unique skills Preacher."

"Something is either unique or not. There are no degrees of uniqueness." Preacher whispered back.

"That's your mother talking."

Lance just looked at him and squinted. The fact that Seibel knew about his mother's nasty habit of correcting others' misspoken words and statements should have surprised him.

"What now?" Lance raised his eyebrows.

"Now you get in the car with me and we go get some dinner."

"And then I sleep with the fishes?"

Seibel laughed again. "No, even worse."

"Worse?"

"You join the Army, Private Priest."

"But dinner first right?" Lance asked.

"Right." Seibel smiled.

"Can TJ and his boys come along?" Lance asked.

Seibel turned from Lance and his demeanor once again changed completely. He was truly a chameleon. He put a broad smile on his face and raised his hands up above his shoulders and lowered them slightly. It was a signal. With that, each member of his team turned and walked from the corner. The two suits split; the black woman headed East on E Street. The sports coat turned north on 6th and got into a car idling at the curb that Lance had seen but not included in mix.

Seibel turned toward TJ and reached back slowly to his back pocket to retrieve his wallet. From it he pulled several bills.

"Thank you for the use of your corner sir." He spoke in a cockney accent. Damn funny.

TJ didn't take the money right away. He looked to Lance. "Looks like show's over hombre. You cool?"

"All our friends are leaving." The streetwise urban accent Lance had affected moments ago was gone as well. "Thanks for your help."

TJ took the money from Seibel and stuffed it in his pocket. "If you say its cool brother."

Lance laughed. "Don't know about cool. But I guess I'm gonna get some dinner out of the deal."

"Make sure you get a good steak and order two bottles of champagne. Let the feds spend a pretty penny on you." Lance and his new gang leader friend took a step toward each other and shook hands. It seemed like Lance's handshake had a little more soul in it than TJ's. "Keep it cool my brother."

"Cool and easy G." Lance clasped TJ's hand in both his and laughed. TJ's walk away from them was pure street. He had worked on it for years. Lance and Seibel stepped over to his Mercedes. Just then a police cruiser pulled up behind Seibel's Mercedes with lights flashing. Seibel waived at the officer and hopped in. Lance got in the passenger side.

Seibel put it in gear and turned to him. "Why do I think this police car isn't just here because of my illegal parking?"

"I'm sure Officer Salinas back there has been watching all this fun from a safe distance." Lance replied.

"Officer Salinas?"

"He's originally from Jacksonville, Florida and has a son starting at defensive end for an Alexandria high school team as a sophomore. He's already thinking college, SEC schools are watching him."

"Nice." Seibel turned back to the road and his driving, but the smile stayed on his face.

Lance smiled too. He had no idea who the police officer in the car behind them was. He'd never met him, never seen him before. But details make all the difference to a good lie.

Chapter 17

This operation took only 17 days, instead of 11 weeks.

Marta pulled the trigger of her Glock and the man's right foot exploded. He collapsed to the ground screaming and moaning. Still trying to catch his breath.

She and Nir, her closest confidant in this new life as a rogue KGB operative, had chased the man across a bridge, through four apartment buildings and into this alcove next to the Sava River in Belgrade. It was 3:14 a.m. Their chase lasted a half hour and covered some very picturesque properties. But none of them had stopped to take in the beauty.

His name was Jordan Ostrovic and he had run from Marta because she knew what he'd done. He'd sold Soviet secrets to the west. Ostrovic knew his jig was up the instant Marta, instead of his contact, showed up at the designated location. He didn't know, couldn't know because it had just happened, his contact would never meet anyone ever again. His head now had a couple of extra holes.

Upon seeing her, Ostrovic took off into the dark. Marta and Nir expected this and had worked out their plan to split up in advance. Marta tracked Jordan from the west side of Branko's

Bridge south along the banks of the Sava. Nir took a route up above them on the street to cut off the KGB double agent.

A Belgrade native, Ostrovic knew his way along the trail and into a series of low buildings nearby. He crossed a dimly lit street just ahead of Nir with Marta trailing. She motioned for Nir to stay to the right as they approached an intersection. She veered left to stay with Ostrovic. The KGB mole turned a corner 50 feet ahead of Marta. She could see him slow too much for the turn so she took a wide berth that brought her into the middle of the street as she reached a point where she could see around the corner. She dove to the pavement and rolled just as he fired four shots at her. Still rolling, she returned fire. With neither of their guns silenced, the quiet calm of the early morning was shattered.

Ostrovic was up and running a second later. She took off after him. His route took him into an apartment commons with four buildings stacked next to each other in the finest 1960s Soviet architectural style. Ostrovic ran into one and considered hitting the stairs, but Nir entered from another direction forcing him back out into the night. Marta came upon him then and was taking aim when he fired three shots at her, barely missing. He was a good, capable agent, at least in a firefight.

He took advantage of her dive behind a short wall to turn back into the darkness near the river. Nir was now closest to him as they left streetlights behind. Nir hung back on purpose. Ostrovic had already proven his ability to fire his weapon. Nir wondered whether the KGB turncoat had a spare clip with him or if he was down to just a few bullets?

Marta gambled that Ostrovic would turn south again when he reached the river so she broke off in that direction which put Nir and the man he was chasing hundreds of yards away. She was nearing the riverbank when she heard three more shots fired. They weren't far away, maybe 150 yards to the north. She turned in that direction and took a few steps before plastering herself to a wall, blending her dark coat and pants with the shadow.

In the darkness, her mind wandered for a few moments. She thought about love for some reason. At 26, Marta still had her virginity intact. Not because she despised the act or even the thought of sex, no, she had refused to give anyone, any man, a semblance of power over her life.

She enjoyed the company of men and certainly thought she would have found a good partner to share her love with by now, but had been disappointed every single time she laid down her rules to those she was close to accepting.

Every time, every single time, she had gotten the same response. The look of fear in their eyes was unmistakable and all too predictable as she let them know any betrayal afterward would be met, not merely with death, but slow, painful agony followed by slow but certain death. The first time she asked this of a man was at the age of 17 while at school in a Moscow suburb. The 19-year-old boy didn't even try to hide his fear. He ran from the room and let it be known throughout the university that Marta was unhinged, dangerous even. She had embraced this reputation and found the respite from boys' advances quite peaceful. It wasn't long afterward that she earned the same reputation from the girls at the school after setting one of them straight on her relational needs. She had let the girl kiss her and then taken a small bite of the young lesbian's ear along with a stud earring for payment.

Her values had not changed over the years. Love was something she had yet to experience. In its place she had drive, persistence, creativity. She believed she had done so well in her profession precisely because she did not have the encumbrances of relationships weighing her down. What she lacked in love and empathy she made up for in ingenuity.

Her gamble paid off. Ostrovic came running toward her on the path beside the river. She could easily put a bullet in his head as he ran under a lone streetlight. But she needed him alive, at least for a few minutes. When he was within a few paces, Marta stepped out while crouching and simply stuck her leg into his path. He tripped over her and hit the ground hard. Before he could recover, she was on him kicking him viciously in the gut and putting her boot onto his neck with gun aimed at his head. She could see him think about pointing his gun up at her, but she would surely drill him with a bullet clean through his forehead before he could get his gun in position.

"Drop it." She said it in Russian, knowing full well this Serbian spoke the language. He complied. A few moments later, Nir rolled up on them. For good measure, he kicked Ostrovic in the mouth, obviously not happy about being shot at earlier.

Nir grabbed the double agent's gun and pointed it at him as Ostrovic got to his feet holding a hand over his bleeding mouth. He struggled to pull oxygen into his lungs.

"Where is it?" Marta didn't go into details with her question.

Between breaths, Ostrovic replied, "I threw it in the river back on the bridge when I saw you."

She laughed at him. "So funny. You just threw away your only bargaining chip. Not likely Jordan."

"I did. I tossed it in the water."

"You're wasting our time. Do you just want me to shoot you and get this over with?" Marta stepped closer, the gun just a foot away from the man's face.

"No, wait. Please, I have children." Ostrovic went all soft, like most men do.

"You should have thought of them before you passed secrets to the French and long before you started dealing with the Americans. You sentenced your offspring to a life without a father, at least until your beautiful widow marries another man to provide for her children and warm her bed." Marta was cruel and direct as usual. She had never met Ostrovic before tonight, but had done her research on his personal, as well as professional life.

"No please, I have it." He pleaded.

"Then hand it over. I may find some mercy for you if you don't waste all my patience." She replied.

He reached into a pocket. Nir stepped forward and jammed his gun into Ostrovic's side. He pulled out an envelope and held it out to Marta. She let Nir reach for it. Nir stepped back and opened the envelope while Marta kept her eyes locked on Ostrovic. The mole looked from her to Nir and back.

"It is the disk and three photos of the schematics." Nir spoke, also in his native Russian.

"Excellent." Marta smiled and lowered her weapon to take aim at Ostrovic's foot. The shot rang out across the Sava River. As Ostrovic knelt and wrapped his bloody hands around his shoe, Marta leaned down over him. "It would be so easy to finish you right now. You are disgusting, a rat. But I'm not going to."

Ostrovic heard the words and became silent. He did not expect this. Did not expect mercy.

"Yes Jordan, you get to go home to your kids and beautiful wife. You get to wake up in the morning and thank your God that you are alive. But you will also know when the morning sun lights your house that you are now a slave. You are property, my property." The words cut him.

"Okay, anything." He actually smiled through the pain.

"Don't start begging yet," Marta bent down on a knee. She was not doing this for mercy's sake. She had no benevolence in her DNA. The former KGB agent was letting this individual live so he could serve her, help her. Nothing more. "You work for me now. Your life is mine and you may wish for death before long. You will continue to deal your secrets to the West. You will simply provide copies of everything to me. In turn, you will be given the opportunity to live a long and tortured life always looking over your shoulder, wondering when death will save you."

Her harsh words were delivered in such a pleasant tone that Ostrovic was mesmerized. Nir stood a few feet away. He smiled at her impeccable performance. She was a master at molding the human psyche. "You will work through others we send to you. You will never see me again while you are alive. If you ever see my face again, it will be the last image you witness before you open your eyes and feel the flames of hell flicking your skin."

She stood, turned and walked away. Ostrovic was about to call out and thank her when Nir kicked him in the temple. He was out cold. The Russian reached in to take Ostrovic's wallet to make it easier to tell the police and his wife that he was mugged. Explaining why he was down here beside the river at 3 in the morning was his problem.

1,057 miles to the east and north, Smelinski waited. Like his American counterpart Seibel, he had an array of resources in the field feeding him information. Those tasked with monitoring Marta and her activities did so under the auspices of keeping tabs on former KGB agents who were soon to be eliminated. Smelinski let it be widely circulated that anyone who stepped too far out of line after leaving the agency would be made to suffer.

Some of his underlings had begun to talk under their breath, but always out of his earshot. Maybe, just maybe, the old man was beginning to lose his iron grip. If he let Marta and her growing band of misfits run wild through Europe, how much control did the old man truly have?

He liked that people were talking. It provided additional cover and obfuscation for his secret. Marta was indeed overstepping boundaries, but she was also reeling in loose ends with every assignment.

Marta was closing networks and eliminating unsanctioned operations without anyone suspecting it was all being done under his direction. She did it with such flourish, such chaos, such flare for the dramatic, that it could not possibly be coordinated.

This early morning, Smelinski waited to hear if she was successful in shutting down a leak that fed both organized crime and the West far too much top-secret information. The fact that she could eliminate problems like this under the guise of taking them over for her own profit was truly genius. Gregor the Terrible anxiously awaited word from Belgrade.

Chapter 18

Lance Porter Priest joined the Army just days before Christmas in 1987.

It was the second time he had walked into the recruiting station located behind a Toys R Us in Tulsa. The first had been during his high school senior year. He'd always seen himself as a patriot and thought he would look good in uniform, but when actually handed the paperwork, he hesitated. In point of fact, he chickened out.

It wasn't that he didn't think he could cut it. No, it was the exact opposite. He could see himself excelling within the military structure and actually finding both a home and life there. A structured life that provided a direct path for advancement was just something he could not abide by. At least that's what he convinced himself.

This time, he told the recruiter, a sergeant from Dubuque, Iowa, that helicopters had always intrigued him. Especially in the period after the failed attempt to rescue the American hostages in Iran in 1980 – Operation Eagle Claw. The top-secret mission failed when a US helicopter crashed in the open desert outside of Tehran. "How the hell did they crash into each other in the middle of that big ass desert?" Lance asked the sergeant with full-on Oklahoma accent. The recruiter had no idea. He hadn't even heard the story, so Lance gave him the details memorized from a military encyclopedia.

Lance proceeded to take the ASVAB test the following week. He scored a respectable but not gaudy 42 on the test and apparently showed real promise in the area of vocabulary and language comprehension.

Preacher underwent the requisite medical and mental examinations at the Military Entrance Processing Station (MEPS) in Kansas City. He sat down with a service counselor and selected his Army job. Recruit Priest shared his initial interest in helicopters with the counselor. Not flying them, but maintaining and repairing these modern miracles of flight. He was assured that a job or Military Occupation Specialty (MOS) in helicopter maintenance awaited him after completing boot camp. Lying to recruits is standard procedure by pretty much everyone. The Army has jobs to fill and the personal preferences of lowly privates are not the main concern.

Private Priest arrived at boot camp at Fort Leonard Wood in Southwestern Missouri in January. He wasn't thrilled about being assigned to Fort "Lost in the Woods," as alumni often refer to the base. He had hoped to go to Fort Benning in Georgia or Fort Jackson in South Carolina. But again, the Army doesn't care much for your preferences. Private Priest, like all the other recruits, was left in Purgatory soon after arriving at base. Purgatory being, in this case, Army Basic Training, the Reception Battalion. Reception is the Army's first attempt to push new enlistees to their psychological limit by forcing them to do literally nothing for days on end. Recruits sit around for days getting an occasional shot in the arm or hip and always perking up when someone walked into the room. Lance served his time in Reception sitting on the floor reading and re-reading a road almanac of Europe. He memorized streets and highways all through Western Europe and what was available of the roads located in the Soviet Bloc of Eastern Europe.

Sitting there for endless hours, he struck up a conversation with a bright young recruit from Yuma, Arizona. Lance knew the small town near the Mexico border that explodes with snowbirds from points north each winter because his grandparents from Montana were among those making the annual trek south in their Winnebago. He had visited them in Yuma for a week back when he was 10 and memorized the drive from Fort Worth to far southern Arizona. He had been hypnotized by his first views of the desert plateaus of New Mexico, the distant Rocky Mountains getting closer. The lava fields right next to the highway just outside the town of Grants, New Mexico got him deeply interested in volcanoes, for about a month.

Further on, the Petrified Forrest National Park mesmerized him even more as he reached out and brushed his fingers along stones that once stood as towering trees 225 million years ago. The signs for the Meteor Crater in eastern Arizona beckoned his 10-year old soul but his Mom wouldn't pull over; just as she wouldn't get off I-40 for a quick stop in Winslow to see if the girl in the flat bed Ford from the song was still there.

Along the way, he'd look out at the two-lane blacktop that made up old Route 66 running along beside I-40 and envisioned travelers from generations past making their way westward. After a brief stop in Phoenix, the rest of the trip along I-8 showed Lance a part of the world he had always wondered about. The desert along the US and Mexico border was hard and cold during winter. He didn't even want to think about the place in the summer when temperatures in Yuma often reach 120 degrees.

The young private from Yuma talked about his first time going north to Flagstaff and seeing snow. Lance cataloged the look in his new friend's eyes under amazement. He looked away from "Yuma" and perfected the look for future use.

After a full week in Reception Battalion, Lance and his recruit class were approved and turned over to their drill sergeant. Sergeant Martinez greeted his new pupils or puppies as he referred to them with utter disrespect and hostility as they assembled before him for the first time. He had them stand at attention or in "parade rest" stance for hours at a time in the freezing cold. A hand raised to scratch a nose or wipe sweat out of an eye meant an immediate 20 push-ups. All during this time, the Sergeant kept up a steady stream of orders, rules and insults. His platoon would be the sharpest, the cleanest and the preparedest when they left here in nine weeks. Lance felt the need to correct the word "preparedest" but remained silent.

"Don't let me catch you taking even a minute off when we are together. You all came here little boys pissing your pants and you will leave here soldiers!" Martinez stopped right in front of Lance and leaned to within inches of his face and memorized his name as he had the other members in the platoon. He did this by spitting the name out in syllables, even when there was only one. "Pre-eest. I like that boy. I'll bet everyone has a lot of fun with your silly name right little Preacher boy?"

Chapter 18

"Yes Drill Sergeant!" Lance answered obediently, looking straight ahead not making eye contact and not wiping the Sergeant's spittle from his cheek. He thought back for a flash of a moment about the first time someone called him Preacher.

It was in Fort Worth when he was 9. An older boy who lived in the same apartment complex invited Lance and a couple of other younger boys to join him and his friends down by the creek. The pleasant invitation came with a threat of violence if refused, of course.

When they got there, the older boy and his menacing friends stuck out a pack of cigarettes at the younger boys and rather politely asked them to light up, under further threat of pain. Jimmy Bell, Lance's closest friend at the time, took one. His other friend Bart also did so, but reluctantly. Lance just watched as an older boy struck a match and lit the two younger boys' cigarettes. Jimmy did exactly as one would expect. He sucked in a big breath and proceeded to just about cough his lungs out. Bart just blew on his cig.

The older fellas got a good laugh at their expense. One then stepped in close to Lance and offered the cigarette pack to him.

Lance politely refused. Another one of them said rather innocuously, "Come on Priest. What are you a Preacher?"

Lance responded by knocking the pack out of the boy's hand. He took a nice little beating from them but gave as good as he got. No big deal, except his two friends proceeded to tell the story to others in the complex and at school. They innocently included the one boy calling Lance "Preacher" and how he stood up to them like a golden hero. It wasn't two days later that a kid he barely knew called him Preacher on the playground. Lance could have made a fuss and maybe knocked the snot out of him, but truth be told, he kind of liked it. *Preacher stuck.*

About the only thing about the nickname that ticked him off was the connotation the word implied. Because folks called him Preacher, it was assumed had to be either a Pastor's son or an evangelical in training. He took it upon himself to read the Bible before his 10th birthday. He actually liked some of the stories and memorized a good bit of scripture to fit certain situations.

He thought about blurting out a certain line and verse to Sergeant Martinez, but decided to play it cool.

"I'll bet you have little boys calling you father this and father that, right boy?" Martinez continued.

"No Drill Sergeant."

"Did you have little boys and girls wanting to confess all their sins to you behind the curtains or maybe out back behind the shed Preacher?"

"No Drill Sergeant."

"I'll bet you took a few little boys' and girls' hands and led them in a special little prayer behind those curtains."

"No Drill Sergeant."

"Did you play let's show all the little alter boys my little pecker? Huh Pre-eest?"

"No Drill Sergeant; only the little girls Drill Sergeant." Lance continued looking straight ahead and only broke a hint of a smile at the corner of his mouth.

Martinez didn't skip a beat having been through this little exercise countless times before. "Well done then Preacher. You keep that little pecker in your pants around these little girls here though."

"Yes Drill Sergeant." Success. Memorable moment established; the name Preacher shared with all in earshot. Lance became a mini-legend among the platoon for knowing just the right moment to push the button on Sergeant Martinez' ego control panel. His fellow platoon members would tell others of Preacher's innate ability to drive up the blood pressure on their drill sergeant while never incurring his wrath or vengeance.

Chapter 19

Private Lance Priest completed Army Basic Training in March 1988 with the other surviving members of 2nd Platoon. He ranked right in the middle of his group, receiving no commendations but no Article 15 punishments either. Lance stayed right in the middle of the pack amid the endless PT drills. Ranked smack dab in the middle in basic rifle marksmanship; was slightly above average in map-reading and didn't get hurt during RBT – rifle bayonet training. Having an M-16 placed in his hands the first time was more of a rush than he expected. He just wished he could shoot the damn thing and hit his target. He stayed perfectly average during it all, as instructed.

Private Priest was presented with a change in plans his ninth week in basic. A lieutenant called him into his office and told Lance his country would benefit more from him applying his skills outside the aviation maintenance track. Instead, he could better serve the nation's interests applying his exceptional abilities in vocabulary and language comprehension at the Defense Language Institute (DLI) in Monterey, California.

Lance's military records provide the details of his decision to change from aviation maintenance to linguistics as his Advanced Individual Training (AIT) specialty. Lance loaded up his trusty1979 Honda Civic and drove from Missouri to California with a requisite stop at home in Tulsa to see his mom and stepdad. During the short visit, he tried like heck to avoid conversations that always came up about dropping out of college. She just couldn't understand why he couldn't wait until he graduated next year to join the Army.

Along the way to California, he saw the same desert Southwest landscape he'd seen a decade earlier. This time, he stopped off at the meteor crater and stood on that corner in Winslow, Arizona, just like the Eagles song.

He also listened to and memorized two cassettes. Played them non-stop from Oklahoma, right through New Mexico, Arizona and up through California. He screamed along with the lead singers and mercilessly finger-fretted the steering wheel during every guitar solo.

He was speechless as he crested the hill coming into Monterey and saw the Pacific Ocean for the first time. His breath was taken away again by the view of the bay below from the Presidio on the top of the hill where the DLI was situated.

At DLI, he spent eight months learning not one but two languages – Russian and Arabic. The first an obvious choice for the Cold War. Arabic was a little bit of forward thinking. He had to attend extra classes on the many Arabic dialects. He did indeed have an innate ability to pick up languages. Words, sentence structures, the connections between meaning and pronunciation were like maps. He could simply see the associations among the words as if they were roads connecting cities and towns and nations.

The pressure-packed curriculum of learning two languages kept him busy day and night. He did get out on occasion and one time borrowed another student's motorcycle which he road up and then down the PCH – Pacific Coast Highway. He stopped for a couple of hours in Carmel just south of Monterey.

Lance looked from sea to hills coming right out of the water and immediately labeled the quiet little town the most beautiful place he'd ever seen. He laughed to himself when he uttered the Russian word *krasivyĭ* instead of the English equivalent "beautiful."

His successful time at DLI-Monterey was followed by months of signal intelligence training at Goodfellow Air Force Base in San Angelo, Texas. At Goodfellow, Private First Class Priest spent hours on end learning the intricacies of listening to radio transmissions from around the world and deciphering their content, especially those emanating from well behind the Iron Curtain. Messages from the other side were broadcast to points west and intercepted by NATO and US satellites and listening stations. Lance learned to "assume the position" with one hand pressing the earphone while the other took notes, almost without thinking. It was a dictation of sorts. Those dictating spoke various languages and dialects from Eastern Europe and Asia.

Lance learned to scan the dials seeking frequencies and identifying certain individuals by their word use, cadence, accent and phrases. He excelled in his courses at Goodfellow and left the installation after six months as Specialist Priest.

His permanent station would be Gablingen Kaserne, better known to its US military residents as "Gab." The facility, featuring a dazzling assortment of satellite dishes and antennas, was located just outside Augsburg, Germany, which lies just outside Munich and therefore just a few hundred miles from the Soviet Bloc.

Specialist Priest was stationed in Augsburg for the next two and a quarter years and served ably without distinction during this time. He listened intently each day to conversations between radio operators in Prague and pilots flying over the Eastern Mediterranean. And eavesdropped on static-filled commands from Generals in Moscow excoriating their inferiors in Minsk, Warsaw or Budapest. He was there to hear the increased chatter all over the region in the days and weeks leading up to November 9, 1989 when the Berliner Mauer, better known to those in the U.S. as the Berlin Wall, was breached and finally collapsed under the weight of freedom.

This record of service, while not exemplary, was impressive enough. That is if it were true.

In reality, only about 25% of Lance's military record featured fact. Yes, he did enlist and go to "basic" at Fort Leonard Wood. But unlike his fellow boot campers, Private Priest left base for extended periods. Sometimes days, sometimes weeks. All excused by his superiors and their superiors.

He did choose DLI over aviation maintenance, but the option was never presented by a lieutenant. It instead, came from high-ranking military officials; guided by the unseen hand of Seibel.

Lance did learn Russian and Arabic at the Defense Language Institute. But again, unlike the other students attending daily classes, Lance would disappear from base for weeks at a time. Yet he always passed every class. His grades were good, in the top quartile.

San Angelo, Texas is a place virtually no one would go voluntarily. That fact may be the very best reason the nation's once, current and future spies and snoops go there for training. Private Priest was indeed assigned to Goodfellow AFB for SIGINT training, but again was not in class for a good portion of his lessons.

His tour at Gablingen Kaserne in Augsburg was an exciting time for the world as the Cold War went through a major defrost. Specialist Priest would have surely enjoyed the camaraderie and fellowship of his Army buddies had he been there. But Preacher wasn't around much. Aside from orientation and a few select weeks of duty with those super-sensitive earphones planted on his head, Lance was basically an anomaly to others stationed in Augsburg. Anyone who took it upon his or herself to ask questions about Specialist Priest and his intermittent appearances would be told to mind their own business in no uncertain terms.

In fact, Priest was something of a minor mystery to everyone who encountered him during his first three-plus years in the US Army. He was there enough to be remembered, but unremarkable enough to have left only a bland impression. Ask any of his basic training platoon mates, DLI classmates or Augsburg station mates and the one consistent answer would be, "He was always nice." Never got into a fight; never got into trouble; never cost anyone extra miles running or time in the stockade. Priest was the epitome of a military wallflower. And Geoffrey Seibel wouldn't have it any other way. He kept his pupil fairly busy training to one day save the world.

Lance did as ordered for his completely non-illustrious military career. He was present and accounted for, nothing more. He was there enough to be remembered if brought up, but little more than a face to most he met.

Instead of Missouri, California, Texas and Germany, Lance Porter Priest spent the majority of his time from the winter of 1988 through late summer 1990 in the marshlands along the eastern coast of North Carolina. To be exact, Lance was a regular guest at Harvey Point Defense Testing Activity Center. This out of the way little base outside Hertford, NC is known in certain circles as the world headquarters for US counter-intelligence training – your basic land of the CIA spook. Not those plain vanilla CIA agent types either. No, Harvey Point produced a more virulent strain of operative. Graduates of the facility were schooled in close-quarter killing, killing from a distance and sometimes just plain killing everyone in sight.

Harvey Point was the official, and therefore unofficial, training and proving grounds for the CIA's National Clandestine Service and more to the point, the playground for the Special Activities Division. SAD is the home of the CIA's black ops units who famously destabilize nations, assassinate criminals and hunt and kill terrorists. Harvey Point is where most of these operatives get their uniquely violent training. Seibel's SAD teams receive special treatment at the Point because of their secrecy and distinctive assignments.

As one of the nameless visitors of Harvey Point, Lance was exposed to the razor sharp point of cutting edge training in the art and science of murder and mayhem. Explosives, firearms, laser-sighted munitions, radio-frequency jamming, blade-inflicted evisceration, spinal separation by way of bare hands and any number of brutal forms of pain infliction and immediate death are basic courses for those visiting the Point.

And unlike the US Army, where Private, Specialist and later Corporal Priest achieved generally unremarkable marks at every level, Preacher excelled and impressed all comers at every turn at Harvey Point. He earned a reputation among fellow nameless students of counter-intelligence and instructors alike as a blatantly ruthless individual. *The kid was scary*.

Preacher, as he would again and again be referred to by those at the Point, was noted for the only recorded, which of course would never be recorded, perfect score at Harvey Point. He was a sponge for all that was taught to him. Literally, everything.

And he was downright lethal in the application of his learned skills. If only his marksmanship scores were even in the middle of the pack. Try as he might, Lance just couldn't shoot for shit. He could hit the target, but he could count on one hand the times he'd hit a bullseye.

But in every other component of his training, Preacher was a phenomenon. His ability to immobilize, disarm and generally annihilate those positioned opposite him in virtually every drill caused concern for Harvey Point instructors tasked with producing qualified counter intelligence CIA officers. He would not just learn the tactics taught to him by some of the world's leading lethal experts, he would absorb their tutelage. It was like violent osmosis. Lance's abilities to mimic, to replicate almost any sequence of motions, allowed him to eventually become his instructors. He would soak up their every word, move, inflection and intent.

During martial arts training, young Mr. Priest would take severe beatings but then so utterly overpower and outmaneuver his counterparts, no matter their size or strength, that others would choose not to face him. Foreign intelligence officers brought to Harvey Point would take one look at Lance's intermittently empty then explosive eyes and question his sanity. Facing someone so utterly malevolent was unsettling, even to veterans of decades of Cold War battles. These hard men, and a few stony women, took with them the knowledge that some humans are indeed to be feared. This young man they only knew only as Preacher was one of these freaks.

Harvey Point was an awakening for Lance. He had never known such freedom, such endless and boundless opportunity. His first trip to the Point two weeks after beginning basic training at Fort Leonard Wood was a metamorphosis.

It was also a close cousin to the satisfaction the first time a sniper rifle fitted with a scope was placed in his hands at a firing range situated on a gentle rolling hillside at Harvey Point. If only he could shoot the damn thing and hit his intended target. After several months and several thousand rounds fired, he at last felt the satisfaction at making the perfect hole at the perfect center of the target 600 yards away. But he could never replicate that one shot. The days, weeks, months and years to follow at Harvey Point taught Lance that satisfaction was, and is, the result of control.

Being thrown by a master Filipino martial arts instructor with decades of preparation and experience was a prelude to the satisfaction of controlling the instructor's fall within six months. Proving the throw was no fluke in ensuing classes cemented the unreserved feeling of satisfaction found only in control. The interruptions of his intense multidiscipline training at Harvey Point in order to put in a showing at basic, DLI, Goodfellow and Augsburg were periods of frustration.

Preacher couldn't wait to get back. He had found something at the Point that brought complete satisfaction. Something he had felt only sporadically during his first 21 years. The Point was both playground and kingdom.

He knew in the minutes after making the deal with Seibel that his life would never be the same. He was embarking on a journey that would lead far from home into a wilderness without boundaries. It would very likely lead to his death. But maybe, just maybe, he could do a little good along the way. Give back to his country by killing bad guys.

The road atlases he had memorized did not contain the map he was to follow. He figured because explanations were so few and vague coming from the likes of Seibel that the one thing he would sacrifice would be control. He was delighted to find just the opposite.

Control was the heart and soul of his journey. And it was the defining element Seibel had recognized in him well before the moment they met in Dallas. Lance was a disciple of control. And that made him a weapon his country could use. It was not long before he was called upon to serve.

The room was dark, purposefully dark. The meeting about to take place required secrecy. The lone man sitting in the room waiting for the other party was impatient, tapping on the tabletop. Dim light lit the features of his face just enough to show his ethnicity. He was Arabic, possibly Persian. He was an emissary for a great leader on a mission that would change the balance of things. He hated to wait.

Chapter 20

"I'm not a good person." The short statement broke five minutes of silence. Lance had been sitting with eyes closed thinking and drifting and listening to Ike and Tina Turner sing about a river. One of his mother's favorites.

Braden had seen this before during their sessions over the past year and a half and let Lance take as long as he needed. Braden had no idea that during this silence a disembodied Lance hovered overhead reading his notes, looking at the photos of his wife and children on his desk and working the New York Times crossword puzzle folded on the table. Three across was tricky, but Lance finally got it – seven-letter word for wholeness -- *gestalt.*

"Why do you say that?" Braden was willing to play along, although he didn't believe for a moment Lance thought of himself as patently bad.

"Because it's true. I don't have a problem with it like others do." Lance opened his eyes. He was calm, collected and in his element sitting in an armchair next to Braden who was seated in his own armchair. They were like co-conspirators. The office was all about comfort with warm colors, subdued lighting and the window cracked to let in a pleasant breeze. Lance leaned toward the psychologist with a new look on his face.

"How do you do that?" Braden abruptly changed subjects and shook his head. He couldn't help himself. The psychologist was willing to go down the "I'm not good" track, but Lance's chameleon-like behavior was on full display today.

"Do what?" Preacher was all innocence. Happy the subject had changed so abruptly, his face altered again, right shoulder sagged, right foot bounced.

"Right there, you just did it again. I'm sitting here watching you and you are the third different person sitting across from me in the last minute. Your face, your eyes, your body language, they all just changed again." Braden had his hand up to his chin with his elbow on the armrest. "You're obviously our Preacher, but your physical manifestation completely changed right there. Very European."

"How so?" Lance was nonchalant in his response, even putting his hand to his chin and elbow on the armrest mimicking the psychologist. His voice a playback recording of Braden's.

"Jesus, there you go again. You just switched to me didn't you?" Braden shook his head.

Lance's next move was lightning fast. He reached out and plucked Braden's glasses and put them on and grabbed the psychologist's notebook and pen. When he settled back into the chair, his slouch, crossed leg, raised eyebrow and tilted head were an exact duplicate of Braden. It was unsettling for the shrink.

Lance smiled gently at his patient. "Tell me about your childhood. Your parents divorced when you were three. How did you feel? What was your reaction? Did you act out in any particular manner? Wet the bed? Suck your thumb?" The words, accent, inflection and slight rise of the voice in the last question were Braden. It was eerie, freaky.

The psychologist sat back, the real one, not Lance. "Man."

Lance laughed. "You asked how I do it. I can honestly say I have no idea how, only that I can. It's as natural as breathing. I know that response is unsatisfying to your practiced curiosity, but it's that simple. You, everyone really, are a culmination of a series of actions and decisions that brought you to where you are right now. You are a map of your life. I can look at you and read it, see your story. Just as you like to play your little 'book by the cover' game with people. I guess I can just see a little deeper below the surface, below the cover." He said all this as Braden, still in character. It was too easy. Lance sat back in the chair and handed the glasses, notebook and pen back. He was Lance again.

"But why? Where did it come from? When did it start for you?" Braden was leaning forward on his elbow. His fascination was palpable. This was case study material.

"Isn't that your job to tell me?" With that, Lance was done with the subject. Braden had learned in the two years he'd been involved with Lance Porter Priest that Preacher could literally turn himself on and off. And a switch had just been flipped.

Braden returned to his notes and scanned the page. "Oh, I had one more question here from last time, probably from the first time we were together really."

"Shoot."

"How long can you go without lying?"

Lance laughed at that but didn't answer.

"No really. What's the longest you've ever gone without lying?" Braden was casual in his delivery, but he was digging for foundational stuff here. He got more than he expected.

"Seventeen days, four hours and 33 minutes." Lance was matter-of-fact.

Braden jotted it down but couldn't keep from smiling.

"Really." Lance followed up. "You think I'm joking?"

"I know you're messing with me. But that's just part of the game with you."

Lance turned all serious for the moment. "I would think that as a professional, you would do better at analyzing your subject. You asked a question and I gave a truthful answer. Those are admittedly hard to come by with me, so you'd better be cognizant of this."

"You're serious." Braden tilted his head.

Lance continued, "Heart attack. And I know that is longer than most people can go. Think about it, how long have you ever gone without lying? One day, two? Be honest. What did you tell your son when he stunk it up at the plate last week, fanning at everything thrown at him? What did you say to your wife after she tried to cook tandoori chicken last month? Or when Seibel asked you about me doing this session with a different shrink this time? I think it goes without saying that you told little white lies in response to each of those."

Braden steered clear of bringing himself into it. Lance had successfully done that in the previous sessions. "Seventeen days? I don't think you've ever gone 17 hours or even 17 minutes without at least a little white lie. You're like that joke about politicians."

Lance knew the joke and gave him the punch line, "You can tell they're lying because their lips are moving."

Braden laughed. "Right."

"You know, that's only a little insulting."

"How so?" Braden's eyebrows furrowed.

"For you to consign me to the category of those who betray others' trust through lies. That is somewhat hurtful." Lance nodded.

Braden's eyebrows furrowed deeper. A "V" appeared on his forehead and his procerus worked overtime. "Isn't every lie a betrayal of trust? Doesn't every lie hurt someone just a little?"

"Ah hah." Lance got a little excited. "I love the opportunity to educate the educated. And I'll do that with a single question. Can you show me, in one concrete example, where my proclivity for prevarication hurt someone?"

This was the most lively Braden had seen Lance. "Easy. You told your mother you were joining the Army to find yourself. A boldface lie."

"And she was happy and protected in that knowledge." Lance responded.

"She would be hurt to know the truth."

Lanced raised a finger. "Now, there are your semantics at work. You see my telling her a nuanced version of reality, a partial truth if you will, as a potentially hurtful thing. When truly her reality is protected. She is at peace with my decision regardless of my true purpose."

"Now that's semantics. You're slicing and dicing it there." Braden chuckled.

"And the beauty of my nuanced, shaded and finely crafted fabrications is their ability to change, to grow and evolve to become reality." Lance raised his hands for effect to complete the lesson. "I don't lie, I tell future truths."

"Damn." Braden could only look down to his notes. He would give up his license and his years in the business to spend more time with this chameleon, this shape-shifter who had created his own reality. This was not schizophrenia or psychopathy. This was sheer control, power. There was no delusion here.

Braden was sitting just feet away from easily the most diabolical mind he'd ever encountered, and he'd seen his share of really messed up humans. But the undeniable truth behind the wall of lies was just that, undeniable. It was real. And Stuart Braden was proud to be part of it.

The kid was certainly messed up big time. But he was also brilliant. Scary brilliant. Braden could never tell a soul or share this experience with his peers. He could only delve into the particulars with Seibel. And Papa wasn't buying any of it. Braden was pleased as punch to be the one probing this kid's psyche. He was also thrilled this kid was on his side. Better to have a natural born killer on your team than on the other side.

Looking up from his notes, Braden had just one more thing. "I want to get back to your statement that you are not a good person, but I have this one lingering question. What makes you happy Lance?"

Most people, upon being asked this question, quite naturally take a deep breath, run through a barrage of joyful memories in their life and then recite a litany of topics tied to happiness. Lance didn't need to take a breath or make a mental list. His reply was immediate, concrete and one word. "Nothing."

This was the fourth time Braden had sat down with Preacher. As usual, he was left with more questions than answers. The psychologist reached over to the table beside him and grabbed the thick file folder. Lance was comfortable watching him.

After leafing through several dozen sheets, Braden stopped at the page he'd been looking for. "I know we're basically done with our pleasant chat here. You've got your little wall up and we both know Seibel doesn't give a shit about these evaluations anyway. But the law's the law and your field deployment comes with a few strings attached. And I'm one of them."

"And?" Lance asked.

"And, how the hell does someone score a 71 on an IQ test one day and an exact 100 point increase to 171 the next day?" Braden looked through the papers.

"I don't know. How could that happen?"

"Obviously it can't with a normal subject."

"Exactly 100 points?" Lance smiled.

"Yep. Impossible, statistically speaking. Someone would have to be really smart to do something like that."

"Smarter than 171?" Lance arched his eyebrow. "Isn't that like the genius range, anything above 165?"

"Of course you would know that. And of course, you would know that 71 is basically on the line between borderline and actual mental disability."

"Huh," Lance's laugh was genuine, believable. "What's yours?"

"130 something." Braden smiled.

"Damn, pretty smart buddy. That's in the gifted range right?" The look on Lance's face was 100 percent impressed.

"I know I'm not going to get a straight answer out of you. But I just want to know why? Why do you choose to be this way?" Braden looked a little frustrated.

It was Lance's turn to sit back now. He made a little production out of stretching his back and raising his arms above his head. They were sore from his morning workout. "You make it sound like there is a choice. Like there is freewill at work."

"Don't play with me." Braden was a little irked by the perceived condescension in Lance's response. "Of course there is a choice. Every moment of every day comes with a choice, a set of decisions."

"I think that is a rather naïve response from a shrink of your caliber Stuart. You know much better than I that there are any number of disorders that limit one's ability to act in accordance with freewill."

"I wasn't speaking of everyone. I'm talking to you, about you. There are those who lack the mental faculties to be able to make choices. You know what I'm talking about. You become a real prick when you get like this."

"That's it right there. I'm glad you got here yourself." Lance pointed a finger.

"What, where?" Braden's irk was now perturbed.

"You should know by now how it works with me. I raise or lower my game depending on the competition. I respect you and consider your job a difficult one. I know you can't come in here and leave your bias behind. Your methods are steeped in psychoanalysis and existentialism. You believe from your training and two-plus decades of experience that there is an explanation, a diagnosis and treatment for my disorder."

"And…" Braden interrupted.

"When I get like this." Lance pointed to his chest for effect. "You are under some misperception, a misconception that I change, that I become someone and something different. You are missing the obvious. I never change. Haven't since I was two. I am remarkably consistent in my inconsistency. I don't get *like* anything. I am, have always been a real prick, an asshole, a 100% cold-blooded, sinister and undeniably recalcitrant being. I am not a good person. And I am quite comfortable with who I am. There is no choice, no freewill at work here."

Braden saw an opening he'd been looking for. "Ah. Then that begs the obvious question. Why are you doing this? Why join the CIA, the Army, put yourself through an inhuman training regimen, constantly studying and in continual pain from pushing beyond physical limits? Why not wrap yourself in your lies, string your webs and build your little world where you are protected, in control?" Braden was now smiling and had obviously been looking to ask these questions for some time but had never been presented with the opportunity. But here again, he was going to be disappointed by Preacher.

"There you go again. You assume there is something more, something I'm about to discover, some self-exposition I'm about to realize through catharsis. And then I'll share my unburdened feelings with you." Lance laughed and reached out to grab Braden's forearm. "Stu, everything in that file, everything you've seen me do, everything you started reading almost two years ago; every video and audio tape, every single word I have ever uttered to you or Seibel or my mom or my imaginary friends in the sandbox. It is all made up. None of it is real. I am light and air. I am heaven and hell. *And I am become death, destroyer of worlds.* I am a blasphemer in the House of Allah. I am *nichego* - nothing - in my beloved Russian. I am Oakland, California to Gertrude Stein. *There is no there, there.*" His peaceful smile worked on Braden who couldn't help but smile back, hypnotized.

Lance squeezed Braden's arm. "Stu, there is no Lance Priest."

Chapter 22

The tension in the early afternoon summer air was as thick as the mist drifting down from King Fahd's spectacular fountain situated on a man-made island in the middle of the bay. Lance sat on a short wall eating a sparse meal of pita bread and goat cheese purchased at a shop along the Corniche, which runs along the beach. The towering fountain created a shadow that danced on the dazzling water below. Lance took in the sites and sounds and faces of those watching the water splash back down from 900 feet. Because he had no control of it, he didn't question why his brain had chosen to play a selection of songs by Pink Floyd over the last hour. He just listened and tapped his foot. He occasionally sang along, in Arabic.

Visitors from all over the Muslim world marveled at the manmade wonder that welcomed millions to Jeddah, Saudi Arabia's western port city.

As the call for prayers bellowed from speakers all around, pilgrims from around the world traveling to Mecca, just up the holy road from Jeddah, kneeled and prayed toward the holy city. Lance snapped a few photos of the scene.

He replayed the conversation with Braden from the week before in his head for a sixth or seventh time. He hadn't been

100 percent truthful with the psychologist, but then again, when was he ever truthful. He laughed at his own joke.

At 23, Lance didn't feel it necessary to share his deeper feelings or explain his motives to anyone. He simply felt lucky, some would call it blessed, to have been born in the greatest nation in the world. The United States provided him the means, the opportunities to become anything he dreamed of. He didn't fancy himself a patriot, but the foundation upon which the nation was built was worth fighting for, even dying for. Freedom had its price and he was willing to fight for it. He didn't make grand statements and admittedly wasn't good with sharing his own feelings, but Lance truly felt honored to be asked to serve his country. Not many people get the chance to do what he was about to do.

Seibel had walked away from Lance minutes earlier; leaving him in a foreign land with fake papers and a false identity as a contract photographer on assignment for a major U.S. magazine. His first NOC assignment. Which translated into non-CIA acronym lingo, means not official cover. He was live and without a net. Finally.

Lance had studied and perfected his new persona for two months and felt he had everything he needed to carry off being Peter Drummond from Surprise, Arizona. Lance knew the history of Peter's parents Jen and Mike, stayed in regular contact with his sister Kate in Santa Barbara and visited his Grandpa Mort in Newark whenever he traveled to or through New York City.

Peter had lucked into a semester in Cairo as a junior in college and developed a love of the culture and language. Now, as a professional photographer, he returned to the region to capture its beauty for others around the world. He turned the camera lens on the towering pillar of water, but trained his ear on those around him. He noted that most spoke the hejazi dialect, prominent in the Mecca province.

He kept his eyes on the mist floating down while listening to a conversation between a father and daughter walking nearby. He silently mouthed a few words to match their inflections. He repeated the daughter's last sentence in precisely the same cadence. *"I respect your wishes father and do not want to cause you any discomfort."*

It was the only conversation Preacher had overheard during the last couple of hours that did not involve Kuwait or Saddam Hussein or what George Bush and America would do now. Iraq's invasion of Kuwait three weeks prior on August 2 had received international condemnation. The world would not stand for such naked aggression. And the United States could not allow a democratically elected government to be deposed by a tyrant like Hussein.

This was complete bullshit, of course. Most US citizens, like those of virtually every other nation outside the Arab Middle East, couldn't find Kuwait on a map and didn't have strong or really any feelings about the small nation. Except, of course, for the billions and billions of barrels of oil lying below the tiny country's desert sands.

"What do you know about Kuwait?" It was two months earlier, June 1990, and perhaps the third or fourth time Lance had ever heard the country's name mentioned. Seibel asked the question as he entered Lance's tiny room at Harvey Point.

"Right between Iraq and Saudi Arabia on the Persian Gulf. About 2 million people smack dab on top of about 7,000 square miles of desert." Lance had memorized the facts from the CIA World Factbook.

"Correct. And what does Kuwait do?" Seibel asked.

"Oil."

"Besides that?" Seibel leaned against the doorjamb and crossed his arms. He surveyed the room as he always does any room he enters. Immediately judging total space, steps between objects, any signs of misplaced items.

"Piss off Iraq?" Lance replied.

"Exactly." Seibel brought one hand up to his bearded chin to rub the graying stubble. Lance had already noted the growth and deep tan. Seibel had been away for several weeks. "Kuwait has done an excellent job pissing off Saddam, especially since the end of the war."

"Which one?"

"Iraq-Iran; the Imposed War; the Holy Defense as it was called in Iran." Seibel rolled his neck to stretch. "Kuwait bankrolled billions in war costs for Iraq and when the bloody massacre ended in 88' they held the debt over Saddam's head. He doesn't like anyone wagging a finger at him."

"Not even us, huh?" Lance snickered.

"Nope. A US diplomat tried to scold him once and barely made it out of Baghdad with his head. Saddam is truly as ruthless as you've read. Kuwait is about to feel his wrath."

"I've heard little bits and pieces around here, especially sitting down at lunch next to the Jordanians the last two weeks." A smile crept onto Lance's lips at the thought of listening in on Arabs unaware of the language skills possessed by some of their Caucasian counterparts at Harvey Point.

Seibel assumed his usual Socratic pose. "Ah, yes. But have you picked up their different dialects? Those from Amman sound markedly more robust in their pronunciation than their friends from down near the Gulf of Aqaba."

"Subtle, but different." Lance acknowledged.

Seibel stepped over to the bookshelf. It held several volumes, most in Russian and Arabic. "Those little bits and pieces you have been hearing about Iraq and Kuwait; what do you make of them?" Seibel was almost never direct in his questioning. Like Socrates, his favorite philosopher, he answers questions with questions and constantly pushes for self-exposition of the facts. Lance had become used to his Socratic methods in the now hundreds of times together since their first meeting in Dallas nearly three years earlier. He likened their conversations to a dance, a waltz.

"Action is not far behind." Lance replied to the question.

"Such as?" Seibel played his usual role of Socrates.

Lance played his part in answering with details, "Direct, deadly, crushing. The war with Iran is not even two years passed and Iraq has plenty of veterans in the Republican Guard ready to take out their frustration on the nominal military of Kuwait. Would likely be over in a few days."

Seibel smiled. "Quite in-depth analysis for a few tidbits picked up here and there."

"Maybe."

Seibel turned back to Lance with the smile still holding. "What then?"

"After Iraq invades poor little Kuwait?" Lance asked.

"Yes. After the loss of life and sovereignty in their kingdom."

"I guess that's what you're here to talk to me about."

Seibel's smile broke broader and he belted out a laugh. "Ahead of me again as always. I come in with a set agenda and you are three steps ahead. Never fails."

"Not always. You had me fooled last year with your little birthday cruise around Manhattan." Lance smiled.

"That's right, that's right." Seibel laughed. "You thought I was going to have you, how did you put it – 'pop your cherry' with that Turkish pimp on the boat."

"I was sure you were going to hand me a silenced Walther P5 and tell me to put two in the head and toss the body overboard." Lance shook his head.

Seibel's laughter exploded at the memory. "And all I did was have the waitress bring over your birthday cake so you could blow out your candles and make a wish in the shadow of the Statue of Liberty."

Lance snickered. "What do you think I wished for?"

The laughter immediately turned to a sparse smile as Seibel looked him square in the eye. "If I know you, and I think I probably do better than just about anyone, you wished for a Walther P5 with a beautiful new shiny black silencer so you could kill that Turkish prick."

Now it was Lance's turn to laugh. When he finished, he stood up to meet Seibel eye to eye. "He was a prick wasn't he? Blowing that putrid smoke our way all during the cruise and cursing his girls like that. I would have been doing a favor to everyone on the boat."

"Undoubtedly. But our plans for young Preacher extend well beyond a common nuisance blowing smoke." Seibel's tone took on his Blueblood origins.

"Do they extend all the way to Kuwait?"

"I can honestly tell you that was not the plan as recently as four weeks ago. But dynamics on the ground in the Middle East have superseded those in Eastern Europe."

Lance nodded. "So, no Sarajevo?"

"As you know, your orders are need-to-know. And right now, you need to know that all plans in place for years are being reworked, adjusted as we speak. Resources once destined for points East and West will now be positioned in the Middle."

"A riddle. Not exactly like you." Lance rubbed his chin.

"Timing is under adjustment right now. December or January as originally planned will now likely be August. Your destination and assignment will most likely involve direct regional involvement."

"Regional?"

"Yes. Once again, our government is discovering that we may have been orienting too many resources toward one adversary and missed the explicit requirements of another."

"The Soviets are yesterday's news and here come the Arabs, tonight at 11?" Lance added in perfect anchorman speak.

"Right to the heart as usual Lance. And in misjudging the environment among the Arab states, our country has not developed enough assets with your basic skills."

"To be able to count to 10 in Arabic?" The smile back on his face.

"Correct again." The sound of footsteps in the hall was followed by a CIA station hand delivering a box to Lance's room. Seibel turned to the man delivering the package, "Thanks Rich. Right on cue." He took the box and handed it to Lance.

"For me, not even my birthday."

"Actually it is."

"How's that?"

Seibel tapped the box lid. "This is the birth of your first cover. Today is the first day of the rest of someone else's life."

Lance set the box down on his desk and pulled out a used camera bag with a Nikon camera and several lenses inside.

Seibel stepped over and put a hand on his shoulder. "The beginnings of your new life are in this box. I don't have all the details yet, but you need to learn how to take and develop first-rate professional quality photos."

Lance pulled out a bulky three-ring binder titled Subject C-1763 – Photographic Specialization. "Photographer?" he asked.

"Pretty cool, heh? And I'd plan on being assigned to Saudi Arabia."

"Pictures of sand." Lance asked examining the camera.

"Not just pictures; you are Peter Drummond, professional photographer. You will be taking photos that touch peoples' hearts and souls. Remember that girl with striking blue eyes on the magazine cover a couple of years ago? You need to capture the essence of the things in your lens, not just what is on the surface. See the soul beneath the surface"

"That's pretty good. You read that in a photography manual?" Lance pulled out a larger three-ring binder simply marked Subject Matter.

"Read up on all that. It's Peter's life story. The parts up till now at least." Seibel added.

"I'll bet his life is about to get interesting."

"Oh, it's been interesting for me for a couple of years now." Seibel stepped to the door and turned. "I'll let you know timing and particulars as soon as I can."

Lance looked up from the box, "It'll be real this time. No drills."

"No drills. Live and without a net. Our investment – your investment will now start to pay off." Seibel turned to leave and then pivoted back to Lance, "Happy Birthday." He left with the smile still hanging in the air.

Lance turned from Seibel to review the other items in the box. "I'm ready." He shook his head.

Seibel. The guy shows up after more than a month and is gone 10 minutes later for who knows how long. Lance didn't ever question his boss about his other duties, his other subjects. He wondered every now and then if there were other special projects like him out there. *No way. No one like me.* He smiled and cracked himself up with his little joke.

The mist from King Fahd's Fountain found a new breeze and turned in Lance's direction. He quickly closed the case to protect the expensive camera, lenses and film from the moisture. He finished the last of his cheese and picked up his things to make his way back to the inexpensive and inconspicuous hotel before heading off to dinner again with his local guide.

Seibel had surprised him 20 minutes earlier when his shadow fell across Lance's meager lunch. Preacher should have been surprised by his mentor's appearance, but dozens of personas assumed by Seibel over the previous three years had accustomed him to surprises from the man. Lance should probably have been disappointed to see him here because he was supposed to be on a live mission, without a net. Seeing Seibel here in Jeddah could mean only one thing – plans had changed.

Chapter 21

How often can a couple of humans walk out of a room knowing they just changed the world?

Evgany Korovin and Nikolai Kusnetsov knew they had done just that as they left the dilapidated hospital room in Dombarovsky, Russia. True, the world had not been changed yet, but the unpleasant conversation the two former KGB operatives had just held with a teary-eyed father of a recently deceased child and husband of a severely injured wife would soon lead to change.

In the two-plus years the dynamic and despicable duo had been separated from their former employer, they had planned, schemed, maneuvered and executed their vision. The previous nine minutes of conversation with the broken man was a culmination of the one phase and the beginning of the next. The final phase.

The man was the key. His name was Andre Davidovich Resparin. He came from a long line of proud southern Russia stock who served the Soviet Union through military service. At the conclusion of his active military deployment, Resparin accepted a position as a guard at a former nuclear missile launch site near Dombarovsky in the foothills of the Ural Mountains.

This facility, once a Cold War beacon, a lighthouse of freedom against the endless aggression by the West, had been decommissioned. No longer would intercontinental ballistic missiles be ready at a moment's notice to deliver their nuclear payload down upon the enemies of the Union.

Instead of active missile silos housing harbingers of death, the facility now functioned as a storage unit, a warehouse. The contents of this particular underground warehouse were what interested K&K. They knew precisely what lay underground because it had been their duty seven years earlier to develop security and counterespionage plans should the missile base ever be penetrated, infiltrated by agents from the West.

Their plans had been so thorough, so complete, that they were adopted throughout the Soviet Union. You'd think that this alone would have gotten them killed by now. How had they been allowed to live, let alone leave the KGB after becoming so deeply familiar with the workings of nuclear missile facilities? Yes, plans and procedures had been changed over time, but not much. Taking a facility out of commission did not change the underlying physical structure, the placement of gates, the thickness of doors or the mindset of guards. They knew all of this and more, much more.

K&K had been planning this little caper well before they killed a bureau chief in Kiev, their official resignation letter to the KGB. The seeds for this elaborate mission were sown in Afghanistan and nurtured along the way by their growing hostility toward leadership who had put them out in the field with little or no support, forcing them to develop their own support structures. It was Korovin who was originally tasked with developing security protocol for nuke sites. He requested assistance from Kusnetsov and the fix was in.

During the ensuing years, K&K kept all planning on this one to themselves. No other party was brought in, until now. They had communicated with each other using a codeset and radio language they uncovered while in the inhospitable burning deserts and equally inhospitable frostbit mountains of Afghanistan. The codeset was only used for a brief 18 months because it was determined to be too difficult and mistakes were made as a result. K&K found the code both unique and memorable because it was the period they began their partnership, their relationship.

Execution of this latest phase of their long-term plan required a strong message delivered to Resparin. They chose to deliver the message at 75 miles per hour on a winding road with the head guard's wife and 15 year-old son in the car in front of them. Korovin was behind the wheel as the powerful sedan moved alongside Mrs. Resparin's Lada VAZ-2101 sedan rounding a particularly tight turn. Kusnetsov was in the passenger seat and he looked with unemotional eyes into the bulging eyes of the woman just as his partner slung the wheel causing their powerful sedan to immediately veer to the right where it made contact with the Resparin's vehicle. The barrier on the side of the road over the steep terrain below was no match. Mrs. Resparin and her son were launched over the edge and down hundreds of feet to a ravine below.

On the way down, the vehicle rolled multiple times, struck several large boulders and finally landed on its crushed right side. The couple's son stood no chance and had mercifully died quickly from the trauma. The poor wife and mother could only reach out with a broken right arm and touch the boy's shoulder. Because she was basically hanging in the air over him, her tears ran down her face and fell upon her dead son's lifeless body.

Security protocol procedures for nuclear missile sites and storage facilities had taken into account employees who could be blackmailed by having their families kidnapped or threatened. K&K were intimately aware of this detail, because they devised and wrote the security plans. One guard would not be enough. So the two had visited this particular brand of murder and torture on three other guards who worked under Resparin. This resulted in all the guards on one shift being convinced to both allow and assist in the removal of three nuclear warheads stored in the facility. The lives of their remaining family members depended on their compliance.

The short discussion K&K had with Resparin as his wife lay near death had cemented the deal. They handed the broken man a bouquet of flowers and then proceeded to recite details about the facility even he did not know. They showed him photos of additional family members, including brothers, a sister, two beautiful twin nieces and his extended family. The effect of presenting the schematics, photos and other details to Resparin was to basically put the man into a state barely more alert than his wife. He was shaken, shocked by their words and their unspoken implications. They had him.

To further bolster his acceptance of his new lot in life, Korovin handed Resparin a file detailing all sorts of sordid details, nasty habits and secret kept lovers by his higher ups. The major he reported to had a number of vices that made him all but useless. The colonel the major reported to was even more depraved. The two officers would be destroyed by this theft and there was nothing Resparin could do to stop it.

It was a brilliant plan. Brilliantly conceived and executed. And brilliantly monitored by a young woman and two members of her team. They watched from afar with binoculars, listened in with wire taps and planted moles in the operation. They knew many of the details and all the players. It was almost as if they had the playbook K&K were operating from.

Marta, like her fellow former KGB counterparts, had gravitated downward into more and more despicable acts during the previous two years. And now, she simply could not allow a plan as potentially dangerous and lucrative as this one to proceed without her. She wanted in and she had a little help from others who wanted her in. Wanted her to step in and steal the nukes.

There were moving parts galore in this one. That made it particularly dangerous and particularly fun. The fact that millions could potentially die as a result made it exceptionally interesting.

Standing in a darkened alley across the street from the hospital entrance in Dombarovsky, she smiled to herself. Marta knew a little secret K&K and others didn't.

Chapter 23

Subject Report: Nawaf al-Ghamdi

Not his birth name. No, all indications were this gifted and ruthless oil businessman had assumed his name in the early 1970s after returning from the West Bank where he had been a "freedom fighter for the PLO" after the Six Days war in 1967. His name change was likely a protective measure to escape the wrath of Israel's Mossad intelligence agency.

He returned to the Saudi Peninsula to begin a new life and a new career in the oil and natural gas. His legend started as a laborer on eastern oil wells and the Sea Island of Ras Tanura. Although educated at Oxford, al-Ghamdi chose to gain his oil education with dirty hands and sweat working alongside laborers from Yemen and Oman. The knowledge he acquired during these years, along with the seismic shift of Aramco ownership from America to Saudi, provided opportunities for someone of his nature.

He was an employee of Saudi Aramco for several years in the middle 70s and then started his own exploration business, blessed by the King, of course. His small business grew as demand for oil around the world skyrocketed through the 80s. His interests now stretch from the Mediterranean to Indonesia.

Along with exploration, his holdings include transport, some refining and manufacturing of petroleum products. His company became a major producer of natural gas on the Saudi Peninsula. His business acumen presented him with opportunities in neighboring countries, especially Kuwait and its developing natural gas fields. Al-Ghamdi brokered deals between the Kuwait Oil Company, which was nationalized in 1975, as were a number of exploration firms. His price for his expertise was always a small ownership stake. Add up these many small pieces and al-Ghamdi had quietly become one of the wealthiest men in the country, outside the royal family. His holdings in Kuwait made him a player on the international level and therefore an interest of competing global interests, whether US, Russian, Chinese or any of the upstarts.

The recent invasion by Iraqi forces could spell trouble for al-Ghamdi but most thought his connections in Baghdad would insulate him from loss.

His Jeddah estate, just off the coast, is a marvel of modernity. Although exuding a traditional Arabic architectural facade on the exterior, the inner workings are high-tech, high quality and nothing but the best. From appliances to security cameras, the latest technology is always being installed.

Subject Report: Hassan al-Bakr

Overseeing all of al-Ghamdi's security operations is Hassan al-Bakr. This diminutive figure, standing only 5 feet 4, was recruited by al-Ghamdi not long after returning from Palestine where he too fought the Jewish infidels. His skill at stealthy assassinations was only superseded by his fondness for gambling and women. This penchant caused him to be careless on occasion.

In Monte Carlo in 1981, he enjoyed the company of two women until late one evening and nearly missed an assassination attempt on al-Ghamdi by an Egyptian crew hired by Syrians. Al-Bakr basically stumbled over the assassins while returning to al-Ghamdi's hotel at 4 a.m. In dispatching the assailants, al-Bakr accidently killed several others, including two American tourists who were actually CIA specialists involved in a totally separate matter. This small mistake brought knowledge of al-Bakr into the CIA orbit and resulted in painstakingly detailed analysis that now covered most weeks of his life.

But the incident and loss of two agents turned out not to be al-Bakr's highest crime against America or freedom itself. As well as heading up al-Ghamdi's security detail, al-Bakr had been freelanced out by his employer to various governments, corporations, secret organizations and assorted jihadist fronts. By merely tracking al-Bakr's movements, which is indeed a challenge for even the best intelligence minds, the agency had uncovered leads, key players, previously unknown locations of terrorist organizations and a treasure trove of intelligence. He had unwittingly brought a mountain of evidence into the hands of the CIA.

Al-Bakr's associates over the past decade included leaders from Iran, Kuwait, Syria, Hezbollah, PLO and others, including Iraq. His services for governments and terrorists were reported to include electronic surveillance, sabotage, assassination, torture, security consulting and more torture. For his services he has been paid well and al-Ghamdi earned the eternal gratitude, general good will and, of course, business from al-Bakr's clients. It was win – win – win.

Thus explains al-Bakr tightly zoomed by a lens attached to Lance's camera. The security expert stood next to the front gate of al-Ghamdi's residential complex.

Watching al-Bakr close-up from nearly a mile away, Lance reviewed his mental notes again, for the 11th time today. His mission, originally to capture al-Bakr at a family wedding in Jordan and transport him to a secret interrogation facility, had been altered. Along with the dangerous and deadly assassin head of security, Lance and his newly assembled team were to remove and relocate al-Ghamdi. It didn't make much sense to Lance, but he was up for the job.

"Wunderbar." Lance whispered.

Someone at the other end of his radio responded in kind.

"Herzlich miene freunde?" It was Fuchs, of course. The veteran CIA operative was initially introduced to Lance nearly three years ago as Pete Grisham.

Seibel had moved quickly. Lance hadn't been thrilled to see Mikel Fuchs when he arrived back at his hotel 20 hours ago. The German lay in Lance's bed reading a magazine.

Sitting on the end of the bed was another familiar face from Harvey Point. Tarwanah looked up from a book and smiled at Lance. And if Tarwanah was here, his fellow Jordanian partner Jamaani couldn't be far away. A toilet flushing down the hall in the communal bathroom answered the question. Lance stepped back out his door to watch Jamaani walk toward him.

"Stomach still bothering you?" Lance stepped into the hall to allow the Jordanian into the small room.

"Still." Jamaani muttered walking by.

Lance followed him into the room and closed the door. "I guess you all just walked right in the front lobby together. Huh?" Lance dropped his camera case on the bedside table.

"Of course," Fuchs lowered the magazine to his chest. "We asked the front desk for their CIA special and they said they only had one room at that rate – yours." His German accent definitely northern; north of Berlin by Lance's estimation.

"Let's just go ahead and shout that." Lance shook his head.

"Relax meine freunde," Fuchs held up a hand. "Tarwanah scanned the room with his little bag of electronic goodies as soon as we entered. Its clean."

"So you all felt it necessary to come here?" Lance leaned against the wall. "That Lockstock's new orders?" Lockstock being Seibel's operational code name for this mission.

"I know this is all a little disconcerting," Tarwanah smiled up at him reassuringly. "Changes of plan always are challenging. But always a part of the game. In fact, change is the only thing you can count on with any mission."

"I'm beginning to think that maybe this change is only news to me." Lance smiled back.

"What makes you think that my friend?" Tarwanah, always civil.

"Oh, just the little fact that the three of you were at HP training at the same time and we just happened to go through the forced retrieval exercise several times together."

The smile broader, Tarwanah looked to Fuchs and his countryman. "There were several others involved in those exercises if you recall."

Lance nodded. "I do. And I'm wondering if I'm going to see any of them show up here too."

Fuchs sat up in bed and swung his feet to the floor. "No. Just us; and we need to discuss plan changes. But not here." He abruptly stood and grabbed a bag from under the bed. He pulled out four radio units with belt clips, wired earphones and microphones and handed one to each man. "Our frequency is programmed. There are four variable frequencies that automatically adjust when one of us changes. Range is two miles. Meeting time is," he looked to his watch and the three others raised their wrists to make sure of synchronization. "23 minutes in the Souq al-Alawi bazaar. Gentlemen, be sure your watches are set on local time. I have 19:37."

"Check." The other three said in unison. Lance said it in Arabic.

Fuchs turned to Lance with his smile, humor and German accent suddenly gone. "Preacher, drills are done. Plan goes live now. This project is a stretch for an eight-man SAD team with weeks of immediate project training. With the four us, and only a few weeks of training together months ago, we will be outmanned, out-gunned and likely out-maneuvered within minutes of escalation. Body count will undoubtedly be high. We are not to be among those counted.

"The fact that you are on this mission means that either Lockstock is failing in his judgment with age or you are everything you have been made out to be. You did very well in drills at the Point but you will not get a second chance after escalation tomorrow. No blanks in their guns this time. Are you 100 percent sure you are ready?"

Lance kept Fuchs' eyes for a second and a half and then looked to the Jordanians. Their casual smiles were also gone. He looked back to Fuchs immediately realizing he had underestimated this supposed German who walked slow and talked incessantly about beer. He was obviously not the part he had played the previous durations they had been together at the Point. He was no slouch and without a doubt, he was the leader of the mission, as he undoubtedly had been many times before.

"Sixteen doors total, all dead-bolt and electronically alarmed. Forty-one windows also electronically secured. Thirteen men in the security detail, with five always on duty. Three dogs, 21 cameras, directional boom microphones at all four corners. Sixteen-foot gate and fence on the street or south side. Fourteen-foot wall with trip wire on the other three sides. Three wives; nine children, six vehicles, penicillin and ragweed allergies and one nasty-ass head of security with 21 known kills and no morals outside his nominal Muslim faith." Lance recited a few of the facts surrounding al-Ghamdi.

"Very good, but are you 100 percent sure?" Fuchs was insistent.

Lance maintained the stare between the two, but broke into song as well. His choice of songs in this instance a 1970s rock radio standard with lots and lots of over the top guitar.

"What? Is that a yes? This is no joke."

Lance turned from Fuchs humming the song, one of his favorites by The Outlaws. He stepped back over to his camera bag to gather it and his small duffle.

The German accent returned, "You're definitely not right in your head Herr Preacher, but sometimes that is an advantage." Fuchs looked to Tarwanah and raised his eyebrows. Tarwanah could only smile at the situation. Jamaani remained passive as always. Irritable bowel syndrome was his major concern anyway.

"He was ready before we completed the last drill Foxy." Tarwanah's obvious familiarity with Fuchs showed. Jamaani only bent to pick up his bag without a word.

"Preacher, you will be given the precise plan. Any deviation from the plan and we fail. Do you have a song for that?" Fuchs asked.

Lance completed the last verse again and strummed his air guitar. "Nothing for that right now. I'll think about it. Twenty-one minutes till gather, right?"

"Twenty-one." And Fuchs was the first out the door. He turned left to head for a set of stairs on the backside of the small hotel popular with Western pilgrims during the hajj. Jamaani and Tarwanah, both decked out in full Saudi attire, left together with their mission items carried in stylish leather bags slung casually over their shoulders. They headed for the elevator. Lance waited another two minutes. During that time, he checked the room for any traces left by his three team members. There was nothing, of course. They were pros.

He then wiped down any surface he had touched over the last three days. Since he had worn gloves most of the time, it took only 30 seconds. He made sure he had cleaned up all his paraphernalia for creating a dark room in the closet. He gathered his camera bag and duffle and walked down the hall to the main stairwell. He walked out of the building with nothing to hide.

Chapter 24

"Danka, Herr Baron." Lance responded to Fuchs over the radio. Their brief conversations now were all either in code or in a variety of languages not likely to be recognized by anyone scanning radio frequencies in Jeddah. The verbal code in place for the operation was a compilation of aviation terminology commonly used by Australian bush pilots. Not a lot of them around in Jeddah.

"No joy. Block RNC." Tarwanah chimed in to silence Fuchs and Lance before their German greetings were expounded upon. Tarwanah sat in the rear cargo area of a white van parked 800 yards southeast of the al-Ghamdi compound main gate. Event escalation was only minutes away.

For all the technology, surveillance, intercepts and dogged espionage employed in the weeks and months leading up to this morning, the basics of the plan about to be executed were a classic smash and grab. Al-Ghamdi's convoy would be three cars. Just as it had been each of the last 11 times he had left the compound during the previous two weeks. The caravan would be made up of three Mercedes sedans all featuring super powerful engines and bulletproof glass. Al-Bakr would accompany al-Ghamdi in the middle vehicle. The head of security usually rides in the front passenger seat.

The plan had been played out several times in exercises at Harvey Point, most successful, some not. Lance silently laughed to himself again seeing the whole exercise laid out from beginning to end. He had practiced this exact scenario well over a dozen times but had not picked up that it would be applied to al-Ghamdi and al-Bakr. Seibel had worked his obfuscation masterfully. In fact, young Lance had been brought into the situation with the assumption that al-Bakr would be taken while either in or en-route to Amman, Jordan at the end of the month. He thought it a bit funny that it was all a ruse; all subterfuge to keep his mind loose during the three-vehicle smash and grab exercises. Seibel was indeed a master of deception.

Through his telephoto lens, Preacher watched al-Bakr emerge from the guardhouse just as al-Ghamdi walked out the door on the west side of the home. "VFR maverick." Lance's words were all that was needed to put the other team members on final alert for their target's departure. He put the Nikon and lens back in the slots of the camera case and nonchalantly walked back across the rooftop of the three-story warehouse he had chosen because of its unique view of the Red Sea coastline just a half-mile away. From this vantage point, he could also see the water reaching its apex after being shot up more than 900 feet by King Fahd's fountain. He stopped briefly and took in the expanse of the marvelous site again. For some reason, the song that started playing in his head was an 80s hit by a Scottish rock band singing about the highlands. The song didn't have anything to do with this desert by the sea he found himself in. He turned toward the door leading from the rooftop singing the tune.

He whistled the rest of the song as he made his way down the narrow stone stairs of the abandoned building. At the first floor, he grabbed a duffle stashed behind a low bench. Preacher quickly pulled out a thawb and keffiyeh and put them on. He placed his camera bag inside and retrieved his two weapons, an Uzi and SIG Sauer P226 handgun.

"Confirmation VFR maverick." Fuchs' muted voice on the radio confirmed al-Ghamdi and al-Bakr were both in the middle Mercedes.

Lance exited the warehouse, walked around the corner of the building and could have just as easily been at Harvey Point. The scene was not only very similar to that practiced by the group, it was nearly exactly as planned. Three target vehicles moved slowly out of the gate and picked up speed three quarters of a mile away. Low buildings lined the street on both sides. In some stretches, walls replaced buildings. The scene made for something of a shooting gallery, which made it all the more surprising that al-Bakr would guide his employer's caravan in this direction upon leaving the compound. He evidently placed great confidence in the armor plating and bulletproof windows of the vehicles. Either that, or he had gotten lazy, which was highly unlikely.

Tarwanah had parked the white cargo van about 200 feet ahead of Lance. Jamaani stood 75 feet or so past the van dressed in ragtag attire and pushing a peddler's cart. A goat, struggling at the end of a frayed thin rope, was tied to the cart for effect. A hundred yards passed Jamaani, Fuchs walked toward the Jordanian on the same side of the street with a canvas bag slung over his shoulder.

The target vehicles were now within a quarter mile of the escalation point and picking up speed. Lance walked toward the location on the opposite side of the street from the other three team members. He surveyed the entire scene as best he could then went up to about 1,000 feet to take it all in. Just as sketched out by Seibel during planning and training sessions, a few pedestrians and other vehicles dotted the area. Innocent casualties were unfortunately expected.

Go.

As planned, with the vehicles 100 yards away and moving at about 30 miles per hour, Jamaani began pushing his cart across the street. His stooped demeanor and outstretched hand begged the forgiveness of the approaching Mercedes convoy, which had to come to a stop. In a flash of a microsecond, Jamaani dove to the ground with a cylinder a foot tall and approximately 8 inches in diameter in his left hand. He placed the device under the engine of the lead car and rolled to the left a few feet. At this same moment, Fuchs approached the Mercedes bringing up the rear of the convoy and placed a similar device under the rear of the car. Just as quickly he moved 15 feet behind the vehicle. When he made eye contact with Jamaani they each pressed a detonator button for their respective devices. The result was more of an intense flare than an explosion, but instantly, each of the vehicles were engulfed in flames as the devices continued to emit what looked for all intents and purposes to be a welding torch.

Within three seconds, each vehicle was immobilized. The front vehicle's forward axle had been completely severed by the fury of the intense flame. The Mercedes at the rear had no back tires, only melted rubber and twisted metal. Fuchs and Jamaani stepped back approximately 30 feet to the sides of the front and the rear Mercedes. Each pulled out an Uzi prepared to annihilate anyone emerging from the flaming vehicles. The driver of the first car had apparently been knocked out by the concussion of the rapid flame and smoke. His passenger, with hands raised, looked at Jamaani from behind the protective glass. He knew his fate should he open the door. Smoke was filling the vehicles' interiors. It would just be a matter of seconds.

Fuchs got action immediately as driver of the rear vehicle burst from the smoke-filled insides with gun blazing. Before he could breath fresh air into his lungs, Fuchs filled his flesh with dozens of bullets from the Uzi. With a short step to his right, he executed the rear Mercedes' passenger, a guard fumbling for his gun. From his position, he also kept one eye on the Mercedes in the center.

Twelve seconds had now passed.

Tarwanah backed the cargo van onto the sidewalk on the left to within 30 feet of the first Mercedes. With the van in park, he leapt out of his driver-side door with a shoulder rocket grenade launcher. He pointed the Russian-made RPG-7 at the Mercedes in the center of the now disabled convoy. The driver's eyes bulged upon seeing the weapon. Bulletproof glass would not protect him from a rocket propelled grenade. Seventeen seconds now passed.

Simultaneously, Preacher emerged from his position directly to the side of the middle Mercedes with al-Ghamdi and al-Bakr inside. From the training, he knew he had to trust Fuchs and Jamaani to take out anyone getting out of the front and rear vehicles as he carried out his assignment. From his duffle, Preacher pulled a third and fourth Flasher -- flare cylinder. He placed one under the front and another under the rear. He then stepped back and pulled out the ignition switch for the super flares and held it up for all in the vehicle to see as he stepped back. Twenty two seconds gone by.

Time slowed to still frames in moments of extreme danger and violence like this. Preacher had barely glanced over at the rear vehicle a moment ago as Fuchs unloaded more than 40 shots into its driver and passenger. Their screams were muted, not really human and not registering in his focused and taught mind. Jamaani had not fired on the front vehicle because no one had tried to exit. With the detonation button under his right forefinger, Preacher surveyed the men inside the middle vehicle a dozen feet in front of him. He looked first to al-Bakr in the front passenger seat now closest to him. The driver continued to look in the direction of Tarwanah and his RPG his hands raised in surrender. Al-Ghamdi and a bodyguard shared the back seat. Both men appeared truly terrified.

Looking back to al-Bakr, it was obvious from his expression the head of security was not terrified in the least. In fact, a distinct, yet toothless smile danced on his lips. He looked directly at Preacher. No blinking. No fear. Preacher took two more steps back onto the sidewalk on the right side of the road and raised his left hand even with his raised right. He kept his gaze square on al-Bakr and pointed with his left index finger at the detonator device in his right and then opened his hand to show all five fingers. He then mouthed the number 5 in Arabic – *khamsa*. He closed his thumb and counted 4 – *arba'a*. Then three fingers and *thalatha*. At *ithnan*, or 2, al-Bakr did something that should have been totally unexpected except for the prediction of the very act by Seibel.

Al-Bakr pulled out an Uzi of his own from behind bulletproof glass and without any hesitation spun around and killed the other three men in the car; including his employer al-Ghamdi. There went one of the targets. *Damn*.

Blood from the close-range executions splattered the windows at the rear and left side of the car. The bulletproof glass kept the bullets from exiting the vehicle. Al-Bakr turned back to Preacher with the exact same expressionless look on his face and dropped the gun between his legs to raise his hands.

Preacher still had both hands raised and closed his left ring finger to signal one and mouthed the word in Arabic - *wahid*. He nodded his head at the door while keeping his eyes glued to al-Bakr's. The Arab did as signaled and reached for the door handle. Preacher took the opportunity to reach into his belt under the thawb and pull out his Sig handgun. Al-Bakr tossed his Uzi out and pushed the door fully open. Perfect timing, a Rolling Stones tune started the moment al-Bakr's foot hit the ground. Preacher shook his head and his foot began to tap in rhythm.

Jamaani circled to his left behind Preacher to provide additional cover. Thirty-two seconds gone.

The security expert and renowned killer raised his hands. But Preacher noted they weren't raised any higher than his shoulders.

"Get down." Preacher ordered.

Al-Bakr only smiled and stared back at him.

"Down." He repeated and raised his gun. No reply and no reaction. Preacher knew instantly what al-Bakr wanted. He wanted to draw Preacher to him. There could be an explosive device strapped to his waist, but that was unlikely.

In the blink of an eye, Lance saw the scene from above. He looked down on Preacher standing 14 feet from the Arab killer. The distance was too far for al-Bakr to attack him but too close if he had a little explosive device under his off-white thawb. Lance just couldn't see that happening. Al-Bakr was too vain for suicide. This was going to be hand-to-hand. The older killer wanted it that way. He needed to get closer. In the next blink of an eye, Preacher was back in front of al-Bakr and ready to have a little fun. Maybe dance a two-step. He took a step toward his deadly dance partner.

Preacher didn't like that the plan would soon fall behind schedule if al-Bakr continued to delay. He processed the situation again and without hesitation lowered his gun's aim and put a bullet in the Saudi's right knee.

Al-Bakr should have gone down but he only swayed to his right, then left. The smile left his face for a fraction of a second then came back after a wince. Thirty-nine seconds gone and

Lance's internal clock forced him into his next action. He stepped forward within four feet of al-Bakr.

The next sequence of actions was a ballet of movement taking place in microseconds. A blade flashed into al-Bakr's right hand and with his good left leg, the Arab assassin lunged at Preacher with the dagger pointed directly at the center of the young American's chest.

The already slow as molasses scene playing out before him now turned to stop-action photography for Preacher. Kind of like a strobe light in one of those haunted houses he ventured into as a kid. He knew, absolutely knew, that al-Bakr would attempt some type of offensive action and he was ready. Whether a knife, a gun, a chop of the edge of his hand; it was undoubtedly going to happen. The blade appeared from nowhere and slashed toward him, but Preacher remained unnaturally calm.

Al-Bakr knew he was the real prize of this exercise and fully expected to take a pound or two of flesh in exchange for his capture or death. But what he didn't know was just how much the very young American approaching him knew.

For instance, Preacher knew that al-Bakr had killed at least four men with a knife; one of them an experienced Israeli intelligence officer. He also knew that this particular Arab had trained with the finest martial arts instructors in Indonesia. And that al-Bakr was actually left-handed but hid this from almost everyone. In the Middle East, this alone made him deadly.

Al-Bakr also didn't know what this young American had been doing for the last three years. There are assuredly people out there, people such as distance runners who have put in more miles running than Lance during the past three years. But not many.

Likewise, there are weightlifters who have put in countless hours in the gym. But few had pushed themselves to build stronger, leaner muscles than Lance. And undoubtedly there were academics who studied their particular field hour upon hour for years. But few had read more words and memorized more information than Lance over the past 34 months.

He did not know what awaited him in the days, weeks and now years since he got into the car with Seibel in DC. But he never failed to excel, to overachieve, to impress. He was never satisfied with his performance. Never will be.

The result of three years, a lifetime really, of this pushing, pressing, bleeding was a rock-hard body with coiled muscles that brought equal amounts of speed and strength when flexed. Preacher was both lion and cheetah. And maybe worst of all, he was indifferent toward his opponent; completely lacking in empathy where pain and misery were concerned. Years or decades of training could not instill the one thing he came by naturally – a killer's instincts.

Hours, days and months in martial arts training with killers and those who train killers exposed him to real pain at the hands of men. This training also taught him the power that exists in each person's toes. And it was there that Lance first responded to the flash of al-Bakr's knife. He knew from anatomy encyclopedias that the primary muscle flexing the primary phalanx, or big toe, the flexor hallucis longus muscle, was actually in his calf. But no time to discuss this with al-Bakr right now.

With his toes, he pushed ever so slightly into the soles of his boots to gain a millisecond of momentum, to leverage his weight to the left and turn his body away from the approaching blade. The knife, aimed directly at his sternum a quarter second ago, was now headed for Preacher's upper right arm. Al-Bakr was deadly and fast and he surely expected to inflict a lethal wound with this particular lunge. However, with the lean and twist to the left, only a few strands of fabric were penetrated. As the razor sharp blade made contact with Preacher's upper right sleeve, it was already too late for al-Bakr to prepare to bring the knife back for another attack.

From his left-leaning position, Preacher lifted his right hand from underneath to grab al-Bakr's right wrist. And with speed that surprised both he and his opponent, Preacher used the toes in his left foot to reverse his lean and throw his momentum back to the right. The stop-motion photography of the moment immediately showed him his opponent's vulnerable spot – *the elbow*.

Preacher brought his left arm up cocked and he drove his own elbow into al-Bakr's outstretched arm. Because Preacher held the man's wrist in such a vice, the Arab assassin's elbow exploded in the wrong direction under the fierce blow. Cartilage and bone snapped as the elbow broke and bent in the exact opposite direction is was designed to operate. The pain instantly removed the smile from al-Bakr's face. It was replaced with a look of surprise and a primal scream of pain. The knife was released from al-Bakr's right hand and began its slow motion fall to the street.

Preacher could have been done with this battle with this excellent move. But something inside, something almost evil, made him pivot off of his right foot, release the wrist and reverse all movement and momentum back to the left while spinning. He glanced at al-Bakr's head position for reference, began raising his right arm while bending it and then completed a reverse spin. The result of this unexpected, unplanned move was an elbow traveling at a radical speed making contact with al-Bakr's spine at the base of his skull. A sickening thud caused the Arab's head to whiplash back and then fall to the ground with the rest of his limp body.

Preacher should have really been done with this latest move. But again, momentum, creativity and utter ambivalence guided his next action. He glanced back at Jamaani, rolled over al-Bakr's body and reached under the Mercedes to pull out the flash cylinder he had placed under the front right wheel. With lightening speed, he retrieved the heavy canister and set it on the ground beside al-Bakr. Preacher rolled the Saudi assassin over onto his back and grabbed the broken right arm to place the assassin's hand directly on top of the cylinder. Jamaani saw what Preacher was planning and took a step toward him. Preacher shot him a look and shook his head to stop the Jordanian in his tracks. He then moved to his right but still with a strong grip on al-Bakr's right arm he reached into his pocket and pulled out the dual ignition device. Preacher turned his head to the right to avoid the heat and pressed the small button.

A thick, searing, white-hot pillar of flame shot 13 feet into the air. The heat was intense, so intense it took with it the flesh and then bone below al-Bakr's wrist. The jolt of extreme pain awoke al-Bakr from his concussion with a howl that could almost be heard over the intense flame. Foam leaped from the corners of his mouth and he gnashed his teeth but could not move because of Preacher's superior strength holding him in place. Preacher pressed the button again and the flame died. To quiet al-Bakr's screams he put a knee in the assassin's diaphragm and a hand to his throat. Preacher looked into al-Bakr's eyes and gave him the same smile that only 20 seconds earlier the assassin had given him as he tried to plunge a knife into his heart.

Tarwanah backed the white cargo van a few feet from them and the back doors flung open. Preacher stood up, picked up al-Bakr and tossed the assassin's broken body into the back of the waiting van. Al-Bakr screamed again when his dangling and shattered right arm made contact with the metal floor. The cauterized wound at his wrist where a hand had been moments earlier slammed into the floor and he screamed again. Preacher turned to Jamaani who was not pleased.

"You're actions have cost us valuable time." The Jordanian said.

"And if he had stabbed me with that knife, that wouldn't have cost us any time?"

"Far outside the mission." Jamaani was angry but needed to be brief.

Fuchs, who had moved up to take the RPG from Tarwanah to allow him to get back in and drive the van now walked up to Preacher and Jamaani at the rear of the plan.

"We will talk about particulars later. Fifty-two seconds and a second detail is just now leaving the compound. Gather the unused Flicker and be ready to move in 15." He turned from them and walked deliberately back passed the rear Mercedes now engulfed in flames. Another white Mercedes was speeding up the road toward the scene. Fuchs let it get within 150 yards and fired the RPG. The explosion was deafening. Debris shot well into the sky and the flaming husk of the vehicle continued forward, but now only at a crawl. It's bulletproof glass no match for the rocket fired grenade.

Lance had stepped back over to the alley to gather his camera case. Fuchs came rushing back to the van as Lance jumped in the passenger door. Jamaani closed the rear door behind Fuchs and Tarwanah floored it.

Lance looked at his watch and then at Tarwanah who refused to look his way. He turned back to Fuchs who kneeled in the back beside al-Bakr.

"One minute 18 seconds," he called out over the roar of the engine. "Four seconds faster than our best time at the Point."

Fuchs finished putting tape on al-Bakr's wrists and ankles as Jamaani put a strip over their captive's mouth. "I imagine we could have saved eight seconds without that little flamethrower bit." Fuchs was not agitated like Jamaani, but then again he had not looked into Preacher's eyes during the brief tussle.

Lance turned back to look out the windshield. Tarwanah had slowed as they moved onto other city streets. "An eye for an eye. A hand for a hand." Lance said to no one in particular.

"You were reckless." Jamaani piped in.

"I guess I should have just shot him a couple of more times."

"Yes." Jamaani was always brief.

Fuchs laughed. "That would have been too easy for you. You wanted to get in closer to the action. I think you wanted to look death in the eyes. Maybe feel it. But you put the rest of us in danger with that shit." Lance didn't comment, but he found it interesting that Fuchs had completely lost his Berliner accent in the van and in the moments just before leaving the scene.

"Next time, just shoot the asshole in both knees and cut off the hand instead of incinerating it. That was somewhat gruesome." Fuchs smiled as he said this last bit. He turned to Jamaani who was also smiling. Between them they shared a look that belied their years of field service. Each would have liked to have just done what their young teammate had accomplished. Tarwanah looked in the rearview mirror to share their smiles. They had their man. And they had their own assassin.

Chapter 25

Artistry. That was the only applicable word to come to Seibel's
mind after taking the binoculars away from his eyes. His
vantage point from a darkened window on the fifth floor of an
office building just over 1,000 yards from al-Ghamdi's
compound provided an excellent view of the show Lance,
Fuchs, Jamaani and Tarwanah had staged below. He had just
seen an artistic minute and a half production that rivaled any
three-hour ballet performance he'd ever been forced to sit
through.

The veteran of three-plus decades of espionage at the
highest, and sometimes lowest, levels turned to Wyrick who
was busy taking apart a video camera from a tripod. "Good
footage?"

"Good stuff. Especially the blowtorch hand removal. Might
even be a classic." Wyrick responded without looking up from
his work – a technician through and through.

"Then I didn't just imagine that, huh?" Seibel raised his
eyebrows and turned back to the window to watch as the van
turned out of sight. "That was something…" He struggled for
the next word. "Unexpected."

"Fucking crazy is more like it." Wyrick had a smile on his lips so he went ahead and whistled.

"Ever seen anything like that? Anyone move like that?" Seibel asked the question to Wyrick, but was really asking himself.

"Foxy maybe 20 years ago. But he didn't move with such *decisiveness*." The way Wyrick put emphasis on the last word, it was evident he had selected that particular description for Lance's style well before now and chosen just the right moment to use it. Excellent timing, Seibel thought.

"Decisiveness. Yes." Seibel spoke the words, but his mind was miles and years away watching through binoculars as a young Mikel Fuchs took down three mercenaries in Zambia. Fuchs had shot one between the eyes at close range, sliced another's throat and then ended it with a broken neck for the third poor soul. Excellent work, and fast. But as Seibel recalled, Fuchs did take a knife to his back and several blows from the future broken neck before prevailing.

Either way, Seibel began to swell with pride at bringing a new resource to the National Clandestine Service just as he had done with Fuchs nearly 20 years prior; and his other protégé a decade ago. His current pupil had just confirmed his early worth in capturing al-Bakr alive without being severely injured himself. Seibel had been confident in the days and weeks leading up to the operation, but he knew the danger al-Bakr presented to even the most experienced agent. Lance had so easily responded with such brute force to the knife attack that the outcome was truly decided before al-Bakr began his initial thrust. *Decisiveness*.

Seibel closed his eyes and turned to slide his back down the wall to sit on the floor as Wyrick finished packing up his video gear. The veteran reviewed the 1 minute 18 second operation just completed. He would watch the videotape dozens of times and maybe show it to a few key individuals before destroying it. But here and now, he replayed the scene in his head where he could see it fresh, in 3D in his mind's eye.

Fuchs and his team executed the plan masterfully. The Jordanians were solid, always dependable. Lance fulfilled his duties and then chose to step in with al-Bakr. Seibel replayed Lance's approach to the assassin. In the young agent's movement he did not see overconfidence or braggadocio. No, it was expediency. He had placed one bullet in al-Bakr's knee as instructed during training. But the Arab's reaction showed that two, three or even four bullets would not move him from his position. Lance confronted him and placed himself within attack range to move the scenario and situation forward to completion. He baited al-Bakr with his body.

His response to the knife attack, now that was something else. Seibel had witnessed a good deal of Lance's martial arts training and noted his significant progress over nearly three years. But the coordination of movement, leverage and application of violent pressure on a vulnerable joint was exceptional. The reverse spin and elbow blow to al-Bakr's neck was exceptional as well. The next move, however, that was pure creativity. Violent, no, malevolent stewardship of a target. Seibel smiled with eyes closed as he replayed the extremity amputation by way of flash cylinder.

"Fucking crazy." Seibel opened his eyes and repeated Wyrick's words from a few moments ago. "That's the kind of stuff legends spring from. Too bad we can't tell anyone. That footage would be something on the evening news."

Wyrick shook his head. "Can you just imagine what that's like? Having your hand basically disintegrate before your eyes. Christ, I don't know about legends, but Preacher boy made himself a lifelong enemy with that stunt."

Seibel stood up and straightened his thawb and headscarf. "No doubt. His new enemy will likely never see light of day again, but he will undoubtedly remember our young Preacher every time he tries to scratch an itch or pick his nose and his hand is no longer there." Seibel nodded to Wyrick and walked across the empty office. "See you back at the ranch Mr. Wyrick." The contract agent simply nodded back at him. The two of them had been through years of this stuff together.

As he exited the building, made his way to a private airport and then departed the Saudi Peninsula for the time being, Seibel worked through his mental notes. He would be reporting back to Account One in Washington in 36 hours before journeying to an undisclosed location to participate, only at the periphery mind you, in the interrogation of al-Bakr.

He glanced at his watch and out the window of the private jet bound for Nicosia, Cyprus. From there he would grab commercial flights to Rome, JFK and D.C. The trip will total 22 hours travel time.

Once home, a nap, shower and shave and then a personal appearance before the members of Account One. Seibel is the only operative who reports to this particular committee, which is comprised of the heads of the CIA, NSA and White House intelligence office. Account One really did not exist in any form other than an assemblage of this august body. There is no paperwork, no documentation, no minutes kept, no calendar appointments referencing the meetings and no one ever willing to admit the existence of the group's actions and directives. Congress is never informed of their activities. The President is never told in advance of their meetings or topics of discussion. Plausible denial is more than a necessity for the members of Account One. Seibel was given the responsibility to act on behalf and report necessary progress or setbacks to the committee more than a decade ago. Since then, his actions had taken on urgency and priority. His projects were never questioned, at least never more than once. Likewise, his requests for resources and recruits were never held up. Results were demanded of him and he always delivered. Account One was job one.

The members of the group would be disappointed to hear about the loss of al-Ghamdi but quite pleased with the al-Bakr acquisition. He would leave out almost all of the details but inform the Account members that their investment in a new agency resource over the past few years had borne fruit. Seibel knew that as much as these heads of huge labyrinthine organizations wanted results, they also enjoyed hearing exotic and bizarre bits and pieces of the spy game. They had been updated on Lance's progress, without mention of his true identity of course, and would be delighted to know he not only played a role, but actively participated in the acquisition of al-Bakr.

A smile came to Seibel's lips under his fake moustache and beard at the thought of giving these unelected kingpins a few morsels of red meat on Lance's actions from this morning. Just as they have marveled over the years at Seibel's brief tales involving Fuchs and a few other select resources, they would salivate and then walk away with a warm feeling in their hearts knowing their country had a new killer-in-training like Lance Priest to turn loose in the field. Especially with the heat turning up and all eyes looking to Kuwait and points northwest in Iraq.

Chapter 26

Lance pressed his right forefinger into the earphone to increase the seal against the skin around his ear, which improved the sound quality. The conversation he was listening to was taking place on the outskirts of Baghdad 1,986 miles away from where he sat at his listening station in Augsburg.

A commander was excoriating a subordinate in the same manner a farmer might berate and then beat a dog that had failed to protect the flock from a coyote. Lance tried like heck to concentrate on the conversation, to pick up on any between-the-lines elements that might tell a deeper tale. The commander screamed on and on about the road south from Umm Qasr. Lance didn't need to glance up at the map pinned to the wall above the long bank of recording equipment. He had the entire region memorized.

He jotted down on his log the particulars of the conversation. The commander's dialect placed his hometown in the vicinity of Tikrit north of Baghdad. Therefore, he was most likely a member of the extended Hussein family. No surprise he treated his underlings likes dogs.

In his previous stints at the base, Lance's listening ears had been aimed at Eastern Europe and the disintegrating Soviet

Union. Since Saddam's march into Kuwait City on August 2nd, resources had been repositioned to the Fertile Crescent.

Lance still thought it slightly humorous that he had learned both Russian and Arabic at DLI. Seibel had suggested he "double up" in his short time in Monterey. Because he learned both languages simultaneously, they often overlapped in his mind. Even though they were significantly different in their phonic and tonal origins and qualities, the languages did have some common characteristics. Mesopotamian Arabic made its way up into the "stans" just as Russian had crept down into Southwest Asia. Each had been carried by winds of colonial expansion, and, of course, human brutality.

Since August, Arabic had taken preeminence. After returning to Augsburg from the gig in Jeddah, Lance found himself a hot commodity. He was immediately tasked with spending every available hour listening in on transmissions as the radio operators brought new frequencies and transmissions online. In the two weeks he'd been back in Germany, he had put in 16 to 18-hour days eavesdropping. His only day off had been a 26-hour overnight trip to a top-secret facility in the Balkans where he spent a little over an hour with his new friend Hassan al-Bakr and then three hours with Seibel and Fuchs reviewing the Jeddah operation. The meeting with al-Bakr in an undisclosed location outside Athens three days ago still occupied his mind, kept getting in the way of his undivided attention on his interception and translation duties. He knew the session with the prisoner was yet another test engineered by Seibel. Part of the learning process; no surprise there.

Lance received nothing but utter and unabashed respect from al-Bakr when he walked into the interview room. He had been told in advance by the Arab assassin's interrogators to expect to be spit upon and cursed at in the most profane manner. Al-

Bakr's left wrist was chained to the floor. No reason to chain the right, of course. First of all, there was no wrist and second, the elbow was shattered with tendons and ligaments ripped and torn. He couldn't see the man's legs because of the table, but the damaged right knee was down there somewhere.

He was greeted instead with a smile. The first thing al-Bakr did was painfully raise his bandaged right stump and break into outright laughter. "You really did a number on me." Al-Bakr blurted out in English while trying to stand. His arm was in a sling, but had not been set in a cast as it should have been. All part of the breaking process, of course.

"That was something." Lance spoke in Arabic and sat in the chair across the table from his new friend. "Got caught up in the moment I think."

"Surely you did. I was sure I had you with my blade and then a moment later, my skull nearly crushed and my hand gone – poof." Al-Bakr used his left hand and opened all his fingers to make the international poof sign. The chain rattled as he raised the hand slightly. "You were too fast, I think maybe too young and strong for me. I guess I'm getting old."

"I just reacted. No conscious thought or planning. I suppose I didn't like nearly having a knife in my chest. So I don't think I'll apologize." They let the moment hang there, just looking at each other.

"Of course not." Al-Bakr broke the silence. "Why are you here my young friend? Hopefully not to join these dogs in their amateur torture games." Lance thought about that for a moment and envisioned al-Bakr torturing others in an expert and extremely brutal manner. He imagined how a professional butcher like al-Bakr viewed with disdain the unprofessional manner in which his interrogation had been conducted.

"Actually, they did bring me here to ask you a few questions." Lance added.

"So the information they are getting from me through other means has been deemed unreliable?"

Lance sat back and took in al-Bakr as a whole, at least from the waist up. He had watched from behind a small two-way mirror a few minutes earlier as two interrogators worked together to question the detainee. One of them had stepped behind al-Bakr and pulled his hair, snapping his head back. They had not struck him in the few minutes Lance watched. But looking at al-Bakr now, he could see multiple wounds that had been administered in the two weeks since he was captured in Jeddah. The right side of his face was swollen and bruised. A small gash above his right eye was fresh enough not to have scabbed over. Bruises around his neck indicated trauma. His one remaining pinky finger had been broken and not set. All this on top of the damage Lance had inflicted in Jeddah. Basically, the Arab assassin was a mess. But he wasn't broken; far from it.

"From what I hear, they haven't extracted much from you at all." Lance answered after some delay. He had spoken with Fuchs for a few minutes in the next room. But the conversation was short, hesitant. Felt to Lance like Fuchs only told him what he was supposed to; as if from a script. The rest was up to him once he entered the room. Another in Seibel's endless tests.

"I have provided names, locations, phone numbers." Al-Bakr added.

"But nothing of real use. Just periphery. Second and third-rate players." Lance replied.

"So what do you want to ask me?" The smile grew again on al-Bakr's face.

"I'm only interested in one thing." Lance smiled back and continued to lean back in his chair.

"Shall I guess what that is?"

"Please do."

"My bet would be that you are interested in al-Ghamdi activities in Kuwait."

"Close," Lance leaned forward and put his elbows on the metal table. "I'm interested in your activities in Kuwait."

"But I work-," he stopped for a moment to correct the statement. "Worked for al-Ghamdi. All of my efforts have been to assist in the growth of business, security and relationships for my employer."

"Come on. I only got to see a handful of files and your work went way beyond al-Ghamdi. I'll go as far as saying al-Ghamdi was your cover, your puppet."

"Please do not disrespect such a man. He is surely with Allah now." And with that, Lance had his unexpected opening.

"Oh, like 'please don't spray my brains all over my car.' That kind of disrespect?"

"I was merely saving him from my fate. I knew that he would not do well in a situation such as this," he waved around the room for effect; the chain rattled. "He would not last long here. He was strong, but in business and negotiations, not in this way."

"So what you did was humane. What about the other two gentlemen in that car? Do you think they appreciated your act of humanity?"

Al-Bakr let that thought run through his mind for a moment. It was clear to Lance that this killer had not given one moment to the memory of the other two men he executed at extremely close range. So close that their blood had spattered his face. "They were good men. Men I hired and trusted and they would surely appreciate my concern for them."

Lance's smile widened. "Man. You're quite a friend."

"To those who earn my trust." Al-Bakr replied.

"Great. So let's get back to Kuwait. Do you think you are going to find it in yourself to tell us a little more about what we need to know."

"I have told you what you need to know. All of it." The Saudi sat back to signify his act of sharing, his openness. "Everything."

"You know what, I'm no good at this interrogation stuff. I don't really know why they brought me here. As if seeing me might put fear in you, right?" Lance sat back.

"Maybe something like that. Maybe to remind me of this," he held up his stump. The act of moving the arm caused him significant pain. "As if I need reminding."

"Maybe, but I don't think that's it. Sitting here, I think the reason I'm here is to let me see a dead man. Talk to a dead man, breath the same air as a dead man. I think I'm really here for my benefit. It's part of my training, my learning."

Al-Bakr rubbed his beard for a moment. The act of doing it with his left hand obviously still foreign to the assassin. "Interesting. Not a bad hypothesis. I know I'm a dead man. Maybe not today or tomorrow, but I won't leave here no matter what they say or promise me in exchange for more information."

"Right." Lance nodded his head in agreement. "Dead is dead, whether today or tomorrow or next year. When you accept it, you come to peace, right?"

"Exactly. It is peaceful. As if nothing can touch me." And with that, Lance pounced on the opening al-Bakr exposed a minute earlier.

"Until Izrail comes for you, heh?" Lance sent up a trial balloon.

"Ah, yes. The Day of Judgment is not far away for me. I am ready."

"For the fires of hell, right?"

"No, no. Paradise. I will surely be shown into Paradise by the angels." The assassin smiled.

"What the-? Are you serious?" Lance's procerus went to work tugging his eyebrows together.

"Of course."

Lance played up incredulous. "You're the definition of an evildoer. Your personal angel has recorded what, 40, 50 deaths by your hand. You are a murderer, torturer, adulterer. Your sins against Allah are almost countless."

"Disbelievers. Infidels. Their deaths were just, ordained. I did Allah's will." Al-Bakr was dismissive to a fault.

"Jeez. You don't believe any of that. I don't think you believe in heaven or hell or even Allah. You've never cracked open a Quran, except maybe to pull out some papers to wipe your nose. Nothing you've done indicates any actions within the pillars of faith. Come on." Lance sat forward and put his arms on the table to bring himself just a foot or so from al-Bakr.

The effect of Lance's comments was immediate and obvious. Al-Bakr had never been spoken to in this way. Had never been disrespected in such a blasphemous manner. He went from ice cold to boiling behind his eyes. Lance saw it and knew he had a wedge.

"Do not blaspheme me or God." Al-Bakr sputtered.

"Me blaspheme you? Hell, I'm a better Muslim than you and I don't believe a word of it."

"Infidel! Demon." Al-Bakr gave away a weak spot. Lance didn't hesitate to advance the conversation and take advantage of this momentary weakness. He, unlike his adversary, knew every word of the Quran.

"Yes, you are. An infidel. A disbeliever in the scriptures. Your life is a sin and when Izrail comes for you in a matter of days, your soul will be ripped from you and cast into hell for all eternity. I have no doubt about that my friend."

Al-Bakr struggled at the chains, tore at his handcuffs in an effort to rise. He kicked at the chair he sat in, but it was bolted to the floor and didn't budge. The pain he felt in his right knee and right arm stump were evident, but he was possessed. He slammed his damaged right arm on the table. The pain was excruciating but he had lost control.

Lance was a little baffled by this display. Surely the interrogators had tried this ploy with their pseudo-Islamic captive. Lance stayed right where he was as al-Bakr struggled and screamed and breathed fire in his direction. Exasperated, the assassin collapsed back into the chair. He pulled his right arm to his chest and brought up his left arm to cradle it.

"You're serious. You actually believe that you're going to paradise with 72 virgins and eternal bliss. Unbelievable." Lance sat back with an incredulous look on his face. After a few moments, he reached down into the satchel on the floor he had brought into the room with him. Out of it he pulled a manila folder and out of the folder he pulled dozens of sheets of paper and photos. One by one, he laid them on the table. As he placed each sheet or photo on the table, Lance said a name and date. After a dozen or so, al-Bakr finally did what was expected and spat on him and on the papers before him. Lance disregarded the warm spittle and continued with the parade of murder and mayhem left in al-Bakr's wake over the last two decades.

When he finished, more than 40 pieces of paper and photos were spread out on the shiny metal table. It was entirely covered by death, destroyed lives, desolated families. "Paradise. You asshole; you're going to hell on the angel of death express, no $200 dollars, no passing go, no 72 virgins. Straight into the fire. Burn, baby burn."

Al-Bakr bowed his head and began to chant silently. He was finished with the conversation and his friend. But Lance wasn't.

Lance took his arm and swept the assemblage of papers and photos of individuals and families no longer living off the table to the floor. He reached down into the satchel and pulled out another manila folder. And like a few moments earlier he began laying pieces of paper and photos on the metal table top, this time saying only names, no dates. Al-Bakr stopped his chanting and opened his eyes. After seven, al-Bakr tried his damdest to slam the table with his left hand, but the chains only let him reach so far.

"Bastard. Fucking bastard infidel!" Al-Bakr howled, but Lance kept laying the photos on the table and saying their names. "I will kill you! By Allah, I will slaughter you and take your heart!" Without missing a beat, Lance continued to place the photos on the table one by one until he had laid all 36 down.

When he was done, he sat back and let al-Bakr yell, scream, curse and grow redder with every breath. After a minute of the show, the caged assassin slumped back in his bolted-down chair and began to cry, maybe for the first time in his life. Before him on the table laid photos of all of his children, even those conceived and raised outside his marriages. Also pictured were his brothers, uncles and father.

"I don't believe in heaven or hell or Allah or the angel of death or paradise. I do believe in payback. And you have earned an amazing amount of payback for what you've done." Lance gestured to the photos, "The Israelis have been given the names, locations and photos of your children. The French and Germans will divide up your brothers and their families. And the British will take those living in England. But I get the very best job."

Lance lifted his left arm to look at his watch, all for effect. "I will personally pay a visit to your father." He smiled and waved his hands over the photos. "All of them will be dead by day after tomorrow. No prisoners, that was the rule to play in this game. No one sparred. Then the photos of each of their dead bodies, with all the men decapitated of course, will be brought back to this room and laid before you on this table and you'll have your eyes pried open so you will be forced to look.

"All except one, because here's the best part. I am bringing your father back from his village, back to this room to sit him right here and look at all these photos plus those on the floor. And we are going to tell him all the evil you have done. Then I am going to hand him the knife that he will use to slice your throat. Lastly, I'll hand him a gun with one lonely little bullet so he can blow his own brains out and join you in hell; his retribution for spawning a demon like you. Izrail will come for both your souls and that will be that."

Al-Bakr burst into tears and full, babbling crying. A broken man. A man now ready to betray the trust of those he had dealt with in Kuwait, Iraq, Saudi Arabia and anywhere else. "No." It was all he could get out.

"Yes." Lance looked at his watch, "In 36 hours, most will be gone and I should be sitting down for tea in your father's tent."

"No. No. I can give you more information. I will tell you."

"Sorry, I don't want information. I want your family dead, all of them. This is where it gets good." The look in Lance's eyes was ice, lifeless. He showed al-Bakr the face of evil.

And with that, Lance got up, grabbed his satchel and walked to the door as al-Bakr pleaded with him.

"No! Please no. They are innocent."

Lance turned back to him. "I've got several calls to make and a plane to catch. Should I send the amateurs back in?"

"Yes. Please send them back in. Now. Please." The assassin pleaded.

"Unless plans change, I'll see you back here in two days with my new old friend accompanying me." Lance couldn't help but smile as he left.

Once outside, Lance was greeted by Seibel who stood looking at his watch.

"13 minutes." Seibel said.

"That long?" Lance replied.

The CIA spymaster turned to Fuchs and smiled. "Two weeks these so-called specialists have been working him and our boy turns him to bucket of piss in 13 minutes." Fuchs just laughed and shook his head.

"Lunch time?" Lance grinned at them.

Seibel shook his head and sighed. "In a minute. I need to get with the boys to discuss next steps. You two go ahead and I'll come join you." Lance and Fuchs started down the hall. Seibel called to them. "But Lance, I suppose if Fuchs had handed you two folders with pictures of butterflies and blue birds five minutes before you walked into the room you would have used those to convince al-Bakr you would kill them all, in 36 hours was it?"

Lance thought for a few seconds. "If it were butterflies and blue birds, I would have told him I'd already killed his children and given a butterfly and bird for each one to his father. Probably would have made something up about their souls being as free as winged creatures fluttering on the winds of fate. Or something along those lines. Telling lies, you know. It's what I do, in case you weren't aware."

"I know. Your specialty." Seibel smiled and turned to his interrogators who had been watching Preacher's performance from an adjoining room.

Chapter 27

"Operation Sandal Rash has proven quite successful, even more than initially reported." Seibel sat at the far end of a plain oak conference table in a nondescript conference room somewhere outside Washington D.C. The members of Account One sat on both sides of the table with the current head of the National Security Agency sitting directly across from Seibel at the far end. His briefings on his SAD, Strategic Activities Division, operations were often the highlight of these leaders' month.

They had each been listening intently to his report, but all perked up in the last minute as he began his update of activities surrounding the killing of al-Ghamdi, capture of al-Bakr, and resulting intelligence gathered through interrogation of the assassin.

Seibel's initial telling of the capture four weeks prior had elicited a good number of questions from the members of this ultra-elite group of intelligence professionals. He had dropped bits and pieces about the operation and sprinkled in a smattering of Preacher magic dust with a reference to the Saudi no longer possessing a right hand. He left out the details of Lance incinerating the Arab's appendage from his body. But he let it be known that during direct contact, hand-to-hand, he asked them to pardon the pun, the Account's youthful prize investment not only held his own against an experienced killer, Preacher completely and utterly dismantled the terrorist's ability to ever pull a trigger with the stump. Let alone shake hands, since Muslims do not shake hands with their left.

It seemed, sitting here in this tight little room full of powerful people with war and invasion on the immediate horizon, these intelligence czars wanted more details about al-Bakr's capture and the value of his testimony as much as they wanted anything else. They also let it be known that they wanted an update on Preacher – his latest activity and future projects.

"The value of our subject's early confessions was minimal, almost without merit. The details provided were only at the surface level. Hardly worth the time and effort dedicated to the sessions." Seibel always spoke this way when addressing this group. He almost never gave actual names; used coded words and phrases and spoke in generalities. Protocol did allow for divulging explicit information, but this was generally done only in the sole company of the Director of Central Intelligence who went by the codename Marvin. Every once in a while, a member of Account One would pat or even slam the table and demand that Seibel stop speaking in code and tell the group in no uncertain terms what needed to be said. This was rare, however.

"The quality and complexity of this information changed substantially 10 days ago when the subject received a visit from Preacher."

Before Seibel could continue, the White House intelligence advisor butted in, "Did the subject lose the other hand?" Members of the group couldn't contain themselves and all chuckled. Seibel allowed himself to join them with a smile.

"No. The subject did not have his other hand severed by way of inferno like his right one," Seibel let another bit of information from the Jeddah operation slip.

"Inferno?" The NSA Director at the opposite end of the table asked. "How was the hand removed?"

"Incinerated sir, blasted away for all of eternity by a Flasher."

"Christ," this time the CIA Director weighed in. "Literally burned away, gone?"

"Completely, right above the wrist. Gone and cauterized in seconds," Seibel added for effect.

"I know I don't recall amputation being a part of your plan," NSA followed up. "But use of a Flasher for this purpose seems extraordinarily cruel."

Seibel did not hesitate, "Extraordinarily indeed. The time it took young Preacher to disarm, take down and remove the hand was 15 seconds. I witnessed it in person and have watched the tape dozens of times since to evaluate the operation. Each time, I am still shocked by both the speed and effectiveness of his methods. Nothing short of amazing. I would have been pleased if any of our resources could take, let alone break, the subject in man-to-man combat. Preacher did what maybe 10 others in the world could do when faced with such a lethal attacker, armed with a razor-sharp knife mind you. As I said last month, our investment is showing early signs of paying dividends. His visit with the subject last week moved us even closer to payback and break-even."

Seibel went into the details of al-Bakr's testimony garnered after his visit from Lance. The room was generally accepting of his assessment about their investment. They had their man in the field.

After a few minutes, the conversation turned to other topics. At the top of the list was Seibel's take on KGB operations and his assessment of latest developments in that sphere. He updated Account One on the fracturing away of KGB operatives from central command. Smelinski was losing his iron grip.

His update of K&K operations took several minutes. Former KGB agents Evgany Korovin and Nikolai Kusnetsov had set up a network that would undoubtedly require the CIA to take action even with Iraq heating up and resources needed there. Their scope of work had broadened from strong-arming local and state leaders in Ukraine and Belarus to black market trafficking of exceedingly dangerous weapons. They had possibly begun operations that could result in weapons of mass destruction coming onto the market. He assured the group he was on top of it.

Seibel took another 10 minutes updating the file on Marta Sidorova, another former KGB operative building a network of current and former-KGB elements. Her operation had expanded out concentrically from Eastern Europe into France, Germany and southeast to Turkey. "Very impressive for someone only 26 or 27 years old."

Seibel qualified his comments on Marta because in actuality, very few hard facts were known about her or her network.

His analysis of other things KGB concluded the meeting a half-hour later. It wasn't surprising to Seibel that conversations between members of the elite group returned to Preacher and his accomplishments. Everyone loves a bad ass; especially a bad ass on your side.

Chapter 28

He indulged himself for an extra minute under the hot, almost scalding, shower. In a moment, he'd turn the water to cold like he always did. But he liked it warm to help him think, to relax. Just let the water hit the back of his neck while rotating his head side to side, up and down. The ritual was rhythmic habit from way back.

It was 5:15 in the a.m. and Lance had just come back in from a brisk well-before-dawn five and a half mile run through the quiet streets of Augsburg. It had taken him a little more than 31 minutes, which kept him nicely in the six-minute per mile range. Two hundred pushups and 200 sit ups rounded out the morning workout. The shower was the reward. He'd learned at boot camp and on several of his assignments, including four weeks at Green Beret training, that showers are indeed a luxury Americans far too often took for granted.

One of the great benefits Seibel had worked out for Lance was his own apartment. Most single soldiers were required to live in barracks on base. That just wouldn't do for one of Seibel's operatives. A long shower with hot water was another benefit those in barracks didn't get.

This particular shower allowed him to consider the events of the previous 24 hours. He'd actually been enjoying the days and days of monotonous listening to his new friends in Iraq, Kuwait, Saudi Arabia and a few here and there from Jordan, Syria, Iran. The variety of foreign tongues and dialects challenged his abilities. He would finish listening to a conversation and practice the dialect until the next conversation was piped into his headset.

He had heard it all in the past few weeks. From simple troop and armory movement orders to oil pipeline sabotage by locals outside Mosul, Iraq who were then summarily executed; to an Iraqi colonel in Kuwait crying to another officer about his wife's inability to give him a son, only daughters. Lance especially enjoyed the sessions where those communicating over the airwaves attempted to speak in some sort of code. Most of it was downright hilarious. And quite obvious that the counterparts were not working from the same code sheets. They would often try it for a few minutes, then curse the damn codeset and speak in Arabic for all to hear.

But it was two specific conversations yesterday morning that perplexed Lance as he stretched the shower well past another minute of comforting warmth. He had already gone over the conversations last night and during his run this morning. So the shower was actually the third or fourth time he'd rerun them in his mind.

The first started out like most others from the past few weeks. Two Iraqi individuals exchanged military pleasantries across the miles. One was stationed outside Mosul and the other on the outskirts of Kirkuk. Both cities were in northern Iraq dominated by Kurdish populations. The boredom in their tones was obvious and it was clear after a few sentences that both would rather be down in Kuwait where the action is. Their conversation was grade "A" boring, right up until the moment the guy in Kirkuk mentioned an incident the day before at a roadblock. Four soldiers were killed by a small group in a single vehicle. Nothing too strange there. But his detailing of eyewitnesses seeing a young woman doing most of the killing was strange.

Lance jotted this little tidbit of info down for consumption by NSA analysts who would be reviewing his work. He put the conversation in a compartment in his brain for later digestion. Then, near the end of his shift, his tracer/interceptor brought online a conversation that had just started up.

"Coordinates confirm source location is Baghdad. Feed is live as of 48 seconds ago," the handler piped the conversation into Lance's listening station and got off the line to search the frequencies for another conversation happening somewhere else in the world.

Lance joined the conversation in progress and didn't notice for a full seven seconds that he was listening in on an exchange being spoken in Russian. He sat up and buzzed his handler in the next room.

"Are you sure this is Baghdad?"

"Confirmed. Coordinates put it in the southeast sector of the city." Corporal Billock from Oregon responded.

"Did you notice this is Russian?"

"Yah. That's why I shoved it over to you. These other guys have all been brought in during the past month for Arabic, Hebrew and Turkish. You're my only regular Russian on the clock right now."

"Got it," he wasn't quite done. "Russian from Baghdad. You don't think you should have told me that up front?"

"I thought it was a little funny to pass it to you blind."

"Funny. Thanks." Lance pushed the button again to sever the line and turned back to the Russian conversation. He knew right away it was a coded language exchange. The speaker in

Baghdad had a pronounced lisp. Sounded fake. His accent sounded educated, but that also fake. Sounded like an Englishman doing a bad Russian accent.

"Pyotr is not embellished by the paradigm."

"Is the maze distracted?" was the reply.

"Torrential downpour. Illusory." The Englishmen/Russian replied in turn.

Lance buzzed Billock again.

"Yah?"

"Location of receiving party?" Lance asked.

Lance could here him shuffle a couple of papers. "Not able to confirm."

"Region?"

"Radio signature indicates Eastern Europe. Probably the Ukraine; maybe Romania. Just guessing though."

"Nothing more?"

"That's it."

"Thanks." Lance clicked off and returned to the coded conversation. He pressed the earphone to try to put him closer to the one in Baghdad. Tried to see his mouth speaking and then his face."

"Partial retainer payment received."

"Maze completion?"

"The benefactors must be incorporated. Benefactors polished."

Lance concentrated only on the one he considered the Englishman.

"Portions in hallmark and gratuity." The speaker from Eastern Europe changed subjects.

"Ballast competitive. Portions ship after shave." Lance saw the mouth speaking. "Ballast front, left of front." He saw the mouth working to control an accent, not a natural act. Contrived.

"Farm to sea."

"Venice before rain." The words ended the conversation. The radio went quiet before becoming static. Lance repeated the words in Russian, "Venice before rain." He'd heard them before, more than once, just as he'd heard "farm to sea, ballast, portions and maze." They were words he'd heard while listening to countless conversations over radio traffic and sometimes phone lines emanating out of the former Soviet bloc. He knew their meanings because NSA and CIA had broken their code several years ago. This particularly rare codeset was a definitive legacy of Russian attempts at colonial expansion in that garden spot of the world otherwise known as Afghanistan.

Venice before rain simply meant same time tomorrow. The two pseudo Russians obviously planned to speak again tomorrow at a planned time. This implied military protocol and precision. Lance picked up something else. It was in the way the words were spoken. There was affection in them. When the gent in Iraq signed off with his partner somewhere in Europe, it was quite evident to Lance that he was saying goodbye to his lover. He jotted this down.

Farm to sea was an order given to agents in the field to continue as planned. Orders given to KGB agents.

Ballast usually meant the contact or element being contacted. *Portions* referred to a meeting or discussions, maybe dealings. *Maze* definitely equated to a transaction. Put it all together and the conversation indicated meetings involving a transaction were taking place in Baghdad between some Russians, or at least fake Russians, and someone else.

Lance let the static ring in his ears as he wondered how quickly NSA computers could analyze the earlier conversation along with this one and get back with likely meanings. Probably 48 hours.

That was last evening.

Lance turned off the cold water and dried off. At 5:22 a.m. his phone rang in the next room. It rang just two times. Seibel calling. Were the events of the day before and this early morning beacon connected? Lance was fairly adroit at recognizing patterns amid the flotsam and jetsam of seemingly everyday life. He'd only gotten better over the last three years. A roadblock massacre led by a woman and a coded Russian conversation during the same day followed by a very early morning communication alert from Seibel were not happenstance. The little fact that Lance was schooled in espionage, Russian and Arabic languages and deciphering basic codes all led to the same conclusion. He wouldn't be in Augsburg much longer. If he had to guess, he was probably headed back to the desert.

He put on his uniform and headed out the door at 5:45 sharp. Walking from his unremarkable apartment less than a mile from Gablingen Kaserne – his base, he considered the pay phone options at his disposal. He knew of 41 within a 10 minute walk from his apartment. He chose Adolf von Bayer Strasse, which didn't take him too far off course from his usual trek to the base. He'd used that phone one time two years prior.

As he began his stroll over to the base this early morning, he saw the usual light activity for a Bavarian morning, plus one person way out of the norm. The individual Lance spotted about 200 yards from his apartment moved from shadow to shadow well behind him.

Now, this really elevated the activities of the past 24 hours above coincidence. Lance had only been followed twice outside of training. Once in Dallas the first day he'd met Seibel. The other in London after leaving a drop site a few blocks from Piccadilly Circus. The tracker in that instance had been particularly good and obviously experienced at urban maneuvers. Lance successfully shook both tails.

What was this about? He hadn't been anywhere outside Augsburg in the last month except his day trip to visit al-Bakr. Before that, he'd been in Jeddah for two weeks and at Harvey Point for two months prior to that. His training for eluding trails had been thorough, maybe a bit over the top, but Seibel and Fuchs had been adamant. The training included elusive and aggressive points.

Lance decided this situation called for interaction with his follower. He turned left on Bergstrasse and then ducked into a doorway on the right side of the road where he could view Bergstrasse to his left and Ludwig-Hermann Strasse on his right. About 35 seconds later, he spotted the individual moving from one shadow to another. In the flash of a streetlight illumination, he saw it was a man wearing a hat and holding a large device to his ear. A cellular phone. Lance knew the network for cell phones in Augsburg was still tiny and talking on a mobile phone was basically talking on the radio. The frequency was easily detectible and decipherable. Basically not smart unless you didn't care about your conversation being overheard by fairly low technological means.

The lone man approached the intersection of Berg and Ludwig-Hermann. He avoided the streetlights at the intersection and crossed 50 yards earlier than Lance had. He walked past Lance's hidden location on the other side of the street scanning side to side. Lance didn't like the way the guy had his left hand in his jacket pocket. It wasn't natural. It wasn't resting in the pocket. It was rigid, holding something. All bets were that it was holding a gun. *What the hell?*

Just then it flashed for Lance. He never forgets a face. He'd seen this guy before. Harvey Point. Maybe 18 to 20 months ago. He was Spanish, at least he spoke only Spanish at the Point.

And he was always with another Spaniard. Seibel had brought them in to work with Lance and three other youngsters. Their four-day drill involved radio recon, detection and rescue of multiple captives. It was Lance's third live-action drill and he'd shot several terrorists with live rounds. They were terrorists with sandbag bodies and mops for heads, but it was satisfying to see the dust splatter out the backs. The two Spaniards expertly determined location, room specs and numbers of captors and hostages using radio and audio listening capabilities. He'd never been offered or inquired about their names.

Lance knew if this one was here, the other Spaniard must be at the other end of the phone line. As he watched from his hidden vantage point, Spaniard One increased his pace as he went under the Gersthofen-Bergstrasse overpass and continued to the corner of Am-Flugplatz. Lance leaned out and took a few steps to be able to see several hundred yards down the street as Spaniard One was indeed met by Spaniard Two at the street corner just a couple hundred yards from the base's main gate. He could see them take their phones from their ears and look around in all directions -- obviously looking for him.

As he pushed back up against the building for cover, a hand suddenly slapped down on Lance's shoulder. It scared the hell out of him. He instinctively spun his leg and lowered with a force and violence that flipped the individual behind him to the ground as Lance's leg met the other's ankles. Lance was on top of him in a flash and had him by the throat ready to twist and rip out vocal chords.

It was Fuchs.

"Jesus, you scared me." Lance blurted.

Fuchs wanted to speak but his throat was momentarily immobilized. He shot up his own leg and popped Lance in the back of the head and rolled over to get back up to his feet. They stood and faced each other as Fuchs gathered his breath and rubbed his throat. "Christ. You nearly broke my neck."

Lance once again heard no German accent. "What are you doing here? What are *they* doing here?" He waived in the direction of the Spaniards.

Fuchs was getting back to normal and smiled briefly, "I forgot just how friendly your reaction to surprises was." He continued to rub his throat. "A little surprised I caught you so off guard there. You didn't hear or see me at all."

"Isn't that your specialty? Sneaking up and silently killing?" Lance stepped back and realized he'd just been totally fooled by Fuchs. His attention was on the Spaniards several hundred yards up the road and not behind him where one or more others could be following. "Crap, I focused in on them and forgot my flank. Completely missed you."

"I know." Fuchs grinned.

"How far back were you?"

"A hundred meters behind Espinoza." The German accent was back.

"Crap. Didn't make you at all. Foolish."

Fuchs stood back to full height and brushed his jacket. "Seibel sent in a little crew to ensure your safety. It was my job to observe and report."

"What's the concern? Has my operation been made?"

"No indications there, but he wanted to be sure on a couple of levels. Activity has increased significantly over the last couple weeks."

"What kind?"

"All kinds. You'll get a full update day after tomorrow when he arrives." Fuchs turned to look at the Spaniards up the street. "A new operation is in development. You will be moving within the week."

"Iraq?" Lance asked, already knowing the answer.

"That's my guess." Fuchs nodded.

"You going to?"

"Not been told." Fuchs leaned in close. "I believe you are being pushed from the nest on this one. On your own out there in the big desert."

"When will Seibel be here?" Lance asked.

"He'll contact us when he's ready. In the meantime, he asked that you stay on base for tonight and maybe tomorrow night. Sleep in the radio room bunkhouse."

"What's he worried about?" Lance laughed.

"His investment. Almost three years and a couple of million dollars."

"But why. What is he worried about for me? Anything I need to know about?" Lance could feel something amiss.

"I think he is just going on lock-down mode. Wants everything wrapped up tight to initiate the operation. I've seen him like this before." Fuchs was convincing, but Lance wasn't fooled. Something else was up.

Lance began to walk away, then stepped back into the dark. "I think it's a coalescing of things Arab and Russian."

"That too." Fuchs remained in the shadow. "Your intuition serves you well. I think that as time and events pull at the edges, the center cannot hold. The breakup means the end of one war and the beginning of the next. From cold to hot, if you will." Fuchs undoubtedly had just repeated something he'd heard from Seibel.

Lance took this as his cue to leave and walked down the street toward Gablingen Kaserne. Up ahead, the Spaniards took positions on either side of the street and remained silently in shadows as he passed. He turned on Am Flugplatz and walked down the last street before walking through the gates to the base. It all seemed a little much and didn't take any great brains to see something else was at work here. Something else was blowing in the wind if Seibel felt it necessary to bring in resources just to get him three-quarters of a mile to his base. Something had changed. A leak had been detected. Someone had been compromised. Regardless, it was all pretty exciting. And the months of waiting around were about to come to an end with a real assignment, something with deep cover and an extended timeframe.

Lance saluted the guards at the entry gate and presented his ID. He couldn't help but smile. The guards found his smile a little irritating in the early morning.

Chapter 29

Operation Desert Shield was in full swing and then some in the first week of December 1990. The Bush doctrine of protecting the world's oil supply originating in Saudi Arabia necessitated action in the days after Iraq's invasion of Kuwait in early August. The U.S. military build-up in Saudi Arabia included active and reserve Army, Navy and Air Force personnel and a bunch of pissed off Marines still smarting from the Beirut bombing in 1983. This purely defensive force included a coalition of troops from England, France, Canada, Australia and other countries looking to show their support of freedom, and free-flowing oil, of course.

On November 29, the United Nations Security Council had passed Resolution 678 authorizing all necessary military action to remove Saddam's forces from Kuwait. The resolution took effect beginning on January 15, 1991. Odds-makers around the world favored an Iraqi pullout before then. The leaders of the United States intelligence community possessed a vast amount of intelligence that foretold a different story. Saddam planned to dig in and keep Kuwait as the 19th province of Iraq by any means possible. These means included bringing other Arab nations into the yawning gap by goading Israel into military action. He planned to launch as many missiles as possible into Israel. And he hoped that at least one of these missiles would carry a nuclear payload when it landed in Tel-Aviv or Jerusalem.

The intelligence community had solid proof of missile capabilities, partly because portions of these systems had been sold to Iraq by U.S. intermediaries during the Iran-Iraq war. The possibility of obtaining nuclear material for warhead delivery had been uncovered in the preceding months. Geoffrey Seibel briefed the leaders at CIA, NSA, FBI, White House and military intelligence the day before Thanksgiving with news of former KGB agents offering nuclear fissile material for sale to Iraq. Competing KGB factions were confirmed in Iraq recently. Updates to this activity included intercepted communications and confirmed sightings.

"Just yesterday we received confirmation from Soviet resources that three nuclear warheads were discovered missing from a storage facility. The missing warheads were removed from decommissioned 1970s era SS-X-15 ICBM missiles being stored underground outside Dombarovsky, Russia." Seibel said soberly.

The CIA Director had already been briefed by Seibel on this breach. "We have confirmation from multiple sources on the credibility of this information. This is one that the Soviets actually feel compelled to share with us. We are working together to track and recover the warheads."

Seibel nodded and added, "Information is scarce, but all indications are that security workers at the facility were pressured to allow the theft to take place with the lives of their families threatened. Some were killed to get the point across."

"Damn, this is nightmare stuff." The NSA Director chimed in. "Just what we've feared the past decade since Gorbachev came to power. Certain elements within the former Soviet

Union are significantly less interested in openness. Less money to make."

"Correct." Seibel wanted this meeting to move quickly so that he could get approval of his plan. He needed military buy-in and funding, and he needed it yesterday. "All of this has been confirmed, as we suspected as recently as last month. Since then, we have been developing plans that involve direct involvement with the sellers and the buyers."

"Do we have any more information on each?" White House spoke this time.

"We do. Our resources have identified several key players in the Iraqi government and intelligence arm – the Mukhabarat. We are tracking their activities as we speak. Not easy, but we are on it."

"So your approach will be to watch the buyers and catch the sellers when they show up, like a drug bust?" NSA again.

"Not quite so passive. We have placed additional resources in the market to intercept the sellers and the merchandise or potentially offer a counterproposal." Seibel replied.

"To buy it from them?" White House this time.

"Something like that."

"What kind of budget are we talking about?" NSA's turn again.

The CIA Director took this cue and spoke. "We are prepared to offer an amount in excess of $100 million. This has been approved by oversight."

"Damn." White House exclaimed this time. "That much?"

"Less than 40 cents for each US citizen," CIA added.

"Point taken, if you put it that way."

Seibel interrupted. "We don't expect to actually pay the sum. But if required, we need to be prepared. Folks, I need signatures for this one."

CIA pulled a document out of his briefcase. "I have already signed." He passed it to NSA. "This has been approved by legal oversight and POTUS." The President of the United States, for those not versed in government-speak.

The White House intelligence director butted in, "I didn't know this had been signed off."

"Just about an hour ago," CIA confirmed. No time for turf wars.

After signatures were obtained, the Military Intelligence representative invited to the meeting finally spoke. "Your operation has received clearance from the Joint Chiefs. Not thrilled, but they understand the need for military cover in the theatre."

"Thank you. With that, I have what I need to proceed. I thank you for your time and hope to have better news to report the next time we meet." Seibel rose and gathered his things.

"Before you go," NSA held up a hand. "Can you enlighten us about your plans?"

Seibel had already stood. He leaned on the table with both hands and met everyone's eyes before speaking. He turned back to NSA.

"You and your predecessors have asked me for a good many years to take the necessary actions to uncover nefarious behavior directed toward our country. I appreciate the leeway you give me and my chosen team members. While I cannot give you specific details, I can confirm what you are all thinking. We will employ the most sophisticated, newest and if called for, the most deadly resources at our disposal. Yes, this will include team members you have heard of for many years with Foxy leading a select team and our young Preacher deployed into the field. We will call upon military resources including Delta Forces. The enemies we are dealing with are capable, talented and many of them have years of covert intelligence experience.

Add thousands of soldiers in the theatre and a vast desert full of uncertainty and this thing is the perfect recipe for something going wrong. It's my job to keep that from happening."

He looked each member of Account One in the eyes and nodded. "We will be successful. We have spent years preparing for this." He exited without another word.

Chapter 30

While there was no shortage of sand, wind, lung-coating fine particle dust and sun -- endless frigging sun -- in the vast Arabian Desert, there was a serious scarcity of US military Arab linguists. So it was that Corporal Priest arrived with other supplies and reinforcements in early December.

The Corporal had gone through an amazing transformation in the previous two months. He sported a sparse, shaggy beard, a deep tan and dark, almost black eyes. Seibel had taken Lance to a cosmetic specialist a month prior. He entered as a somewhat tan Anglo with dark brown hair and came out two days later deeply, darkly tanned with black hair, eyebrows, eyelashes and even pubic hair. His finger and toe nails had been dyed three shades darker. His teeth seven shades yellower and therefore darker. The contacts adhered to his pupils were basically permanent until they were removed surgically. Lance appeared to all the world to be an Arab.

The transformation involved significant weight loss as well. He had seen for himself in Jeddah and trips out to the surrounding towns how the desert sapped excess body weight from those who lived in this arid climate. He dropped from 178 to 159 pounds and felt more cheetah than lion. He retained muscle, but dropped all excess fat.

Also required from this transformation was adherence to the tenets to Islam. Lance took on this role with gusto. He had learned during his Arabic language training that words and their meanings were deeply tied to Islam. He took this cue and integrated all aspects of the religion into his daily life, through diet, exercise and prayer. He was on his knees before Allah five times each day. A darkened bruise at the top of his forehead was evidence of his devout life. He went entire days and weeks without speaking English. To fully understand the words of the Quran, they must be read and lived in Arabic.

He told anyone who asked and anyone who ordered him to shave his beard that it was necessary to form stronger relationships with the Saudis and Iraqis when allied forces eventually moved over the border.

The company's Captain, Reese, a hard ass from Cedar Rapids, Iowa, wasn't satisfied with Lance's answer and wanted the beard gone *pronto*. He wouldn't have anyone in his outfit looking like a slob. Lance was very respectful but was also very insistent on keeping the beard. If the Captain had any problems, he could call General Hardwick at Centcom who had personally signed Corporal Priest's deployment papers. This was of course a bluff, but Lance loved saying it to officers who had nothing better to do than ride a poor corporal's ass when there were much bigger issues facing US forces in this "godforsaken desert."

In his endless hours of Arabic language studies over the past couple of years, a deep understanding of the desert and Islam and the interconnections of these two was a continuing theme. Lance had come to this land as much a Muslim as anything else. Hell, he knew more about the religion than he did any other. Raised Mormon and moved to the buckle of the Bible Belt in

Texas and then Oklahoma, he had been exposed to Christian beliefs his whole life. Islam offered a different communion with God.

It wasn't hard though to see the cultural strife between US Army personnel and local Saudis. There was conditional respect for neighbors from the Arab hosts; and general, sometimes overt, disdain shown by the US visitors. "Towel heads" and "camel jockies" were common colloquialisms used by the "Ugly Americans." Lance stayed quiet and continued to soak it all in. Walking among the locals in Hafar al-Batin, a tiny village along Highway 85 where the squads, platoons, companies and battalions comprising the 24th Infantry Division had built camp, he absorbed the language, the culture of the desert. Lance mingled with locals whenever possible, making friends daily and pissing off commanding officers something fierce. He pissed off many others as he stayed in character.

A few days after arriving, he was climbing into his bunk after praying when he was approached by a small group of soldiers wanting to know just "what the hell he was doing here?" Was he American or a heebie jeebie? Lance played it cool and told the three testosterone junkies that America was a coat of many colors stitched together in one big cape that covered everyone in warmth and comfort.

They laughed and stepped in close for a little "rastlin" with the newbie. The other soldiers in the barracks sat up on their bunks to watch the show, expecting to see a little ass-kickin. Lance was still in his thawb while his new friends were down to pants and t-shirts. The closest guy swung for Lance's gut with a hard right. He was more than a little surprised when he hit nothing but solid mass in Lance's midsection. The shot stung, but Lance didn't show it. He smiled at the blow and gave each a look and a moment to let them think about this.

His Arab accent disappeared, replaced by a smooth Oklahoma drawl, "Boys, do you really wanna dance?" His smile was even smoother.

The private second-class in the middle began to wind up for a punch. Preacher exploded with three straight and sharp blows. Each started from his toes, of course.

First to the one in the middle's throat, second to the groin of the guy who'd just punched him, and lastly, a shot right below the sternum for the ringleader on the right. Three simple blows, delivered silently with blazing speed and yes, decisiveness. Delivered with such force that all three went down to knees and then on their sides. Each stunned and unable to make a sound. Lance thought his Brazilian Copoeira and Jiu Jitsu instructor at a special academy he attended for five long weeks outside Rio de Janeiro would have been pleased with the speed, brevity and effectiveness of the moves.

He bent down on his knee to ask the private who had punched him if he was okay. He told them all he hated to resort to violence but hoped they understood he didn't come all this way to take a beating from his fellow Americans. He was here to give Saddam and his buddies a good *whoopin*, not his fellow Americans.

A few other soldiers came over to help the three up. They had expected more entertainment and a different outcome. But each had been given the same message about their new bunkmate. *Don't*.

The platoon gathered around. Lance immediately fell back into his Arabian-English accent and proceeded to tell them all a few stories about the desert and camels and Bedouin women. He told how he had come to America from Jeddah as a teenager and worked as a busboy and dishwasher in restaurants in Fort Worth while finishing high school. His uncle, who owned several convenience stores had paid to bring him over to give him a shot at the American dream. Lance made up the stories there on the spot. But man, these fellas enjoyed them. His telling of his first time cruising Camp Bowie Boulevard in Fort Worth to pick up chicks on a Friday night had them all laughing hysterically. They made him retell the story again at lights-out when everyone had returned from patrol.

Corporal Priest was told he was to be at the disposal of Captain Reese 24/7. When Reese didn't need him around, he could do whatever he wanted. But when the Captain called, he better come running. Reese had been frustrated for weeks not able to adequately communicate with Arab unit commanders.

Lance accompanied Captain Reese and other leaders, including a mash-up of Majors, Colonels and the occasional General, on visits with their Arab counterparts. They came to trust Lance, or Amjad, as he called himself in Muslim company, for his translation skills. He not only capably imparted the spoken words, but their deeper meanings. For some reason, he was able to see things, details others couldn't. And because he was always reverential with Arabs, they shared more details.

During one particular excursion 25 miles north toward the Kuwait border, Lance asked that the motorcade stop so he could talk with a small band of Bedouins camped out a hundred yards off the road. Major Elles allowed it and ordered the drivers to pull over. No one liked the idea much because they would be out in the open, but damn, you could see in all directions for miles. Sentries were sent to the front and rear as Lance, Captain Reese and Major Elles, accompanied by a few badass Rangers, trekked across the sand to the Bedouins.

Lance, dressed in his flowing robe-like thawb, led the expedition and approached several men seated in an open tent having a spot of afternoon tea. "As-salaamu 'alaykum," Lance had his right hand raised and his left hand over his heart as he stopped about 15 feet from the tent.

"Peace be with you." The Arabic reply came from a haggard man with a long grey beard.

"May I speak with you on this fine day?" Lance bowed as he spoke. The Army contingent standing behind him stayed back a respectful 20 feet as Lance had asked.

"Yes. Please join us for tea." The haggard one was obviously the leader of the nomadic band of travelers numbering 30 humans a dozen or so camels and several dozen goats.

"Thank you. Can my leaders join us?" Lance motioned to Reese and Elles.

"Yes. Please." The desert man stood up and motioned the four other Bedouins sitting around the teapot to make room.

Reese stopped and whispered in Lance's ear as he passed. "Five minutes. We need to meet the Saudis in half an hour."

"Sir," Lance bowed his head as Reese walked by.

Reese and Elles greeted the group with a round of "Peace be with you," just about the only Arabic they'd learned.

Lance joined them and introduced the Captain and Major to the Bedouins. Their host responded most respectfully. "Welcome, welcome to our traveling home. I am Ramses al-Anfar. We are desert people. Goat traders and goat milk, of course." Lance translated.

"We are very pleased to meet you and gracious for your hospitality," Lance spoke to Ramses and smiled to the four other men seated beside him. "We are guests in your land. Here to protect Arabia from invasion."

"We have encountered many military men in recent days. Allah help us from war and keep us all from death."

"Yes. Allah protect us all." Lance's response elicited a chorus of "Allah Akbar's" from the tribesmen. Lance turned to Reese and Elles. They too bowed their heads in respect.

Reese and Elles accepted the pungent tea offered by the Bedouins and drank to their discontent. Lance accepted the small cup that hadn't been washed in years and drank on cue. "Wonderful, wonderful," he said and smiled to all. They smiled in satisfaction.

"We have just a few minutes before we must depart, but wanted to know if you can share any knowledge with us," Lance kept the smile on.

"What knowledge can we impart?" Ramses raised his hands to signify his humble place in this world.

"You know the desert better than any. What can you tell us of the lands to the north? Who will we meet if we leave the road and travel across the sands?" Lance pointed northwest.

"Only Bedouins like us." Ramses followed Lance's gesture northwest. "Nomads, wonderers. People of the sand."

"Anyone else traveling through recently?"

"Always strangers, but yes, there were our brothers from the north, from the old city just the other day." Ramses added.

"The old city?"

"Baghdad."

Lance kept the smile. "All the way down from Baghdad? Why would they be out in the desert so far from home?"

"They told us they were searching for friends. Friends lost in the sand." Ramses let his eyebrows raise slightly with this last part.

"Friends? So far away from home? That seems strange. They must have been very lost. Allah protect them." Lance replied with some questioning in his voice.

"Their story was not convincing, but their search was a serious matter." The Bedouin nodded his head.

Lance let the conspiratorial notion of the Arab's statement pervade his own response. "So they were searchers, but maybe they sought more than knowledge of their friends. Maybe they sought knowledge, like us?"

"Perhaps." Ramses again raised his hands in submission, a humble man of Allah.

"Perhaps they were seeking information about anyone you had encountered?" Lance raised his eyebrows now.

"Everyone seeks knowledge." At this Lance smiled and laughed. He turned to Reese and Elles.

"Our friends here came across a scout patrol the other day."

"How far, where?" Reese looked from Lance to Ramses.

Lance turned back to Ramses. "How many days ago did you meet these wanderers? And can you tell us how many were in there party?"

"Two days ago," Ramses was glad to provide helpful information to his new friend. "There were six."

"How did they travel?"

"Land Rovers in excellent condition."

"Two?"

"Yes. Very nice. Leather interiors." Ramses said. Lance laughed at this level of description.

"I prefer leather as well." He bowed to his host and rose. He turned again to Reese and Elles. "We need satellite imagery and maybe a flyover looking for two Land Rovers." He turned back to Ramses. "Thank you again for your hospitality. We must be going. Can we offer you anything in return?"

"Have you any chocolate? The children are never happier than when they have a piece of chocolate."

"Of course." Lance turned back to a specialist 20 feet away. "Chocolate bars my man. How many do you have in that backpack?"

"How many do you need?"

"Pass out a handful to these fine men if you will." Lance swept his hand quite dramatically and the corporal reached into the backpack and pulled out several thick chocolate bars and walked up to the tent. Bedouin children playing a few yards away saw the bars and started laughing and screaming. The men in the tent gratefully accepted the bars.

"Thank you again Ramses al-Anfar." Lance bowed to his host. "Your hospitality is most gracious."

"Anytime my friend. Peace be with you, although I think peace will be hard to find soon."

"I hope peace can be among us all." Lance waved for Reese and Elles to step away. They bowed accordingly, shook hands with their hosts and walked ahead.

As he walked, Major Elles spoke straight ahead, "So let me get this straight corporal. You just learned about an Iraqi advance scout patrol from that little exchange?"

"Yes sir. Allah be praised." Lance walked behind his commanders.

"So intelligence that usually takes weeks to dig up, you just gathered in about five minutes."

"Yes sir."

"Captain Reese do you think that maybe there's more to Corporal Priest than meets the eye?" The Major asked.

"Sir, my guess is intelligence of the central variety is probably a good reason we have Preacher with us in this big ol desert." The Captain replied.

"I was thinking just that." Elles replied.

"I got the general idea when I asked someone up the ladder about his raggedy ass and was told in no uncertain terms that Corporal Priest is A-Okay. A real asset to our military and our nation." Reese said all this with a smile.

"This young fellow is likely a TLA." Elles added.

"Agreed, sir." Reese smiled at Lance.

Lance couldn't let that just hang there. They had just about reached the convoy back on the road. "Major Elles, sir. A TLA?"

"That's right corporal. TLA – three letter acronym."

"Oh, like GLF." Lance smiled.

Elles turned to him just before opening the door on his jeep. "GLF?"

"Good looking fella, sir." Lance just grinned.

"Yah, something like that. What was that you called him Captain?" Elles asked Reese.

"Preacher."

"Preacher? Don't think that fits, but I guess you could probably charm a confession out of a snake or maybe even the last dollar out of a sinner." Major Elles got in his jeep and grabbed the radio. He called in satellite imaging services for the area and asked for any sightings of two Land Rovers over the last few days.

Turned out the two vehicles were just six miles away in the blowing desert northwest of Highway 50. The next morning a special ops squad choppered in on the Iraqi scout patrol, killed three and returned with three helpful men willing to trade their secrets for their lives. Excellent intelligence by any standards. All for the price of some chocolate on the side of the road.

Chapter 31

Gregor Ivanovich Smelinski didn't like losing control. And he didn't much care for his long-cultivated and developed agent resources turning on him and the Komitet Gosudarstvennoi Bezopasnosti – The Committee of State Security. The KGB, for the rest of us.

As Director of Intrasecurity, Smelinski was charged with keeping the heads of regional KGB units in line. There were only three men above him at the KGB and no one who knew more about the individual agents and their operations. Not many citizens of the Soviet Union had traveled more than he over the last 33 years. After a requisite stint in the Soviet Army, he had worked his way up the ranks of the KGB from Prague to Paris to London to a brief stay in the United States before returning in 1980 to assume his current role as resident tough guy and strategic knuckle breaker.

Gregor the Terrible had kept order among the KGB ranks with an iron fist, even as the Union broke apart at the end of the 80s. The leaders of the organization had come to rely on him to bring order to chaos, take out the trash and remove regional department heads summarily, without hesitation. Many had disappeared -- without warning. His reign over KGB resources was as ruthless as his exchanges with CIA, MI6 and other western intelligence agencies. Smelinski was old school, but his knowledge of current events across the entire union was unsurpassed. It was this fact and reputation that tore at him most when agents went rogue, AWOL. And rogue agents were becoming the norm. Perestroika brought with it the freedom for KGB agents to consider new ventures, to become entrepreneurs.

And too many knew how and where to obtain valuable materials much sought after in desperate and troubled places around the world. AK-47s were in demand throughout Africa. Opium is always in demand in Europe. And nuclear warheads, or at least, nuclear materials capable of being weaponized, were the ultimate prize for an array of terrorist organizations and third-world governments.

It was this last element that necessitated the call Smelinski had just made from a phone booth outside a quaint little restaurant in Kiev. At the other end of the line had been an individual the KGB legend had battled for decades. He'd beaten him on a few occasions, lost to him many times, but had never been successful in killing this particular nemesis. They'd come face-to-face a few times and even fired on each other once in Sierra Leone, but neither had been able to eliminate the other. Respect between them was mutual. As was hatred.

Times had indeed changed, Smelinski thought to himself as he rubbed the graying stubble on his chin. Seibel sounded sincere just now in his appreciation of the information the KGB master shared. The American didn't question his Russian counterpart's motives for the call. He even seemed to be a few steps ahead of the storyline he'd just been told -- always the way it is with Seibel. No one worked harder to obtain usable information. No one cultivated more resources in more places.

Smelinski had always been envious of this aspect of their relationship. Always a step behind. But this problem needed to be shared; needed to be acted upon by both sides. Rogue KGB agents had finally done what all had forever feared. Nuclear materials had been stolen. Communications had been uncovered between KGB players and elements within the governments of several Middle East and South Asian nations. Seibel knew it was Iraq.

"This is perhaps the single most dangerous situation we have ever faced," Smelinski spoke bluntly into the phone, his breath fogging before him in the tiny phone booth. "I cannot overemphasize the severity of this matter."

"You have confirmed all of this in the field?" Seibel already knew the answer, but wanted to get verbal confirmation from the long tenured enemy.

Smelinski replied, "Confirmed. Materials have been removed. Photographic confirmation relayed directly to my hands. And since, communications have been traced. Players are being identified."

"Do you have leads on these players?" Seibel already had a pretty good idea.

"We do. They are former employees who have left of their own accord. Left without notice. No forwarding address. No severance."

Seibel's words to Account One in previous months were being confirmed now. He knew Smelinski better than most in the KGB. This call was no subterfuge. This was a cry for help from someone no longer able to keep a deadly secret. KGB agents had left the farm and taken their game to a new level.

"Next steps?" Seibel cut to the chase.

"You have resources in the desert?" Smelinski asked.

"Of course."

"January 15 is only three weeks away. Action prior to the deadline may be required." The United Nation's deadline for Saddam's Iraqi forces to leave Kuwait was fast approaching and everyone knew he wouldn't evacuate voluntarily.

"We read the newspapers over here as well," Seibel replied sarcastically. "We know about the deadline and fully expect to be in the field at the time, as I'm sure will you." Seibel felt the conversation had served its purpose and knew Smelinski had told all he had to tell on this secure line. "I appreciate the call Andre. Talk to you soon."

Smelinski smiled to himself walking away from the phone booth. Andre was the cover he'd used in Brussels in 1968. Seemed like a lot more than 22 years ago now. He had turned a Nepalese representative much to the chagrin of Seibel and others who thought they had the opportunity to work the back channel into China. Instead, Smelinski saw to it that the tepid relations with their fellow communists in China were protected on their Himalayan flank. Such is the spy game. One side wins, the other loses. Those caught in the middle always pay.

With the call to Seibel complete, Smelinski figured his next steps would be tracking his former agents. He had enlisted the CIA as a last resort, but was not surprised to learn from the tenor of Seibel's voice that he knew quite a bit already. Secrets were hard to keep, especially with war on the horizon.

He'd fully expected rogue activity from Korovin and Kusnetsov. He'd practically begged them to work outside the system as they built up their operations in Ukraine. Their leverage was a deep understanding of their country and culture, it's roots beneath the Soviet topsoil. They had been remarkably successful in penetrating networks, from criminal gangs to local Army stations. And because their presence was so pervasive, they were instrumental in Smelinski's efforts to keep control of all things KGB within Ukraine. That they were now entrepreneurs working freelance in a new Eastern Bloc free market economy was not unforeseeable. Just unfortunate timing.

They could have remained on KGB payroll and still worked their side businesses. But Smelinski had sensed they were in league with others. Others looking to capitalize on glasnost and perestroika and the end of centralized government. The age of capitalism was coming and K&K were merely embracing the dawning of this new day. Their choice to enter the nuclear arms sales business was unfortunate as well. They could have reaped the whirlwind for years in any number of developing black market industries affiliated with arms sales.

But the theft and marketing of nuclear weapons was simply going too far. K&K were in touch with certain elements within the Iraqi government. Negotiations were underway and the fate of a tiny invaded nation lay at their hands. Saddam needed oil to sell and to barter for necessities. And he needed the hundreds of millions and billions of dollars the oil below Kuwait could generate to complete the acquisition of his Mother of All Weapons. He was ready to trade oil money for nuclear supremacy. K&K were just the renegade types to provide him his needed tools, for the right price.

Their bravado had signed their own death warrants. They would never live to spend any of the hundreds of millions they hoped to gain. And whoever among the nascent but growing class of oligarchs was supporting them and investing in their venture would also crash and burn. Gregor the Terrible would see to that. Heck, he might just kill them himself.

"So much greed." Smelinski muttered to himself. "Such a waste of talent."

Containing Korovin and Kusnetsov would not be easy. He planned to turn over their key attributes to Seibel and let the

American and his resources be bloodied in combat with K&K. He'd relay all pertinent information to Seibel within days through a reliable channel in London.

Smelinski did have another card to play. Marta, like K&K, had operations in Iraq. She had "eyes" on K&K's operations that Smelinski did not even know about. As the deal got close, Marta would simply one-up their ruthlessness with cunning and skill the two older agents did not possess. *Hopefully.*

Smelinski shook his head as he continued walking through the chilly Ukrainian night. He loved Kiev pretty much any season, but especially during winter. It was warmer and much more alive than Moscow. He wasn't thinking of Kiev or winter or spitting snow. He was thinking of nuclear explosions in Tel-Aviv or Riyadh and the ensuing destruction, war and repercussions that would follow. Like Seibel, he had worked to build up and protect his country for decades. Nuclear weapons were the deterrent to offensive behavior by either side. Now they were in play like never before. Deterrent could soon be exchanged for nightmare if his former agents were successful in consummating their deal with the Butcher of Baghdad.

Chapter 32

January 13, 1991 started with a cold morning sun rising over an endless desert. All preparations had been made. Elite teams of the British Special Air Service were deployed into Southern Iraq three days earlier. Their reconnaissance and reports back from the field detailed position and placement of Iraq forces. The allied air campaign was set to begin in two days. The Iraqi military had become very adept at hiding their forces, especially tanks and Scud missile launchers, from satellite and aerial surveillance. Eyes on the ground were invaluable.

The British reports were of great interest to Seibel and Fuchs as they put the teams of Delta Force commandos through the plan one last time. Seibel had made the decision to keep Lance under full cover as a translator and avoided any public contact. Lance was embedded in one of three Delta Force teams being inserted into Iraq. The teams were tasked with traveling under cover of night through the eastern deserts of Iraq to the outskirts of Baghdad. They were to arrive at a location highly suspected to be the transaction zone for nuclear materials smuggled into the country by Korovin and Kusnetsov.

The intelligence utilized to determine this time and location had been incredibly difficult to obtain. It resulted from combined espionage resources working both sides of the quickly deteriorating "Iron Curtain." Seibel and Smelinski had spoken twice more, which was more than they'd conversed in the previous two decades.

K&K had been ultra-secretive in their efforts to contact, negotiate and deliver nuclear arms to a now fully rogue Iraqi government. But their secrets were discovered along the way.

Marta and her network had remained much more illusive. Tracking their activity and progress had been significantly more difficult. Gregor the Terrible shared a theory with Seibel that Marta was working at an entirely different level than Korovin and Kusnetsov and even monitoring their progress from inside.

He believed that Marta's nascent operation was playing all sides against each other and didn't intend to deliver anything to anyone. Instead, any funds garnered from her operation would be funneled back into a ghost government of oligarchs springing up in Russia. Seibel considered it an interesting theory.

Meanwhile, back at the ranch in the cold Saudi Arabian desert outside Hafar al Batin, Seibel and his team had set up operations a quarter of a mile from the 24th Infantry headquarters. His team, headed by Fuchs and joined by the Jordanians, worked closely with military intelligence.

The Delta Force teams had been training for several weeks now, including a week at Harvey Point, where Seibel could issue orders directly. Colonel Franklin, the commander on scene for Delta, had questioned Seibel and his methods within minutes of meeting him at the Point. The two men stepped aside for a brief conversation.

Not surprisingly, Franklin did not question Seibel again. Papa had a way of convincing individuals that his plans and approach were the most likely to succeed. Colonel Franklin stood across a table from Seibel as they poured over a map lying before them and the three captains who were to lead the Delta teams the next day.

"Newest data coming in from the field, thanks to our British friends, is just as we expected. Most Iraqi resources are either in place or being moved to Kuwait or the northern Iraq theatre. Baghdad is being emptied of its military elements," Seibel swirled his finger around the ancient city at the center of the map as he spoke. "Every day they move more troops out. They continue to reinforce this area directly north of our position. Troop and transport movements are being captured by aerial and satellite reconnaissance."

"As we have discussed at length, we will circumvent these forces by entering Iraq from further to the west," Colonel Franklin spoke and moved his finger from Hafar to the west and up through the deserts of Saudi Arabia into southern Iraq. "Your entry point will be here, west of Nisab." The small desert outpost along the Saudi/Iraq border was little more than a gathering of small huts surrounded by hundreds of miles of barren desert.

Franklin added, "No changes there. Black Hawks will transport your teams to the drop zone outside Mahmudiyah. The choppers will remain there until you signal them for extraction."

Captain Alan Doster, commander for the second Delta Team leaned in. "So no changes for entry. The route from Mahmudiyah is still this surface road? No changes there?" He traced his finger along a line south and east of central Baghdad.

Colonel Franklin responded. "Correct. That corridor is unprotected, no checkpoints detected. And those that spring up will be low-level. Still provides ideal access to the transaction location without having to utilize major thoroughfares or highways except for the one bridge across the river."

The group of a dozen men stood around a table and continued the planning for another 45 minutes. To the side stood a silent but observant shaggy faced Corporal Priest, a translator. He had been briefed, debriefed and over-briefed in secret by Seibel and Fuchs late into the evenings. Lance had memorized every detail of every report Seibel and team could obtain on K&K, the Marta Squad, as he had come to call them, and the players on the Iraqi side. He'd also read up on deactivating nuclear warheads. *Boring stuff.*

During the previous month and a half, he had continued to assimilate to the desert environment and culture with daily tanning, dying his hair and beard jet black again. His voice projected the dryness, the utter dust-filled dryness that pervades the kingdom. He drank little water, never washed his hands and dropped even more weight he had carried into the desert from western civilization. He looked to anyone who gave him a moment's attention to be a local – a creature of the desert.

He kept up his fitness routine by running barefoot up and down desert hills each morning before sunrise. He was in seriously deadly shape.

His transition was nothing short of remarkable. He was an Arab. He had taken to changing into a thawb and keffiyeh and walking around amongst the locals in Hafar any chance he got. He had spent more time with several traveling Bedouin families of peddlers to improve his acting skills. Try as he might, he couldn't take on their hardscrabble persona in a convincing manner. Their total independence from any other aspect of Arab life made them a challenge to any actor, let alone a 24-year-old Oklahoman. Still, he worked at it every day.

Fooling Americans and westerners was no problem. Lance had been subjected to rude and crude treatment at the hands of American soldiers and been berated for being in a secure area by a French lieutenant who went as far as pulling his sidearm to motivate an apologetic Lance to leave the area immediately.

Captain Reese had gotten used to Lance's need to assimilate and enjoyed being in on the ruse. He had come to rely on Lance and his translation skills daily. The main character Lance had developed was Ismail, the son of a fisherman in Jeddah who wanted to help his country fight off the demon and unholy Saddam. He had become an expert in the types of fish, ideal locales and preeminent weeks of each season to bring in the best catch from the Red Sea. Reese would at times have to interrupt Lance and his tales of fishing along the coast to bring the conversation back to the matter at hand. Lance would bow and praise Allah for his bountiful seas. Invariably, everyone sitting around them would also bow and thank Allah as well.

"The sea is a desert Allah has given us with the bounty below, just like the desert sands," Ismail would add, also to general agreement from those around him. Reese would smile and try to keep from laughing.

If anyone ever took it upon themselves to question Ismail's seemingly western features beneath his tanned skin, Lance would tell them the story of his grandfather, also named Ismail. He had traveled the world as a sailor and met the love of his life, a Spanish beauty in Barcelona, and brought her back to Jeddah. In telling this tale, he invariably brought in Muslim pride at conquering a good portion of the Spanish Iberian Peninsula 1,500 years ago. The Moors were Muslim Northern Africans who left their marks on European culture in the forms of architecture, government and, of course, dark skin and coal black hair.

It was as Ismail that Lance stood at the back of the room as the final elements of the plan were nailed down by Seibel, Colonel Franklin and Delta Captains Parkhurst, Doster and Hubbard. Lance had been assigned to Doster's squad to ride shotgun alongside Tarwanah who would drive one of the three trucks from Mahmudiyah northeast into southern Baghdad. As the group broke, Doster turned to Lance and smiled.

"You got all that Corporal Ismail?"

"God willing, we will be successful," he was in character more than not most days.

"I get the feeling you are my lucky charm on this one," Doster looked back at the other captains. "Don't know why I got you, but Seibel seems to think you'll be able to handle yourself and the product when it is secured. You think so?"

Lance responded by singing a newly classic song and strumming his air guitar. By the time he was done with the song, Doster and everyone else in the room was singing alone. They continued singing and humming the song as they left.

"Always infecting others." Seibel smiled a telling grin.

"Music is my life," and then just as quickly back in character, "Allah gives us music to allow us to focus on his majesty, his word."

"Ah yes." Seibel nodded.

"Allah be praised," Ismail answered.

Seibel kept the smile, but stepped in close to Lance and whispered into his ear. "This one is turning into a goddamn crapshoot and quick. Intel on the items in transit has been spotty the last two days since the truck passed over the border from Iran."

"I thought you had 24/7 surveillance, satellite and fixed wing?" Lance asked.

"I thought so as well, but a couple of generals have seen fit to pull my recon for other intel, especially with go-ahead day after tomorrow."

"So have we lost contact with the vehicle?" Lance asked.

"Only for short periods, a little more than an hour a few times. Confidence is high that nothing has changed and the package is still on board. Point and follow vehicles have not changed. Satellite imagery has confirmed Korovin in the follow vehicle. He got out to take a piss yesterday morning and the bird got a perfect shot."

"Of his pecker?"

"No," Seibel laughed. "His bald head."

"Oh you mean this," and Lance proceeded to grab his privates, relax his shoulders and raise his head, releasing a quiet groan of satisfaction felt during urination.

"Exactly, except he is left-handed." Seibel corrected.

"I knew there was something else about that guy I didn't like. He's a brutal killer, an extortionist, but by God, he's wrong-handed as well. I'm going to enjoy killing him."

Seibel stepped back to ditto Lance's comment, "Allah be praised."

Chapter 33

The CIA and US Military Intelligence were not the only ones with eyes on the beat-up transport truck currently parked beside a roadside café in Al-Kut, Iraq. As both the US and Russian government resources scrambled to track the vehicle from its origins in the Ukraine through Azerbaijan and Iran, a collection of individuals witnessed a good many of the miles driven by the truck. They watched from another vehicle, from a plane overhead or even better, from a seat in a vehicle accompanying the convoy. Marta Sidorova had her people positioned along the route and, of course, within the K&K operation.

She, perhaps more than most from the motherland, was positioned to capitalize on this situation. Unlike many of her former counterparts in the KGB, she was not weighed down by the baggage of years of service and a known network of associates, resources and possible leaks. Best of all, if one can look at it that way, she had no family. No husband, no children. Marta was free to roam, to network, to infiltrate and build connections. She put it another way when telling an acquaintance once. She said she had no anchor, nothing keeping her in place, keeping her from moving on a whim. The KGB

had been her only family. Smelinski her father figure. *How
messed up is that?* She asked herself on more than one occasion.

Her relative anonymity had been her secret weapon as she
built a loose affiliation of resources before she dropped off the
grid in 1987. Because she was still a new and mostly unknown
player in the game, very few of those she worked with knew her
operatives, her methods and most of all, her means.

Marta sat motionless in a nondescript room in a nondescript
portion of southern Baghdad the morning of January 15, 1991 –
D-Day for Saddam Hussein. She sat so still because the
headphones on her ears were lousy. She kept hearing a buzz
when she wanted to hear the conversations taking place between
Iraqi soldiers and their commanders in the field. She was most
interested in their status reports on troop movement to and
through Al-Kut. The precious cargo convoy had been halted on
the road between the small town and Baghdad 80 miles to the
northwest. The driver and co-passenger in the cargo truck had
special papers giving them clearance to travel to Baghdad, but
security was heightened with the UN deadline at midnight.

The Iraqi secret security personnel coordinating the
transaction were apparently not willing to travel outside the
capital city because of leaks at every level. If the outside world
needed an update on just how fragmented Saddam's
government had become, the Iraqi Intelligence Service, or
Mukhabarat, was the only place they need look. It was the Wild
West. Roving teams of bandits working under the auspices of
"clearance from Saddam himself" wreaked havoc throughout
the country.

Details were excruciatingly sparse, but as best Marta could
piece it all together, those within the Mukhabarat who had
brokered the deal with K&K for the Soviet warheads had

secured and delivered $20 million in funds with promises of $180 million more coming after delivery.

Her plan was to swoop in at the last moment before delivery and elevate the deal to the highest levels on all sides to expand the $200 million to over a $1 billion. Smelinski would be pissed. Her plan was as fluid as it was daring and crazy. Changes at this point were troubling.

"Nyet, nyet," she whispered in her native tongue as she listened in on an Iraqi commander reporting that all traffic on all roads was to be inspected. She needed that truck in Baghdad tonight, before the UN deadline expired and the Americans started clogging up the sky with their bombers. Marta turned to Josef, her number three, sitting pensively across the room. "If that truck is not moving within the hour, we will need to implement the backup as planned."

"Certainly." Josef answered with one word, Marta's preferred form of response. The backup plan, should it need to be implemented, required Josef to travel out to meet the cargo truck with the packages on board and work with the two embedded operatives in the convoy to kill everyone else. Simple.

Marta took the headphones off and picked up a cigarette, her only weakness. She needed to think through the next few hours. K&K were a concern, but not as much as US intelligence, which was certainly in on at least the basics of the nuclear weapons sale to Iraq. If they weren't, then she would be disappointed, because their involvement was a must to expedite the securitization of hundreds of millions in funds within a day or two.

Marta closed her eyes and worked through a couple of elements of her serpentine and labyrinthine plan. She had it all between her ears. Nothing written down so nothing could be passed to others who might foil her plot. She had kept her team to eight this time with a newly rich entrepreneur friend in Russia at an arm's length funding it all. He would be the key afterward with his ability to "wash" hundreds of millions of dollars and bring it into Russia in a number of unaudited methods.

On her direct team there were only Josef, a former Turkish secret policeman, and Nir. These were the only two she had worked with for more than a couple of years and the only two she trusted with details that brought together more than 50% of her plan.

Each of them had learned in working with Marta that she rewarded them well for their service, just as long as no questions were asked. Each was wealthy beyond either of their wildest dreams because of her. Yet each wanted to continue working with her because she offered them something no one else could -- the opportunity to change the world.

Their allegiance was unwavering and their commitment proven by multiple murders on her behalf. Nir beheaded a mobster in Minsk at her request and served his head to others at a backroom dinner party to get a point across. Josef, an excellent marksman, had proven his worth to Marta with four kills from over 500 yards each. Again, all four murders proving a point to her adversaries. Now, it was Marta and her team against the world. She liked those odds.

"I need to move a little. Contact Nir to let him know we are coming his way to go over logistics again," she rose from her seated concentration. "He will undoubtedly have new information for us from the scene." She had been holed up in the room for two days and needed to get out for a bit.

Marta gathered her things and put on her hijab or headscarf to conceal her western looks. She had grown accustomed to wearing the hijab or sometimes a niqab, a full face-covering veil, in the Middle East and other Muslim countries.

She found it liberating and appreciated what she had heard from Muslim women. Wearing a veil allowed them to be free in a controlled society. She thought on more than one occasion that wearing full face-covering scarves or even a burqa in the West would make the spy business a whole different game. She could have easily increased her kill count well beyond the 30 or so people she had executed if she could have gone about her business covered by a hijab, or better yet, a burqa.

Chapter 34

Just as Marta and Josef left the hotel room, three US Army Delta Force teams with a sprinkling of CIA Special Activities Division operatives pulled out of Mahmudiyah 30 miles south of Baghdad. Loaded in three cargo trucks, humorously labeled by Seibel as Mushroom, Pepperoni and Sausage, their route would skirt the southern reaches of Baghdad until they crossed the Tigris River just three miles from the transaction spot. The trip so far had been without event, which made it a rousing success.

The teams' helicopter flights from Hafar northwest to Al Jumaymah and then across the Iraq desert in the black of night to the west of Karbala and to the north side of Mahmudiyah had gone without apparent detection. No shots had been fired on their birds. They landed safely in a clearing 200 yards from a warehouse where the three trucks sat parked. The cover of night and their low altitudes had secured their entry. The two helicopters were refueled and covered by huge drop cloths that made them virtually undetectable from the air.

The Delta Force commandos were veterans all. Each had seen action in theatres from Grenada to Panama to Libya.

Before being diverted to this mission, they had been training for a recon strike mission along the coast just south of Kuwait City.

Situated now in the cargo holds of the trucks, they each wore nondescript clothing that would fit in well in Baghdad or the Bronx. Bulletproof vests added a little weight. Some had beards, hair had been died black, skin darkened. All could pass for locals for a brief period if necessary. One thing they all possessed was a look of determination; a single-mindedness for the mission ahead of them. They had trained non-stop for three weeks for this Baghdad smash and dash, beginning the day after Seibel had received the call from Smelinski. He knew with no time to plan an extensive mission, he would need his Delta Force friends. A call to the general in command of Special Forces was all that was required to reorient the three teams for his mission.

In stark contrast to the serious and stern looks shared by the Deltas riding in the rear compartment of his truck, Lance sat smiling beside Tarwanah in the bouncy cab. Jamaani drove the truck 200 yards behind them on the dirt road. The lead truck a mile ahead was being piloted by Abdullah, a Seibel-secured resource who had worked in Iraq for so long it was his home more than the small village outside of Cairo he knew as a boy.

He wasn't in the convoy, but Lance could feel Fuchs' presence. He knew that Seibel would not allow the operation to fail. Putting everything in Lance's young but capable hands was a stretch. Tarwanah and Jamaani could only be called upon to do so much. He expected the satellite phone in his pocket to ring at some point with Fuchs on the other end, serving a role and purpose only he and Seibel knew about.

"Fourteen minutes ahead of schedule." Tarwanah looked from his watch to Lance and smiled. "Always good to be a little ahead so that there is room to massage the timeline, right?"

"I'm trusting you on that aspect," Lance responded still looking out the window at the surprisingly lush landscape passing by as they traveled the dirt road.

"Your trust will not be misplaced."

Lance turned to his Jordanian counterpart. "So this is number two for us. How many Seibel missions does this make for you?"

Tarwanah laughed at the question. "I can't recall the exact figure, I'm sure it exceeds two dozen, maybe three. But remember, some of them lasted months. Why do you ask?"

"No reason really. Just like to know the motivation for my character."

"This motivation comes from inside, does it not?" The Jordanian smiled again at his much younger mission mate. "Motivation is not hard to find for this mission."

"Not this mission. I'm thinking in more general terms. Why we're doing what we're doing." Lance turned back to the window.

"Good and evil. That simple." Tarwanah was a man of few words. "We are in a battle every day. We choose sides and do what we must." The Jordanian looked over at Lance with a quizzical look. "What are you thinking?"

"I know the good and evil stuff. I understand making that choice, I just wonder where it all fits sometimes."

Tarwanah added, "You must concentrate on the mission. That gives you the answers. Everything else has no importance until the mission is completed. And then of course, there is the next mission."

Lance turned from the window and smiled at Tarwanah. "Don't worry about me brother. Failure is not an option." He turned back to the window. "I just like to let my mind wander when I'm riding in a car and can look out the window and see the world here and now. I wonder about it all."

"I understand. Don't like your timing particularly well, but I understand." Tarwanah's voice was soothing.

Lance leaned his head against the window glass and closed his eyes. He started humming and then singing. The song his brain chose for the occasion was both melodic and touching. It was one he had come to truly love in the two years since he first heard it driving from San Angelo to San Antonio to catch a flight. It told the tale of a young woman trapped by society, by her loyalty to others who let her down at every turn.

"This is nice," Tarwanah responded. "It is a love song, yes?"

"No. It's about loss, poverty, unrealized dreams."

"It is a fast car, no?" The Jordanian asked.

Lance smiled. "The car is just a vehicle, it isn't the way out she thought it was. Just a car."

They rode in silence for several minutes. They passed farms, groves of trees, canals bringing water's lifeblood from the Tigris River into the fields to grow the plants that feed the people of the land of Eden.

"So the car in the song is fast, but it isn't fast enough to escape reality?" Tarwanah asked.

Lance opened his eyes and laughed. He reached over and smacked Tarwanah on the shoulder. "Exactly, my man. You nailed it." He said this in Arabic. "He can leave or he can stay and face the world as it is. Deal with responsibility or move on down the line."

"Yes, he's got to make a decision. Now here is my problem with America." And Tarwanah looked stern for the moment.

"How's that?"

"Americans always dream of a better life, more money, more things. They think they can get it all just by changing, by leaving one place, one home for another."

"Go on…" Lance nodded.

"He thinks because he has a car he can get a better life and she thinks that because he has this car he can give her a better life. Nowhere do they talk about work, struggle, commitment, dedication."

Lance's turn. "Ah, now here is the problem I have with Arabs. They jump to conclusions without all the facts. They assume that because some Americans have nice things that everyone wants nothing more than a fast car, nice house or worst of all, to be famous. You didn't hear the rest of the song."

"I assume it will be the usual American story of boy meets girl, boy loses girl, boy wins girls back. Everyone lives happily ever after. The end."

Lance smiled and laughed at this. "You realize, you've said more to me in the last few minutes than you've said in the weeks we've been together before."

"This is what I do when I am riding in a car and have time to think." Tarwanah smiled.

"Very good, that I understand." Lanced turned back to the window and the groves of trees. "Let me sing the rest of the song for you."

"Please."

Lance closed his eyes and tapped his hands on his thighs to get the rhythm back. He sang the whole song from beginning to end. It is a great song.

Tarwanah took it in for a few moments. "Now that changes everything. I see now it is about working, caring for others, dreaming of a better life but realizing the better life cannot be found with the one you love. It is a song of loss. Very sad."

"Yes. But what is really sad is the number of people who live life just like that. Never getting out, never giving your children a better life. Letting the cycle perpetuate itself."

"Man, you're getting me down." Tarwanah said this in English with a very good New York American accent. Lance cracked up.

"That's just life my man. Can't put all your hopes in a fast car." He turned to Tarwanah. "Or all your fears in one bomb."

"How about three bombs?" Tarwanah asked.

"Now that's scary. Three bombs in the wrong hands is a reality I don't like." They let that be it for a while. Ten minutes later they were on a stretch of highway and across the bridge into southeast Baghdad. Still about 15 minutes ahead of schedule.

They had traveled in radio silence for the duration as planned. As they crossed into the city, Lance took out the small radio in his pant pocket under his thawb. In Arabic he relayed instructions to all three vehicles. "Honey agenda. No sales." The short staccato words confirmed no changes in plans. Since the satellite phone in his other pocket had not rung, Lance had to assume no changes in plan had been proffered by Seibel.

Tarwanah hummed and sang the song from a few minutes ago. Lance liked how it sounded when sung with a pleasant Jordanian accent.

He closed his eyes as they crossed the Tigris River and exited the highway. As the vehicle crossed under a highway overpass and Tarwanah negotiated the path that would bring them to the transaction spot, Lance kept his eyes closed and saw the three moving vehicles on a satellite map below from 5,000 feet. He had memorized Baghdad roadways and made a couple of suggestions to Seibel on routes.

He went ahead of the trucks on his mind map to the location they were heading toward. The warehouse district where the meeting was to take place was ideal. Few people, lighter traffic and multiple entrance and egress options. Eyes closed, he went from map to timeline to plan of attack to nuclear warhead disarming.

He opened his eyes and looked at his watch. The mission was still ahead of schedule and no news over the satellite phone meant the transport truck carrying the nukes traveling up Highway 6 was moving on schedule. He didn't like it. Too easy, too clean. There had to be something Seibel had missed.

"You feeling good about this?" He turned to Tarwanah.

"Not at all. Haven't liked this one from day one. Iraqis, Russians, KGB, Mukhabarat, Delta Forces, nuclear weapons. Too many moving pieces." Tarwanah replied.

"You trust Seibel though." Lance asked.

"No one is better." He smiled again as he kept his eyes on the road. "I fully expect you to be as good one day. But that is many years and many missions away."

"You trust me?"

Tarwanah smiled. "I am here aren't I? I could have taken any of the other vehicles, but I know where you are will be the most likely opportunity for action and therefore the opportunity to try to control an uncontrollable situation."

The satellite phone rang. Lance clicked it on and put it to his ear. The message was brief.

"Time and time again. Affirm."

He heard the words and became a different person.

A switch flipped; a door opened. His melancholy vanished. His eyes lazy and languid from a two-hour drive on bumpy dirt roads tightened and squinted.

He brought the radio to his mouth and spoke in flawless Arabic. "The morning calls us to prayer in the light of day. The smoke spirals." The spotters and team leads in the other two trucks heard the words and sat up, tightened belts, secured firearms in holsters and said a prayer if inclined. They were here to do a job. A job, which likely entailed killing others, many others. And maybe saving the world along the way.

Lance surveyed the warehouses up and down the street in Baghdad's Al Wahdah district. The transaction was to take place three hours from now less than a half mile from their current location. Lance had asked Seibel just once a little more than three weeks ago why they couldn't just take the merchandise out on the highway in the middle of nowhere. Swoop in, take out all players, snag the warheads and hightail it back over the border. Seibel's answer was direct and to the point, much more so than normal.

"We need a large body count on this one. Need to eliminate players on all three sides in a most deliberate manner. No loose ends. We need to send a message." Seibel was usually very eloquent, more literate in his delivery. Lance could tell that this one was important. This one was for the ages. And Lance liked being a part of that.

Still, he would have preferred to take the convoy out on the desert highway instead of in a warehouse district where there were corners, darkened windows and shadows lurking in doorways. Not to mention a bunch of Iraqi soldiers around. He rubbed his hands down his thighs and instinctively brought his hands to the handles of the guns under his thawb. He would kill someone, maybe several someones.

He searched himself for a moment and found no emotions. No fear, no anger. He'd gotten into this position and, like many things in his life, he didn't find it all that hard. He thought to himself as he absently squeezed the grip of a gun in his right hand -- *is today the day?* He might be one of those among Seibel's body count on this mission. Again, he didn't feel any emotional tug at that thought either. He turned to Tarwanah who had been watching him out of the corner of his eye.

"What?"

"What do you mean what?" The Jordanian hunched his shoulders.

"You're sitting there eyeing me. I see your wheels spinning. You're thinking something."

Tarwanah smiled. "I'm always thinking something. Maybe I'm wondering what you are thinking."

"I was just thinking of another song, like usual." Lance lied, as always.

"Which song, let's hear it."

Lance just smiled. "That's all right, I'll keep this one to myself." He turned back to the window and thought for a moment about exactly which song he would like to hear one last time before he died. He was only 24, but music had been his constant companion. He thought of being a child and riding in the tiny storage area behind the back seat of his mother's VW Bug. A song by Elton John was his favorite then.

A little later on, a classic by Mannford Mann's Earth Band was his theme song. His teenage years were dominated by U2. That was it. No question, no more debate. U2 was it. That is the band he'd like to be listening to when the light faded to black or whatever happens when you die. Pretty friggin lame to be thinking about something so trivial. But then, isn't life just a series of trivial events punctuated by moments of chaos?

"I think I can say without an ounce of doubt that I am scared." Lance changed subjects.

"You wouldn't be alive if you weren't afraid." Tarwanah swung the wheel of the large truck to turn down a tight alley just two blocks from their appointed location. His calm demeanor told nothing of fear. "We all live in fear every moment, the question is what you do in the next moment." He put the truck in park and exhaled a deep breath. "We are all going to die. What we do while we're alive is all that matters. There is nothing else."

"That doesn't sound very Muslim."

"Allah is not here and Allah won't stop these assholes from getting an atomic bomb and killing thousands, maybe millions. This is our challenge." He rubbed his eyes and stretched his arms to the ceiling of the truck's cabin. "What I know of you my friend Lance, is that you aren't afraid of dying or being hurt. You are only afraid of one thing."

"And that is?"

"You are afraid of failure. That and maybe about being wrong."

"Everyone's afraid of failing. What do you mean being wrong?" Lance asked.

Tarwanah looked at him for a few moments. His two decades longer on this Earth showed in the lines of his face. "You'll figure it out. You are smart."

Chapter 35

Pittsburgh's Three Rivers Stadium is called such because its location at the confluence of three rivers – the Ohio, Allegheny and Monongahela. Two coming in, one going out. Lance let this geographic trivial fact he'd heard during a football game broadcast slip into his mind as he walked down a narrow alleyway between two warehouses. The word *confluence* got him thinking. The next two hours would indeed bring together a confluence of forces, interests and ideologies. This mash-up would mean death for many of its participants. That was fine, as long as nuclear weapons did not fall into the hands of those who would gladly kill millions more.

He walked past a worker sitting on stairs outside a warehouse side door. He nodded to him and looked up to the sky. It was clear blue and would make for easy targeting by pilots who would be filling the skies within hours as midnight approached. The air portion of Operation Desert Storm, was soon to begin.

Lance assumed he knew something others on this mission did not. At least one satellite had his current position in view. Another tracked a truck traveling northwest up to Baghdad. The order had already been issued if the operation was unsuccessful, the location was to be inundated by a barrage of bombs sure to destroy the warheads, kill all those in the area and possibly set off a nuclear explosion. If it did, well that's the chance Saddam's lackies took when they embarked on a mission to obtain weapons of mass destruction. Thousands would be killed, but that would still be thousands less than might be doomed if nuclear warheads rained down on Tel Aviv or Istanbul or Tehran. Lance's radio headset chirped to let him know Team 2 was in position.

About three blocks from where Lance made his way down an alley, Marta sat backwards straddling a worn kitchen table chair. Resting her elbows on the chair back, she looked through a pair of binoculars from a window on the third floor of an apartment building. Nir stood beside her looking out the same window through another pair of binoculars. The small radio beside her on the table chirped. She picked it up and spoke in Arabic.

"Yes."

"AZ cleared."

"Shukran." She said thank you in Arabic and set the radio back on the table. Josef walked in from the bathroom where he had washed the blood from his face. Killing the family that lived in the apartment until a half an hour ago had been messy.

"Update?" Josef nodded to the radio.

"Kadim radioed that the transport has moved through Al Aziziyah. Should arrive in 45 minutes."

"Any changes?" Nir asked.

"Nyet." Marta turned back to the binoculars to see a small group of men in a warehouse near the building where the exchange was to occur. The group was armed and awaiting further orders from their Mukhabarat leaders. Marta knew that this was just one of four groups stationed near the warehouse the transport truck would enter and the keys handed to Mukhabarat Iraqi Intelligence personnel. How she knew all of this was a mystery. "No movement yet. We still wait for their move."

She moved her gaze from the men gathered outside the warehouse past a cargo truck parked down the street with a driver inside smoking and another man leaning against the side. She knew why the truck was parked there as well.

Approximately 330 yards from Marta's position, Nikolai Kusnetsov sat a few feet back from a window in a two-story office building looking through a pair of binoculars at the same truck. There was something he didn't like about it being there.

He had worked for months to get to this moment with his prized possessions less than an hour away and another $180 million dollars soon to make its way into he and Korovin's untraceable bank accounts. The year and a half of planning, scheming, putting practice into action and ruthlessly covering up loose ends had brought them to this day.

No one had ever pulled off one like this. It was at its heart a basic crime. Steal from one group, sell to another. Simple and clean. Cover every angle and remove all loose ends. There were plenty of spy games involved. But it took having the balls to do it. K&K had them.

Things would get even more interesting in the coming days when they let their friends back in Moscow know about the transaction and the fact that only two of the three warheads had actually made their way into Iraqi hands. It would cost another $200 million for the remaining nuke not to be sold to another rogue regime. He smiled at the bravado of it all. With financial resources like this at their disposal, he and Korovin could truly change the world. Or they could buy a small island or two and set up a new country. Or maybe just take a permanent vacation from 20-plus years of spying and killing.

The satellite phone on the floor beside him rang. He answered silently.

"Blissful entreaty. Rarified elation." Kusnetsov still smiled at Korovin's insistence on utilizing the code language. Their time together in the Red Army stationed in the living hell of Afghanistan in the 80s had introduced them to the archaic code talk. They had all but forgotten the code language during years of service as elite members of the KGB. But their defection from the agency two years ago necessitated extreme measures. Having a codeset that few could recall, let alone decipher, was a nice treat.

This last message from his partner was a confirmation that everything was on schedule. Blissful entreaty was Korovin's pleasure being relayed. *Rarified elation* had no code meaning. Korovin merely wanted his partner in crime and life to know he was excited about the prospect of consummating a plan they had put into action 19 months ago.

K&K had served their country well. They'd killed dozens, maybe hundreds. Who kept count? Their years of valuable service were always tainted, of course, by their not so hidden brand of sexuality. The two Russians fell in love within moments of meeting each other as young KGB agents inserted into the military and sent to their death in Afghanistan. Even though they had proven themselves countless times on the battlefield and in all things espionage, they were never able to be at ease. Others condemned their relationship and some had tried to rid the world of them and their particular stain. These people usually ended up dead after K&K applied their skills at destroying individuals and their entire world. K&K didn't merely kill their enemies. They annihilated families, villages and businesses without a modicum of remorse.

Kusnetsov didn't think of these things now. He concentrated on the next hour and what he had to do to complete this transaction and extricate himself and his partner from the area before literal hell fell from the sky. They had all the pieces laid out perfectly on the chessboard. The Iraqi intelligence players were positioned around the warehouse. The CIA, KGB, MI6 and Mossad were focused on a transport truck making its way up Highway 6. The diversion had been successful on a number of levels. Smelinski had done his part right on cue as expected. He was always predictable. The illustrious Seibel had taken the bait along with the rest. Sources had seen and even interacted with him in Hafar.

K&K discussed several times the risk Korovin was taking by riding in the convoy's follow car. But the ruse would be so much more convincing with him along for the ride. He had been sure to stop the vehicles and get out to piss and at a border checkpoint in northern Iraq where several obvious watchers kept the road under surveillance. It was another nice show for the cameras around him and above in satellites.

Amir Rezzon al Tikriti leaned against a wall in the hallway of a low-slung building across the street from the designated warehouse. Saddam himself had enlisted Rezzon several months earlier to coordinate the nuclear weapons transaction. It was a great honor. And a great pain in the ass.

By virtue of the location of his birth, Rezzon shared the same hometown and familial lineage as the great leader. Thus, he earned the right be called a friend by one of the century's prolific mass murderers.

Rezzon had excelled in the Saddam regime and rose from foot soldier to number three in command of the Mukhabarat – the despised secret intelligence service. Rezzon possessed a well-developed sense of suspicion. This whole thing had set his senses on high alert the moment he first heard of it.

The price tag of $200 million had not been the source of his doubt; it was something else. The Russians running the deal kept their identities hidden. Rezzon's resources did not reach high enough into the KGB. He had gotten as far as authenticating K&K as ex-agents and obtained a few key biographical elements.

He had also confirmed the theft of the nukes, but had not been able to crack the armor of the operation. And that irritated him. Here in his home country, he knew everything, all players in every situation. His network stretched throughout the region into Europe, across the sea to America. But the damn Russians and perverse KGB were so incredibly dysfunctional that getting reliable information was damned near impossible. The Russian mob was more organized and easier to work with.

The particular conduit based in Saudi Arabia he had been forced to work through the previous year delivered excellent, unquestionable proof of the nuclear warheads. The contact had even handed Rezzon a key and code needed to activate one the three warheads. The Mukhabarat commander had met one of the Russians briefly in Azerbaijan, but the room had been kept dark. The conversation moved the transaction to the final stages, but had not set Rezzon at ease. Arranging for the initial $20 million to be transferred was a bit of fun. Saddam himself had been required to supply a portion of the funds because the country was still bankrupt from the long war with Iran. The transfer of the funds confirmed delivery of the warheads today. Rezzon looked at his watch – *just minutes now*.

He stood smoking a cigarette across the empty street from a warehouse while the men around him stewed in their own juices. Each of the men in this building was armed to the teeth. They were the elite of the elite when it came to special ops.

Ready for anything and anyone. All of this seemed surreal with the United Nations deadline just hours away. What if the CIA knew all about this little transaction and had the warehouse targeted for the first bombs?

The radio in his left hand beeped. He answered with a stifled grunt.

"The truck has entered the city and will be at the location within 30 minutes. Traffic ahead is light." The spotter at the other end of the radio was brief, as Rezzon preferred.

Rezzon put the radio in his pocket and pulled out another radio with his right hand. "Vehicle has entered the city. All units will be prepared to move in 20 minutes. No mistakes, no other vehicles are to enter the zone. Foot traffic is to be observed and anything suspicious is to be eliminated without delay. No mistakes."

Rezzon wanted to move. Wanted to get outside of this piece of shit building. But the orders had been explicit. No questions. Rezzon was to be at this exact location, next to this phone hanging on the wall.

He cursed the phone again. He didn't like being told what to do or where to be, except by Saddam. This leash, this tether on him seemed to be more than a simple request by the Russians. By keeping him here, they kept him from seeing something else. And that was what made him most suspicious. He could easily carry a cellular or satellite phone and be reachable wherever he was. But no, they had insisted he be here by this phone. *Maddening*.

All of this confluence was set amidst doom and gloom as the allied forces of the United States, England, France and dozens of other coalition countries prepared to enforce UN 671. Dark was only hours away and all of Baghdad knew that with night came terror from the skies. Saddam would refuse to budge on

Kuwait. Everyone knew this just as everyone in Iraq knew the pain of war.

The long struggle with Iran had ended only a few years ago. The pain, suffering and general misery of that 8-year struggle had hardened the 36 million residents of Iraq. But they had never come face to face with the might of the American Devil now on their doorstep. The general consensus was Saddam would keep a stiff upper lip for a while as his military resources around the country were battered from above. Just how long was a matter much debated.

Chapter 36

Lance passed one such debate between three elderly men in the street. They each had an opinion and none of them were afraid of either the US or Saddam. Their words were brave, at least.

Lance was two blocks from the warehouse and about to walk up the steps of a three-story apartment building that provided an excellent view of the warehouse district below. He had been told to step into a third-floor apartment that had been cleared out weeks prior. He knew just where to find the building. He'd looked at it and everything else on maps and satellite images. He knew Baghdad better than most locals.

Approaching the steps, he spotted a man standing and smoking and trying too hard to be inconspicuous. A sentry; and not a very good one at that. Lance, wearing his thawb and keffiyeh and carrying his leather satchel, walked past him without a word and pushed the door open to enter the apartment building. He took a few steps into the lobby to see if anyone was around. No one was. He stopped to double back to the front door. Peeking through the small window in the middle of the beaten and battered door, Lance could see the sentry raise a radio to his mouth and speak. The man turned to look in the direction of the door and Lance stepped back into the dark. A few moments later, a young woman, a girl maybe 17, came up the stairs and pushed the door open. Lance turned to walk slowly toward the stairs.

The girl came through the door and quickly caught up to and passed Lance on her way to the stairs. Lance stepped aside and bowed slightly. "Shukran," She shyly thanked him for letting her take the stairs ahead of him. Lance let her bound up the stairs before he took them much slower. When she rounded the first landing, he stopped on the first step and looked back to the door and waited a few beats. The sentry didn't enter. Lance looked around the small lobby again. A couple of chairs sat against the wall and two prayer rugs lay on the floor in the corner. He turned back to the stairs and made his way up.

He saw nothing of note on the second floor landing and was halfway up the third flight of stairs when he heard the loud knocking from the third floor followed by the pleas from a girl. He assumed it was the girl who had preceded him. He was near the top stair when she knocked harder, more open-handed slapping of the door than knocking.

Her pleas were more serious this time. And her next statement caused Lance to freeze on the last stair. He peeked around the corner to the end of the hall where the girl stood. "Open the door. Amal, what are you doing? Why won't my key work?" And she slapped the door again. She was the picture of an impatient teenage girl forced to wait. "Amal, open the door!"

Lance could have stepped up onto the floor and walked the other direction three doors down to the empty apartment waiting for him. But he stayed where he was. The sentry outside; the girl's knocking and pleading; warnings went off in his head. Before she could knock again, the latch of the door turned. The girl's demeanor lightened but she was still pissed. "Finally, what have you been doing?" Those were sadly her final words.

The door opened only an inch or two and Lance spotted the silencer. Just as quickly, a single shot was fired into the girl's forehead. Lance pulled his head back after seeing the minuscule blood droplets spray out the back of the hijab covering her head. He heard her body collapse to the floor with a thud and kept his back to the wall as he reached into his robe to pull out his own silenced gun. The door swung open and someone stepped out and quietly pulled the girl's dead body into the apartment. It took another few seconds for the door to close.

Lance waited for 15 seconds before lowering himself to the floor and peeking around the corner from foot level. The hall was clear. Aside from a small bit of blood, there was nothing else out of order. No other sign a young life had just been extinguished.

Something changed. Preacher furrowed his brow. A life he knew nothing about minutes earlier was over. Innocence lost. It was wrong. It ticked him off. And he was going to do something about. *Something bad.*

He stepped back down the stairs and listened for any sounds below. It was faint, but he could hear a television from a second-floor apartment. He took a few more steps back to the landing between the third and second floors. He calculated the possibilities and quickly came to the obvious conclusion this incident was related to the nuclear weapons deal.

Someone seeking a view of the scene below had taken over the girl's apartment and killed everyone inside. Instead of arranging for an apartment with a view of the neighborhood to be cleared by credible means, the person or persons now inside that apartment killed its tenants. Quick and easy. *That was cold.*

That also meant they were pros and quite comfortable taking lives. Preacher ran through all of the players Seibel had informed him of over the past weeks. He didn't know why, but this felt like Russians. If he had to choose, he'd guess this was the work of the mysterious Marta and crew.

"Dumb friggin' luck." He whispered to himself. He needed to focus on getting back to his assigned duties as lookout and radio point man, but he also needed to act on this new information. If he had truly stumbled on Marta's operation, he needed to either inform others or handle it himself. He could simply walk back up the stairs like any resident and make his way three doors down where he could report in. But he couldn't requisition resources at this late juncture. The Delta Force teams were in or nearing positions. Tarwanah and Jamaani could be conscripted into an impromptu side mission, but they were blocks away and supposed to keep their trucks at the ready for repositioning. The plan, although built with flexibility, did not allow for a reapportioning of resources less than half an hour before going live.

Preacher decided his next actions in an instant. He continued down the stairs passed the second floor to the first floor lobby. He spotted a door just beside the stairs and opened it. It was a closet as he assumed. The lobby was still clear. Preacher could sense the siege mentality of the place. People were in their homes behind locked doors; seeking security and information from their televisions and radios. They were thankfully not congregating in the lobby. Preacher crossed the small reception area and stopped at the front door.

The sentry was still standing and smoking. Preacher opened the door, looked both ways down the street and saw only a few people moving about. No vehicle traffic. He stepped silently down the four steps and reached the sentry without being noticed. He then delivered a savage blow the side of the man's neck. The guy was instantly stunned and breathless and collapsed. Preacher pulled the man's arm over his shoulder and pivoted him so he was facing the stairs. He laughed and said to anyone within earshot, "I know my friend. You are tired, troubled by these times as am I. Let me help you home."

The sentry gasped for breath but had no strength to fight back. Preacher yanked the man's arm tightly around his own neck and with his left arm reach around the man's torso to apply great pressure on his abdomen; this kept him from getting a deep breath. A few seconds later he had the sentry up the steps and through the door. Once inside, he headed for the chairs against the wall. He sat the sentry down in a chair, put a knee in his chest and from a sheath strapped to his leg pulled a knife. The sentry's eyes bulged when he saw the blade come up to his throat. The tough sneer on the man's face faded.

"I can kill you fast or drain you slow. Which do you prefer?" Preacher leaned into the Iraqi's face with a menacing smile. "Or didn't you know you were going to die today?" With that, Preacher stuck the razor sharp knifepoint into the man's throat a half inch and twisted. He brought his left hand up to cover the sentry's mouth. Blood streamed down the man's neck

"Scream and I cut your head off. Quickly now, I have no time. Tell me your name. Any lie in your eyes and I plunge my knife deeper into your flesh."

Preacher removed his hand slightly from the Iraqi's mouth.

The sentry, a trained killer without a soul moments ago was reduced to a child, a stuttering infant. "Nimad," he whispered through the pain. His tough exterior shredded by the look in Preacher's eyes. This stranger *wanted* to kill him, wanted blood.

Preacher put his hand back over Nimad's mouth and moved the knife's point down to the hollow of the neck below the Adam's apple. "Good. Nimad, you were standing guard outside this building. I can tell you are a professional. My guess is you are local talent hired because you are expendable. I watched the girl get killed upstairs. And I saw you radio to them before she came up. You killed her as much as they did. Tell me before I kill you, how many Russians are up there?"

Nimad made no motion to speak. Only further widened his eyes. Trying hard to be a killer.

"You can live if you tell me what I need to know now. Or I will count to three and then open every artery and vein in your neck. You can watch yourself bleed to death and then drown in your own blood. One, two."

He blurted something. Preacher moved his hand an inch. "There are three in the apartment. Two Russians, a man and one woman. The other is Turkish."

"Shukran." Preacher thanked Nimad in Arabic. He needed to move onto the next phase of this off-assignment project and couldn't let this man go. He couldn't just knock him out and have him wake up in minutes. Preacher already knew what he had to do. He knew he would do it the moment he saw an innocent young girl take a bullet. *He was going to kill them all.*

Protocol of a knife kill called for him to cover Nimad's mouth and squeeze his nose to cut off air flow and insert the 7-inch blade at a 45 degree angle down through his neck, basically reaching into the chest cavity, maybe his heart. This movement would slice through esophagus, trachea and a variety of arteries. Death would come 30 seconds later.

But Preacher didn't want to follow protocol. He wanted to send a message to whoever finds Nimad that this man had done wrong.

Preacher violently sliced the knife across and into the sentry's neck. The blade eviscerated veins, arteries and muscle, cutting all the way to vertebrae. Instantly, blood gushed down his neck but Nimad could not move. Preacher put incredible pressure on his mouth and his knee remained pressed to Nimad's chest. The sentry struggled violently, but for only a moment. He was dead in nine seconds.

Preacher knew he had taken a chance capturing and killing the man here in the lobby, but time was lacking and he needed basic information. He left Nimad's blood-soaked body seated and dragged the whole chair to the closet near the stairs. He shoved the bloodstained body and chair into the small room. There was a trail of blood on the floor, but nothing too bad. He didn't have time clean accordingly. He grabbed the radio from the dead man's pocket, closed the door and turned to the stairs.

Moments later he was up the stairwell, taking them two and three at a time. He stopped on the second floor landing and brought the radio close to his mouth. He turned the sound down to its lowest level. He assumed the sentry had a single radio on one frequency and the remainder of the operation was on other frequencies. This place was hoppin with radio traffic on multiple frequencies and about to get a whole lot busier. The satellite phone in his left pocket chirped. He turned it to silent.

Last chance. Preacher could step up onto the third floor to the empty apartment and complete his mission. Or, he could do what he already knew he was going to do and walk the other way down the hall to the apartment currently occupied by at least one Russian killer and likely more. He couldn't just burst into the room and start shooting. He needed a diversion. The small radio in his left hand was a good place to start. He stepped back down to the second floor and pushed the transmit button.

He did his best to imitate Nimad's accent as he whispered into the radio. "This is Nimad. There are police."

He left it hanging there and waited a few moments.

"What do you mean?" The male voice spoke in Arabic. But it was not natural. The accent was foreign. Russian.

"Police in cars and on foot. They are coming." Preacher added.

"How many?" The voice asked. Lance did not answer immediately. He waited a beat.

"They are coming-" He abruptly cut his transmission before he finished the last syllable. Now he had to see how his diversion would be responded to. If there were other resources close by they could call them from other locations to converge on the apartment building. But Preacher was banking on the other option. The apartment unit the Russians were in was on the other side of the building from the lobby so they could not see if indeed the police were approaching. Preacher was convinced they would send someone to the lobby to check.

He leaned against the wall and listened. He held his silenced handgun with the safety off. Seconds later his answer came. A door opened and closed up above. Rapid footsteps made their way to the stairs. The footsteps came down the stairwell, turned at the landing above and a moment later the man was on the second floor pivoting to step down the next flight.

In this instance Preacher, plastered to the wall just feet from the man, saw three things. This dude was armed with a compact assault rifle; he was dressed in local Baghdad apparel and wore a cap. And this lone man was not Russian. Most likely he was Turkish like Nimad had said. As the Turk pivoted to step down onto the next stair, Preacher whispered, "Hey."

Josef was surprised and turned his head to the voice. Preacher had his gun leveled at the man's head and pulled the trigger. A perfect hole appeared in the Turk's forehead before the clack of the silenced gun was heard.

"Bullseye." Preacher whispered in Russian.

Blood splattered the wall as the man fell to the floor with a loud thud. Preacher was on him in a flash pulling the body down the hall away from the stairwell. He rifled through the dead man's pockets and found a radio just like the one in the pocket of his thawb. Preacher depressed the transmit button and left the line open for a moment and released the button.

It achieved the desired result.

"Report." The same voice as before. Now irritated.

Preacher was even briefer than before. "All clear. Coming back." He spoke in Arabic with his best attempt at a Turkish accent.

The male voice responded with annoyance. "Where is Nimad? What about the police?"

"Nothing. Everything fine." Preacher said this into the radio from a distance so that his voice was even more faint. "Coming back." He bent down over the Turk and pulled the cap off the dead man's head and put it on his own. He then stripped the jacket off the man and put it on. Just then, a woman carrying laundry came out of an apartment unit several doors down. She gasped at the dead man and spreading pool of blood underneath him. Preacher turned the gun on her and could have easily put a bullet through the woman's brain to silence her. That would have been expedient. Instead, he lowered the gun.

"Go back in your home. The war has started; they are here. If you come back out you will likely die."

She didn't protest and turned back to close and lock the door behind her. Preacher turned and bounded the stairs to the third floor with the dead Turk's assault rifle in one hand, his silenced Sig in the other. He moved down the hall and stood outside the door for a moment before knocking. He thought briefly that he should have gone into the empty apartment reserved for him to get a lay of the land -- a better understanding of the apartment's layout. The unit behind the door before him was likely laid out in a similar design. No time for that now. He knocked on the door and bowed his head so only the brown cap and jacket could be seen through the peephole.

He heard the footsteps approach; could sense the weight of the person on the other side lean in to look through the view hole. The latch turned and the door opened. Before Nir could react, Preacher reached in with the Sig pointed up and sent three successive bullets up through the bottom of Nir's chin which then traveled up and out the top of his head. Before the body could fall or the airborne blood droplets dissipate, Preacher grabbed Nir to lay him down gently. A moment later, he was several steps into the unit.

He was in a living room with a kitchen to his left. Preacher could see into that small kitchen. No one was in there. He turned to his right and burst into short hall with a bathroom immediately to his left and two bedrooms a few more steps down the hall.

He was there in a flash and once in the doorway, saw a woman getting up and turning around from a backwards chair. She had been looking through binoculars out the window and was turning to the door as he stepped in. She had the binoculars in one hand and a radio headset in the other. Her holster and guns lay on the bed four feet away. She glanced down at the guns and thought for the briefest moment about diving for them. And then she simply relaxed her shoulders as their eyes met.

She was beautiful in a way Lance had not seen in his 24 years.

How much life can be lived in one second? Just how much can someone be affected, changed in one brief moment. The earth turns. The sun shines. A child smiles and laughs. Another cries.

What is love? Is it a thought? Maybe it is just a mixture of chemicals that come together in perfect amounts at a precise time.

Love has to be more than a certain look in one's eyes, or does it? The eyes that answered him now offered something he'd never seen or felt before. Did she have any idea how much she had just changed his life. He would never be the same after this one moment. *Never.*

And then the second is over. In the next moment, he saw what was surely a true and accomplished killer. He could see in the fluid movement of her eyes taking him in that she was dangerous, deadly. For the next fraction of a second he felt like the youngster, the rookie he was. He was an amateur in her midst.

"Hello Marta." Preacher smiled and said in Russian.

"Hello Lance." She answered in impeccable English and smiled right back.

He should have been surprised, dumbfounded even. But for some reason he wasn't. She was comfortable in his presence. Preacher broadened his smile to a shy toothy grin and expertly put a silenced bullet through Marta's right thigh without taking his eyes off of hers. He was getting better with his aim.

Chapter 37

Most people when shot through a major muscle from a distance of 12 feet will scream, curse, flail about and make a general ruckus. Marta Illena Sidorova did none of these. She did wince and drop to her left knee to apply pressure to her thigh above the damaged leg. The smile did leave her face as well. But aside from that, someone watching this scene from afar might think she had merely stubbed a toe.

Lance studied her reaction for a few moments before speaking. He was impressed with her pain tolerance and control. "Toss the radio onto the bed and sit back against the wall." He gestured to the wall to the right about five feet from the bed. She did as told and limped over to the wall, turned around and eased down the wall to the floor. Lance took a step closer but not too close. "I can see from here that you are dangerous with a very high tolerance for pain. I'll bet you have at least two other weapons on you."

She wore dark brown pants, a slightly lighter sweater and brown boots. "I can see you have a knife strapped to your left leg. Makes me wonder if you are left or right handed. Or are you equally dangerous with either?" She pulled the knife and tossed it on the floor.

He stared at her and she back at him. Something finally flashed across her eyes. A thought, or strategy maybe. She was thinking, assessing. "I am right handed."

"Good. Hold up your left then." She slowly raised her left hand and Lance put a bullet through the center of the palm. The bullet passed through and into the wall behind her. This shot elicited a little more reaction from her. She flinched and brought the damaged bloody hand to her chest and gripped it with her right hand. But she did not scream or cry.

"Jesus, why don't you just kill me?" She finally whispered and showed some emotion. Her English impeccable.

"Like you killed the family who lived here until a little while ago? Too good for you. You need to suffer a bit." He took a step to the bed. "I don't know how you know my name and I'm going to guess you probably aren't going to tell me. But right now I don't have much time. Which, of course, you already know." He pulled the satellite radio from his left pocket and dialed. "Kaleidoscope?"

Seibel replied. "Where have you been? Been trying to reach you."

"No time. I am in the company of Green 3."

Seibel hesitated, obviously caught off guard. "Location."

"On lookout scene. Down the hall."

"Down the hall? Down the damn hall? Sit rev?" Seibel stuttered.

"Captive." Lance replied. No emotion.

"Number?"

"Green 3 only. Others eliminated." Preacher was clinical with his words.

"Allah be praised." Seibel inserted this in place of shouting 'Jesus Christ.'

"Finish?" Lance inquired about his next steps.

"Hold. 30." Seibel ordered him to wait 30 seconds.

Lance moved the phone from his mouth to speak to Marta. She beat him to it.

"Getting your orders from Seibel? You have to do what Papa says." Her English was flawless. The fact she knew Seibel's codename was troubling. Just what else did this killer know?

"I was going to tell you he said to say hi." Lance smiled. Something about her beckoned to him. He just looked into her eyes for a few seconds more before speaking again. "I'm pretty sure he's going to come back on the line and tell me to put a bullet in your brain like I did to your friends. Anything you want to say before I get that order?"

"I don't think so Lance." She was in pain but still managed a smile. "You'll catch up before too long." Her comfort in using his name was a little unnerving. "I guess this is where I'm supposed to plead for my life? Maybe offer up my sources, my network in exchange for my life?"

"No, not that. I already have all that." Lance lied and squinted his eyes. "No I was hoping you would say something like 'geez, you're better looking in person than photos.' Or maybe even tell me how good at this I am. Something to feed my ego, you know?" And with this, he raised the gun in his hand to silence her. Seibel was back.

"Co-opt transfer." Seibel ordered.

"Serious?" Lance didn't like this. Seibel wanted her captured, not killed.

"Yes." Seibel replied.

"No. Solid no." Lance protested.

"Leave unfinished and get back out there. *10*." Seibel confirmed the truck was 10 minutes out.

"Unfinished?" Lance was incredulous.

"Now, move." The boss ordered again.

"One more." Preacher had more to say.

"Go."

"Green 3 knew. Looks like she knows everything, even about you." Lance added.

"Of course." This last statement from Seibel was a thunderbolt.

Lance pressed the disconnect button on the bulky phone and pursed his lips. "Huh. The boss gives the orders and I don't follow them. Guess that's adios." He raised the gun to level with Marta's forehead.

"Okay, okay, I'll plead for my life. Please don't kill me." Her words lacked conviction. She even started to giggle.

"That sucked. You didn't even try." Something didn't jibe.

"What could I possibly say to keep you from killing me?" Her giggling continued.

"What did your father say before you killed him?" Her file was sketchy, but Lance had read between the sparse lines of her back-story. "What did your brother say?" Seibel and Lance had brainstormed Marta's sketchy life story just last week and built an impromptu psychological profile of this born killer. He looked at his watch. Nine minutes and the truck loaded with nuclear warheads would be pulling into the warehouse 300 yards from where he stood.

"My father? My brother? You fool. You've taken it all hook, line and sinker."

He just looked at her.

She continued. "Okay, you want to hear my father begged. My brother never saw it coming. None of the others got much warning either. Some were tortured, of course. But most were dispatched quickly. That's what the file said right?" Her eyes and mind went somewhere else. Lance could see it. Sitting here slumped on the floor against the wall, this mysterious and dangerous killer was not who he thought or had been told she was. He could see the little girl, the lonely and scared creature who would become an evil murderous villain. But it was an act. He could see it now. There was not time for this.

"Can't believe I'm saying it, but I'm actually sorry to have to do this," he took aim between her eyes. In those eyes he finally saw what had been troubling him since that he first looked into them.

"Go ahead, I'm tired." She was resigned and apparently relieved at the prospect of dying. She looked much older than 27. She seemed old and shrunken and tired.

Lance realized what it was that was nagging at him. He was looking into a mirror. He saw himself in her. From the first moment he'd heard of Marta from Seibel about a year ago, through the brief dossier compiled on her life and ruthless accomplishments, right through this moment looking into her eyes, he had been faced with the stark reality that this human looked at and lived life just as he had.

She had undoubtedly seen a whole lot worse than he. But like him, she had never really been alive. Obviously never known love and never found the value in the lives of others. It was there on her face. Like a map.

Great. Here he was about to try to keep nuclear weapons from falling into the hands of known mass murderers and he was having something of an epiphany. He stepped back and sat on the bed but kept the gun leveled at Marta's head. He didn't need to look at his watch to know he now had eight minutes.

Marta seemed to recover from her disappearing act and saw the change in Lance. She was in a whole bunch of pain and not really seeing things clearly, but she should be dead right now. She deserved to be dead. Why hadn't he killed her? As she looked into his eyes, she could see he was off somewhere. He was struggling. He'd killed Nir and Josef without much apparent effort but couldn't bring himself to kill her.

He didn't know the truth about her. Seibel hadn't told him.

"Seibel already has the nukes." Her words were clear, concise.

The words brought Lance back to Earth from planet self-doubt. The words shocked the hell out of him. What did she mean? How would he already have the nukes?

Then it clicked. The answer was stupid obvious. They weren't on the truck. She knew.

"What?" He answered, playing dumb.

"They never had them."

"K&K?"

She shook her head. "Of course. All Seibel. All his work. Just like me, and you. Brilliant, as usual. Moving at a level far above us mere humans." Lance tried to keep up with what she was saying, but needed to see the deeper meaning. She had been relying on Korovin and Kusnetsov to complete the transaction as well. She most likely had someone on the inside of their operation. She had been a few steps ahead.

But now Marta was telling him the CIA already had the nukes. But if they weren't on the truck, where were they? "You had to learn sometime Lance. Why not now?" She smiled.

Preacher had to move. Had to alert the Delta teams. Eight minutes. "Bullshit. You act like you don't care if you live and you come up with some last minute scheme to try to stay alive."

"I don't care if you kill me or not. I'm done after today. Free." She responded.

"From what? The KGB? You are already out. From what then, Smelinski? He'll never really let you go."

"He never had what he thought he had." She looked at the ceiling.

"From who then?" Lance thought a few moments more and then the bell went off. "Seibel."

"Yes, from that bastard. He has run my whole life."

"Smelinski you mean." Lance needed to go, now.

"They're all in this together. They run it all. On opposite sides but running the whole game." She looked like she was drifting now. Starting to fade into unconsciousness. Not making sense. "Seibel is God and Satan. Smelinski is his understudy."

He leaned in close to Marta and put the silencer to her forehead. And just like he'd done in done in Dallas three years earlier with Seibel, he didn't pull the trigger. "Bang, you're dead. You're free."

He leaned in even closer. "You should be dead and I know for certain I'll regret it, but I think maybe you are already gone. So now you get to live. You get to be free after today right? What you do is up to you." With that, he lowered the gun and kissed her. There was no hesitation, no delay in her reaction.

She came to life in the kiss. As he began to pull away after a moment she used her good hand to grab his neck and pull him closer. She had him right there and had the strength left in her to grab his Adam's apple or plunge her thumb into his eye, but she didn't. She just pulled him closer for that lasting moment.

They kissed deeper, came closer. Finally, they released and looked into each other's eyes. "Goodbye." Lance smiled and suddenly, violently brought the butt of the gun up to her temple delivering a blow that slammed her head back against the wall and knocked her out cold. He ripped a portion of her sweater and tied it around her leg and then her arm to slow the blood loss. He ripped more fabric and tied it around both injuries to apply pressure. Twenty seconds later he was up and moving.

"That may go down as the shortest, most screwed up affair in history," he said turning away from her to leave. To be safe, he grabbed the radio headset and Marta's guns from the bed.

He was further snapped back to reality as he hurried down the hall, stopping only briefly to see the pile of dead humanity Marta and her friends had left in the bedroom across the hall. He just shook his head and walked to the living room and into the kitchen. He found a grocery bag for the extra guns and radios he had accumulated over the past 15 minutes. Before leaving the apartment, he dialed the satellite phone again.

Seibel answered obviously irritated and rushed. "Go."

"Whole thing may be screwed. No packages on the truck according to Green 3."

"And?"

"Someone on the inside. She knew all along. Thinks we have them already. Says you knew, you know it all. Bullshit."

Then Seibel said something that surprised, better yet, shocked the young agent. "Green 3 correct. Continue mission."

Lance stopped in his tracks. He was 24, a trained killer standing alone in an empty room in Baghdad, Iraq on the eve of war. And he had been lied to by his boss and mentor. "What did you say?"

"Continue. Mission is unchanged." Seibel's words were Spartan, antiseptic.

"And how do we do that?" Preacher asked.

"Green 3 has been neutralized?"

"Si."

"Green 1 and 2 are to be engaged and eliminated as well as Yellow 1." Lance understood immediately what Seibel was saying. This mission was a hunting and killing party from the get-go. The loose nukes were a ruse. They had been acquired, most likely purchased by someone working with or for Seibel. A light went on.

"Fox in the hen house?" Lance used the code words and nickname for Fuchs.

"Confirmed." And with that Seibel disconnected the line. He had confirmed what Lance had wondered and felt all along. Fuchs had to be involved, he had likely led negotiations or infiltration or even another corresponding mission and already obtained the warheads. Lance's job here was to kill all those involved, from K&K to Marta's gang to the Iraqi intelligence people lurking in doors and windows around the warehouse. He had learned everything he could about nuclear warheads in the past few months. Studying this information had kept him busy, occupied. It had also been part of Seibel's disinformation and diversion plan. Lance was a pawn. And he had four minutes until that truck pulled into the warehouse three blocks away. He could pull the radio from his right pocket and give an abort order to the Delta Force teams. He could give Tarwanah and Jamaani a secret code and they could walk away from the total chaos about to break out.

Lance opened the door, peeked out and then stepped into the hall. He was near the stairwell when the door to the apartment three doors down past the stairwell opened. It was the unit Lance was supposed to be using as a bird's eye view of the activity below. He was shocked for the second time in minutes when out walked Seibel followed by Fuchs.

Chapter 38

He just stood there at the top of the stairs, shook his head and laughed. He realized in an instant that he was a schmuck -- just a punk kid playing a man's game.

"Don't just stand there. You have your assignment; the mission is still a go." Seibel was all business. His demeanor emotionless. There would be time later to discuss and rehash and bitch and scream. "The truck is three minutes out."

Lance didn't say a word. First Marta knew his name, then he learned the nukes were already captured, or maybe never stolen, and now Seibel shows up. Actually, he was here already. Lance turned to look back down the hall at the door he had just left.

"She's not dead. I guess I'm a softie." He nodded toward the door.

"I'll bet she said a thing or two that surprised you." Seibel was brief. No time.

"She seems to know you." Preacher turned to go down the stairs. Fuchs was right on his tail. They raced down the stairs and out the lobby into the street. He put the headset and microphone on under his keffiyeh as he and Fuchs ran between the apartment building and a bazaar. Fuchs already had his headset on.

"Baghdad beckons." Fuchs' words brought a short response from team leads for the Delta squads. All reported ready and in position. Everything was brief in case anyone was monitoring the frequency.

"Eyes on shopping cart?" Fuchs asked.

"Rolling; 1.5." The truck was estimated at 90 seconds out. Lance and Fuchs slowed to a stroll as they rounded the corner on the street the truck would be turning onto any second. They split up on each side of the street. Lance looked over his shoulder to see the cargo truck come round the corner a quarter mile down the street. He looked over at Fuchs to see him casually scanning every window with a view of the scene. He was looking for something, someone.

They passed the first truck holding a Delta team. Abdullah, the driver, leaned against the hood. The Egyptian ignored them and concentrated only on the last puffs of his cigarette.

"One," the eyes down the street chimed in to put all teams on the 60-second warning.

Fuchs slowed his pace and stopped to pull out a cigarette. He made brief eye contact with Lance. Lance continued to the next street where a security checkpoint had been set up within the last hour. The truck Tarwanah had driven and Lance had ridden in was now 30 yards behind this impromptu security blockade. Lance crossed the street to get some distance between him and the soldiers manning the checkpoint.

In just a minute, the cargo truck supposedly carrying the warheads would be at the checkpoint and surely be waved on. Also down the narrow lane, Lance saw dozens more soldiers positioned on each side of the street. The clandestine meeting had become a militarized exchange of goods.

Seibel's voice suddenly buzzed in Lance's ear.

"Alfalfa. Go to 13." This code simply meant switch the radio frequency to channel 4. Lance kept walking while reaching into his pocket to turn the dial to the new frequency. Once there, he was joined by Seibel, Fuchs, Tarwanah and Jamaani. All said go.

"This frequency just opened up and is brand new, only we can use it for now," Seibel was slow and deliberate. "Gentlemen, plans have changed. All resources are to be employed to take out Green 1 and Green 2 as well as Yellow 1. Cargo is not the target. No prisoners. None. Be advised, sources are confident Yellow 1 is on or near the scene. Most likely in a four-story office building 800 meters north. All resources are to be employed to ascertain and exterminate. Good luck. Back to ops frequency now."

Ten seconds later Seibel came on the radio frequency for the entire mission. "All units. Blue cashmere sweater. Answer is negative on package. Shopping to continue. All store clerks to be tipped. One hundred percent." His orders were clear. Everyone dies.

Captain Hubbard sounded off. "Cashmere, come again on package?"

"Repeat. Negative." Seibel replied.

Hubbard cut him off, "Source?"

"Repeat. Negative on package. Confirmed by higher authority. Continue shopping. Mushroom move position to four-story structure one click northeast. Position is east side of the building. Yellow 1 is possibly inside structure. Confirm when in position."

Hubbard was pissed. The other Delta Force captains were likely just as ticked. The mission had been changed with less that a minute before escalation. If it were anyone besides Seibel, they would abort the mission. But Seibel was beyond reproach. He had the confidence of both military leadership and the boots on the ground. He had been here before.

"Blue skies." Hubbard confirmed his new orders and ordered Jamaani to move the truck to the position Seibel ordered.

Plans change all the time. This had been drilled into Lance from day one after signing on to join Seibel's private espionage army. This however was no mere change. A plan built entirely to capture nuclear warheads, disarm them and evacuate the area via helicopter had now been repositioned as a hunt and kill mission with K&K and Iraqi intelligence as the targets. But even more so, Saddam Hussein -- *Yellow 1* -- was believed to be on scene. Most likely to revel in the acquisition of his precious nukes at last.

Flash bulbs kept going off for Lance. The plan, the entire plan, was a ruse, a fake. He stood on a street in friggin Baghdad, Iraq with a dumbfounded look on his face. It was all Seibel.

The realization was a gut blow. The mission was never meant to capture nuclear warheads. They came to Baghdad to kill people. They were here to kill all actors in this play; here to find and kill Saddam Hussein when he showed up to witness his greatest achievement. "Damn." Lance whispered to himself as the truck supposedly carrying the precious cargo reached the checkpoint just yards away. A soldier conversed briefly with the driver and waived the truck and two vehicles behind it to turn down the barricaded alley. "*This whole thing was a set-up from the beginning. All of it.*" Lance said in Arabic to no one.

Seibel was the unquestioned expert in compartmentalization. He had created several sets of reality and controlled the participants in each, just as a director controls actors on a stage. Lance was merely a piece of an intricately layered puzzle Seibel had amassed in the years leading up to this moment. He smiled to himself as he thought the brilliant plan through. *Brilliant.*

First, identify the one thing Saddam wanted more than anything. Second, arrange for three nuclear warheads to be "stolen" from the Soviets. Three, trick rogue KGB agents to act as brokers to contact Iraq. Put a supposed rogue KGB agent and her team on their trail so they can watch the whole thing. Four, switch out the nukes sometime before they begin their trip to Iraq, if there ever were real nukes. Five, get Saddam's intelligence folks so consumed with the deal they bring the great leader himself into the transaction and its ensuing celebration. Six, kill Saddam and as many bad guys as possible at the scene of the crime.

Something about that thought made Lance look to the sky. If Seibel knew Saddam was here on this block at this time, would they call in a missile hit? That could probably kill three Delta Force teams and a CIA squad with he and Fuchs. But that would merely be collateral damage for taking out the world's greatest threat. Preacher didn't think that sounded like Seibel though.

"Shopping cart available." The words were brief and awaited a reply. The Deltas were all set. The cargo truck had pulled into the warehouse.

"Green 1 located." Another spotter had located a high value target and relayed the info.

"Two, take position on Green 1." Fuchs' order was brief.

From his vantage point, Lance could see down the long alley. He had watched the van disappear into the open doors of the warehouse about 200 yards away. He scanned the street. A look left revealed little traffic. To the right, there were a few vehicles moving at the end of the block. The army barricade across the street from Lance had seven men. They, of course, didn't know they were dead.

Lance replied, "Baghdad beckons. Come home." Four simple words spoken in Arabic. But with those words came action, thundering explosions and death; lots of death.

Lance walked across the street to the small troop of seven soldiers manning the street barricade. They were in no mood for small talk so he got right to the point. He saw that behind them

Tarwanah approached on foot. He looked over his shoulder and Fuchs walked toward the group. Lance smiled at the soldier who stepped up to get in his face. In the four seconds after that deliberate smile, Lance killed the soldier and two others with his silenced SIG. Tarwanah took down two and Fuchs silently killed the remaining two. It was all done quietly, right there in the middle of the street. Their silenced guns made audible pops that blended with the sounds of the city. The Iraqis did not get a shot off.

The three of them turned from the spot and walked away. The second Delta Team truck pulled up to and past the empty checkpoint. Lance and Fuchs walked down a side alley. Tarwanah returned to his truck and started it up. The mission's new mission-- Seibel's real mission, was now underway.

Chapter 39

People die every day. Lots of people. They die in fires, auto crashes, hospital beds, swimming pools, front lawns, motel beds, everywhere. On January 15, 1991, lots of people died in Baghdad, Iraq. Most died when bombs started falling from the night sky just before midnight. But hours before this man-made cataclysm, hundreds of people died from gunfire in the warehouse district of southeast Baghdad.

In the fading afternoon light as shadows grew, the sounds of gunfire, screaming, explosions, racing engines and flailing helicopter blades all meshed to bring about a whirlwind of death. Lance Priest was right there in the middle of it.

In the moments after a beat up and dirty transport truck pulled into a nondescript warehouse, Iraqi soldiers began pouring out of a building three down and across the street. Amir Rezzon slapped several of them on the shoulder as they ran by him. He was cursed to stand by the phone. But he knew that just as soon as he walked away from it, the phone would ring and at the other end would be the Russians, or even worse, Saddam. For now, he had to trust his instincts in sending out nearly 100 well-trained and experienced Republican Guard soldiers to lock down the scene and take possession of the warheads, regardless of how the Russians wanted the transaction to be conducted.

On the highest rooftops, Rezzon had snipers accompanied by Mukhabarat agents to relay information. He knew his plan was risky, but he couldn't chance anything going wrong at this late date with American warships flying overhead. He cursed the phone again.

Kusnetsov saw the Iraqi soldiers come pouring out of the north end of the street a few moments after he witnessed the execution of seven Iraqi soldiers at the roadblock. That had to be either CIA or Mossad. Not unexpected. He moved his binoculars and looked up ahead at another truck to see men dressed as laborers jumping out of the back. They obviously weren't laborers; Americans most likely.

From his window, he could see it all unfolding below. He'd expected some diversion from the orders he had given to the Iraqis, but hundreds of soldiers converging on his nuclear warheads was not cool. His partner was about to get caught in the middle of all of it and he needed to point this out now. He raised the radio and depressed the transmit button so Korovin could hear him speak and then picked up the phone and dialed the phone Rezzon stood beside.

"Yes." Rezzon picked up at a half of a ring.

"So many soldiers, what is this?" Kusnetsov asked in Arabic.

"Insurance." Rezzon responded in Russian.

"Of course, but why the lack of trust?" Kusnetsov's voice was full of pleasantries.

"Just making sure all is well with our purchase Igor."

"Well, I have to report that all is indeed not well with your purchase." Kusnetsov smiled a little.

"What do you mean Vladimir?"

"So funny Amir. Yes, I know your real name Amir Rezzon al Tikriti and your address and family. I get to know my business partners quite well."

"Fine, Kusnetsov, me too. What do you and Mr. Korovin need to tell me about my purchase. What has changed?" Amir snarled in reply.

"Very good Amir. You have done your work as well." He really was pleased to learn the Iraqis had looked into he and Korovin's backgrounds as KGB agents. They knew they were dealing with serious men.

"You have other interlopers moving in on your location, I just saw three of them kill your roadblock on the south end. But that is not the change I am calling you about."

Rezzon did not reply. He was on the radio with his snipers to confirm the activity at the south end of the street. He got confirmation and then relayed to the colonel in command to bring in more troops on the periphery of the scene. Damned if they were going to get his bombs.

"Why then are you calling me?" He replied calmly to Kusnetsov.

"Inside the warehouse, my partner was ready to hand over your next instructions, but now with all your soldiers and what looks to be CIA or Mossad or MI6 on the scene, we will be unable to complete this part of the transaction."

"What do mean instructions? You are to hand over the firing keys for the weapons now or you will not receive another penny." Rezzon fumed.

"I know the plans as you were told them. But that was never going to happen Amir. My partner is carrying a set of instructions that tell you where you can find the firing keys here in Baghdad. But as I said, with all this military might around, the plans have changed. You will now provide my partner and his men safe passage out of the area. If safe passage is not provided now, you will not receive the instructions. Oh and 30 seconds after you hang up this phone, you are to call the banker and arrange for the remainder of the money to be transferred or you will get absolutely nothing, no firing keys, no nuclear weapons and I think I will pay your family a visit as well."

"This is not what we agreed to Nikolai. You will hand over the warhead keys now, or we will kill your partner and his men and then pay your remaining family members in Kiev a visit. The keys better be handed over to my men in the warehouse, now."

"Amir, they are not there. My partner cannot give them to you. Provide them protection and safe passage, or you will not be able to use your new little toys. There is no time Amir." Kusnetsov lowered the phone to his side and spoke into the radio to Korovin.

"See my brother, you should never have gone into that snake den unnecessarily. Holy hell is about to break out down there."

Inside the warehouse, Korovin could not see the confluence taking shape around the building but he had a good idea from the conversation he'd just overheard. "So tin soldiers are coming? How many?"

"Many, and our other friends are here as well. Ahead of schedule." Kusnetsov added.

"But not unexpected." Korovin added.

"We'll have to agree to disagree again on you being in there. But as you've heard, protection of sorts will be coming in a few moments so you better follow our plans. Now please."

With that, Korovin turned to the others in his transport group and told them to fortify the doorways. An attack was coming, not protection. They raised weapons and headed for the front and rear doors. Korovin, on the other hand, dipped around behind the truck with the only other Caucasian in the crew. While he bent for a small handle barely visible on the dirt floor, the other man hopped in the car to move it. Korovin pulled the handle and a door opened to a small crawlspace and tunnel below. He jumped in and closed the door behind him. The car was rolled up a few feet to hide the door again.

K&K had made special arrangements several months earlier when they rented this warehouse. They had a tunnel dug that ran nearly 90 feet to the east into a crawl space under a squat building next door. They had concerns that the Iraqis might not act in good faith when the deal was finally to be consummated.

The tunnel was insurance, but Korovin always thought he'd be using it. That's why he worked closely with the three-man crew who dug the passageway using shovels, jackhammers and picks. He had crawled down with them often, made sure their way was lit and well ventilated and that they always had water and food when they crawled back out from their day's work. Because he wanted the work done quickly, he had them stay in the warehouse for the week. When done with the project, he gratefully thanked each as they climbed out of the tunnel for the last time. He gave them all a cold drink of water and a hug. He finished thanking each by putting a bullet in their heads, silenced of course.

Kusnetsov returned to the telephone conversation with Rezzon. "Amir, I am hanging up now and in less than a minute, I will call the bank in Cyprus to confirm the transaction. If I do not get that confirmation, you will not get your bombs." He hung up and looked at his watch.

Rezzon cursed the Russian but did as told. He dialed a number only he knew. The banker at the other end of the line was pleasant and had been told in advance to expect this call. "Good afternoon."

"Benefactor 34613. Confirm." Rezzon had no time for small talk.

"Next phase?" The banker followed protocol.

"Brazil 64992."

"And phase three?"

"Oscar 11286."

"Thank you sir. Your authorization code is confirmed. Transaction will be completed within one minute."

Rezzon hung up and punched the wall. He had just approved $180 million dollars being moved to a clearinghouse account that he could not track. He knew a good portion of the money had come from resources stolen from Kuwait, but it still pissed him off.

Kusnetsov let the minute pass and dialed the number only he and Korovin knew.

"Good afternoon, may I be of service?" The voice was pleasant and professional.

"Account transaction confirmation please."

"Yes sir. Account and authorization please."

Kusnetsov provided the necessary information and was delighted to learn the amount of $180 million dollars had just been received in his account. He instructed the bank coordinator to make seven pre-arranged disbursements of various amounts to other accounts at banking institutions on four continents. He and his partner were very wealthy men, for the moment.

But alas, moments are fleeting.

"I'm nearly out." Korovin relayed to Kusnetsov over the radio as he reached the end of the tunnel three minutes later. In the crawl space under the next building he put on clean clothes waiting for him and emerged expecting to see few or no people. He was surprised to find two armed men waiting for him. Fuchs and Lance stood there smiling.

Before Korovin could draw his weapon or open his mouth, Fuchs drilled a clean hole through his forehead that silently exploded out the back in a cloud of red mist. Fuchs bent and picked up Korovin's radio. But first he spoke into his own headset.

"Green 2 terminated. Proceed with Green 1."

"No hold." Seibel cut in. "We need another minute, hold position. Wait for my signal."

Watching from the window previously occupied by Marta, Seibel continued to take in the action below. He wasn't quite ready for the next step in the newly revised plan. He needed confirmation of Saddam Hussein's presence. His binoculars were trained on the top floor windows of the four-story building a half-mile from the warehouse. He peered into the windows wondering if the country's great leader was watching as his dreams of nuclear blackmail went up in smoke.

Seibel got up from the chair and picked up the satellite phone from the windowsill. He dialed the number assigned for this mission only. While waiting for the line to connect, he took two steps over to the bed and sat down next to Marta who began to stir. She was in a lot of pain but would have to tough it out for a while longer. He had given her a pretty good dose of painkillers that helped her drift off to sleep. Her wounds were not life-threatening. But she was going to be seriously pissed when she got her wits about her.

He brushed the hair from her face. Marta opened her eyes and looked at him as she had done many times before. He smiled down at her as he had many times before. She was his investment just like Lance, but on a more personal level. He had brought her into this business to save her as much as help him fight the cold war. She was his most precious cargo. He loved her as much or more than his own daughters.

A technician 11,000 miles away answered immediately on the first ring.

"Pedro's Pizza, how can I help you?"

"Eagle Eye summer sparklers; 74819 delta." Seibel responded.

The tech knew it was Seibel but still punched in the code as required by protocol. "Sir, how can I help you?"

"Update on movement in the vicinity of our target location." Seibel referred to the four-story building five blocks away.

The tech had been watching the location for the last hour as ordered and referred back to his notes. "Vehicles meeting the description of Pearly Gate arrived at 17:24 local time. Multiple figures emerged from the vehicles and entered the structure."

"Thank you. Are the vehicles still there?" Seibel asked.

"They were moved to the east side of the building at 17:29 and were still there as of one minute ago sir."

"Any other activity of note?"

"Only sparse vehicular and pedestrian traffic," the tech replied efficiently.

Seibel chuckled. "You'd think these people were expecting an attack any moment, huh?"

"Yes sir. Not many people out, especially for rush hour."

"Expanded view. Out one mile. Any troop movements to this location?"

"Thought you might ask for that sir. No movements towards location but lots of activity several blocks over outside and around a warehouse of some sort."

"Excellent. Thank you. Out." Seibel was watching that same activity in the streets below.

Seibel rubbed Marta's shoulder and rose from the bed to return to the window. In the 55 seconds he had been away the scene below had changed significantly. Two Delta Force trucks were moving toward the four-story building. The Iraqi soldiers had the warehouse surrounded and the sharp shooters on rooftops were all aimed at the same building. Their Mukhabarat handlers beside them spoke into radios. The situation was tense. That made it excellent.

He could see several soldiers shouting into the open warehouse door with their weapons pointed at those being shouted at inside. He needed this situation to hold for another minute so the teams could reach their destination. The first truck was just seconds away with the other 30 seconds behind.

He trained his binoculars on the left-most window on the top floor of the office building. The glare from the fading sun made it difficult to see, but lights from inside illuminated the rooms somewhat. The first window was still empty, as it had been when he scanned the windows a few minutes earlier. The second window showed no movement. The third still had a man looking down with binoculars of his own. Seibel drew in his breath hoping to see someone in the last two windows. In the fourth, he could see two men talking. One of them certainly resembled the illustrious leader. The fifth window was empty.

Returning to the fourth, he squinted to tighten his vision and focus. The man on the right wore a jacket and black shirt underneath. He had a mustache, like most Iraqis. He also smoked, also like most Iraqis.

"Come on, take a little step forward." Seibel whispered. He knew Fuchs was getting antsy down there and wanted to get moving toward the office building, but he needed a little more proof before the next action. On the radio he heard Team 1 report on scene and unloading.

He watched the man on the right speak to the younger man beside him and raise his hand in a very dismissive motion. Unmistakable. Seibel had watched hours of footage on Saddam. He was notorious for having body doubles in public. But in those moments when the unquestioned leader was caught on tape, his overbearing, overly secure state of being oozed from every pore. And dismissing others with the flick of the back of his hand was an unmistakable Saddam action. Seibel had the proof he needed.

"Go for 2." He spoke into the radio.

And the third truck, Pepperoni, carrying Delta Team 2 raised the heavy fabric flap to expose a Delta member holding a rocket propelled grenade launcher. There was a reason this truck had stayed back from the other two and parked where it did. Where it now sat, the Delta sergeant aiming the weapon had a perfect shot at a second-floor window one block away from the warehouse.

Fuchs spoke into Korovin's headset, "Brother Kusnetsov?"

"Yes." A hesitant reply.

"Your plans have changed."

Kusnetsov, anxiously waiting for word from his partner, now stepped foreword to the window and trained his binoculars on the spot where Korovin should be walking around the side of a building. Instead he saw Fuchs standing looking up directly at the window.

"Fuchs." It was one word and it was resignation. "How did you?"

"Your radios. For more than a year now. Your time in Afghanistan gave you and your codes away; quite easy actually."

"Such good code though," Kusnetsov smiled in the face of death just moments away.

"And then your communication with the Iraqi Mukhabarat. A little bird in Jeddah sung a tune for us and here we are today." Fuchs' matter of fact vague detailing of the information was curt. Lance, standing right beside Fuchs recognized right away the meaning behind the singing bird. Al-Bakr's confession had been the key to everything. Lance had not put two and two together before now. He smiled and shook his head. Seibel had indeed been masterful in pulling together this symphony. And Lance had unwittingly played his part to perfection.

"You and your master have been busy," Kusnetsov made reference to Seibel. These were his last words.

"Goodbye." Fuchs spoke into the open radio, "Go."

K&K were world-class agents; top operatives in the business. They had risen to the pinnacle of their profession, broken away from their handlers in Moscow and formed a multi-million dollar operation that appeared on the verge of garnering $200 million in exchange for Soviet era nuclear warheads. Problem was, they had chosen to use a dead coded language from their Afghanistan tours 15 years earlier. By using that codeset during the last 18 months, they had been intercepted by listeners in Augsburg, Germany. And by tracking their radio frequencies in the ensuing year and some months, Seibel and his team had followed their every move and even been a few steps ahead. The theft of nuclear warheads already made inert and incapable of detonating from the Dombarovsky storage facility was sheer brilliance on Seibel's part. The intel developed after Lance's capture of al-Bakr had put all the pieces together.

Before Kusnetsov could breath in his last breath or think about turning from the window, or begin to mourn the loss of his partner, the RPG was fired by a member of Delta Team 2 on the street below. Kusnetsov and the entire office he occupied exploded in a deadly fireball that set the building on fire. Fuchs and Lance took the explosion as their cue to take off running toward the office building six blocks away.

Lance went out of body for the moment, rising five thousand feet into the air to look down on the scene below. His view was enhanced by his exposure to satellite imagery. Instead of a map or static photo from months or years ago, he had viewed the very scene he saw below just yesterday evening.

He had of course memorized the image. He saw the streets, parked cars, building tops, walking citizens and other intricate details. Because the satellite image was so vibrant, detailed and fresh, he could see it in his head like a movie, like a three-dimensional image.

He watched himself and Fuchs run through the streets as two cargo trucks carrying the Delta Teams moved toward the building a few blocks away. He saw the battle beginning to take shape on the street fronting the warehouse where the nuclear warhead exchange was supposed to take place. In a flash, he was back in his head racing two steps behind Fuchs.

Seibel kept his binoculars trained on the fourth window and the leader of this nation soon to be under siege. The explosion of Kusnetsov's office caused the man's easy demeanor to instantly change from dismissive to agitated. He stepped closer to the window and his face was now unmistakable. Saddam Hussein was pissed.

"All units. Yellow 1 is located in position previously identified. Visual confirmation now. Top floor east side, fourth window to the right. Team 3 fire now."

With that, the flap on the back of Delta Team's cargo truck flipped up and another RPG appeared less than 100 yards from the office building. As the Delta soldier took aim, Seibel watched as someone from behind Saddam pulled his shoulder to move him.

"Now dammit!" Seibel shouted. Precious milliseconds passed.

The rocket-propelled grenade was launched and reached its target less than a second later. Seibel closed his eyes and pulled his head back as the window and surrounding building structure exploded. Direct hit.

The sound of the explosion reached him a few seconds later. Delta Team 1 was already in the building, entering through the main lobby. Open radios relayed shouts and gunfire. Delta Team 3 members were near the building as well establishing a perimeter and engaging any security personnel outside the building. Team 2 was 40 seconds from being on scene. Fuchs and Lance raced over on foot and would be there within 30 seconds.

Seibel could hear gunfire from the Iraqi soldiers and remaining members of K&K's doomed crew inside the warehouse. That part of the equation no longer mattered to him. He looked back at the office building. A huge hole had appeared in the side and roof, as if a bite had been taken out of the structure by a 60-foot monster. It spewed smoke and flames. But he couldn't see whether there were bodies strewn in the room. He could see movement through the door into a hallway. Someone was moving. He wished that he had put men in the building earlier to be sure the RPG had done its job or to do the killing themselves. But he knew he couldn't have people everywhere at once.

He spoke into his radio. "Kill not confirmed. All units are to secure and move into structure. Yellow 1 is priority one. No prisoners. Eliminate on site."

Seibel picked up the sat phone again and dialed. This time a communications officer in Riyadh answered.

"This is Aunt Mae. Connect me to Uncle Jeb immediately."

"Yes sir." The communications officer transferred Seibel to the three-star General in charge of Desert Storm.

"Go." The particular general was always short.

"Action underway in the city. I do declare there is oil in them thar hills."

"Who is this? Seibel?"

"Fuck you Mears, never use an operative's name on a telephone. Never."

"What is it, what do you want?" The General was chagrined.

"You are to begin actions now General. Begin airstrikes." Seibel ordered.

"We are on plan. You know that. Air strikes will commence as planned and not before."

"General, you know that my orders are direct from the President. Begin strikes now on targets in sector 23. Now General, I want to hear bombs dropping in five minutes. I know the birds are up there, I can here them."

"You are a prick." General Mears responded.

"100 percent, Grade A. Now General. Your orders come from the top cause that's who I'm calling right now when we hang up. Oh, by the way, do you hear this?" Seibel opened the window to let in the noise of gunfire from the warehouse.

"Who is firing? Where are you?"

"The war has begun general. That's Baghdad right now outside my window. Bring the rain general, now." He disconnected the line.

And with that, Geoffrey Seibel started Operation Desert Storm and the US involvement in the 1991 Gulf War. He wished he had a better view of the streets around the office building but would have to trust that the Deltas did their jobs. He knew Fuchs, Tarwanah and Jamaani would do theirs and he hoped Preacher would keep his head down.

He dialed another number and a US Marine helicopter pilot playing cards with three other pilots in a warehouse 40 miles away answered.

"Boulder dam." The pilot answered.

"Wings up. Pick up in 10. The boys need you bad." Seibel disconnected the line to return to surveying the office building for signs of Saddam or his Delta Teamers. He turned to smile at Marta for a moment. She smiled back and then turned away. The sound of gunfire outside soothed her.

Chapter 40

Lance rounded the corner hot on Fuchs' heels. Up ahead, the Delta Force teams had done a number on the Iraqi security personnel around the office building. He glanced up at the smoldering hole blown out of the building and hoped it had hit its target. From inside the building they could hear lots of gunfire. Glass blew out of a window on the third floor. A woman screamed. More shots.

Three Iraqi soldiers came around a corner in front of Fuchs. He shot all three without slowing his pace. Lance was amazed at Fuchs' skill. He was a machine and Lance was basically riding his wake. As they reached the intersection, they saw other soldiers coming at them from a side street. Both men dropped to one knee and took out the group of five soldiers. Their screams now filled the street along with their blood. Fuchs was back up in a flash and heading for the building.

"Sit rev for building." He shouted into his mic.

"Perimeter secure at the moment, but more shit is on the way less than two minutes out." A Delta sergeant replied from beside the transport truck.

"Do we have eyes in the sky?" Fuchs replied.

Another Delta member replied. "I'm on the rooftop next to the target. I can see soldiers moving this way from the warehouse. Maybe 40."

"Foxy and Preacher are entering target location now. Update me on any signs of Yellow 1." Seibel cut in.

Lance and Fuchs made it to the building, ran into the lobby and to the stairs. Bullet holes pockmarked walls everywhere. Saddam's security personnel had been shredded, blown away by the Deltas. They passed a Delta Teamer manning the stairwell and keeping an eye on the lobby. They nodded to him as they ran up the stairs. Their target, Yellow 1 - Saddam Hussein couldn't have made it out of the building. His security team was likely holed up on the fourth floor still recovering from the RPG explosion. If they were alive.

"Third floor clear," Captain Hubbard spoke into his mic. "Multiple enemy casualties, no sign of Yellow 1."

Fuchs stopped on the second floor landing beside a Delta lieutenant stationed there. "Increase casualty count. No prisoners, no sanction." Lance watched Fuchs and his control of the situation in a completely new light. Fuchs was no back-bencher. He was a low-key, no-nonsense and lethally efficient killing machine. He turned to Lance and smiled. "Sorry to keep you in the dark on this little side mission, but how do you feel about killing the main asshole?"

"I'd love to." Preacher replied.

Fuchs stepped aside and Lance headed up the next flight to the third floor. Another Delta was posted there. He had been shot in the shoulder but gave no indication it caused him any pain. "Where is Hubbard?" Lance asked the sergeant.

"Other end of the hall. About to go up." He replied.

Lance turned back to Fuchs. "I'll go to the other end. You go up here."

"Not supposed to let you out of my sight."

"Got to let me spread my wings sometime," and Lance started down the hall. He looked back and smiled, "First one to put a hole in Yellow 1 gets a gold star on their forehead."

"Just keep your head down." Fuchs started up the stairwell.

Sledding up to this point had been a little too easy. The Delta Force teams had more than done their jobs and killed dozens. Only one Delta had been lost and a couple injured. But every perfect mission must face reality eventually. In this case, reality came in the form of the reverberating sound of helicopter blades beating the air.

As Lance made it to Hubbard heading up the stairwell at the far end of the hall, the unmistakable sound of choppers overhead made them both think the same thing – "*the roof*" they said in unison.

"Eyes, give me eyes on the birds coming in." Hubbard demanded an update.

"Four I can see. Moving fast. Three spreading out, one heading for the rooftop." The sentry on the roof next door reported back.

"Godammit. I need those birds taken down." Hubbard shouted.

"On it." The sergeant stationed at the closest truck, Mushroom, jumped into the back to procure a SAM – surface to air shoulder-fired missile launcher. But unfortunately, at the same time, a dozen Iraqi soldiers came around the corner and spotted him raising the SAM to take aim at the incoming birds. Before he could lock on any of the helicopters, he was blown away in a hail of bullets. As he fell, he pulled the trigger and the missile fired directly into a storefront across the street. The structure exploded and a fireball went up into the darkening evening sky. Abdullah had tried to cover the sergeant, but also fell in the barrage of bullets.

"SAM is down. Mushroom is out." The rooftop sentry now turned his attention to the soldiers filing into the street. He took aim and took down four of them. Unfortunately, the helicopters and gunners coming on scene could see the muzzle flashes from his M-16 plain as day on the rooftop. He was nearly cut in half by a 50-caliber machine gun. A third Delta Team member was gone.

Just over 800 yards away, Seibel watched the copters come in and the fireball go up. He knew the mission was over. He just knew it.

He watched the chopper land on the roof of the office building and he knew Saddam was still among the living. A call had gone out, a rescue mission had been launched to save the Iraqi leader. Seibel had listened to the Delta radio traffic and knew the situation his men faced. He spoke into the radio with a voice significantly calmer than his demeanor.

"Pepperoni, Sausage, prepare for departure. Now." Papa ordered the two remaining trucks to get ready to evacuate.

Lance and Hubbard heard the words and shook their heads. Tarwanah and Jamaani jumped into the cabs of their trucks and moved to the east and north sides of the building. The Delta Teamers in and near the lobby stepped out to the perimeter to take aim at the approaching Iraqi soldiers.

Lance felt the tug at his shoulder and turned to look at Hubbard. The mission's lead captain started down the stairs. Preacher should have followed. Should have been right on his tail. But instead, he turned to the door knowing full well someone with a loaded gun stood on the other side. Hubbard turned back up to him.

"Soldier, move now. We are out of here in 30 seconds."

"Sorry sir, we're too close. If he is through that door, then we need to take him down. Papa did not put all this together to have it fall apart when we're this close. I'm going in."

And with that, Lance fired a dozen shots through the door leading into the fourth-floor hallway. He kicked the door open and rolled inside. As he rolled, he fired into the hallway killing three security guards. Pretty good stuff. But a fourth guard fired his machine gun in Lance's direction striking him twice, in the right thigh and hip. Lance winced but returned fire blasting the man backward with four rounds center chest. *Getting better with a gun all the time.*

He rose to one knee in firing position and realized in an instant he was back at Harvey Point working his way through a training mission completed several dozen times. Preacher noted that he'd never been shot in those training sessions, but what the hell. First time for everything.

With the hall clear, he got up on his wounded leg and advanced to the other stairwell, which had roof access. As he approached, he heard gunfire at close range behind the door. Suddenly, Hubbard passed him. With a wounded leg, Lance was slower than normal. As they reached the door, they silently coordinated their entrance and burst through.

He and Hubbard stepped through the doorway and annihilated two of Saddam's remaining security guards positioned above on the stairs firing down the stairwell at Fuchs below. With these men down, Hubbard ran up the stairs leading to the roof with Lance limping behind. Fuchs and Marsh, a Delta Sergeant, came up quickly behind them.

Hubbard looked back at them and signaled a four-direction entry onto the rooftop. He threw open the door and all four of them spilled out onto the roof firing in all directions. Just over 40 yards away stood two security guards firing back at them. Ten yards behind the two guards, the helicopter revved up its whirling blades. Getting onto the chopper were two men, one seriously wounded, bloody and limping badly. It was Saddam.

Injured but not dead.

All four of them fired on the security guards. They went down in the hail of shots. But behind them, a gunner firing a 50-caliber gun took aim on them. They had to spread, jumping, rolling, twisting in all directions. In this precious succession of seconds, the pilot put the chopper to full throttle and lifted off the rooftop. Hubbard regained composure and expertly put three bullets into the gunner's head, but the chopper began to lift and bank away.

All four took aim at the bird and in just a few seconds fired hundreds of shots into glass and metal and hopefully flesh. The pilot expertly turned away from the barrage and dropped the bird off the edge of the 50-foot tall building.

The bullets fired into the helicopter were all that the team could do. A few moments later, the whirling helicopter rose back into their view. They raised their weapons to take aim again, but at the same time one of the three other choppers moved in from the west and opened fired. Hubbard was struck in the back and hurled forward by the 50-caliber round. Fuchs turned his aim at this new chopper. Lance and Marsh moved to grab up Hubbard and pull him inside the protection of the stairwell.

Once they were all back inside, Lance and Marsh put Hubbard's arms over their shoulders to carry him down.

"We are coming down. The bird got away. We will be at rendezvous in 30. Hubbard is hit." Fuchs reported.

"Pepperoni in position and ready." It was Tarwanah.

"Sausage ready," Jamaani added from the cab of his truck.

The remaining Delta Teamers gathered in the lobby of the building laying down suppression fire against the Iraqi soldiers gathering at the end of the block. Everyone in the team knew the next steps. Evacuation was as important as entry exercises for Deltas. The exit route required the two working trucks to transport team members to the rally point where the two choppers that dropped them off this morning would retrieve them and hightail it back to the desert and across to Saudi Arabia.

That all looked a whole lot better when there weren't helicopters buzzing overhead. To a man, they knew the prospect of getting out of here in those trucks without getting the shit blown out of them by the guns mounted on those choppers was none, not even slim. They needed a miracle.

As if on cue, Seibel's miracle came through. The ground shook beneath their feet and a fireball lit up the sky less than a mile away. High overhead, US aircraft had unleashed a little hell on military and essential command and control targets in Baghdad. Lance knew from his memorization of Baghdad the explosion was a refinery. As he, Fuchs, Marsh and a badly wounded Captain Hubbard reached the first floor lobby, a second ground-shaking explosion went up. This time to the east.

"Power plant." Lance whispered. Moments later all lights went out. With the sky mostly dark now, the loss of electricity would make it more difficult for the helicopters to make out what was happening below. Getting away might just be merely impossible now.

Fuchs assumed mission control with Hubbard injured and barely hanging on. His demeanor was complete command. Fuchs spoke into the open radio, "Everyone. We exit east and north ends of the building and board the vehicles. Put down fire in all directions. No delays, no one left behind. Go." As they split into two groups and made their way to the trucks, another explosion rocked the evening sky. This one was closer. It shook the building and knocked out a few windows. Glass shattered all around as they made their way to the waiting trucks.

Before the last man was on board, the vehicles were rolling toward the pick up spot just less than two miles away. Each man reloaded weapons and took up positions with their sights set on either the surrounding landscape or up at the sky.

It took the choppers only seconds to begin their assault on the moving vehicles. The first one swooped in with the gunner opening fire. Usually, a helicopter with a 50-caliber weapon sweeping in from above has a significant strategic and tactical advantage over those below. But usually those below are not Delta Force teams and trained CIA killers. As the gunner opened fire, two team members returned fire and literally blew the gunner's head off. It exploded as it was struck by a dozen rounds. The pilot's vision was obscured by multiple shots striking the glass in front of him. He pulled up and made room for the next attacking chopper. One down.

Tarwanah and Jamaani had worked out their routes to the pick up spot in advance. They took different streets that basically ran parallel toward the destination. The Jordanians pushed the trucks to their speed and control limits. Traffic was extremely light as all of Baghdad prepared for the midnight deadline just hours away. Undoubtedly, explosions starting just after 6 p.m. put millions in shock.

Lance was sitting in the cab next to Tarwanah with an M-16 pointed out the window. An Iraqi army jeep appeared from around a corner and Lance was the first to take a bead on its passengers. His spray of bullets killed the three soldiers inside. The vehicle rolled lifelessly forward into a parked car.

Word had definitely gone out and several more jeeps appeared ahead. The Deltas standing in the rear of the truck focused their weapons on the vehicles and a deadly barrage of bullets took out those inside and exiting from the jeeps. The two cargo trucks hurling through the streets of southeast Baghdad were a killing parade leaving carnage in the streets behind.

With the open field now in view, Lance got excited about maybe getting out of here. One hell of a story to tell. He looked at his blood-soaked pants. The pain was slightly past severe but not much he could do about the wounds right now. He'd have to hit the first aid kit on the Black Hawk. A radio staple by Journey started up in his head. His foot tapped along on the floorboard.

He was going out of body when a helicopter gunner overhead took aim and scored a direct hit on the right front panel and tire just feet from where Lance sat. The tire basically imploded and the radiator spewed steam. Smoke shot out through the holes and the truck rocked back and forth as Tarwanah expertly maneuvered the vehicle on three tires and a sparking bare wheel.

The Jordanian knew right away they were sitting ducks. He spun the wheel and maneuvered the truck into an alley where they would have a little protection from the chopper and be able to fight off soldiers approaching on foot. It wasn't ideal, but stopping in the middle of the road was suicide.

As they came to a stop, the Delta Teamers automatically disembarked from the vehicle and took up positions without a word. Their actions now were instinctual, based on years of training and real-world experience. Lance got out and stepped up on the runner bar to take a look at Hubbard lying on the truck's bed. He was bandaged and in bad shape but still managed a smile and thumbs up.

"Foxy, Foxy. We are hit and disabled approximately a quarter mile from rendezvous." Lance spoke into his mic calmly. As if he'd been here before.

Fuchs and his fellow passengers were a couple hundred yards away fending off the other helicopter. Shots being fired in succession made it difficult to hear him. "What is your position, exactly?"

Lance could *see* exactly where they were on the map in his brain. A little red "you are screwed" circle flashed on his mind map. "Approximately 500 yards southwest of the pickup on the road. We pulled into an alley after losing a tire." Lance could see the helicopter buzzing the other truck.

"We'll be there in two minutes. After we blow this damn chopper out of the sky." Fuchs' German accent 100% gone.

Another benefit of Tarwanah bringing the vehicle to a stop was the opportunity to fire the remaining SAM without burning the skin off everyone in the truck bed. Marsh grabbed the shoulder-fired missile launcher and stepped up to the front of the building to peak around. The chopper was banking around; coming in from the north. He flipped the activation switch. The high-pitch whine revved up. To get the shot off, Marsh needed to move out into the street. Lance stepped out in front to lay down covering fire against the soldiers coming up on foot.

Both Lance and Marsh spotted them at the same time. Coming in fast from the south were two more helicopters. But these were Black Hawks -- the units that dropped them off early in the morning. The Black Hawks separated about a half-mile out, one destined for the chopper swooping in on Lance's crew the other targeting the bird harassing Fuchs' group. Marsh switched the SAM off, not wanting to fire the missile and have it hone in on the heat signatures from their own birds. He and Lance stepped back behind the building's corner.

The Iraqi pilots didn't have a clue what was about to happen. The Black Hawk swooped in behind the first unsuspecting chopper. The Hawk's co-pilot had moved to the M60 machine gun. When they were within 200 yards, he opened fire. It was sitting duck city.

He strafed the Iraqi bird mercilessly. Within seconds, smoke appeared and the copter began to falter, the engine and rear rotor hit. A few seconds later it exploded in a fireball a block away.

The Iraqi soldiers who had been advancing on the alley stopped and took up aim at the Black Hawk. The pilot had to bank hard to move out of firing range. As the closer bird lifted away, the other Iraqi chopper less than a quarter mile away started its rapid descent. It too had been riddled by the second Black Hawk's M60. Two more down.

With the harassing birds out of the air, both trucks could have proceeded to the pick up spot and got the hell out of Dodge in minutes. But trying to make it to the pickup spot on three tires would make Lance and crew an easy target.

"Should we run for it?" Marsh called to everyone.

"Almost a quarter mile, but out in the open and we need to carry Hubbard," Lance replied.

Tarwanah came around the truck. "If we stay here we will be sitting targets for them in three maybe four minutes."

"Can the bird land right here in the street and pick us up?" Captain Doster this time.

"Do you think we can lay down enough fire to keep them back?" Marsh looked around the corner and saw three jeeps coming and what looked like several dozen Iraqi soldiers running.

"Foxy, how far away are you?" Lance called to Fuchs.

"We will be turning onto your street in 30. What does it look like there?"

Lance joined Marsh to look around the corner of the building. "The locals are restless and coming. Maybe 45 seconds to a minute and they'll reach us."

"Pepperoni, this is Beaver 1. We will come back around in a flash to run off some of those wild Indians. Where is Mushroom? We see only you and Sausage en route." The pilot of the first chopper called in while banking around.

"Mushroom is out. All team members are in the two remaining trucks. And now we are down to one. Pepperoni's wheels are SOL. Sausage is swinging around to come to our rescue." Lance responded.

"I see." The pilot radioed his counterpart. "Beaver 2 we need to lay down a little cover to allow these boys to join up and make it over to the rendezvous."

"Got it. We'll come around at 3 o'clock for a run and hit their position." Beaver 2's pilot replied.

"Beaver 1, what else can you see from up there? How many more locals do you see rallying to our location?" Lance posed an important new question.

"Tough to tell with lights out. Looks like another firefight is going on a few blocks back. But I see more headlights moving your way. We need to get ya'll outta there quick-like." The pilot could see the warehouse battle still raging, but indeed vehicles appeared to be gathering to follow the action.

In the distance, another massive explosion went up illuminating the night sky for a few moments.

"All units, all units. Gather up your stuff now." Seibel weighed in after listening for 10 minutes of non-stop action. "Grab Hubbard and throw him onto Sausage when they reach you. You two birds lay down a shitload of cover fire and escort the Sausage mobile to pickup. Get everyone out in five minutes. Move."

Seibel's commanding words set everyone in motion. Marsh and Ricks jumped back into the truck to lift Hubbard. He moaned but stayed conscious. Lance stepped around the corner, the enveloping darkness made it difficult to spot the Iraqis. They had extinguished their headlights and were moving up on foot. A few moments later Beaver 1 moved overhead and lit up the Iraqis with a spotlight. Lance and three other Deltas used the brief swath of light to pick off more than a dozen soldiers. A barrage of shots from the Iraqis required the helicopter to pull up a few seconds later. Moments later, Beaver 2 came in from the opposite direction with the M60 blazing as its spotlight lit up the gathering jeeps and foot soldiers.

Fifteen seconds after that, Fuchs and crew came barreling up to their location. The team had Hubbard lifted to be loaded. The nine in the group were ready to join the other nine remaining mission mates on their truck and get the hell out of town. Lance looked over his shoulder at the Iraqis being lit up from behind by Beaver 2 and saw the one thing he would rather not. Two Iraqi soldiers were bending down to one knee with RPGs on their shoulders. They were about 90 yards away, which meant they stood a good chance of hitting what they were aiming at.

Lance yelled, "Everyone out. RPGs!" In a flash, Jamaani opened his door and Fuchs was right behind him. The Delta Teamers jumped out of their working truck as the RPGs fired.

The elapsed time from Lance's recognition of the threat until the rocket-propelled grenades reached the vehicle totaled 4.5 seconds. Lance had saved everyone's life as they dove into the alley or to the ground as both grenades struck the side of the truck. The explosions were fierce. Shrapnel caught a few of them including Lance, but no one was hurt seriously. Well at least, any more than they were already banged up. Lance felt a burning in his back where the metal shard struck him, but it added little pain to his already throbbing leg and hip.

The extreme reality of the situation quickly set in. They were just over a quarter mile away from their pick up with no means of transportation. Each member of the team, when healthy and uninjured, were in excellent physical condition and could cover the distance in two minutes or less. But undoubtedly, several and quite possibly most of them would get picked off if they made a run for it down the street now. Facts were facts. This had turned into your basic shit sandwich.

"What about the rooftop?" Marsh pointed up as Fuchs and the others from the other truck scrambled to their feet. "The bird can land up there and haul us out of here."

Fuchs got his bearings and stood up. "They'd just shoot it up and anyone else up there. Not enough time to make it happen."

"I'm guessing that was Sausage going up?" It was Seibel.

"You got it," Lance replied and peaked around the corner to take a few shots at the Iraqis.

"What is your position, exactly?" Seibel replied.

"Basically screwed," Preacher smiled as he looked at Fuchs.

"An alley right now. Approximately 500 yards west of pickup." Fuchs shook his head.

"Exactly 487 yards to the west," Lance corrected. His mind map was never wrong.

Fuchs smiled. "We are exposed on the north and at the other end on the south."

"How far away are the hostiles?" Seibel asked.

"About 100 yards east for now. More are on the way and will likely have us surrounded within minutes." Fuchs added.

"Fortify your position. I am calling in more air support." Seibel picked up the sat phone and called General Mears again.

Fuchs stood tall and addressed everyone in the group. "We are to stand and hold this position for now. Cashmere Sweater is calling in more air support which probably means F-16s." He ordered four Deltas to the other end of the alley and Tarwanah and Jamaani to the roofs of each building to give them eyes a little higher up.

Fuchs radioed the choppers. "Beaver 1, Beaver 2. We are to hold our position for the moment. Can you make another run at these guys to light them up for us?"

"You got it boys." Beaver 1 replied.

Fuchs turned to Lance leaning against the wall beside him. "This one isn't quite as easy as Jeddah is it?"

"This is nothing. Try hunting with my stepdad. Your life is on the line every moment and very few make it out alive." Lance kept the smile on his face. He really was enjoying this.

Fuchs let his face turn a bit harder as he spoke his next line, "You do realize that other people in this mess actually care if they live or die. Many of these guys have families back home."

"I know that." Lance looked at him a little quizzically. "But I have the great luxury in life of not giving a shit about anyone or anything, right? That's why you folks brought me into this deal isn't it?"

Preacher continued, "Don't get all sanctimonious with me Foxy. We came here to kill people plain and simple. Some of us were just kept in the dark about the real mission."

"Need to know." Fuchs turned away.

"I guess I didn't need to. Now this whole thing turns into a piece of shit because you and Daddy O didn't think to have someone take a SAM or RPG up to the top floor so we could shoot ol' Saddam's bird down. Details Foxy, details."

Beaver 1 came roaring in from above with gun blazing and spotlight putting Iraqis on stage for all to see. Fuchs and Lance rolled out into the street with three others and put down another dozen or so soldiers in the brief moment they were illuminated.

"We have troops moving in from the east over here." It was one of the four Delta Teamers at the other end of the alley. "I can see three jeeps and a troop truck.

"Cashmere, we are going to be pinned in here in about three minutes. Any word on that air support?" Fuchs barked.

"Hold." Seibel issued a one-word response.

"Sure would love to have a couple Apaches come to this party," Marsh said as he rolled back into the cover of the building.

"I think Cashmere is calling in a little bigger bird. Should light this place up plenty. Just hope we don't get caught in the scraps." Fuchs looked around the corner at reinforcements joining the other Iraqis 100 yards back up the street.

"I'm thinking something," Lance was flat on his belly. But he was also 2,000 feet in the air looking down. A light bulb went off and he saw a plan. "I'll bet if we put down a shitload of cover fire and one of our birds shot em' up at the same time, the other Hawk could land right out here in the street and fly a good many of us out of this. They can hold 10 or 11 right?"

"You know that's not the dumbest thing you've ever come up with kiddo," Fuchs pulled his head back around the corner and thought about it for a moment. "Half or more can get out. Let's make that happen." Again, the German accent gone. Lance thought Foxy sounded like he was from the Midwest, maybe Chicago.

Fuchs relayed Lance's plan to the two helicopter pilots. They agreed it offered the best chance to get most of the 18 remaining mission mates out, especially the injured. Fuchs then spelled out the plan to Seibel.

He too liked it and commended his young protégé with another one-word comment. He also informed them that two fighters would be on scene within five minutes.

"All players listen up," Fuchs spoke into his radio mic. "Plan is to evacuate as many as we can on Beaver 2. Landing spot is right here on the street east of this burning Sausage mess. We will keep the locals occupied and push out to them to give time to load up half of us, especially the wounded."

The teams reloaded and two grabbed Hubbard again. Another seriously injured Delta was hoisted up by one of his comrades. Tarwanah and Jamaani on the rooftops moved out closer to the Iraqis. Inside a minute, all were ready for the pickup. On cue, both choppers came in, keeping close formation. At the last possible moment, Beaver 2 turned on his spotlight to see the landing space below. And simultaneously

almost every member of the team began firing at the assembled
Iraqi troops. Marsh and Lance stepped out around the corner
and pushed toward the line 100 yards off. At the other end of
the alley, two Deltas also stepped out a few feet to pin down the
Iraqi troops coming up from the rear. On the rooftops,
Tarwanah and Jamaani inflicted heavy casualties on any and
everyone they could see down below.

Overhead, Beaver 1's M60 mercilessly sprayed the Iraqi
line. Another vehicle exploded when a round struck the gas
tank. The explosion served another purpose in lighting up Iraqi
soldiers positioned around it. They were sitting ducks and many
were killed quickly by the expert Delta shooters.

Hubbard and other wounded were loaded onto the waiting
bird. Fuchs basically pushed several others onto the helicopter.
Some objected and wanted to stay, but he wouldn't have it.
Eleven of the 18 were loaded and the bird lifted off. The
remaining seven included Captains Doster and Parkhurst,
Marsh, Fuchs, Tarwanah, Jamaani and Preacher. To be sure he
wasn't shoved onto the chopper, Lance had been one of the two
pushing out. He and Marsh were furthest from the chopper. He
knew Fuchs would have hoisted him onto the bird because
Seibel wanted it that way. And truth be told, he was seriously
injured. But he wasn't going anywhere.

As the helicopter climbed into the night sky, another sound
could be heard. Two F-16s were screaming toward the scene,
the explosion set off by the jeep gave them a precise location to
hit. The remaining members of the mission hit the deck. Two
missiles were loosed and came wailing in. The explosions they
set off made the jeep and Sausage blasts seem less than tame.
Just a hundred yards down the street, dozens of Iraqi soldiers
were blown into little bits of burning flesh and bone.

That was it. Cue to leave. Exit stage right.

"We move." Fuchs was first on his feet and made his decision within a second. Fifteen seconds later all team members had assembled back at Pepperoni. "On foot, single file we have just over a quarter mile to the pick up. Stay close to the buildings. Lets hoof it fast, now. Beaver 1 we are heading to pick up on foot. We may need suppression fire along the route."

"You go boys. I got your back." The pilot responded.

Marsh took the point. Each filed out after the one in front of him. Fuchs brought up the rear just behind Lance. They hugged the fronts of the buildings as they ran. Fuchs looked back over his shoulder. He hoped the aftermath of the missile strikes would cause a few minutes of chaos among the Iraqis. That might just be enough time to get out.

Preacher's leg was beyond killing him. The shrapnel in his back didn't feel all that great either. He did his best to hide his limp, but this running thing was just about the last thing his aching and bleeding leg and hip wanted to do. He did a little calculation as they ran at about three-quarter speed. Back in his high school track days, he could cover a quarter-mile, or 440 as they called it, in 52 seconds. Not the fastest, but fast enough to get him to the state finals.

He didn't know if it was the pain or maybe blood loss, but for some reason he thought of that state final race in Edmond, Oklahoma. He was behind from the starting gun, but out in the 6th lane he didn't know it. He kept his eyes on the lane before him and the poor guy out in the 7th. About 100 yards in, he saw three guys come up on his left shoulder. No way they should be up to him this fast. At this rate he was going to be out of it by the 220 halfway mark. He committed to staying with the guy to his immediate left in lane 5. The extra exertion caused his rhythm to be off, but he said dammit all.

By staying shoulder to shoulder with lane 5, he passed the gent in 7 and stayed ahead of the inner lanes. Who, by the way, had won those inner lanes by running faster times in the quarter and semifinal heats earlier in the day. They now had an advantage around the inside turns.

By the 220 mark, it was six-wide across the lanes. All six were even; lane 7 had dropped. With the turn ahead, it was expected that Lance and likely the guy next to him in 5 would drop since they had more distance to cover than the inner lanes. Lance had other ideas. As they worked through the turn, he hugged the line and stayed abreast of lanes 1 through 3 as lanes 4 and 5 fell off. By the end of the turn with 110 yards remaining, it was down to 1, 2 and 6. Lance was stride for stride with them and felt like he had a good bit more to give.

As usual, at this point in the race, Lance started hearing a song in his head. Always happened; never failed. Whether he was running a 220, 440 or 880. He always took this opportunity to sing along with the song; sometimes he sang out loud. It undoubtedly caught other racers off guard hearing another runner waste breath singing. But Lance just couldn't help it.

He took a look left at the guys in 1 and 2 at 90 yards and gave a little push to their pace. He'd gone ahead by a half-stride by 80 yards. The guy in 1 cracked which left him and 2 to duel it out down the stretch.

He turned from 2 to look at the finish line. It was out there at 60 yards now. Eight, maybe eight and a half seconds away. The pounding rock song in his head; his lungs barely taxed; his legs full of spring. He had a state championship if he wanted it.

And then that new reality and its consequences set in. State championship meant his name at the top of a list, maybe in the newspaper. The local paper might mention him and the school paper could write an article about him. That would put a crimp in his greatly prized anonymity. There was peace and security and power in being anonymous, or at least second place. He knew this when he'd won the district and then took a close second at regionals. But he kept going because he'd something to prove to a coach who questioned his heart in front of everyone on the team.

Now with the finish line 50 yards ahead, he realized he'd proven himself. He'd shut that fool coach up and shown he could beat the best in the state, no problem. At 40 yards he had a full stride on lane 2. With the crowd cheering in the stands and his coach looking on with stopwatch in hand at the finish line, Lance eased up. Just a little, but enough to give the guy the opening he needed to catch him. By 30 yards they were even and by 20 yards, lane 2 was half a stride ahead.

With the song in his head into its dual chorus and the crowd cheering at the top of their lungs, Lance Priest eased in for a second-place finish and just kept on jogging after the finish line, right off the track and over to his duffle bag. He picked up the bag without stopping and jogged right out of the stadium. He didn't ride the bus back to Tulsa with the team and didn't catch a ride with his parents who were proud of his silver medal they accepted from Lance's coach after he missed the medal ceremony.

He did that night for the first time what he'd done dozens times since. He went off into a town he didn't know and made his own way home without calling a friend or family.

Lance smiled to himself at that thought as he limped along with the others in Baghdad. He suddenly jumped to the right and stopped, letting the others move ahead. His leg appreciated it immediately. Fuchs stopped and grabbed him by the arm.

"Preacher, keep going."

"No, I'm good. You go on." Preacher bent over to put his hands on his knees.

"Now. Let's go, there's no time." Fuchs was in no mood.

Preacher swung his arm to knock Fuchs hand away. "No, I'm cool right here. You go on, I'll get home on my own."

Fuchs went from irritated to pissed. "This is bullshit. You are jeopardizing everyone. Let's go now." He subtly moved his gun to point at Lance.

"Don't point that fucking thing at me and get going. Go on." In that instant, Preacher had produced his silenced SIG and pointed it at Fuchs' mid-section. "Go on, now. I'll see you back at the ranch. And don't call Seibel. Just go on, catch up to them. I'll be fine. I always am."

"Jesus. You are such an asshole. Such a child. You're not worth half the crap we put up with."

"You've read my file more than a couple times Foxy. You know I don't play well with others and I've gotten through life just fine on my own. I'm turning this corner here and walking away. You need to get on the little bird and get the others out of here. Now, go on. I'll see you back at home."

And with that, Preacher turned away, "Don't call Papa. Just get out of here." He said as he walked into darkness. Fuchs watched him take a few steps and then looked at the guys moving away to his left. He turned back to his right to see some activity back at the explosions. Looked like they were starting this way. He turned to Lance.

"Go on little boy." Fuchs called out.

"Adios meine freunde." Preacher raised his hand but didn't look back. He began jogging down the side street hoping Fuchs didn't have a gun pointed at his back. He started singing the song he had sung during that state championship race.

Fuchs caught back up to the others. Thirty seconds later, they were crossing under an overpass and in another 20 seconds they were boarding Beaver 1 waiting for them with blades whirring. Fuchs looked back in Lance's general direction out the door of the Black Hawk. As the chopper lifted into the night, he put on a pilot's helmet to speak with Seibel.

"Everyone aboard and accounted for?" Seibel's mood had lifted after the bird took off. He was watching through his binoculars, smiling.

Fuchs let the question hang there for a moment, with his Bavarian accent back in place he answered. "All but one."

"What, who did we lose?"

"We didn't lose anyone. One of us decided to take another way home."

Seibel now let that hang for a moment. "Why did you let him go?"

"Was I supposed to shoot him?" Fuchs answered.

"You know what I mean. You should have convinced him."

"He picked a most inopportune moment to take his leave. Right in the middle of our little jog just now. He simply turned and walked away. Nothing I could do." Fuchs closed his eyes, exhausted.

"I know, I know. He's done this throughout his life. Did it back in high school the first time. Had his parents worried to death. Always needs to prove something to himself." Seibel shook his head.

"Just like you now, huh?" Fuchs joked.

"Right."

"Do you want me to go back in and track him?" Fuchs asked.

"That'd be useless. He just disappears. Becomes someone else. Quite amazing really." Seibel turned from the window to look at Marta lying on the bed in the darkened room.

"Quite a pain in the ass if you ask me." Fuchs added.

"That too. I'll see you back in Riyadh. Out."

"Out." Fuchs took off the helmet and handed it to the co-pilot. He turned back to Tarwanah and Jamaani. They all smiled. You can't hear a word in a Black Hawk flying at top speed with the doors open. The three of them just looked at each other each knowing full well what was behind the shared smiles. Tarwanah turned away to look into the empty night sky. He hummed to himself the song Lance had sung for him this morning.

Chapter 41

In Edmond, 1984, it was a single mother of two very young boys. In Dallas, 1985, it was a divorcee who needed someone to listen to her. In San Francisco, 1988, it was a poster shop owner who loved to talk about her cats. In Oklahoma City, Wichita, Orlando, Chicago, New York, London, Paris and Berlin it always followed this model.

Each time, it was a female or females. Probably something psychological about that, but nonetheless, it was a proven method. Dive into unfamiliar communities and cultures; meet someone in need; tell them the most wonderful yet utterly believable lies. Sometimes it lasted a few hours. Other times, these detours from reality lasted days. There was always a sexual dynamic even if no sex was enjoyed.

He'd perfected his false selves during these excursions and become comfortable living lives not his own. Yet, a streak of modest chivalry ran through each of these tales. At no time did he hurt his benefactors. Often, he helped much more than he was helped. His aid included dislodging bad boyfriends, encouraging ex-husbands to move out of town and straightening out irrational bosses.

He took no money, other than that used to purchase food or transportation. He never stole, either cash or hearts. He always made it clear from the moment they met that he would not be staying long. Their time together would be brief but memorable.

In Baghdad, 1991, it was two sisters forced home from college by the impending assault by America. With two bullets and shrapnel in him and bombs reigning down from the sky, Lance became Amad, the eldest son of a Saudi leather goods trader. He had traveled to Baghdad to negotiate with a new trading partner but had the misfortune of walking into a robbery.

He couldn't go into details because of police corruption he had witnessed the night before, but he could confirm that two of the robbers would never steal again. The others took his money and identification and shot him. But he had been able to escape death. Amad had lost a lot of blood and was in terrible shape the next morning as he told the girls his tale outside a market. He looked even worse than he felt.

The two sisters took the injured hero to their uncle Hamid. He was an Oxford-trained surgeon who had a booming black market business because he had to practice in secret due to his political views falling on the wrong side of Saddam's Bathe party.

The surgeon took an immediate liking to Amad, especially his love of running. The uncle had run long distance at Oxford and would've loved to compete for the Iraqi national team at the Olympics, but again his politics were wrong.

Amad was welcomed into and recovered in the sisters' home for the next few weeks. The sisters' parents were easily convinced. While there, he was able to fix a persistently leaky faucet and convince a rowdy upstairs neighbor to turn his music down after 10 p.m. The sisters' father considered Amad a gift from Allah and hoped he could stay for an extended period, at least while the bombs fell.

Amad had to fend off very personal healing assistance from the sisters. They offered daily to soothe him, but he feigned weakness from his injuries. He was clear with both that he could not and would not be staying long.

The downtime recuperating allowed Lance to do something else he hadn't done in a good long time. He'd lie there at night and just think, go into a deep trance. During this particular stint of deep thought, he tried to focus on one person -- Geoffrey Seibel. Problem was, he kept seeing another face. Marta would not leave him alone.

He'd been wrong about Seibel. Been guilty of underestimating his boss, his master. Lance had always been able to hold his own with others because of his ability to master encyclopedic, geographic and other assorted bits of knowledge. He, by his very nature, understood nuances and body language and could always dig into someone's psyche without too much effort. He thought he'd done this sufficiently well with Seibel.

He was sadly mistaken.

Lying there late into the night seeing Seibel in his mind's eye and rolling him over and over, he could see there were blind spots everywhere. Seibel kept more hidden than he revealed; much more.

Fuchs, Marta, fake nukes, hunting Saddam; it was all measured and mixed and created by Seibel. Lance realized he was a small cog, more than a piece of dust, but nonetheless, a tiny part in the intricate machine that Seibel had built and labored over for 30 years.

A disembodied Lance looked at himself lying in this bed in this small, quiet room. He moved up to widen the frame. It took complete focus, but he could see Seibel's compartmentalized world below.

As he pulled back further, he saw more and more rooms; hundreds, maybe thousands of them. Seibel had created a labyrinth with twists and turns and levels and layers and overlapping dimensions that expanded out and collapsed upon others. It was a multi-dimensional puzzle box. It was a web.

He wanted to be a much bigger player in Seibel's game. Whatever it was. Lance wanted to know more and see if he couldn't influence the outcome or even better, change the machine's parts and redesign the labyrinth just enough to make it his own.

It was selfish, but that is just Lance. Maybe it was nothing more than selfishness driving him. Maybe.

Lance had never stopped to ask himself about his motivation and he wasn't going to start now. He needed a challenge. It was that simple.

Truth be told, another vision took up a significant portion of his time now. Marta.

Her eyes, when they first met his, brought a new sensation that had infected him. The kiss they shared was also unlike any he had experienced. Granted, he'd never kissed a woman a few minutes after shooting her.

Her eyes and face and mouth haunted him in brief moments when he closed his eyes or turned his head or breathed.

By the third week, Preacher had healed considerably. The surgery and stitching done by the black market surgeon were excellent No infections and no need for follow-up care. The household had come to depend on him, perhaps a little too much. When the sisters' mother intoned one morning that she and he would be alone that afternoon and she had a project that could use his special skills, Amad knew it was time to go.

This time had been different though. Instead of working for himself and a personal goal, Lance had been working the angles; doing the critical intelligence collection thing. He had learned from the sisters, their father, their uncle and family friends how the local network of corruption and skullduggery worked. He had identified the real power players controlling the neighborhood and the identities of those who controlled the neighborhood leaders.

Lance had learned in three weeks what may have taken a year for a network of eight or maybe 10 players. He knew the power broker for the southeast quadrant of Baghdad. Over tea on the floor in the family's living room, a member of the Baghdad inner circle had even bragged that he had direct contact with Saddam. People were willing to share the most amazing things with Amad. He just had that effect on others.

With a wealth of information memorized, Amad told the sisters and their mother he was going out for a walk and would be back before lunch. He walked out the door never to return. Fifteen minutes later, he was on a bus headed for the outskirts of town. An hour after that, he caught a ride on a ramshackle and overloaded truck headed west for the Jordanian border. Getting there was challenging with most bridges blown apart by US bombs.

Two days later, he walked 18 miles around the Iraq-Jordan highway border crossing. And a day after that, he walked down a pleasant street in a quiet and quaint neighborhood in Amman, Jordan.

He knocked on a blue door. The door opened and out stepped Tarwanah. He could only smile and hug the ragged desert rat on his doorstep.

Chapter 42

Four days later, a clean-shaven and very tan Corporal Priest walked onto base in Augsburg with only a slight limp evident. He spent the day listening to an array of Iraqi military conversations. They were all delightfully boring and told the same story – an endless barrage of US bombs had paralyzed the Iraqi military. Operation Desert Storm, with its precision missile strikes, had been remarkably successful.

That evening, Corporal Priest strolled the three quarters of a mile home to his apartment. As he fully expected, a couple of visitors waited for him.

Seibel sat at the table drinking a cup of coffee. Fuchs was in the kitchen scrounging up a meager dinner with the sparse options available. Lance joined Seibel at the table.

"Nice vacation?" Seibel smiled as he put the coffee cup down.

"Nice enough."

"I read your report. Very thorough, but completely lacking any details on your actual whereabouts." Seibel added.

"Baghdad." Lance smiled. Fuchs chuckled in the kitchen.

"That I believe." Seibel sighed as he brought his hands to his face and fingers through his hair. He had obviously come straight from the airport. "Baghdad."

"My sources are credible, but need to remain confidential to protect their identities." Lance added.

Seibel turned away and stretched out his feet. "If I had to guess, you most likely befriended a young female and worked your way into staying in her house, with her parents' blessing, of course. You received medical care on the black market. You earned the respect and trust of the girl's parents while earning the intimate affection of the girl. All the while picking up details from people who came into their lives on a daily basis."

Now Lance leaned back and stretched out his legs. "That sounds like a nice plan. Good model to work from."

"Your model, proven time and time again since you were 17."

"16." Lance corrected.

Fuchs walked in with a box of crackers and joined them at the table.

"I don't think we are going to get a lot of detail out of our boy here. I think we just need to work his intel and see where it gets us." Fuchs was playing good cop to Seibel's pissed off investigator.

"Oh, we'll work the intel, no question. It's good stuff. But I just wonder what we are going to do with our little head case here. Mr. 'play by his own rules.'"

"You knew what you were getting with me." Lance was calm, non-confrontational.

"You knew what you were signing up for. You were told time and again by me and others that sacrifice was the first thing we do. Being team players is the second. You were given ample opportunity to back out of this."

"Yeah, right. When was that, after you sent two guys to track and kill me in Dallas? Maybe at Harvey Point? Or maybe when I shot one of your deep resources in that apartment in Baghdad? Just walk away anytime?" Lance pursed his lips and shook his head.

"You had the opportunity to say no before you got in the car in DC. But you weren't about to walk away. You saw the opportunity to be a part of something that gave you the chance to lie and kill for a living. That was it plain and simple."

"Lie and kill?"

"Plain and simple."

Lance turned to Fuchs. "Is that why you signed up?"

"Can't remember, really." Fuchs kept his smile and German accent intact.

"I would think that a few years later you would know a little more about me. Killing was never the reason I got in that car and joined your little traveling circus." Lance had an authentic look of disappointment on his face. "I've done what was necessary each step of the way. Done just what you taught me. A few people got killed in the process. I guess taking lives just comes natural for some of us." He looked at both of them. There were only killers sitting at the table.

Seibel decided to stand. He stretched again and took a few steps -- a professor about to lecture. "So what role is this you're playing now? You sit there calm and assured; satisfied that you have produced valuable intelligence. But I can see what is really going on. All over your face."

"And that is?"

"Why me? What do you really want old man? Why the hell didn't you tell me the truth about Baghdad?"

"All that, here on my face?" Lance drew a circle around his face like a mime.

"All that and more." Seibel added.

Lance turned to Fuchs again. "Right here on my face, that easy?"

"I think our fearless leader can see more than I can, more than others." Fuchs raised his eyebrows.

"So get to it. Tell me what I'm thinking." Lance turned back to Seibel.

"Nope. No answers from me. You knew coming in that my methods serve a purpose that you aren't privy to." The CIA master shook his head.

"Yah, I knew that. But I didn't know you were going to send me into shit storms under false pretenses. Three times now."

"Three? How's that?"

"Jeddah, Baghdad and Marta." Lance raised a finger for each incident.

"Ah, I think we may be getting to the heart of the matter."

"Almost killed her. That close." Lance squeezed his fingers together for effect. "I've thought a lot about that recently. How you worked her into the story so seamlessly. You had her planted for years didn't you."

"Since she was a little girl. She is bar none the best I've ever had." He turned to Fuchs for support.

"Bar none. She has been deeper than any of us." Fuchs agreed. "No one like her."

"Is she still in then? She implied she might be done." Lance raised his eyebrows.

"Marta is recuperating in an undisclosed location. Someone shot her and whacked her in the head. But I don't think that hurt her as much as something else you did." Seibel left it there, but the implication was clear. "She has some decisions to make." Seibel sat back down to took another sip of coffee. "But you want to know more about her, right?"

"I guess I just wanted to know what it's like for you." Lance ran his fingers through his short hair. "What it is like to put someone in so deep and then leave them dangling; to be killed by someone like me? You always talk about your investment in me. You had a lot more invested in her."

"More than you know." Seibel put both hands on the table.

"So just like that, you send her in where she can be wiped out any moment. After all the time, money, secrets. I guess that's what I want to know. Not her really; I want to know what makes you tick?"

Seibel smiled at that. He turned to Fuchs and then back to his young pupil. "I really have to stop sometimes and remind myself how young you are; how raw you still are and how much you have to learn. You are such a brilliant bastard, such a piece of work and a goddamn cold-blooded murderer. I forget you've only been in for what, three years?"

He stood again and continued, "By the time I was 24, I'd seen too many men die. Killed more than a few myself. Fuchs here was a veteran of combat at 22, a multiple killer. Marta, she was old by 24. What she'd seen and lived through and done makes us all look like amateurs.

"Let me tell you Lance, you've only scratched the surface. Both in what you are capable of doing and in what you will experience." He sat down to emphasize his next words. "I didn't pick you out of thin air, or because you were some good looking punk."

Lance asked, "Why did you pick me again? Was it because I almost shot you the first time I met you?"

"No, that was confirmation of my decision." Seibel smiled, took another sip of coffee and leaned back in the chair. "Do you remember that short little questionnaire you answered in the career center at college, that form number T12A?"

"Yeah, somewhat." Lance lied. He remembered it well. Eleven questions. Eleven answers made up on the spot.

"Well I remember it like it was yesterday. Those single sheets of paper go out to colleges, technical schools and even high schools all across the country; around the world even. Thousands, sometimes hundreds of thousands of kids fill them out each year." Seibel leaned back toward Lance. "How many do you think I receive each year?"

"Dozens, hundreds?" Lance guessed.

Seibel chuckled. "None, zip. Been that way for years. The unique profile that is required to answer those 11 questions correctly is so precise, so algorithmically miniscule in its variance, the way it slices and dices critical concepts, that no one ever meets it. No one that is, until one young man three years ago."

"No one before that?" Lance raised his eyebrows.

"Or since." Seibel nodded.

"What is the profile looking for if it is so precise, so selective? Did you design it?" Lance asked.

"Of course I designed it, with the help of a few psychologist friends, Braden among them. And what it is looking for in a quite precise, quite scientific and incomparably selective process is nothing short of the perfect spy, or better yet, the perfect candidate."

Lance laughed. They all laughed together.

Lanced added. "The perfect spy. Like the novel?"

"Exactly. Except that spy wasn't even close to perfect. No, my little profile tool has been so ingenious that it has kept me from wasting my time, our government's time, on individuals who could never succeed. It eliminated every candidate, until that day I received your answers."

The elder spy looked up at the ceiling, recalling a memory. "It was shocking at first. You know, you answered every question with the exact, the precise words the profile was built to capture. It was astounding when I shared it with those friends

I mentioned." Seibel's eyes went cloudy for a moment as he drifted back to another time. "Imagine if you will, a loner, a pathological liar, an under-achiever in almost every category, a person who worked daily to remain anonymous, would be the one."

"Astounding." Lance chuckled.

"It got me thinking. I had been wrong. I had been recruiting, searching for certain types, for a certain and singular type. People like this guy." He pointed his thumb at Fuchs. "Combat experts, incredible physical specimens, trained killers. I realized that I'd been wrong from the start. The perfect spy, the one, the pinnacle, didn't need to be that type at all. Nothing wrong at all with him, but not the complete package I was truly looking for."

"My feelings aren't hurt even in the least." Fuchs chortled.

"What I was really looking for was a liar, a cheat, a chameleon, an honest to goodness shape-shifter who could move from difficult circumstance to impossible situation without missing a beat. Oh, I'd tried actors, acrobats, even clowns before, but they were not fluid, not adaptable enough."

"And they weren't killers." Fuchs added, matter of fact.

Papa nodded. "Precisely. They could be trained to kill, but it didn't come naturally. There was always a moment of hesitation, a conversation they had with themselves before pulling the trigger.

"So, when I was handed a sheet of paper filled out in Tulsa, Oklahoma by one Lance Porter Priest, I was surprised, but not completely. I had been missing something and you finally showed me."

"So, if can summarize," Lance butt in. "I'm a liar, a cheat, a chameleon and a natural killer. At least according to that 11-question profile."

"Correct. All the makings of the perfect spy." Seibel added.

"Well then I've got a bit of news for you."

Seibel's eyebrows furrowed. "Okay, shoot."

"I lied."

"On the questionnaire?"

"Yep. Faked it all, every question." Lance smiled.

Seibel burst into laughter and the others joined him. After a few moments they subsided. "I know."

"What do you mean you know?"

"You lied on every question, every one. You had to in order to answer it correctly."

"Then my answers weren't real. I'm not who it says I am. You got the wrong guy." Lance laughed.

Seibel pounded the table lightly. "You see, that's just it. That's what I was so astounded to learn after I read your answers, watched the video of you taking that Foreign Service Officer exam and then the surveillance footage of your everyday world. Your entire life, your entire existence was fake. You were never yourself, never. And that's what I was missing in waiting for someone to answer the questionnaire correctly. No one could, no one ever could. Not a real person at least."

"Not a real person?" Preacher asked.

"No, it was impossible. Anyone with even a modicum of empathy would fail. And everyone did. Some got a few answers partially correct, but literally everyone failed. Everyone until you." Seibel now did something a little strange. He got up and walked behind Fuchs and around the table and got on his knees in front of Lance. It was immediately uncomfortable. "I'm not a religious man, never have been. But I believe you were sent to me for a reason. You have a purpose in life."

Lance chuckled at this, but said nothing.

Seibel smiled up at him. "Laugh at me, make jokes, do whatever you need to. I'm down here on my knees because I believe, I truly believe that you are here to do something incredible. You are going to save me and save your country."

"Man. Don't go off the deep end. I'm sure as hell no savior."

"You are. You are special. I am 100 percent certain in saying there is no one else like you my boy. No one. I'm going to ride you and work you and drive you, come close to killing you. But in the end, you are going to do something very special that no one has ever done before, ever." Seibel's eyes even started to tear up. "I know it."

Lance looked at Fuchs. "What's going on?"

"He's been like this for the last couple years. Ever since he met you."

"And all I did was put a gun to his head."

"You did." Seibel laughed and put balled fists on Lance's lap and then brought a pointed finger to his temple. "You put it right here, what more of a sign did I need?"

"Maybe I should have killed you?" Lance squinted.

And Seibel just stopped. Tears gone, he stood up and smiled. "Now that would have been perfect. That would have been something really special." He walked back around and picked up the coffee cup and took a last swallow. "I feel better getting all that off my chest. Really."

Lance sat back. "Well I'm glad. That was quite a show."

"No show. I meant every word. You are going to be the greatest fucking spy, the greatest weapon there ever was. If I have to kill you to prove it."

Lance looked from Seibel to Fuchs. "Well, no pressure there, right? If I decide to stay and play."

They all laughed again. Seibel was first to stop.

"Oh you're in. In for good, for life. I'll make damn sure of that. You need this as much as we need you." Seibel was sure, positive.

"We'll see." Lance was evasive.

"And you better get packed up." The spymaster was done. Just like that, he was the old serious Seibel. Like he'd not just been on his knees or cracked a smile the last few minutes.

"Why's that?" Lance asked.

The CIA legend looked at his watch. "You've got about 11 minutes until some ex-KGB guys show up here looking for you."

Lance pushed away from the table and stood. "What? What do you mean? How would they have found me?"

"Probably because I told them."

"What the hell? Told who?"

"You'll find out. Foxy and I are out of here. You better not leave behind anything that points to any of us." Seibel kept a smile on his face.

Fuchs had been quiet that last few minutes but spoke as he got up. "Just do what he says. Don't stick around."

"Wait, why'd you do this?" Lance took a step after them.

"No more questions, no more answers from me. You do your little disappearing act, your specialty. We'll see you back at the Point."

Fuchs and Seibel stopped at the door. Lance was already into a compartment in the floor retrieving IDs and passports. "Oh, nearly forgot," Seibel turned back and pulled out a piece of paper with coded longitude and latitude coordinates. "Here are directions to that undisclosed location if you'd like to pay someone a visit before coming home. I think she might like to see you."

Lance took it and continued working. "See me or kill me? I kind of shot her you know."

"Never can tell with her. But there are certainly worse ways to die." Fuchs opened the door and Seibel followed him out.

Lance turned to them while stuffing a duffle bag. "You know what, I should just shoot you now."

"Plenty of time for that. Nine minutes." Seibel tapped his watch and closed the door behind him.

Lance stood and looked around the room. He didn't need nine minutes or seven or five. He had nothing invested in the apartment.

He was a consummate chameleon, ready to fade into the night or change colors at a moment's notice. He grabbed the few clothes in the closet and stuffed them in the duffle. He probably had plenty of time to walk out the front door, but Seibel might have been messing with him. Time could already be up.

Preacher stuffed his SIG into his belt, walked into the bathroom, opened the window and tossed the duffle out. He followed it with a tight roll on the ground. No need to look back, there was nothing for him here.

Epilogue

"Are you comfortable talking about it?" Braden's question followed a few minutes of silence as Lance sat with eyes closed. They had just debriefed the details of the Baghdad mission. He told the CIA psychologist about killing 12 people in less than two hours, the frustration of missing Saddam by inches and the need to be alone when he broke away from the team heading to the pick-up spot.

Lance was appropriately emotional about the entire experience. He exhibited remorse at taking human lives and the finality of his violent acts.

He mentioned shooting Marta, but not the feelings she stirred in him. He also didn't mention seeing her this past week or spending several days walking and talking with her, even holding her hand a few times. And he certainly did not confess to Braden how difficult it had been to tear himself away from Marta. Her haunting eyes and surprisingly warm smile. That was personal, private.

Usually, the psychologist let this particular patient break the silence. But Braden was excited about finally getting to a certain subject after three years and multiple sessions with Preacher.

"About what?" Lance knew full well what the question meant.

Braden tiptoed in. "I think you know. The subject we have skirted for years. You were never comfortable discussing it."

"I've been willing to discuss any and every subject in these sessions Stu. I think any lack of comfort on a particular topic was yours." Lance smiled, an innocent grin.

Braden took his time. He wanted to work through this difficult topic and not lose Lance in the process. "Do you know what I was doing the week before your oral assessment in Dallas back in '87?"

Lance considered the question with a surprised look and thought for a moment. "I assume reading my file and doing your psychoanalysis voodoo."

"Aside from that."

"No idea." A boldfaced lie. Lance never, not ever, had no idea about any subject. Basically impossible for him.

"Believe it or not, I was in Fort Worth that week. I was hunting down information on the unfortunate incident that occurred while you lived there."

"As I recall, several unfortunate incidents took place during those four years." Lance was noncommittal. Waiting for Braden to maneuver into his line of questioning.

"I'm referring to the accident, the suicide of your mother's boyfriend in 1978. I think you know that." Braden's voice was smooth velvet. He wanted this to work this time.

"So what brought this up?" Lance wanted him to work a little harder.

"I've brought this up several times before, but you have successfully switched subjects, told a joke, insulted me in your most gracious manner or created any number of diversions to get around it."

"So what makes you think I want to talk about it now?"

Braden smiled and nodded. "I guess, I was thinking since you had been through the Baghdad assignment and seen," he struggled for the next words, "A number of deaths. I hoped that maybe discussing the suicide would be easier for you now. Maybe put it in perspective."

Now it was Lance's turn. "Stu," He was the only person who called the psychologist Stu. Seibel even called him Stuart. "I don't see how my mother's boyfriend committing suicide when I was 12 can be related to the murder and mayhem I saw and participated in over in Baghdad. The two have literally, and I mean absolutely, literally nothing to do with each other. Nothing."

"I know they are not connected in the sense that they took place thousands of miles apart and more than a decade separates the two events. But I believe you have never come to terms with the suicide; seeing a dead person for the first time."

Lance just looked at him. Nothing.

"Am I right?"

"I think you think you are right." Preacher replied.

Braden laughed at that. "There you go again, saying the absolute perfect thing at the exact right time. I swear you have this stuff rehearsed, but-" the psychologist bit his lip to shut his mouth. Lance had taken him off topic with one statement. He centered himself and took a deep breath. He wasn't thrilled that Lance took the exact same deep breath, made it look like Braden was looking in a mirror. "Come on. Don't do this."

"What? Am I supposed to make this easy for you?" Lance increased his smile to full toothy grin.

"This isn't about me. Why don't you let me help you? Just this one time." Braden pleaded.

"I'm sorry. I just needed to be sure you were ready for this since you have obviously been thinking about it for more than three years." Lance smiled.

"This is not about me." Braden repeated himself, almost a mantra.

"Well it's not about me either. I don't spend any time thinking about that suicide or its repercussions. It happened a long time ago."

Braden was glad they were back on the topic. He knew Lance had steered them back to it for some perverse reason, but he was still glad. "I can see how a bloody scene like that could have a lasting impression on a boy. I've seen it hundreds of times in talking with soldiers, operatives and others. Adults who have witnessed far less graphic incidents are often deeply affected."

"So go ahead and ask me your questions. I know you have several." Lance leaned in closer to Braden to make himself appear more open.

"I only have a couple, really."

"Shoot. Bad pun, I know. But go ahead." Lance smiled a perfect smile.

Braden brought his pen to his notepad. "Can you describe the scene for me?"

Lance sat back. He knew Braden wanted honesty here so he put on the full display. "We came home, Mom, Eric and I. It was a Friday night I think. George's truck was in the driveway so we knew he was there. I walked in first and the smell hit me. I didn't know what it was. Of course, I've since learned it was the after affects of the sphincter and other muscles relaxing after death.

"Anyway, I walked down the hall into the living room and saw him sitting in the chair with the blood splatter on the wall behind him. I turned around to stop Eric and push him back toward the front door. Mom had just walked in and I remember looking at her not knowing what to say. She saw something in my eyes and started to walk passed me. I tried to stop her. I said something like, 'Mom don't go in there.' I didn't want to say anything more with Eric right there, he was only 9."

"What did she do?" Braden asked.

"She pushed me aside and rushed into the living room. She screamed 'oh my God' and then came back down the hall to make sure I moved Eric outside onto the porch. She told him there had been an accident and for me to keep him outside. She went back inside and called the police. They showed up in less than ten minutes."

Lance's telling of the story was factual, no embellishments. It was without emotion. And he could tell by Braden's face that the psychologist didn't like it. Too easy.

"That's it really. After the police came, we gave them our statements. The hearse showed up and they wheeled him out on a gurney. He was completely covered. My mom's boss sent the cleaning crew from the office over to clean up the mess. They took the chair away as well. We stayed at some friends' house that night and the next, and we moved to Tulsa a month or so later."

Braden just looked at him. No comments.

"I can tell by your reaction that you were expecting more. Maybe for me to tell you how the image was seared into my brain. Maybe that I cried myself to sleep at night or had to console my mother as she wept for days and weeks. I'm sorry for your letdown Stu, but none of that happened. I never cried. My mom cried a couple of times and then never again and we have never really talked about it since."

"So it was unresolved." Braden wrote a note on his pad of paper.

"Yah, like life. Unresolved." Lance responded.

"You seem defensive."

"Only because you want to make it a big deal. You want this single event in my life to take up some important role in my development. It didn't. I didn't really mourn George's passing. He was not a nice guy. He was not a good person, everyone knew that. My mother had learned it too. She knew she had made a mistake getting involved with him, especially since she had two boys to take care of."

"How was he not a good person?" Braden's question was leading.

"What did the police say about him when you looked into it?"

Lance's reply caught Braden off guard. He furrowed his brow and responded, "What do you mean?"

"You said you went to Fort Worth the week before the oral assessments in Dallas. What did the police say when you asked them about the suicide? I assume you spoke with the responding officer, the investigating officer, maybe a neighbor or two still living on the street." As usual, Lance was ahead of Braden.

"I did. I spoke with the police, neighbors, family members and co-workers of your mother and George." Braden tapped his pen on his notepad.

"Why would you talk to all of them?" Lance tapped his foot on the floor because Pink Floyd had started playing a stoner classic between his ears.

"Seibel and Wyrick and I all had competing theories on the incident. I was doing a little bit of detective work in addition to psych evals." Braden was a little chagrined. He had told more than he planned to.

"What does that mean, competing theories?" Lance put a look on his face that was equal parts shock and surprise. It was also fake. "Theories about what, the death?"

"Yes, the cause of death."

"Oh," Lance rubbed his chin and opened his mouth. He leaned his head back to look at the popcorn ceiling of Braden's peaceful office. He could see Mona Lisa's smile in a pattern. "So am I to assume someone thought George's death was not a suicide?"

"That would be a fair assumption."

Lance smiled and sighed. "Let me guess. Seibel thought it might have been me who did it. Wyrick thought it might have been my mom, right?" He got no reply from Braden, which was a confirmation. "And I'll bet you were the one who believed it was just a suicide."

Braden shook his head. "As usual, you nailed it."

"So for the past three years, you have been waiting for me to tell you the truth about the incident. Doesn't that seem somewhat naïve?"

"How so?" Braden furrowed his brow again.

"Me? Tell you the truth. When have I ever done that?" Lance grinned.

"More than you think you have Lance."

"Hah! Now that's naïve. You should know at least as well as Papa that anything you get from me is suspect at best and most likely a lie."

"So, your telling of the story a few minutes ago, was that true or nuanced?" The psychologist prodded.

"That's for you to decide Stu." Lance turned his hands over palms-up. The epitome of innocence.

"Do you want to know what the Fort Worth police said?" Braden asked.

"Sure."

"They said it was textbook suicide. No doubts from the investigating officer. Case closed." Braden sat back.

"And what did the others say?" Lance prodded.

"It was all variation on the same theme. George was a rough guy. He had a history of violence. The police had been called to his home several times in years past. His coworkers said he was a hothead. His family knew he had serious anger issues."

"And?" Lance could see that Braden had more.

"Did you know he had threatened your mother just a few days before he killed himself?"

Lance squinted. His procerus muscle did its thing. "How so?"

"A co-worker of hers told me that George had asked her to marry him and she politely declined. He got more than a little mad and when she asked him to leave, he said no. He threatened to hurt her and even worse, hurt you and your brother." Braden watched Lance for his reaction to this news.

Preacher was silent for a moment. "So he was a bad man. Just like I said."

"It also brought into play Wyrick's theory that she may have been involved in some way." Braden added.

"But she wasn't, right?" Lance was leading with this response.

"Her alibi that night was airtight. She was at a friend's with your brother. Someone was with her every moment that evening."

"So it was suicide, just plain ol' suicide by a drunk guy who had lost his woman and didn't want to go on." Lance looked at the ceiling again. The look on his face best resembled relief.

"Textbook." Braden was relieved as well. He believed the past few minutes had been truly helpful for Lance. He had helped him move passed a place he had been stuck for 12 years. Braden felt like they had finally achieved something during a session. This was the way it was supposed to work. He added, "It was just suicide. It wasn't your mom's fault or yours. It was nobody's fault."

Lance looked back down from the ceiling. The look of relief still on his face. "Well that's that then, right?"

"Yep. Your mother wasn't involved. You weren't involved. It was just him." Braden looked at his notes for a moment. And then back to Lance with a question in his eyes. "I know your mother was with someone that evening until she left with your brother to go pick you up at 10 p.m. I don't have it in my notes, where did she pick you up from?"

Lance continued the look of relief, even rubbing his eyes with the palms of his hands. Then he looked Braden square in the eyes, "I was at the video arcade." A smile came onto Lance's face as he recalled the place. "I loved to play that game Galaga. You know, where you shoot all the alien ships coming down. I think I set a new record on that machine that night."

ABOUT THE AUTHOR

So, here is where you are supposed to read some information about Christopher Metcalf. Okay, the basics – he's married to the beautiful Diana and they have five, yes five, kids. They live in Tulsa, Oklahoma. You can learn more about the author or contact Chris by visiting www.christophermetcalf.com.

Chris really appreciates your time and hopes you enjoyed reading *The Perfect Candidate*. Lance is quite a character. Chris learns new things about Preacher every day. Be on the lookout for *The Perfect Weapon*. The second book in the Lance Priest series will be published in Fall 2011. Preacher is challenged like never before. He must face a brilliant terrorist bomber, his own mortality and his feelings for a certain former KGB operative. It gets a little messy. Thanks again for your time.

THE PERFECT WEAPON

COMING SOON

February 26, 1993
The billowing smoke was evidence of what could have been. The
buildings still stood. Was it luck? Did they not put enough
explosives in the truck? Whatever the reason, they had still
completed their mission. Their goal may not have been met, but
they had succeeded in declaring war on the United States.

It was an ant.

In the midst of utter chaos chasing Amir Shafiq through the streets of Hamburg, Lance adjusted his footfall to avoid the ant. A single solitary little black one. It was nothing, literally nothing. But it was also something.

In 24 years, he'd stepped on thousands, maybe millions of ants, spiders, roaches and all variety of scurrying insects. He could not recall a single instance in which he avoided stepping on one of these seemingly endless vermin. Killing them was nothing. So why did he just change the trajectory of his right foot to steer clear of this particular fella? Why?

He knew the answer, but he didn't want to think about it, or her. Yes, it was her.

He'd been changed. No matter how small the transformation, he was different. He'd found compassion, if only a modicum. A microscopic sliver of empathy could now be found alongside his general disdain. And he didn't really like it. It felt unnatural to care. Preacher smiled to himself.

So here, with Shafiq only 25 feet ahead of him barreling through narrow and ancient city streets, Lance avoided an ant. Great. What next, call out to the terrorist and ask him to hold up so he could rescue a kitten from a tree? Should he ask the Pakistani bomb maker to stop traffic to help an elderly woman cross the street? Of course, this was just a phase, right? These new thoughts with their soft, beveled edge of feeling, of consideration and compassion, were a temporary state, right?

Made in the USA
Lexington, KY
20 September 2011